Corey pushed the private detective's papers away from her. He had to be wrong—the rich, hard Lili Spaulding had nothing to do with her. There must have been a thousand babies born in Atlanta that month to a thousand unmarried mothers.... *But you were born in Atlanta, weren't you?* And the name on the birth certificate was false....

Lily. That was Millicent's last word, her mother's last word. *Lily....* Lili.

The pain was so ferocious Corey thought she would die from it. She prayed her heart would stop beating so she wouldn't have to face the truth another second. All the years of wondering about her birth mother, fantasizing about some selfless woman who'd cared only for her baby's happiness—

Millicent had left a paper trail for Corey that a blind woman could follow. Her adoptive mother had believed in happily-ever-after endings. She would have wanted Corey to meet Lili Spaulding, to talk to her, to become part of her life.

She would do that for her mother. She would go to New York and meet Lili Spaulding.

And then she would do something for herself. She would find a way to take Lili Spaulding down.

GUILTY
PLEASURES

BARBARA
BRETTON

MIRA BOOKS

MIRA

ISBN 1-55166-170-5

GUILTY PLEASURES

Copyright © 1996 by Barbara Bretton.

GUILTY
PLEASURES

Prologue

December 22, 1995

Lili Spaulding had given up furs, cigarettes and red meat in the name of political correctness but she'd be damned if she gave up her Rolls.

"Admit it, darling," she said to the young woman seated next to her as the sleek gray car exited the parkway. Beyond the tinted windows, the snow-covered Somerset Hills rose gently into an early evening winter sky. "Some things in life are meant to be savored."

"You know my take on this, Mrs. Spaulding." Corey Prescott's voice was low, her tone even. "Conspicuous consumption went the way of the eighties. If you have to ride around in something flashy, the least you can do is buy American. Better for the image."

Lili spread her slender arms in a gesture so inherently graceful it set Corey's teeth on edge. "Darling, this *is* my image. You've been with me how long...one month? Certainly you know what I'm about by now."

Corey leaned back against the buttery leather seat and counted to ten. Twice. *You asked for this job,* she reminded herself. Without her position at Lili! none of her plans had a chance to come true.

She and Lili Spaulding had spent the day at a department store opening in Center City, Philadelphia where Lili! hosted a formal Christmas luncheon for four hundred matrons with money to burn. Lili intended to light the match for them. As director of public relations, it was Corey's job to make sure the spotlight was focused on Lili's perfectly coiffed head while the older woman offered up sound bites like hors d'oeuvres to eager local news crews.

I can help you, Lili's every move had promised the women gathered in the glittering ballroom. *Watch me and I'll show you the way.*

Revlon and Rubinstein had done it. Lauder had turned it into an art form. But only Lili had figured out how to bottle magic and package dreams. No matter what you thought of the woman, you had to admire the tycoon. She'd turned a dying company into a twenty-first century corporation and she'd done it with nothing more than charm and a pair of balls the size of Granny Smiths.

The Rolls purred to a stop in front of a low, rose-colored brick building. The structure was U-shaped; it curved around a stand of dogwood and red maple trees. Tiny white lights twinkled from the bare branches, reminding Corey of Tavern on the Green. Leave it to Lili to bring a little Manhattan to suburban New Jersey. An enormous wreath, complete with red bow, hung above the wide double doors of the main building. Except for the discreet sign that read Lili! it could have passed for a country home belonging to the hunt set. She'd seen pictures of the main plant but they hadn't come close to doing it justice.

She turned back to her boss. "What are we doing here?"

Lili flashed one of her lightning quick smiles in Corey's direction and patted her hand. "It occurred to me you might enjoy a closer look at in-plant operations."

"It's after six," Corey said with a glance at Lili's vintage Cartier tank watch. "Why don't we come back another day?" Hadn't the woman ever heard of the concept nine-to-five? Besides, it was three days before Christmas. Even Scrooge gave Bob Cratchit time off for good behavior.

"I have a surprise for you," Lili said, her smile widening to impossible dimensions. Her teeth were white and even, like the keyboard of a Steinway piano. "The test run for Night-Way rolls off the assembly line in twenty minutes and I'm here to sign the first bottle."

"Twenty minutes?" A buzz of apprehension rippled through Corey. Had Lili lost her mind? "I thought the test run wasn't scheduled for another twelve weeks ."

"Change of plans, darling. We're going to launch in May, in time to capitalize on next year's Christmas trade."

"But that's only five months from now. We don't have advertising in place, the campaign is only half formed—we haven't even settled on a face." Not to mention the potential problems Stephen Gold from R and D had told her about on the phone the other night.

"You'll manage," Lili stated over her shoulder as she exited the Rolls.

"Manage?" Corey sputtered, climbing out after the woman. Her red wool skirt rode halfway up her thighs and Ed, the limo driver, winked as she tugged it back into place. "You're asking me to execute a full-court press for a virgin product in time for the '96 holidays?"

Lili spun around to meet her eyes. "Are you telling me you can't do it?"

"That's not what I said."

"That's what I heard."

"Then you heard wrong."

A perfectly groomed dark brow arched. Lili Spaulding could convey more with an eyebrow than most men could with a loaded rifle.

"You misunderstood," Corey amended, hating herself for letting the woman get to her the way she did. Lili Spaulding's approval shouldn't matter so much. "I was clarifying my position."

"You don't have a position, darling." Corey caught the glint of fire in Lili's sapphire blue eyes. "I take a position, you implement it. If you understand that, then we won't have any more problems."

Lili started toward the front of the building. Her stride was long, her pace as quick as her temper. Other women would tread carefully on the icy walkway. Lili Spaulding dared the ice to slow her down.

"You got off easy," said Ed. "I've seen her leave high heel marks on a man's back."

Corey smoothed the lapels of her short, tight-fitting jacket and touched the strand of pearls at her throat. "Don't worry about me," she said. "I can handle the boss."

"Right," said Ed. "That's what the last publicity director said just before—" He drew his index finger across his throat. "If I were you, I'd keep that résumé up-to-date, Ms. Prescott. That's the best insurance policy you can get around here."

He didn't know the half of it. Corey winked at the driver. "I'm going to be around for a while yet."

"Anything you say, Ms. Prescott," he said, grinning back at her. "Nothing wrong with positive thinking."

It's more than positive thinking, Corey thought as she followed Lili into the building. She'd spent her entire life waiting for this opportunity and nothing was going to get in her way. She'd feed overblown egos, soothe ruffled feathers, do whatever it was she had to do. There was no job too menial, no challenge too great.

Corey's breath caught as she took in the splendor of the front lobby. It had been constructed in the grand tradition of public buildings of the thirties and forties, the kind of building designed to show human beings how insignificant they really were. Carrara marble floors, towering pillars reminiscent of Greek architecture, and the pièce de résistance, a cathedral ceiling complete with stained-glass skylight designed to display the Lili! logo in shades of rose and periwinkle and cobalt blue.

"Good afternoon, Mrs. Spaulding." A sixty-something man with a neatly trimmed white mustache greeted them near the security guard's station. He wore charcoal gray trousers and a plain white shirt. There was something approachable and down-to-earth about the man and Corey found she liked him on sight.

"Ben." Lili leaned in for the obligatory continental kiss on either cheek. She patted his ruddy cheek with a beringed hand. "You've been using Spaulding pour Homme," she said with an admiring nod of her head. "Your skin looks marvelous."

Ben beamed, his ruddy cheeks growing ruddier. "Ruth said the same thing last night, Mrs. Spaulding. I should have started using it years ago."

"Is Ruth still teaching?" Lili asked, eyes wide with interest.

"She retires in June. We're looking forward to doing some traveling this autumn."

"Call me before you make any plans," Lili said. "I have a wonderful travel agent. She'd be happy to help you work out a splendid itinerary."

I've got to hand it to you, Lili, Corey thought. *You've got schmoozing down to an art form.* Lili didn't give a damn about Ben or his wife or what they did on their vacation. She was there to do business.

Poor Ben, however, hadn't a clue. The man positively glowed under the spotlight of her attentions. He launched into a long, detailed story about his granddaughter's upcoming fourth-grade dance recital. Lili's smile never wavered. She asked the right questions, admired a photo of the latest grandbaby, and made Ben feel as if chatting about his family were the sole reason for her visit to the factory.

It was all Corey could do to keep from bursting into applause. Meryl Streep couldn't have turned in a better performance. She doubted if Lili had ever set foot inside a grammar school, much less attended a fourth-grade dance recital, but you'd never know it to listen to her.

Lili turned toward Corey and placed a hand beneath her elbow. "Ben, this is Corey Prescott." Lili paused long enough for Corey to realize the man hadn't the foggiest idea who she was. "My new director of public relations."

"Ben Krementz." He extended his own hand in greeting. "Are you the one who pushed through the Amaryllis promotion Blake Morrow left behind?"

"Guilty."

"We moved a lot of product since Thanksgiving and got some good press. Can't ask for more than that." His eyes met hers and she saw nothing but sincerity. "Great job."

"Great product," she said, warmed by the good-hearted praise. It was a rare commodity in the beauty business. "You make my job easy."

Lili was observing them with a deceptively bland expression on her flawless face. "How wonderful," she said, linking arms with both Corey and Ben. "My two favorite people have become friends."

Ben and Corey exchanged bemused grins over their employer's head. Both knew that was Lili's way of saying it was time to shut up and get down to business.

Ben explained some of the complexities surrounding the launch of a new skin care product as they walked through the winding corridors that led to the conference room.

"We've been having one hell of a time with the animal rights people," he said as they passed the life-size portrait of Lili's late husband Carter Spaulding.

"That's one of the bullet items we'll need to discuss for phase three," Corey said, making a mental note to follow up from the office tomorrow morning. "We can't afford to be anything but cutting edge on this issue."

"I refuse to be intimidated," Lili stated flatly. "Any decisions we make will be based on effectiveness and cost considerations, not on the terrorist tactics of a group of social misfits."

"An enlightened attitude," Corey shot back. "There are alternatives to animal testing, Mrs. Spaulding."

"None of which is acceptable."

"Research shows that public opinion falls on the side of—" Corey stopped cold as Ben opened the door to the mahogany-paneled conference room and a score of expectant faces looked up at them from around an enormous marble-topped table. The best and brightest men and women in the field and their expressions were the same as those of the wealthy Philadelphia matrons at the luncheon that afternoon.

They were looking to Lili for magic and damned if she didn't provide it.

When it was over an hour later, Lili stood in the center of a crush of admirers, fielding more compliments and New Year's Eve invitations than Corey had received in a lifetime. Somehow Lili had turned the simple act of signing a bottle of night cream into a celebration and even Corey had to admit the woman had enough personal charisma to start her own religion.

Ben Krementz was leaning against the doorjamb, a bemused expression on his face.

"She's something, isn't she?" Corey asked, joining him in the doorway.

"That she is." He angled a glance in Corey's direction. "You don't like her very much, do you?"

Corey started in surprise. "I admire her very much," she said carefully. "She's a great businesswoman."

"Right," said Ben with a chuckle. "But you don't like her."

"It shows?"

"A little." He adjusted his glasses. Corey noted the angry red furrows left by the nose piece. "Nothing time and experience won't take care of."

In her three and a half weeks at Lili!, only Stephen Gold had suspected Corey was anything but a wholehearted disciple. "I'll have to work on my poker face." She managed a smile. "I don't suppose you can smoke in here."

The ends of Ben's mustache tilted upward with his answering smile. "That depends on how you feel about the death penalty."

She tilted her head in Lili's direction. "Tell Mrs. Spaulding I'll be waiting by the car."

"Mind if I join you?" Ben asked. "It isn't every day you find a kindred tobacco lover."

They started for the door.

"Ben!" Lili's voice rang out over the din of celebration. "We need your expertise." Her tone made it clear that saying no wasn't an option.

Ben met Corey's eyes and laughed. "Take a drag for me."

"With pleasure," said Corey. She considered asking him to keep her opinions about Lili Spaulding private but somehow she knew that wasn't necessary. Ben Krementz was one of the good guys.

She walked quickly through the quiet corridors, aware of the click of her high heels against the polished marble. The security guard looked up as she approached.

"Is it over?" he asked. A basket of red poinsettias rested on the floor by his desk. She wondered if he would take it home with him.

"Not yet," Corey replied. "Give her another week or two."

Her words lingered as the door closed behind her. What was the matter with her tonight? She'd spent the better part of her life hiding her feelings and now they were popping out everywhere, like stuffing from a rag doll.

Ed was dozing behind the wheel of the limo, the bill of his chauffeur's cap pulled low over his eyes. He'd pinned a sprig of mistletoe to the cap. They had a running bet over how long it would take Lili to notice.

Corey hopped up onto the front fender. She reached into her briefcase for a pack of cigarettes then stopped. The air was cold and sweet with the sharp tang of pine. It actually smelled like Christmas. Smoking suddenly lost its appeal and she leaned back on her elbows and drew in a deep breath.

So far not even the great and powerful Lili Spaulding had been able to duplicate the magic of a crisp winter night.

When Corey was a little girl she used to sit outside and look up at the stars and make a wish. The constellations varied. Her wish never did. A home. A family. Someone to love. She might as well have asked for the moon because nothing good ever lasted.

Corey stifled a yawn as she thought about the things she'd said to Ben Krementz and the security guard. Maybe it was the holiday blues that had made her let down her defenses and risk everything she'd struggled to achieve. The years of searching, of planning, of working twice as hard as anybody else because she'd had to travel twice as far to get where she wanted to be.

But it was almost over. She was so close to her goal, so close to grabbing the brass ring that she could almost feel it, cold and shiny in the palm of her hand.

Voices floated toward her from the doorway. Lili's throaty alto. Krementz's husky bass. An assortment of sopranos and tenors, mingling like the dissonant sound track from an obscure foreign movie.

"...my schedule is so full—" she heard Lili say. "Let me—"

The rest of Lili's words were lost as an explosion rocked the quiet night. The force of the blast threw Corey to the ground. Her knee slammed against a rock and she was aware of hot blood pouring down her leg as she shielded herself from shards of broken glass and chunks of brick falling from the sky.

She looked up to find a wall of flame quickly devouring the south side of the building. The lobby had been reduced to rubble of rose-colored brick and pink marble. The only sounds were the crackling roar of fire and faint strains of birdsong drifting incongruously from beyond the hills.

"Holy shit!" The limo driver appeared at her side. "What the hell happened?"

Corey grabbed Ed's arm and struggled to her feet. "Call for help," she ordered the man. "Police, fire, ambulances—everything you can get. Do it now! There's no time to lose!"

Turning she started to run toward the building.

"You can't go in there!" Ed screamed, tackling her about the waist and holding her fast.

She rammed her elbows into his rib cage then broke free. Waves of heat rippled toward her, thick with smoke and the smell of fear. Her throat burned as she got closer and she was aware of how little air actually made it into her lungs. She blinked rapidly, trying to maintain her focus. Ben Krementz's body lay beneath a pile of brick and stone, resting next to what was left of the security guard. A young red-haired woman in a white lab coat had been thrown clear. She lay facedown on the snow in a splatter of glass and blood and enormous chunks of marble. Corey saw it all but she refused to let it register. If she did, she wouldn't stand a chance.

"You can't help them!" Ed yelled from behind her. "Don't try to be a hero!"

She wasn't a hero. It wasn't courage propelling her forward: it was thirty-two years of anger and pain and loneliness. Thirty-two years of wondering why it had to be this way.

"Lili!" Her voice rose up over the chaos. "Lili, where are you?"

A faint moan sounded to Corey's right. She wheeled about, straining to see through the haze of smoke and the gathering darkness. She made out the slender line of a woman's leg poking out from behind the evergreen bushes that had once landscaped the building.

Moments later she pulled Lili Spaulding's body into a clearing. Blood streamed down her unlined forehead, seeping into the fine fabric of her designer suit. Corey crouched down next to the woman and searched for a pulse at her wrist, her elbow, the base of her throat.

"Come on . . . come on . . . don't die on me . . . don't—" Elation tore through her with the same powerful impact as the blast had only minutes before. "Help me, Ed!" she cried. "I've got a pulse."

Ed stopped ten feet away from where Corey knelt by Lili's side. "Ah Jesus," he moaned, wringing his hands together. "Look at her, will you? Look at all that blood! She's gonna die!"

"She'll live," Corey whispered fiercely as she cleared Lili's air passages then bent down to breathe life into the woman's lungs. "She'll live because I haven't finished with her yet."

Hold on, Mother. This is only the beginning....

BOOK ONE

The Mother

1

Euless, Florida, 1962

The stiff white paper covering crackled loudly as Lilly Ann Barnett shifted position on the examining table. Bad enough that she'd had to lie back, put her feet in the cold metal stirrups and spread her knees wide so Dr. Willis could examine her; now she was sitting there in a threadbare cotton robe that barely covered her thighs while he looked at her as if she were one of those girls who strutted down Main Street on Friday night, hunting for an easy way to make some quick money.

Don't you go smirking at me like that, she thought, sitting up straight as an arrow. *I'd like to know how smart you'd be feeling if you were sitting here with your legs sticking out for the world to see.*

Not that Doc Willis was looking at her legs. No, he was too busy tut-tutting like one of her grandma's friends did whenever Lilly Ann entered the room, as if the whole wide world were going to hell in a handbasket and Lilly Ann was the one to blame. You could almost smell the stink of fire and brimstone swirling around her head.

"Well now you've done it, Lilly Ann," he said finally, pinching the bridge of his nose between his thumb and pointer finger. "Got yourself in the biggest mess a girl can get herself into."

Her heart leaped into her throat and she dug her fingernails into her palms. "Am I—?"

"Three months gone and no wedding ring on your finger."
He shook his head so hard his jowls wobbled like wash on the
line. "I'm glad your daddy is dead and buried so he doesn't
have to bear this humiliation."

Lilly Ann felt the ugly red flush move down from her cheeks
to her throat and chest. *You're a stupid old man,* she thought,
not looking away from Doc Willis's reproving gaze. *You don't
know one thing you're talking about.*

"I know what you're thinking, little girl," Doc Willis went
on, "and let me tell you you're in for a real letdown. If you
think Maisie and Big Earle are going to let Cliff marry the likes
of you—"

She leaped from the table and wagged a finger in his wrinkled old face. "Clifford loves me and he's going to be happy
there's a baby on the way."

"Lilly Ann, we need to call your grandma and talk about
this. There's a home for girls in your predicament by Tallahassee." He sighed deeply, as if the weight of the world rested on
his bony shoulders. "You go to school, have the baby, and get
on with your life like nothing happened."

"No!" The word leaped from her throat like a pack of
wildcats running after a wounded bird. "Nobody's taking my
baby away from me!"

"You're sixteen years old, Lilly Ann. You have your whole
life ahead of you."

"My mama was fifteen when I was born," she argued
smugly, "and she didn't give me away to some stranger to bring
up."

"Your mama's gone, girl," Doc Willis replied in a kinder
tone of voice, "but if she wasn't I don't think she'd be encour-
aging you to follow her example."

Tears welled up and Lilly Ann didn't even bother to blink
them back. "Mama loved me and she'd want me to be happy."

She grabbed up her clothes from the back of the scarred
wooden chair in the corner of the room and darted behind the
screen.

"We're not finished talking, girl," Doc Willis called from the
doorway, "not by a long shot. I'll see you listen to reason or
know the reason why."

"Old fool," she muttered as she yanked on her panties and struggled to fasten her bra. Didn't he realize being pregnant with Clifford Earle Franklin's baby was like finding the pot of gold at the end of the rainbow? That little tiny baby curled inside her belly changed everything, same as if her fairy godmother had waved her magic wand over Lilly Ann's head and made all her wishes come true.

No more talk of waiting until Cliff finished college. No more sleepless nights worrying that he'd decide she wasn't fancy enough or smart enough to hold her own with his snooty family. She was one of them now, part of that big old family who lived at the top of the hill in the fanciest house in Euless, Florida.

Not that the Franklins were all that used to being rich, mind you. They were still rattling around in the mansion like a bunch of marbles in a tin can. Big Earle had only come into his fortune ten years ago with a lucky oil strike on a pitiful little plot of land his daddy'd left him way over in Texas. No, the Franklins were swamp rats just like the Barnetts, born and bred in the hot, humid area around the Florida Everglades even if the last thing they wanted to do was admit that.

Lilly Ann buttoned up the front of her pink cotton blouse then shimmied into her pleated navy blue skirt. The seams strained at the hips and waist, and she had to suck in her breath until she thought she'd faint in order to hitch up the zipper. She'd be needing maternity clothes any day now and she wondered if Cliff's mother Maisie would send her to Glo's Discount Emporium or drive her to the Bon Ton where all of the woman's ritzy friends shopped.

Lilly Ann worried her bottom lip with her teeth as she ran her plastic brush through her hair. Thinking about Maisie was enough to put a cloud on the sunniest day. Maisie looked at Lilly Ann as if she were a speck of fly dirt on their red flocked wallpaper. Back at Christmastime, Lilly Ann had overheard Maisie hollering at Cliff when he'd told his mama he was taking Lilly Ann to the family New Year's Eve party at the Euless Country Club.

"That gal's nothing more than white trash," Maisie had said to her favorite son. "Find yourself a girl from a good family, one that can make us all proud."

Thinking about it made Lilly Ann's hackles rise. Just because she wasn't born with a silver spoon in her mouth didn't make her any worse than those fancy girls whose pictures appeared in the society column of the *Euless Picayune-Gazette.* She was smarter than Lorene Clark and twice as pretty as Suellen Weber with the overbite and bad skin.

Those girls had great big trust funds, but they didn't have Clifford Earle Franklin Junior. No, sirree. Cliff belonged to Lilly Ann and, thanks to the sweet baby growing beneath her heart, there was nothing anyone on earth—not even Maisie— could do to change that fact.

Three days later Grandma Hattie Barnett and Maisie Franklin met for lunch at the country club south of town. Grandma Hattie wore her best Sunday dress, an overblown blue organza with matching hat and gloves. Hattie had worn the same dress to her son's funeral and her daughter-in-law's, as well, and Lilly Ann knew that her unborn baby ranked right up there with death and other family tragedies. The only thing that kept Hattie from disowning her granddaughter right on the spot was the fact that the Franklins owned half the town.

Lilly Ann saw the way Maisie's fish lips curled at her first sight of Grandma Hattie.

Cow, thought Lilly Ann, lifting her chin as they followed the waiter to Maisie's table. Maisie was all done up like a circus clown with red circles of rouge on her fat cheeks and bleached blond curls that danced across her forehead like trained poodles. Lilly Ann's hand itched to wipe some of the gloppy makeup off the pudgy woman and smooth her hair into something approaching style. It wasn't that Maisie was ugly; it was just that all the money in the world couldn't erase the unmistakable look of white trash.

"You're late," Maisie said as she offered one of her cheeks for Lilly Ann's kiss. "I was about to order without you."

Lilly Ann hung on to her smile. "Mrs. Franklin, I want you to meet my grandma, Hattie Barnett."

Grandma Hattie stuck out one blue-gloved hand. "Pleased to make your acquaintance, Miz Franklin."

"Same here," said Maisie, daintily shaking Grandma's hand. The two women locked eyes.

"The Good Lord don't take kindly to fornication," Grandma Hattie said with a disapproving cluck of her tongue.

"The Good Lord ain't the only one," said Maisie with a look at Lilly Ann.

"I didn't raise the girl to spread her legs for every sweet-talking boy who comes along."

"And I didn't raise my boy to waste his time with gold-digging tramps."

Lilly Ann sank lower in her chair, wishing she could disappear under the tablecloth.

"Don't much change the fact that she's in a family way."

"No, it don't," said Maisie with a loud sigh. "So let's plan that wedding before the whole town knows."

Of course the whole town knew before they were finished with their ambrosia. The busboy, one of the Du Bois children from over Whitehall way, overheard them talking and he told the waiter who was the son of Maisie's housekeeper Lottie's sister. The waiter called his mother and his mother called her cousin who worked at the Cut 'N' Curl and by the time Maisie Franklin paid their bill everyone from Euless to Whitehall and back again knew that Cliff had knocked up the Barnett girl and was about to pay the piper.

The next two weeks were the longest of Lilly Ann's life. Half of her friends were so scandalized they wouldn't talk to her, while the other half found the whole thing to be more exciting than Friday night at the Blue Teardrop Lounge.

"We should've just gone to the justice of the peace and got it over with," she said to Cliff two nights before the big day. They were sitting on the front porch of Grandma Hattie's house.

"You know my mama," Cliff said, draping a casual arm across her shoulders like they were already an old married couple. "She says people will forget about the baby but they won't forget the wedding."

There was something wrong with that but Lilly Ann couldn't quite figure out what. She scooted toward the far side of the porch swing. "I wish you weren't having that bachelor party tomorrow night," she said, swinging her bare legs in front of her. She should have used the pale pink polish on her toenails instead of the scarlet. Scarlet looked too harsh against her pale skin.

Cliff grinned and captured her right ankle in his left hand. "Jealous?"

She pulled away from his grasp. "Should I be?" Just the thought of him going all slack-jawed over some bleached blond cow made her want to pitch a fit.

"Maybe," said Cliff, his turquoise blue eyes dancing like lights on a Christmas tree. "I hear Jimbo's hired a stripper from Prattville."

"A stripper?"

"A big-haired gal with titties out to here."

She lashed out at him with one bare foot but he managed to dodge out of the way. "You're going to be a daddy, Clifford Earle Franklin Junior. I don't think you ought to be making eyes at naked women."

"That's how come I'm going to be a daddy, Lilly Ann Barnett," he said, sliding down next to her on the porch swing. "I like to make eyes at naked women." He draped his arm around her shoulders and let his fingers graze the top of her left breast. "You're filling out your blouses real fine these days."

Lilly Ann blushed and ducked her head. In another month she'd be showing for real. She wondered how Cliff would feel about a wife with a big round belly to match her big round breasts. Men were funny about things like that. She remembered back when Charleen Jones got herself in a family way and her husband Frank ran off with a skinny waitress from Miami soon as Charleen's waist began to get thick.

"I love you, Cliff," she whispered, wishing she didn't sound so clingy and young. "All I want to do is make you happy."

"I know that, sugar." He grazed her nipple with his thumbnail and she shivered with wanting him.

She waited for him to tell her that he loved her too, that he was going to do everything he could to keep her happy, but instead he flicked her nipple once more as if it were a cigarette lighter and pushed himself off the porch swing. "Denny and Tom are waitin' on me at the bowling alley."

"I'll come with you." She slipped off the swing and stood next to him.

"Not this time, darlin'," said Cliff, darting a quick glance toward the candy-apple red Chevy waiting for him in the driveway. "Bowl-A-Rama gets real rowdy on Saturday nights."

"It's still early," she protested like a kid being sent to bed without any supper. "I promise I'll leave if anyone kicks up a fuss."

He kissed her on the forehead like an older brother. "Don't want my wife in a place like that. You deserve better, darlin', and I'm aiming to see you get it."

She wrapped her arms around his waist and held him tight. "I'm not your wife yet, Cliff. I'm still your girlfriend."

"Two days," he said, chucking her under the chin. "Two more days and you'll be all mine."

Lilly Ann withheld a sigh as Cliff gunned the engine and roared down the driveway. He said he wanted to take care of her but why was it she still ended up feeling as if she were on the outside looking in?

She sank down on the porch step and wrapped her arms around her knees. *So why are you so surprised, Lilly Ann? You know what marriage is all about.* She'd seen enough dewy-eyed young girls walk down the aisle as brides, only to walk back out of the church as wives with the weight of the world laid across their lacy white shoulders.

She didn't want to end up a housewife, married to a pile of brick and wood instead of a man. Oh, she knew there wasn't much she could do about it right now, not with the baby on its way, but once she was herself again she'd see to it that she was a real part of Cliff's life, not pushed in the background like a wedding present you couldn't return.

She was only sixteen years old, filled with so many hopes and dreams that sometimes she thought her heart would burst like a birthday balloon. There was a whole world out there waiting to be explored and she wanted to investigate every single inch of it before the good Lord said it was time for her to go. She didn't want to end up bitter and dried up like Grandma Hattie or flint-eyed and angry like Maisie Franklin. Marriage seemed to do that to some women but it wouldn't do that to Lilly Ann Barnett. Not by a long shot.

"A good woman stands behind her man," Reverend Walker had said during his last Sunday sermon, "lending support and comfort so he can do battle with the world.'' Lilly Ann had wanted to leap to her feet and say, ''Why can't she stand next to her man and battle right along with him?'' But she knew Reverend Walker would never understand.

She'd be the best wife in the whole wide world to Cliff and the best mother any baby could hope to have, but there had to be more to life than sitting at home, looking out the window while everyone else went off and had adventures. Marriage could be an adventure, too. Together she and Cliff could make a life for themselves and their baby that would be something real special. Something to be proud of.

And it would all begin the moment they said ''I do.''

2

The First Baptist Church was filled with flowers. Pale pink carnations. White daisies. Armloads of baby's breath and Johnny-jump-ups and more roses than Lilly Ann had ever seen in any one place in her whole entire life. It was just the way she'd imagined the church would look on her wedding day.

If it hadn't been for the casket in front of the altar, everything would have been perfect.

''Clifford Earle Franklin was a good son,'' intoned Reverend Walker, his voice breaking with emotion, ''a fine young man cut down in the flower of his youth....''

A loud sob broke the heavy stillness as Maisie buried her face in a lace-trimmed hankie. Big Earle, his jowls drooping like a basset hound's, put a clumsy arm around his wife's shoulders but Maisie shook him off and sobbed even louder. ''Sweet Jesus, you took my baby boy!'' Maisie wailed loud enough to be heard in the next town. ''Take me, Lord! Take me instead!''

A wave of weeping broke out from Cliff's grandmothers and aunts and cousins. Ten rows back, Lilly Ann dug her fingernails into her palms and struggled to choke back her own tears but couldn't quite manage it. She'd done nothing but cry since the morning Sheriff Harland pulled up in front of Grandma Hattie's place to break the news.

"Sorry to come by so early," he'd said, looking real uncomfortable, standing there in the front parlor amid the crocheted doilies and antimacassars, "but I got some bad news for you, Lilly Ann." He tried to smile but couldn't and Lilly Ann knew right then that Cliff was gone.

"I know it ain't much help but Clifford died right away," Sheriff Harland went on, not quite meeting her eyes. "The Chevy shot out over the embankment near Route 22. He never knew what hit him."

All Lilly Ann had to do was think about it and her stomach tied itself up into knots so tight that she was afraid for the baby. Everyone said Cliff had been drinking before it happened. An empty bottle of bourbon had been found next to the body of the girl who'd been sitting in the bucket seat next to him.

She whimpered softly, just loud enough so that the banker's wife turned slightly and cast her a pitying look that cut Lilly Ann to the quick. She knew exactly what that look meant. *What are you doing back there all alone, girl? Shouldn't you be up front where you belong, with Maisie and Big Earle and the rest of the family?*

The knot in her stomach tightened up some more and she bent forward as the air rushed from her lungs in a whoosh. Beads of sweat formed at her temples as she struggled to breathe. The air was so heavy with the smell of roses and My Sin and Old Spice that she she was afraid she would retch.

She rested her forehead against her knees as voices rose and fell all around her. So many voices, all talking at once, talking and talking and not making a whit of sense. This was supposed to be her wedding day, the day she and Cliff stood up before God and took their vows. Instead she was sitting in the back of the church like some crepe-hanging stranger who'd walked in off the street to watch the funeral of a rich man's son.

Up front Maisie unleashed another wail then threw herself into Big Earle's arms, sobbing as if her heart would break.

You're not the only one who's hurting, Lilly Ann thought angrily as she watched Big Earle pat his wife on her shoulder. Her own heart felt as if it had been ripped in two, but she didn't have anybody to hold her close and tell her everything would be all right.

"Now you got yourself some *real* trouble, girl," Grandma Hattie had said last night while Lilly Ann ironed her black cotton skirt on the kitchen table. "I know Maisie Franklin and I know she ain't about to let the likes of you into her house. Not without a wedding ring."

The harsh words still rankled. Lilly Ann knew that Grandma Hattie would like nothing better than to see her brought to her knees, forced to admit that she was no better than her mama had been, a poor little nobody looking to latch on to the first man who could promise her a way out. "Broke my Jackie's heart, your mama did, when she ran off like that," Grandma Hattie had said. "Didn't even stop to take her baby with her."

The old lady never mentioned that her brokenhearted boy's four other wives all saw fit to pack their bags and run away as fast as their feet would carry them. Everyone knew that his sixth wife Dora would have run off too if Jackie hadn't up and died on their honeymoon.

Sometimes Lilly Ann wondered what her life would have been like if her mama hadn't left her behind with Grandma Hattie and Daddy Jack. There was a whole wide world out there beyond Euless, Florida and she had no doubt her mama had managed to see most of it. *Do you ever think about me, mama? Do you ever wish we were still together?*

Lilly Ann placed her hands on her barely rounded belly and a feeling of determination straightened her spine. She had loved Clifford Earle Franklin Junior and she would have made him a good wife, but Cliff was gone now and no amount of sobbing was going to bring him back. She had other things to think about, more important things than her shattered dreams.

Her baby deserved more than a hand-me-down cradle in the back room of Grandma Hattie's house, more than a life spent wishing she were somebody else, wishing she were anywhere but the place she was. Maisie might be able to turn her back on the girl her son had planned to marry but she couldn't turn her back on the mother of his child. Not while there was a breath left in Lilly Ann's body.

Two weeks later Lilly Ann Barnett moved into the big house on the hill.

"I wash my hands of you," Grandma Hattie said the last morning Lilly Ann lived under her roof. "You and your mama brought nothin' but dishonor to my family. Everyone knows what that fancy boyfriend of yours was up to that night."

"Don't you dare talk about Cliff!" Lilly Ann warned as she gathered up the last of her belongings. "He loved me."

It wasn't as if she couldn't hear the whole town whispering about the girl who'd died in the car wreck with him. One of those strippers who popped out of cakes at bachelor parties, the newspaper report had said. Lilly Ann knew you had to look the other way with men, that sometimes they had to sow a few extra wild oats before they settled down with a wife and baby. If he'd lived, she never would have even mentioned the girl.

We could've been real happy, Cliff, she thought as the bus chugged its way toward the other side of Euless where the Franklins lived. She would have learned how to be like his people. He never would have had any reason to be ashamed of the girl he'd married.

The bus driver let her off at the bottom of the hill and she walked the rest of the way to the Franklin house. Hot sun beat down on the top of her head and twice she had to stop and catch her breath. She lifted her hair off the back of her neck and twisted it into a knot. It wouldn't do to show up at her new home looking all limp and bedraggled.

The house was big and expensive, exactly the kind of house you'd expect Maisie and Big Earle would live in. It stood three stories high and was wider than the Euless Township High School. Town gossip said that Big Earle had got himself a mighty nice tax break from the assessor's office in return for a handful of cash slipped under the table but so far nobody'd been able to prove it. Lilly Ann didn't know much about taxes but she did know that if it were *her* house, she'd take down those ugly green-and-black striped awnings that hung over every window and get rid of the pink flamingos on the lawn.

And maybe she'd buy a new doorbell too, she thought as she listened to the boring old ding-dong sound it made when she pressed it. Something fancier, like those church chimes they had in England.

A maid in a black uniform opened the door and stared at her.

"I'm Lilly Ann Barnett," she said, careful to speak real slow and clear the way rich people did in the movies.

The maid didn't smile or say hello. She just stepped aside and waved Lilly Ann into the foyer.

"Ohh!" The sound escaped her lips before she could stop it.

"Miss?"

"I—it's so cool in here," Lilly Ann stammered. "I wasn't expectin' it to be."

"Air-conditioning, miss," the maid said, a snippy little smile lifting the corners of her mouth.

Lilly Ann's face flamed despite the temperature. Of course the Franklins had air-conditioning. Why wouldn't they? They didn't have to pinch pennies to pay the electric bill the way Grandma Hattie did.

"You wait here," the maid said, pointing toward a little bench pushed up against the wall. "I'll get the missus."

Lilly Ann waited in the front hall a good ten minutes before Maisie saw fit to greet her.

"I'll send Jim Bob to fetch the rest of your things," Maisie said as she showed Lilly Ann to her room on the third floor.

"Thank you, ma'am," Lilly Ann said, "but I've got all my things with me."

Maisie stopped on the landing and gave her one of those looks most people saved for dead skunks. Her beady little eyes landed on the two brown Winn-Dixie bags clutched to Lilly Ann's chest. "Everything?"

Lilly Ann nodded. "Everything but my school books and I don't reckon I'll be going back to class until after the baby's come."

Maisie's painted-on brows drew together in a scowl. It was all Lilly Ann could do to keep from spitting on a hanky and wiping those dopey upside down Vs off the woman's face. "Don't you go thinking this is some fancy hotel," she said as she pushed open the door to Lilly Ann's room.

Lilly Ann's breath caught as she stepped inside. The room was bigger than Grandma Hattie's kitchen, a great sunny space with high ceilings and a window that overlooked the fancy swimming pool in the backyard. It was exactly the kind of room she'd dreamed about as a little girl and now it was hers.

Maisie ran a fingertip over the top of the chifforobe then waggled her index finger right under Lilly Ann's nose. "You keep this room clean, missy. I'm not plannin' to waste Lottie's time cleaning up after some big ol' lazy gal like you."

Lilly Ann's face flamed. "I'm poor," she said, "but I'm not trash. I'll keep the room plenty clean."

"Just so we understand each other." Maisie didn't seem the slightest bit sorry for hurting Lilly Ann's feelings. "This is a big house and it takes a whole lot of help to keep it runnin' smoothly, the way Big Earle likes it. If you want to be fussed over, find yourself a fancy hotel to live in."

"I don't want to be fussed over," Lilly Ann said, opening the top drawer of the chifforobe and placing her bras and panties neatly inside. "All I want is a safe place for me and my baby." She turned to look at Maisie. "It's what Cliff would've wanted."

Maisie watched her with hard, cold eyes and Lilly Ann held back a shiver. "You got your way this time, missy, but don't think you've pulled the wool over my eyes. You might've fooled my Cliff but you can't fool me. I know what you want and you ain't gonna find it here."

With that Maisie stormed from the room.

"It doesn't matter," Lilly Ann whispered, turning toward the window. She didn't care that Maisie thought she was nothing but a gold-digging tramp, looking to latch on to some Franklin money. She had as much right to be there as Maisie did. The baby she carried was a Franklin and Lilly Ann wasn't about to let any of them them forget that fact for a minute.

The Franklins ate dinner at five o'clock sharp so Lottie the housekeeper could catch the last bus back to town. Somehow Lilly Ann hadn't quite reckoned on having to sit at the table with the Franklins, making small talk as if she really belonged. Maisie would probably have herself a hissy fit if Lilly Ann made herself a tomato sandwich and took it back up to her room.

The heavy smell of fried catfish slapped her in the face as she made her way downstairs. Her stomach tilted sideways and she stopped on the landing and closed her eyes for a moment. She prayed she wouldn't be sick.

She jumped as a hand clamped down on her shoulder. "You feelin' poorly, girl?" Big Earle's voice sounded right next to her ear.

Lilly Ann shook her head. It wouldn't do to start complaining right from the get-go. "Just tired, that's all." She didn't much like the way his fingers were resting right in the soft spot above her collarbone.

"Don't know what Maisie's thinking, putting you up there in the attic."

"It's a real nice room," she said, meaning it. "Lots of sun."

"Hot as blazes up there," Big Earle said. "You should be on the second floor with the family. I'll tell Maisie to—"

"Really, Mr. Franklin," she broke in, "I'm fine right where I am." She didn't want to be any closer to Maisie than she had to be.

Big Earle's bloodshot blue eyes welled up with tears and before she realized what was happening he'd placed the palms of his hands flat up against her belly. "You're carryin' my grandbaby in there," he said. "All that's left of my son." His voice went all gravelly with emotion. "That makes you the most important person in this whole damn house."

It didn't take Lilly Ann long to figure out just how right Big Earle was. The Franklins were a loud, brawling family and as the weeks wore on, she seemed to be right at the center of every single fight that broke out in the house on the hill. It was as if Cliff's death had taken the heart out of them and they were looking for someone to blame.

Someone like Lilly Ann.

"It's downright indecent the way your belly's growing so fast," Maisie said last week after Lilly Ann's appointment with Dr. Willis. "I only gained sixteen pounds when I was carryin' Corinne."

Lilly Ann was four and a half months along and she'd already gained ten pounds. You'd think she'd committed a crime or something, the way Maisie went on about it. She even went so far as to tell Lottie to serve up smaller portions for Lilly Ann at the supper table.

The bigger Lilly Ann's belly grew, the angrier Maisie got. Sometimes it seemed that Maisie would like nothing better than for Lilly Ann to lose the baby. That didn't make much sense, considering that Cliff had been the apple of his mama's eye. You'd think she'd be jumping for joy that her boy had left something of himself behind.

But not Maisie. She was too filled with hate to realize what a miracle it was that Lilly Ann was carrying her dead boy's baby.

Things weren't all that much better with the rest of the Franklins either.

Nineteen-year-old Teena was scandalized that her dead brother's pregnant girlfriend was living there as if she were one of the family. "Why don't you just go away?" she snapped at Lilly Ann one morning over breakfast. "Nobody wants you here."

Lilly Ann waited for someone to speak up for her but no one did. Cliff would have, she thought. Even when Maisie had threatened to cut him off without a cent, he'd told his mother he was marrying Lilly Ann just the same. "I'm real sorry you can't be happier about this, Mama," he'd told Maisie right in front of Lilly Ann and Grandma Hattie, "but I love this gal and we're gettin' married."

No one had ever stuck up for her before and when Cliff told off his mama, Lilly Ann had felt like the queen of the world.

Fourteen-year-old Bobby forked up some grits and kept his eyes on the sports page of the newspaper. Six-year-old Corinne was more concerned with picking the blueberries out of her pancakes. Big Earle shoved another sausage in his mouth while Maisie met Lilly Ann's eyes across the table.

"Now don't you talk like that, Teena Marie," Maisie said after a moment. "Lilly Ann and the baby are part of the family."

"No, they aren't," Teena argued. "She's not his widow. We don't owe her anything. Why can't she just go back home where she belongs and leave the rest of us alone?" With that Teena pushed back her chair and ran from the room.

Lilly Ann bit her lip and looked down at her toast and plum jam.

"Don't you pay Teena Marie no mind," Big Earle said, reaching across the table to pat Lilly Ann's hand. "Damn gal's too uppity for her own good."

The hand lingered on Lilly Ann's just a split second too long for comfort, but before she had a chance to pull her own hand away, Big Earle went back to eating his breakfast like nothing had happened.

But Maisie didn't miss a trick and Lilly Ann knew things were going to get a whole lot worse before they got better.

"I don't want to hear none of your bellyachin'," Grandma Hattie said the day before Christmas. Lilly Ann had dropped by the house to deliver a bright red poinsettia in a green foil-wrapped clay pot. "You made your bed with Clifford Franklin, now you got to lie in it."

Lilly Ann rubbed her belly as she shifted position on the hard-backed kitchen chair. "I'm not complainin', Grandma Hattie. I'm just saying I don't much like Big Earle."

"And ain't that just too bad." Grandma Hattie took a sip of coffee from her chipped dime-store mug. "Don't seem to me you got much call for complaint, living up there in that fancy house on the hill."

"I never wanted to live with them, Grandma," she replied, wondering why she even bothered. "I'd have been real happy staying here with you." The words had barely left her lips before Lilly Ann realized with a start that she no longer meant it. She had once, but not anymore. The frame house seemed awfully small to her now, more like an overstuffed closet than a home. She would hate to be trapped in there again, praying that something—someone—would come along and take her away to someplace better.

She wondered why she'd bothered telling Grandma Hattie that Big Earle was looking at her the way a man looked at a woman he wanted to take to bed. Hattie couldn't do anything about it, even if it was true. And she was entirely sure it was. A man would have to be awful hard up to give her a second look. Her belly strained against even her biggest maternity dress. Sometimes she thought her skin would burst if she gained so much as another ounce.

It didn't much bother Big Earle. He'd caught her under the mistletoe the other night during Teena's Christmas party and she'd swear he'd tried to slip his slobbery tongue between her lips. Not that anyone would believe her. When it came to things like that, she'd already learned it was always her fault, as if she were sending out some kind of invisible signal that told men she was easy.

"Like father, like son," Grandma Hattie said as she poured herself some more Christmas cheer. "You spread your legs for the boy. Can't blame the man for wanting some for himself."

3

The Franklins left for Augusta the day after New Year's. They gave Lottie a week off which meant Lilly Ann would be all alone.

"Don't you go holdin' any parties while we're gone," Maisie warned as she preened in front of the hall mirror. "Just remember you're a guest in this house, not a member of the family."

"Yes, ma'am," Lilly Ann said. As if she could forget that fact for even a second. She was tired of tiptoeing around, afraid of making too much noise, using too much hot water, or drinking the last of the milk. It would be real nice to be able to watch TV in her nightie and not have to worry about what anyone thought.

"We'll be back home on Wednesday," Maisie went on. "I expect things to look just the way we left them."

What did the old cow think Lilly Ann was going to do anyway, sell off her furniture and run away with the milkman? Truth was, Lilly Ann had lost touch with her school friends. Maisie didn't want anyone coming over to visit and Lilly Ann was too big and too darned uncomfortable to take the bus into town. She supposed she could call Venita or Jacy and catch up with things, but she just didn't have the energy. Her belly was huge and so were her breasts. Her back ached more often than not and she wished the next six weeks would hurry by so she could be her old self again.

But she was never going to be her old self again, was she? She was going to be somebody's mother.

The thought hit her so hard she had to sit down on the porch step as the Franklins backed down the driveway.

Now that it was too late, she finally understood what Grandma Hattie and Dr. Willis and even Maisie had meant when they said she and Cliff were too young to fall in love.

She was only seventeen. She should be going out on Saturday night dates to the movies. She should be daydreaming through home economics about what she'd wear to the senior prom. Instead she was all alone in the big house on the hill with no one to talk to except the baby inside her belly. Cliff was gone. Grandma Hattie wanted nothing to do with her or the baby. Maisie hated her and Big Earle liked her way too much.

All she'd done was fall in love and see where it got her.

She cried for a long time, sitting there on the step. She knew things would have been different if Cliff hadn't got himself in that car wreck but what was done was done. He was dead and buried in the Euless Baptist Cemetery and she wasn't. She was alive and she deserved something more than she was getting.

After a while she struggled to her feet and went inside the house. Lottie had left behind a tuna casserole and some fried chicken but all she wanted was a bowl of ice cream and some leftover Christmas cookies. "You have to think about the baby," Doc Willis had chided her just the other week. "Good food makes good babies."

Well, she was tired of thinking about the baby. She'd done nothing but think about the baby for the past eight months and she was sick of it. It wasn't like she was going to take up skydiving. All she wanted was some ice cream.

Ten minutes later she curled up on the living room sofa with a half-gallon container of vanilla-chocolate-strawberry and a handful of broken gingerbread men. "Love of Life" would be on in a few minutes. And after "Love of Life" there would be "As the World Turns" and "Search for Tomorrow" and "The Guiding Light." She would spend the whole afternoon watching other women handle problems that were even worse than hers and maybe if she was lucky they'd show her a way out of the mess she was in.

Who would have figured Maisie Franklin would be the one who showed her the way? Maisie hadn't been in Augusta visiting cousins at all. She'd been in Atlanta making arrangements for Lilly Ann to move in with one of Maisie's old school friends, a woman named Eileen Fontaine who owned a small dress shop near Peachtree Street.

"We have to save what's left of your reputation," Maisie said as Lilly Ann packed her belongings in the suitcase Maisie had bought for the purpose.

"It's not like people don't know I'm going to have Cliff's baby," Lilly Ann replied as she tucked her bras into the little satin pouch that snapped to the inside of the suitcase.

Maisie cast an admiring glance at her reflection in the mirror over the dressing table. "Just because they know don't mean you have to stick their noses in it."

Eight months along seemed a little late to start worrying but Lilly Ann wasn't about to argue the point with Maisie. Better late than never, especially if it meant Lilly Ann could finish up her pregnancy in Atlanta. She'd never been north of Tallahassee before and the prospect of seeing the big city filled her with excitement.

Besides, she knew that wasn't the real reason Maisie was sending her away. Big Earle's interest was getting harder to ignore. Lilly Ann had taken to spending most of her time in her bedroom with the door locked tight in case he took to wandering during the night. From the look on Maisie's face every time her husband eyed Lilly Ann, Big Earle had done a lot of midnight wandering in his day.

Lilly Ann didn't bother to say goodbye to Grandma Hattie or her school friends. It wasn't as if she were going away forever; except for Christmas cards, she hadn't heard from anyone in months. Sometimes she felt as if she'd never had any other life except the one she was living as a prisoner in the Franklin house. She was glad to be leaving it behind, even if it was only until the baby was born.

"Aren't you the prettiest little thing!" Eileen Fontaine exclaimed as Lilly Ann stepped off the train the following afternoon in Atlanta. "Maisie's description didn't half do you justice."

"Th-thank you." Eileen Fontaine was nothing she'd imagined a friend of Maisie's would be. The woman was dressed like a model in a fashion magazine and she smelled of expensive perfume, the kind that didn't cling to your clothes like last night's dinner. "It's real nice of you to take me in."

"Wonderful manners," Eileen observed as she linked her arm through Lilly Ann's. "Darlin', they're going to just love you here in Atlanta."

Lilly Ann felt as if she'd died and gone to heaven. Eileen Fontaine had a Caddy same as the Franklins, but she also had a chauffeur who wore a crisp black uniform and cap just like in the movies. The car smelled all leathery and new and Lilly Ann settled herself in the back seat as if she'd ridden around in luxury her whole life.

Eileen Fontaine swiveled her long legs into the car with one neat motion then the driver closed the door after her. Lilly Ann was speechless with admiration. Eileen seemed as glamorous as a movie star to Lilly Ann in her fancy pale pink suit with matching shoes and bag. Eileen Fontaine wore her blond hair in a ballerina's bun that emphasized her perfect features, the high cheekbones and straight little nose. She didn't do a bad job with makeup either, Lilly Ann observed as the woman leaned forward to give directions to the driver. Her skin was flawless. Her eyes had been highlighted with a light blue-gray shadow then lavishly mascaraed. The bright red lipstick she wore surprised Lilly Ann. Considering Eileen's fair complexion and the pastel tones of the suit, Lilly Ann would have chosen a clear matching pink. Eileen's choice was unexpected but somehow it worked.

"I'm takin' you to lunch, darlin'," Eileen said, leaning back in her seat and crossing her legs. "Hope you're not too tired from travelin' to meet a few of my friends."

Lilly Ann had been downright exhausted but suddenly she felt a burst of newfound energy. "Actually I'm real hungry, ma'am."

"Ma'am?" Eileen Fontaine threw back her head and laughed. Her throat was as smooth and white as Audrey Hepburn's. "You make me feel positively ancient. I'm Eileen, darlin'."

Eileen seemed to know everything there was to know about Atlanta. She pointed out buildings that had miraculously escaped Sherman's march through Georgia during the Civil War

and buildings that had been built during Reconstruction to re-
place ones lost to the Northern army's destruction. History had
always seemed as dry as old bones to Lilly Ann but Eileen made
it come alive. Lilly Ann half expected to hear a rebel yell in the
distance as the boys in gray charged into battle.

She was almost disappointed when the driver pulled up in
front of a small brick building with a sign that read Miss Melly's.

"You have to excuse us our love affair with *Gone With The
Wind*," Eileen said as she helped Lilly Ann from the car.
"Tourists expect it and we like to oblige."

"I loved *Gone With The Wind*," Lilly Ann told the woman.
"I read it three times before the library said I had to give it
back."

"Charming!" Eileen smoothed Lilly Ann's hair with gentle
fingers. "What a dear thing you are."

The woman's touch was so kind that Lilly Ann found herself choking back grateful tears. She couldn't remember the last
time anyone had touched her like that, as if she were a real
person with feelings, not just an embarrassment to keep hidden from sight.

Eileen linked arms with Lilly Ann as they started up the
walkway that led to Miss Melly's. "We're just going to become the *best* friends, darlin'. I promise you this month will fly
by and before you know it, your baby will be here."

The inside of Miss Melly's was so beautiful that Lilly Ann
half expected to see Rhett Butler stroll in with Scarlett O'Hara
on his arm. Heavy velvet draperies, flowery wallpaper, cherrywood paneling that smelled of lemon oil polish, gleaming
silver teapots and china so delicate you could practically see
through it. In the far corner of the room sat a woman with long
coppery red hair that fell to her waist in waves like you'd see on
a picture of a princess. She was playing a harp, running her
fingers across the strings so gracefully and so fast that Lilly Ann
was surprised the gates of heaven didn't swing right open and
welcome them inside.

"I think our girl is overwhelmed," said Eileen's friend Candy
from Memphis. "Her eyes are as wide as quarters."

Candy's husband Blake chuckled. "First time in Atlanta?"
he asked Lilly Ann. He sounded kindly, like she imagined her

daddy would've sounded if he'd ever once remembered he had a daughter.

She nodded. "First time anywhere."

Candy leaned across the table. Her big brown eyes were warm with friendliness. "So young and pretty!" she said, squeezing Lilly Ann's hand. "You're goin' to have the most beautiful baby in the whole wide world!"

Lilly Ann felt her cheeks go warm with pleasure. "My baby's daddy was real handsome," she said. She hadn't talked about Clifford in forever. It felt good. "And smart too." Though, if the truth were told, she'd always been real partial to pretty people over smart ones. Grandma Hattie said that was another way Lilly Ann was just like her mama.

Candy and Blake exchanged one of those married looks like characters on a television show.

"That's just what I thought, darlin'," Eileen said, motioning for the waiter to bring more sweet ice tea. "Maisie said her boy was somethin' special. Do you have a snapshot we could see?"

Lilly Ann reached into her purse and pulled out her wallet. She had three real nice pictures of Clifford and she passed them around for everyone to admire. It sounded as if Eileen had never met Clifford, which seemed kind of strange to Lilly Ann. If Maisie and Eileen were such good old friends, wouldn't you think Eileen would've met her friend's son? But the next minute both Candy and Blake were peppering Lilly Ann with questions about school and the baby and what life was like in Euless and she forgot she'd ever wondered about anything at all.

She loved being the center of attention. These three strangers made her feel special. As if she were a very important person, one they would do anything for. No one had ever treated her that way before. Even Clifford, who had loved her, had been forgetful and distant sometimes, as if he had other things on his mind.

But not Eileen and her friends. They listened to every word Lilly Ann had to say. They laughed at her jokes. They made sure she drank a second glass of milk and urged her to finish her carrots before she ate her chocolate cake. And when lunch was over and they were saying goodbye in the parking lot of Miss

Melly's, Candy and Blake hugged Lilly Ann as if she were family and, to her surprise, that was exactly how she felt.

Actually it was a whole day of surprises for Lilly Ann.

Eileen Fontaine didn't live in a big house like the Franklins or the other rich people in Euless. She lived on the top floor of a fancy hotel right in the center of town. A suite, Eileen called it, with two bedrooms and two bathrooms and a view from the sitting room window that took Lilly Ann's breath away it was so beautiful.

"I'm sorry the Christmas lights aren't still up," Eileen said as she stood at the window with Lilly Ann. "You would have loved them, darlin'."

Lilly Ann nodded then stifled a yawn with the back of her hand.

"You poor thing!" Eileen exclaimed, placing a friendly arm about Lilly Ann's shoulders and turning her away from the view. "Let's get you unpacked and into something comfortable."

Lilly Ann was too tired to put up a fuss. She was used to doing for herself but she found it surprisingly easy to just sit back on the comfy lounge chair in the bedroom and let Eileen unpack her clothes and put them away.

"These will do for tonight," Eileen said, handing Lilly Ann her pale pink nightie and robe, "but we'll have to do some shopping for you tomorrow."

"Wish I could," she said apologetically, "but I don't have enough money."

Eileen threw back her head and laughed. "Darlin', don't you worry. Eileen will take care of everything."

The woman was as good as her word.

Before the week was out Lilly Ann had two new maternity dresses, silk pajamas, and the most beautiful pair of sling-back high heels she'd ever seen. Eileen took her to a beauty parlor where her long black hair was styled into a smart, shoulder-length pageboy that made her look as if she'd grown up in the city.

Eileen also took Lilly Ann to a doctor who examined her from head to foot and pronounced her and the baby to be in perfect health.

"My guess is Valentine's Day," he said when he spoke to both Lilly Ann and Eileen in his office afterward. "First sign of labor pains, you head for Saint Cyril's. I'll meet you there."

The days passed in a blur of activity. Eileen took her to the zoo, to museums, to lunch a handful of times with Candy and Blake. The married couple were always kind and interested in what Lilly Ann was doing, her plans for the future.

"I don't really know what I'll do," Lilly Ann said during lunch the first week in February. They were seated around a big oak table in the dining room of the hotel. "Guess I'll figure it out once the baby comes."

The three adults exchanged glances.

"Darlin', maybe you should start thinking about it now," Eileen suggested kindly. "Time's movin' on faster than you realize."

Lilly Ann shrugged and spooned up some more vanilla ice cream. "I s'pose Miz Franklin'll have a notion about where the baby and I go, but it's my life. I guess I have some say in what happens." The thought of going back to the Franklin house was enough to make her sick. Truth was, she'd been doing a lot of thinking lately about what the future might hold. Euless seemed a million miles away. She could barely remember what her other life had been like.

Eileen liked her. There wasn't any doubt in Lilly Ann's mind about that. Maybe after the baby was born, she would talk to Eileen about getting a job in her dress shop. She could take the baby with her and keep him in a little basket behind the counter and nobody would even have to know he was there. She could work a cash register and even take up a hem if she had to. She'd scrub floors, if that's what Eileen wanted.

But somehow she knew she and the baby would never go back to Euless.

4

Lilly Ann Barnett's baby was born just after midnight, on February 14th.

"A Valentine's Day baby," the doctor crowed as if he had something to do with it. "What did I tell you?"

Lilly Ann, still groggy from the delivery, cradled her newborn daughter against her chest.

"She's so tiny," she crooned, smelling the top of the baby's head.

"Six pounds, nine and a half ounces," the doctor announced. "That's a good-size baby for a mama like you."

She counted each tiny finger and toe, then counted them over again. The baby was so tiny yet so perfect that Lilly Ann could scarcely breathe. It seemed as if her heart had swelled up so big that there wasn't room in her chest for air.

"Now hand the little one over, honey." One of the nurses stood next to the table and held out her arms. "We have to clean her up."

"No!" The word popped out real loud but Lilly Ann wasn't embarrassed, not even a little bit. "I mean, I want to hold her a little longer."

"Oh, honey, you've got eighteen years of holdin' her ahead of you. Let us have her for just a few minutes then she's all yours."

Eileen came to visit a few hours later.

"Nobody ever gave me roses before!" Lilly Ann exclaimed as she buried her face in the dozens of pale pink blossoms. "Thank you."

"No more than you deserve," Eileen said, perching on the side of the bed. She wore an eggshell linen dress with matching shoes and bag. Her pale blond hair was brushed smoothly off her face and held in place with a black velvet headband. Her only jewelry was a small gold watch on her left wrist. "She's beautiful," Eileen said.

"You saw her?"

Eileen nodded. "I stopped at the nursery before I came here. They have her in the first row so everyone can admire her."

"I know," Lilly Ann said proudly. "They said she's the most beautiful baby they've had here in years."

"Well, they're right. That's a very special little girl in there."

Lilly Ann fairly preened. Surely Eileen would want to keep them both around on a more permanent basis. She leaned forward, about to bring up the subject of a job when, to her surprise, Candy and Blake swept in the door, their arms piled high with presents.

"I know we should have called," Candy said as she spread the gaily wrapped packages on the bed next to Lilly Ann, "but we were just so excited about the baby that we had to come by and see you."

Lilly Ann clapped her hands in delight. She felt as if she were the guest of honor at a wonderful party. "Have you seen the baby?"

Candy and Blake exchanged looks then laughed out loud.

"Guilty as charged," said Blake in his booming, friendly voice.

"We couldn't resist," said Candy, with a graceful shrug of her shoulders. "What a beauty she is!"

They praised the baby's dark, curly hair; her big blue eyes; her perfect rosebud mouth. Lilly Ann drank it all in and still wanted more.

Candy and Blake came back again the second night and the third.

"They're awfully nice," Lilly Ann said to Eileen after the couple left that third night.

"Yes, they are," Eileen said, straightening out the covers on Lilly Ann's hospital bed. "It's such a shame they don't have any children of their own."

Lilly Ann's eyes flooded with tears. "How terrible!" Now that she had her own precious baby, she couldn't imagine life without her.

"It is terrible," Eileen agreed. She sat down on the chair next to the bed. "They've become very fond of your little one."

"I know." Lilly Ann gestured toward the mountain of baby clothes stacked high on the dresser. "They've been real generous."

Eileen leaned forward, her eyes shining. "Did you know that Blake owns his own company?"

Lilly Ann shook her head. "I don't really know much of anything about them, except they're your friends."

"Oh, darlin'! Blake and Candy are both from fine families. Blake inherited his daddy's business about ten years ago."

"That's real nice," Lilly Ann said again. She didn't see why it seemed to mean so much to Eileen that she knew all these things about the married couple.

Eileen went on about the couple's fancy home, their cars, the trips they took to all sorts of foreign places. Lilly Ann listened politely but she was beginning to get a real funny feeling deep in the pit of her stomach.

A nurse poked her head into the room. "Visting hours were over ten minutes ago, ladies."

Eileen rose from the bed and walked over to the door. Lilly Ann couldn't make out what she said to the nurse but the nurse nodded then left, closing the door after her.

Lilly Ann's heart lurched with fear. She swung her legs out of the bed and rooted around for her slippers.

"Darlin', what are you doing?" Eileen rushed back to her side. "Get back in that bed this instant! You're still weak as a kitten."

"I want to see my baby."

"The baby's sleeping," Eileen said, placing a hand on Lilly Ann's arm.

Lilly Ann pulled away. "I won't wake her up. I just want to see her."

"You heard the nurse. Visiting hours are over."

"I'm not a visitor. I'm her mama."

"Of course you are," Eileen crooned. "And you're terribly tired. I'm afraid we just wore you out tonight with all our jabbering."

"I'm not tired." Lilly Ann slipped into the robe Eileen had bought for her. "I just want to see my baby."

"Sit down, Lilly Ann."

Lilly Ann looked at her friend in surprise. She'd never heard Eileen sound that stern before, almost like a parent. She sat down.

"There's something we need to talk about, darlin'," Eileen began. "Something very important."

"Is it—" Lilly Ann struggled to take a deep breath. "The baby isn't—?"

"The baby is fine."

Lilly Ann sagged against her pillows. "Thank God," she whispered. As long as the baby was fine, nothing else could be all that important.

"I'm afraid Maisie didn't tell you the entire truth about me, darlin'," Eileen said. "I'm not really an old school friend of hers."

Prickles of apprehension scratched their way up her spine. "You're not?"

Eileen shook her head. "I've only known Maisie a few years."

Wasn't that just like Maisie, trying to get above herself by pretending she'd gone to some fancy school? "But you are friends?"

"We're friends," Eileen said, "but maybe not the kind of friends Maisie let you think we are."

"I'm real confused," Lilly Ann said, wishing they weren't having this talk. "Why are you tellin' me this?" It didn't much matter to her how well Eileen and Maisie knew each other. It didn't change the fact that nobody in the whole wide world had ever been kinder to her than Eileen Fontaine.

"Darlin', there's just no easy way to broach this subject so I'm going to just jump right in and say what needs to be said. Maisie and I have worked it out so Candy and Blake will adopt your baby."

Lilly Ann started to laugh. "I guess I *was* bein' kind of silly, wasn't I? I don't blame you for teasing me."

"Listen to me, darlin'. I meant what I said. Candy and Blake want to bring up your baby as if she were their own."

"But she's not their own," Lilly Ann said. "She's mine."

"They can offer her the world," Eileen told her in a quiet voice. "Things you could never give her."

"She'll never want for anything," Lilly Ann said. "Not while there's a breath in my body."

"Darlin', I know you mean every word you're saying but that's just not the way it is. You don't have a husband, a job—"

"You can give me one!" Lilly Ann grabbed Eileen's hand in hers. "Everyone says I have a good eye for color. I could work in your dress store."

Eileen frowned. "My dress store?"

"Maisie said you owned a dress store."

"I'm sorry, Lilly Ann, but I don't own a dress store."

Lilly Ann grew quiet. "Where do you get all your money from?"

"My husband was a very rich man," Eileen said. "When he died, he left me a great deal of money."

"Well, if you can't give me a job, I know I'll find somebody in Atlanta who will."

"You're going to stay in Atlanta?"

"Or I could go to New York City. There must be a lot of jobs in New York City." She'd always imagined herself walking down Fifth Avenue in a smart dress just like the ones Eileen herself wore.

"And who'll take care of the baby?"

"I—I'll find someone." Why did adults always manage to ask the one question you didn't have an answer for?

"You're not thinking clearly, darlin'. This whole situation is a lot harder than you realize."

"I know it's hard," Lilly Ann said, leaping from the bed, "but that doesn't mean it's impossible."

"You don't know that for certain."

"I'm a hard worker. I know I can take care of my baby."

Eileen sighed as she looked at Lilly Ann. "And what if you can't? Is it fair to that poor helpless little darlin'?"

"Then I'll find another way." She thought for a moment. "I'll call Maisie and Big Earle. They're family. They'll help me take care of the baby."

"You're forgetting something very important, darlin'. This was Maisie's idea."

"I don't believe you!" She knew Maisie didn't much like her but that baby was all that was left of Clifford. "Family is the most important thing in the world to Maisie."

Eileen looked at her with something close to pity. "This isn't the first time I've helped Maisie do this."

Lilly Ann felt her jaw sag open. "What?"

"Teena," Eileen said softly. "Two years ago. A lovely family in California adopted her son."

"Teena has a baby?"

"Teena gave birth to a baby," Eileen corrected Lilly Ann. "And she loved that baby enough to give him a chance at a better life. You should think about that, Lilly Ann."

"The Franklins have lots of money," Lilly Ann said. "They could've given the baby anything he needed."

"There's more to it than money, darlin'. That poor baby would be labeled a bastard for the rest of his life. Everybody in town would be whisperin' behind his back, saying his mama made a terrible mistake." Eileen paused for effect. "Now who would want to do that to someone they loved?"

Lilly Ann didn't have an answer. She knew that what Eileen was saying was right. People never forgot things like that. Why, Euless still buzzed about the day the Japanese bombed Pearl Harbor and Maybelle Long was caught behind the general store with her best friend's father and that was more than twenty years ago. She could only imagine what would happen if she marched back to town with Clifford's baby and settled down to make a life for them there.

"It's different in big cities."

"Not that different."

"I'm not giving up my baby."

A frown flickered across Eileen's face then disappeared. "It's late," she said. "You must be terribly tired."

It was as if Eileen's words gave her the right to be exhausted. Suddenly Lilly Ann felt all of her energy drain out through the soles of her feet and she climbed back into bed.

Eileen leaned over and smoothed the hair off Lilly Ann's forehead. "I know I've given you a lot to think about." She reached into her purse and withdrew a sheaf of papers. "This document should explain everything." She placed it on the bed next to Lilly Ann. "You read it, darlin', then we'll talk."

* * *

Lilly Ann read the document twice and was about to read it a third time when a nurse came in and convinced her it was time to turn off the light.

"Those papers'll still be there in the mornin', girl. You get yourself some sleep."

Lilly Ann put the papers on the nightstand, then shut off the lamp. She supposed the nurse was right. It really didn't matter how many more times she read the thing. She was never going to understand it.

"Get yourself some sleep, girl," the nurse said again as she tucked the covers around Lilly Ann. "Whatever's bothering you will seem better in the morning."

Lilly Ann doubted that was true but she managed a smile. "You're not going to forget to bring my baby in to nurse, are you?"

"You look real tired," the nurse said. "Why don't I give her a bottle so you can sleep the night?"

"No!" The thought of not seeing her baby tonight scared Lilly Ann to death. "She's my baby. I have to feed her."

"Formulas are better than mother's milk. Why should you be gettin' up every few hours if you don't have to?"

"Because I'm her mother," Lilly Ann said. And for the first time she understood what that meant.

A few hours later one of the nurse's aides brought the baby to Lilly Ann.

"You're makin' more work for everybody," the woman said as she handed the baby to Lilly Ann. "Bottle's good enough for everybody else in this hospital."

"I'm not everybody else," Lilly Ann said, lifting her chin. "And neither is my baby."

"Well, aren't we Little Miss High-and-Mighty?" the aide huffed then stomped from the room.

"Who cares what the old biddy thinks?" Lilly Ann whispered to the baby as she unbuttoned the front of her nighty and offered her daughter her breast. They *were* special, even if the nurse's aide was too blind to see it.

The baby didn't much care about anything but the breast; she latched on to the nipple and sucked hard and a feeling of wonder filled Lilly Ann. How could Teena have given away her own flesh and blood, turned her baby son over to a pair of total strangers? It wasn't as if the Franklins couldn't afford another mouth to feed. Grandma Hattie always said Maisie and Big Earle had enough money to keep the whole darned town in steak and beer. How much could one little baby cost anyway?

But somehow she knew it wasn't about money. Maisie had been running from her own people for as long as Lilly Ann could remember, trying to put as much distance between her and where she came from as she could. Country club daughters got pregnant just like everybody else, but they usually waited until they had the diamond wedding band on the third finger of their left hand.

Having her own precious daughter Teena carrying some boy's bastard child would only remind the town that Maisie and Earle Franklin were just one step away from their white trash beginnings.

"We won't think about them," Lilly Ann whispered to her baby. "We don't need people like that, do we, sweet thing?"

She'd choke before she asked the Franklins for help. People who would turn away from family would do anything at all.

She could almost hear Grandma Hattie laughing at her. *Thought you had it all figured out, didn't you, girl? You thought spreading your legs for Clifford would be the answer to your prayers.*

Her face flamed as she remembered the soft early spring air drifting over them as they did it in the back seat of Cliff's car that first time.

"Don't worry, baby," he'd said as he slid his hand under her skirt. "I'll take care of you."

She could still hear the scratchy sound his zipper made as he opened his fly and the quick rhythm of his breathing.

"Touch me," he'd said, working his finger inside the elastic band on her panties. "Don't be afraid. It won't bite you."

It seemed to mean a lot to Cliff so she held him gently in her hand, amazed at how big and hard he was.

"I'm gonna put that inside you, Lilly Ann," he whispered in her ear as he spread her thighs, "and you'll feel real good."

He slid one of his fingers inside her and she cried out with pain and shock.

"No!" She squirmed beneath him. "I don't want to do this anymore."

"Sure you do, sugar." He was stroking her now, moving his finger in and out, in and out, until her hips seemed to catch his rhythm and rock against him. "Look how nice and wet you are for me."

Wet? She didn't exactly know what he was talking about but his hand suddenly felt so good against her that she moaned out loud.

"I can't," she'd whispered as he pressed himself right up against her. "What if I get pregnant?"

"Don't you worry about anything, sugar. I'll take good care of you."

And you would have. Damn you, Clifford Earle Franklin! Why did you have to up and die that way? Lilly Ann wiped her eyes and leaned back against the clean white hospital pillows. Everything would have been different if Cliff hadn't had that stupid bachelor party. They'd be married now, set up in a nice little house right off Main Street in Euless, with a nursery for the baby and a modern kitchen with maybe even a dishwasher. Cliff would have gone to work for his daddy while Lilly Ann cared for their baby girl and kept the house neat as a pin.

But there was no use thinking about the past. What was done was done. Cliff was gone and there'd be no help from the rest of the Franklins. And Grandma Hattie had made it crystal clear that Lilly Ann and her baby weren't welcome anymore.

Maybe Eileen was right and she was being selfish, thinking she could care for the baby better than Candy and Blake could. She didn't have a husband or family. She didn't have a job or a place to live. She'd read a lot of baby books these last few months and she knew babies needed security and stability, two things Lilly Ann wasn't altogether sure she could provide.

So call Eileen. Tell her you were wrong, that maybe giving the baby to Candy and Blake is the best thing for everybody.

She'd end up just like Sally McClintock who lived over the barber shop with her two sons. Sally's husband had left her for a legal secretary from Tallahassee who had poodles instead of kids. Sally was skinny and angry and who could blame her? She worked days at the Euless County Bank and nights at Ginny's Diner and on weekends she cleaned office buildings. Her kids looked as if they saw a home-cooked meal about as often as they saw a bathtub. Everyone knew it was just a matter of time until the county took them away from Sally.

Lilly Ann shuddered. She'd rather die than end up like that, a dried-up ghost of a woman working herself into an early grave. If she went back to Euless, that was exactly what would happen.

The baby's chubby legs pumped the air and Lilly Ann moved her to the other breast. *Breast milk is free,* she thought, touching the baby's cheek with the tip of her index finger. Some mothers nursed their babies for months and months before they started feeding them solid food. Months where they didn't have to buy special baby food in those little bitty glass jars or fancy formulas in soda cans.

All she had to do was make sure she ate enough to keep her milk flowing. That couldn't cost very much. If there was one thing Lilly Ann had learned living with her grandma, it was how to make a little food go a real long way.

And she'd already escaped Euless. How hard could it be to find a job in a big city like Atlanta? Lilly Ann knew she was pretty, which was a plus. And didn't Grandma Hattie say she could talk the ears off an elephant with all her pointless chatter? You'd think that would be enough to get yourself a job in a beauty parlor. Someplace where there were lots of women who would understand.

A plan began to take shape. It was real shadowy at first but with every second that passed it got clearer and clearer until Lilly Ann wondered why she hadn't figured it out a whole lot sooner. She didn't need the Franklins or Eileen Fontaine or that rich couple who couldn't have themselves a baby.

"We're going to be fine," she told the infant cradled in her arms. "Just you wait and see."

5

Lilly Ann waited until it was almost time for the day shift to arrive. The night nurses were busy filling out all sorts of paperwork and everyone knew doctors didn't show up until well after breakfast. They'd brought the baby to her a half hour ago so she could nurse and Lilly Ann didn't expect them back for a good while yet.

She changed into her regular clothes, bundled the baby up in one of those new outfits Eileen had given her, grabbed a stack of diapers, then slipped out the fire exit. She felt light-headed and shaky on her feet as she made her way down the three flights of stairs to the ground floor. She'd grown used to the way her body felt with her belly sticking way out in front of her like the prow of a ship. It took some doing to keep her balance but she and the baby made it outside without getting caught.

The morning air was cool and crisp. She closed her eyes for a moment and drew in a deep breath. It felt a lot more like January in Atlanta than it did back in Euless, kind of the way she imagined winter should feel. She'd always wanted to live up north, someplace where they had seasons besides summer and hell.

Heart pounding, she started to walk down the street. She half expected police cars to come whizzing around the corner, lights flashing and sirens blaring. The cops would leap from the squad cars, guns drawn, ready to arrest her for leaving the hospital.

Don't act guilty, girl! She's your baby, not theirs. It wasn't as if she were committing a crime. She hadn't asked to go to a fancy hospital like St. Cyril's. That had been Eileen's idea. "Best hospital in the city," she'd assured Lilly Ann. "Your baby will get a fine start there."

Anger burned inside Lilly Ann's breast. How could Eileen have lied to her that way? The woman had been so kind, so loving, so generous and all the while she was in league with Maisie Franklin, looking to give her baby away to total strangers. She hated them, hated all of them, and she hated herself most of all for being tempted.

She walked for a good half hour through the early morning streets before a taxi rumbled up the street.

"Where to?" asked the tired-looking driver as she climbed in.

Lilly Ann hesitated. "I—I don't know."

He blew out a real exasperated sigh. "I been up darn near twenty-four hours, lady. If you don't know where you want to go, you can be doggone sure I don't know where you want to go."

She hugged the baby closer. "We need some place to stay."

"Don't we all." He swiveled around to take a good look at her. "Some place fancy?" he asked, his eyes taking in the expensive winter coat Eileen had bought for her the other day.

She shook her head. "I don't have much money."

"I know a motel but it ain't really the place for a baby."

"Is it cheap?" she asked, watching the meter inch its way up toward the one dollar mark.

"Doesn't get much cheaper."

"Take me there," she said, wishing she felt half as sure as she sounded.

"Hate to do it, miss."

"If you don't, I'll find someone else who will."

He shrugged his shoulders. "You talked me into it."

Ten minutes later they pulled up in front of the Georgia Peach Motel. Lilly Ann handed the driver two crumpled singles then bundled up the baby and climbed out of the car before he could get angry about the fifteen cent tip.

The lobby of the Georgia Peach smelled like the back room of the barber shop in Euless, bay rum and sweaty men. The smell would have been enough to turn her stomach inside out when she was pregnant. She clutched the baby to her breast and approached the desk clerk.

"I'd like a room, please."

The desk clerk barely looked up from the magazine he had spread out across the countertop. "No vacancies," he muttered.

"What was that, sir?" she asked in a sweet tone of voice.

"You heard me," he said, meeting her eyes. "No vacancies."

"I—I don't understand." She shifted the baby from her left shoulder to her right.

"No vacancies, no rooms. You speak English. You know what that means."

Who did he think he was, treating her as if she were dirt beneath his feet? She wanted to tear a piece off his hide like Grandma Hattie would have done, but it occurred to her maybe you really could catch more flies with honey than you could with an acid tongue.

"Sir," she said, her eyes welling with pretty tears. "Excuse me if I'm mistaken, but isn't that a vacancy sign blinkin' outside?"

"What if it is?" he asked in a real belligerent tone of voice. "Still ain't no rooms available."

"Why don't you check?" she suggested. "I think it just might be against the law to turn away a payin' customer when there's an empty room just waiting." She paused for effect, willing a tear to roll slowly down her cheek. "Especially a payin' customer with a baby."

"Six dollars a night," he said, crossing his bony arms across his chest. "Two nights in advance."

"*Two* nights in advance?"

"Yep, missy. I'm not going to be left holdin' the bag if you decide to up and leave on me."

Slowly she handed him a five dollar bill and seven singles. He pushed the key to room 43 across the counter. "One complaint about that baby cryin' and you're out of here."

"She won't cry," Lilly Ann promised. "You have my word."

"Don't cry, darlin'," Lilly Ann pleaded a few hours later. "Please don't cry!"

The baby had been crying almost since they got there, little squeaky cries that sounded like a kitten's mewling. Someone in the room next door pounded hard on the wall and she cringed, praying they wouldn't call the desk clerk. She was so tired she could hardly keep her eyes open and her bottom hurt so bad from the stitches that she felt like crying along with her daughter.

"Are you hungry?" she whispered to the baby.

The baby stared back up at her, big blue eyes wide and wondering. Lilly Ann unbuttoned her blouse and leaned back against the headboard and put her daughter to her breast.

Thank God her own milk was flowing freely. By the time she'd bought cereal and bananas from the small grocery store around the corner from the Georgia Peach, her nest egg was down to $29.37. She'd filched a stack of diapers from the hospital but she'd be lucky if she had enough money to buy the soap to wash them in. She didn't have money for baby clothes or doctor's visits or any of the million things she was going to need for her daughter any day now.

This time yesterday she'd been almost giddy with happiness. Labor hadn't hurt half as much as she'd thought it would, and when it was over, they'd placed a healthy baby daughter in her arms. Best of all, she and the baby weren't alone. They had friends who wanted to help them get on their feet. Friends who wouldn't let anything bad happen to either one of them. For the first time since Clifford's death, she'd been really, truly happy.

She could just imagine how Grandma Hattie would laugh if she knew about this turn of events. *You got what you deserved, girl. Now let's see you get out of this mess.* What a fool she'd been to believe that anybody hooked up with Maisie Franklin could have a drop of kindness in her heart. Eileen wasn't her friend any more than Maisie had been. All Eileen wanted to do was hand over Lilly Ann's baby to that rich couple as if she were a sack of groceries from Winn-Dixie.

The baby suckled noisily and Lilly Ann's heart lurched. She loved that little girl more than she'd ever loved anybody in her whole life but the notion of motherhood scared her senseless.

Think about what they could give her, girl. She'd have a fancy nursery and a layette and a trust fund . . . everything her heart desired.

"Never," she whispered as she moved the baby to her other breast. There was nothing in this world that would make her give up her baby.

Think about how much easier it would be on you. You could go back to school and maybe even get a job in some fancy office in the city. But none of it's going to happen if you're saddled with a baby.

She tried to push the horrible thought from her mind but it wouldn't go away. She could almost hear Grandma Hattie laughing. *You're as bad as your mama, girl. Every bit as bad....*

"We got complaints about you, missy." The desk clerk peered into the motel room from where he stood in the doorway. "That baby's been cryin' too much for most people's taste."

"She's a baby," Lilly Ann snapped at the man. "Babies cry." She'd been crying for days, it seemed, and there was nothing Lilly Ann could do to make her stop. She'd tried rocking her, talking to her, nursing her until her breasts ached, but nothing worked. Her nerves were rubbed raw as her nipples and it wouldn't take much to send her tumbling into a tailspin.

"Don't you use that tone with me, missy." He took a step into the room. "I only let you stay here because it was cold outside and I'm a good Christian man."

"I'm sorry," she said, not meaning it a bit. He was a horrible little man, all bony arms and legs and big old horse teeth. "You were very...kind." The words came close to choking her but his face softened. The baby's cries grew louder and the knot in her stomach tightened.

"What's her problem?" he asked. At least this time he sounded a little less angry.

"I think she's hungry." Lilly Ann scooped her up from her makeshift dresser drawer cradle.

"Don't sound like a hungry cry to me."

"You know about babies?" she asked suspiciously. He didn't look much like anybody's daddy.

"Sure do, missy. Me and Dora raised us up a half dozen of them between us."

The baby's cries grew louder, more frantic sounding.

"Don't mean to scare you but that sounds serious."

Lilly Ann met his eyes. "She threw up this morning."

"That the first time?" he asked.

Lilly Ann shook her head. "She hasn't been able to keep anything down all day." Her voice broke and she drew in a ragged breath. "She can't stop crying and I just don't know what to do for her." She wanted to run away, run as fast and as far as she could, all the way back to before she met Cliff and made the biggest mistake of her life.

The desk clerk placed a bony hand on the baby's cheek. "No wonder she's cryin'," he said, frowning. "This little mite is burnin' with fever."

Lilly Ann pressed her lips to the baby's forehead then burst into tears.

"Don't you start cryin' too," the desk clerk scolded. "One's bad enough."

"I don't know what to do," Lilly Ann sputtered. "If anything happens to her—"

He patted her hand awkwardly. "Nothing's going to happen to her, missy. Not if you get her to the hospital as fast as you can."

"I can't afford a hospital," she said through her tears. "I can't even afford a doctor."

"The little mite's in bad shape. Take her to the hospital," he repeated, "and worry about how you're going to pay for it later on."

"You did the right thing, calling me, darlin'." Eileen Fontaine gave Lilly Ann a warm hug as the two women stood outside the door to the pediatric intensive care unit. "Can't expect you to bear this burden alone." She stepped back and took a long look. "Lord, you're just skin and bones. When did you last eat?"

"I-I don't know," Lilly Ann managed to reply, swaying on her feet. "Before the baby got sick."

"That's five days!" Eileen looked downright horrified. She linked her arm through Lilly Ann's. "Now don't you back talk me, darlin'. We're going down to the cafeteria and I'm going to see to it you get some food in that flat little belly of yours."

"I can't leave her," Lilly Ann protested, gesturing toward the baby who was hidden by all sorts of tubes and scary-looking machines. "She'll be afraid."

"She's sound asleep," Eileen said with a gentle laugh. "Besides I think she'd be a lot happier if her mama wasn't about to pass out on her feet."

She wanted to hate Eileen, she really did, but she was so relieved to have someone to lean on that she couldn't quite manage it. "Some soup would be nice," she admitted.

Eileen took her downstairs to the cafeteria and saw to it that she finished two bowls of chicken noodle soup, a stack of crackers, and a tall glass of milk. Eileen nursed a cup of coffee and a cigarette while she told Lilly Ann what the doctor had to say about the baby's condition. Eileen's words seemed to float toward Lilly Ann through a heavy fog.

"She has pneumonia," Eileen said matter-of-factly, "and a few other problems. Doctor says she'll be in here at least a month."

"A month," Lilly Ann breathed. Her soup spoon clattered to the table. "That's going to cost a fortune."

"Yes," said Eileen. "It will."

Lilly Ann met her eyes. "Maybe Maisie and Big Earle can help."

"You know the answer to that, darlin'." Eileen chuckled. "You called them before you called me."

Lilly Ann's face flamed. "They told you?"

"They told me."

"I didn't mean to lie to you, Eileen."

"I know you didn't, darlin'. You're just alone and scared and way too young to have such problems."

"I don't know what to do," Lilly Ann said, her voice shaking. "The hospital wants to take her away from me because I don't have the right kind of home for her."

"They're worried about her, darlin'. She's going to need a lot of care when she gets out."

"Then I'll give it to her."

"How?" Eileen asked, leaning across the Formica table. "You don't have a home or a husband or a job. You don't even have identification to prove who you are or where you come from. County officials won't take real kindly to that."

"We'll move away," Lilly Ann said. "I'll go back to Euless and get a job waiting tables." At least back home they knew who she was.

"And how will you pay the hospital bill?" Eileen challenged. "And the doctors' bills?"

"A little bit at a time."

"They won't accept that, darlin'. You know they won't."

"They can't take my baby away from me. That's against the law."

"So is stealing."

"Stealing?" Lilly Ann's heart started to pound real hard inside her chest.

Eileen lowered her voice. "They're not very happy with you over at St. Cyril's. They don't take kindly to new mothers walking out with their babies without stopping to pay their bills. They called the police." She shook her head sadly. "They're lookin' for you, Lilly Ann, and I'm not sure I can help you when they find you."

You're bad, Lilly Ann. Every bit as bad as your mama ever was....

"I know why you did that," Eileen went on. "You were afraid, weren't you? So much has happened to you ... you're so young ... you need someone to take this burden off your shoulders...."

Lilly Ann trembled like a leaf as she struggled to hold back her sobs. In the two weeks since the baby was born she'd felt as if she were trapped in a nightmare, one of those terrible dreams where you're running and running but you can't run fast enough to get away from the monster who's about to grab you in his jaws and eat you alive. And the worst part of it was there didn't seem to be a way out.

"You wanted to take her away from me. I was afraid I—" She stopped short and looked down at her hands. Cliff used to say she had pretty hands but now they were raggedy and awful, the nails bitten right down to the quick.

"Go on, darlin'," Eileen urged. "Say what needs to be said."

She couldn't. It was too awful ... too dreadful a thing to admit to anyone. Not even to herself.

"There's nothing to be ashamed of." Eileen's voice was soft and soothing, a mama talking to a scared little child. "I know how you feel...that miserable motel...not enough food...the baby crying and crying and there's nothing you can do to help her—"

Lilly Ann buried her head against the woman's shoulder and sobbed as if her heart would break. That's how it was, exactly how it was with her. She'd done nothing but make one mistake after another, from sleeping with Cliff to believing they would live happily ever after to thinking she could bring up her baby all by herself.

"Will they put me in jail?" She wiped her eyes with the back of her hand but the tears were falling so fast she couldn't keep up with them.

"I don't know." Eileen looked so sad Lilly Ann could scarcely breathe. "They might very well do that."

"They can't!" She grabbed Eileen by the arm. "If they do that, who will take care of the baby?"

"The state, I suppose," said Eileen. "They'll put her in foster care . . . maybe even an orphanage."

"Oh God," Lilly Ann breathed. Her beautiful, perfect little girl growing up unloved and alone.

"My heart goes out to you," Eileen continued in her sweet voice. "Your precious baby deserves so much better. . . ." She deserved a layette with handworked dresses and embroidered caps. She deserved a nursery painted shell pink with fluffy white priscillas hanging from every window. She deserved a mother who could be with her morning, noon, and night—a mother who could do for Lilly Ann's baby the things her own mother hadn't done for her. Things that Lilly Ann would never be able to do for her own child from a jail cell.

"I could get a good lawyer," Lilly Ann said, grasping at straws. "A good lawyer could explain it to St. Cyril's and make it all better."

Eileen's smile held more than a touch of sadness. "That just might happen," she said, "but then what? How on earth is a poor little girl like you going to do for your child?" She sighed deeply. "It's a terrible mess you're in . . . just terrible."

The enormity of it all took Lilly Ann's breath away. For the rest of her life she'd be trying to make up to her daughter for all of her mistakes, trying to explain why she couldn't give her girl all the things she deserved while the girl hated her more with every day that passed. And she'd be a liar if she said it was only the baby she was worried about. She was scared to death she'd end up trapped like her mama and daddy and Grandma Hattie and everyone else back in Euless. Her dreams of a better life were going up in smoke and there was nothing she could do to stop them.

"Please help me," she whispered to Eileen, knowing this was the first step on the road to hellfire. "Please . . ."

"My poor little darlin'," Eileen crooned, smoothing back Lilly Ann's hair with a motherly hand. "Maybe I can find a way. . . ."

Three hours later Lilly Ann boarded a Greyhound bus headed for New York City. She took with her a suitcase full of new dresses and five hundred dollars cash tucked in her shoulderbag.

She left behind her maternity clothes, a pair of lemon yellow flannel pajamas, and her baby daughter.

BOOK TWO

The Child

6

Cincinnati, Ohio, 1969

Millicent and Jack Banning despaired of ever having a child to love. They had been married over twenty years and the Good Lord hadn't seen fit to bless them with a baby and it was beginning to look like He never would.

"It's God's will," Reverend Evans counseled them early on as they sat crying in his study. "He has something else in mind for you two."

"Then He'd better hurry up and figure out what it is," Millicent said, "because we aren't getting any younger."

A year passed and then another and still God didn't see fit to show them what He had planned for them. Jack spent most of his time fishing in the creek out back of the house while Millicent drank coffee by the potful and wondered what she'd done wrong in her life that she was being punished so harshly.

The county adoption agency had told them they were too old to adopt a baby. Too old, Millicent had sniffed, outraged by the very thought. They were in the prime of life, strong and healthy and eager to love a little child. But no. The powers that be didn't see things that way and they stamped a big red no on the Bannings' application blank then filed it away forever.

This wasn't the way it happened on her beloved soap operas. On her shows babies miraculously appeared on doorsteps or were bequeathed to childless couples like silverware or heirloom jewelry. A part of Millicent was still waiting for the knock on the door that would change her life forever.

"I can't take this no more," Jack told Millicent over dinner one night at the Sizzler. "Let's put it all aside, Millie, and get on with our lives." Hoping for a miracle that never came had left him brokenhearted.

But Millicent was made of stronger stuff than that. Oh, she was heartbroken same as her husband, but that didn't stop her. Somewhere out there a baby was waiting for her loving arms and she had to keep on searching until she found him. It didn't much matter to Millicent if the baby was American or Korean or a regular Heinz-57 variety with the best of everybody all mixed up together. She just wanted a baby to love, a tiny little bundle of joy who would belong to only them.

And then one day, out of the blue, it happened. The theme song from "The Guiding Light" had just started when the telephone rang. She glared at the phone from her easy chair. This was the day when Ed and Leslie were going to reveal their true feelings for each other and Millicent didn't want to miss one moment of it. Papa Bauer and that nosy Bert didn't think much of Leslie but Millicent knew she was exactly right for young Doctor Ed.

After a few moments the phone stopped ringing and she relaxed but then it started up again. Grumbling, she got up from her chair and went to answer it.

"Now I don't want you to get your hopes up, Millie," said Reverend Evans, "but I think your prayers have been answered."

She clutched the phone to her ear. "My prayers?" she asked in a quavery voice. She prayed for lots of things these days: for the late Bobby Kennedy, God rest his soul; for those astronauts who were about to walk on the moon; and, even though it was probably pointless, she still prayed for a baby.

"Take yourself a deep breath, Millie," Reverend Evans went on.

Bright red and yellow and blue lights danced behind her eyes as she leaned against the wall for support. She knew she had a better chance of hitchhiking a ride to Mars than she did of getting a baby but hope was a hard thing to kill.

"There's a little girl," the Reverend said in a real careful tone of voice. "She's six years old."

"Six years old?" Millicent fought against a wave of bitter disappointment as she thought of the handworked layette that rested, unused, in her hope chest.

"She's in foster care near Nashville," he went on, ignoring her outburst, "and my sources say she badly needs a home." He told her a sad story about a couple from Tennessee who'd been killed in a car crash when the little girl was less than two months old. "It was a terrible wreck. They were on their way up from Atlanta when they crashed head-on with a van." Miraculously the baby had survived but she'd been badly scarred. "She's a special case, Millie. She needs someone who knows how to love." People these days wanted perfect houses, perfect cars, perfect children. There was no room in anybody's heart for a little girl who fell short of perfection.

Millicent didn't want to love the little girl. She'd waited all the years of her marriage for a baby, for a little helpless infant who would look to her for everything. What would she do with a six-year-old child who'd already known a fair share of heartbreak? The little girl had never known a real family. She'd been shuffled from foster home to foster home, and more than likely she'd be a handful of trouble before she settled down in one place.

"There's probably no point to this," she said to Jack as they drove down to Nashville where the little girl was living.

Jack agreed with her. They'd been married so long that they even thought alike. "We're doing this for Reverend Evans," he said, tapping the wheel of their Ford Fairlane with his index fingers. "He's been real good to us, Millie. The least we can do is meet the little girl."

Millicent nodded. It made perfect sense to her. "Yes, I suppose you're right, Jack. He's never asked anything of us before." She patted his knee. "Besides, I hear Porter Waggoner and Dolly Parton are over at the Opry tomorrow night."

They would check into the motel near to the highway and get a good night's sleep, then tomorrow morning they would drive into town and meet the little girl who had somehow captured Reverend Evans's interest. They would stay long enough to be polite but not long enough to get the poor thing's hopes up, then they would make their goodbyes as kindly as possible. All in all, it was exactly the right way to handle things and Millicent was quite pleased with herself.

"Corey!" Mrs. Zimmer hollered from the foot of the attic stairs. "You come down here this instant!"

Corey burrowed more deeply beneath a pile of quilts and stifled a sneeze. The attic was dusty and dark but it was the only place in the house where she could be alone.

"This is your last chance," Mrs. Zimmer went on. "The Bannings will be here any second. Don't you go embarrassing me by coming down here all dirty."

Corey stuck out her tongue. Mrs. Zimmer was a mean-tempered old witch who only cared about getting rid of her. She liked to make believe she loved Corey the way she loved her own kids but Corey wasn't stupid. She knew that Mrs. Zimmer laughed at her behind her back and was counting the days until she waved goodbye.

Corey wished there was a mud puddle right there in the middle of the attic. A big ugly squishy puddle that she could roll around in. She'd smear mushy dirt over her face and in her hair and paint designs on the crisply ironed blue cotton dress that had belonged to Mrs. Zimmer's daughter Dana. It would serve her right, Corey thought, if she met the Bannings looking as if she lived in a swamp.

"Get yourself down here this minute, young lady!" It was Mr. Zimmer this time and he didn't sound any happier than his fat dumb wife. "These people drove all the way from Ohio to meet you and you'd better be on your best behavior."

Corey stuck out her tongue at him, too. He was even worse than Mrs. Zimmer. He cuffed his own kids in the ear when they sassed him and hit them with his belt just because he felt like it. She knew the only reason he didn't lay a hand on her was because he'd rather hug a snake than touch her. She'd seen the way his face scrunched up each time he looked at her, kind of like he was about to throw up or something.

"You got yourself one long road ahead of you," he'd say, shaking his head like a dog with a flea. "You better be smart because you sure ain't gonna be beautiful."

She never cried when he said that. She just stared right back at him, making him look long and hard at the scars on her face. She'd rather eat a bug than let him know that his words hurt her more than the strap of his belt ever could.

She *was* smart, smart enough to know that the face she saw each day in the mirror wasn't the kind of face that made people smile and want to do nice things for you, like adopt you and make you their own little girl. No, hers was the kind of face people whispered about when they thought no one could hear.

They all whispered about her sooner or later. Even the grown-ups who made a big show out of not noticing the scars that ran down the left side of her face like angry red railroad tracks or the way one side of her mouth was higher than the other. Just when she thought that maybe this time it would be different, she'd hear the same old words all over again. *Poor kid. Who's going to want her, looking the way she does?*

She wanted to fight like a scalded cat when she heard things like that. She wanted to kick and scratch and bite until all the people who made fun of her hurt the same way she was hurting. But that would be the same as crying like a baby each time they said something mean. And she'd never do that. Not in a million years.

She heard footsteps on the stairs and tucked the dusty quilt more tightly around her body.

"You better get down there right now." Ten-year-old Tommy Zimmer poked her foot with his shoe. "Pop's ready to have himself a hissy fit."

Corey giggled and sat up. "Are his ears gettin' red?"

"Red as beets." Tommy tugged on his own big ears. "He thinks these folks are gonna adopt you."

Corey screwed up her face and kicked off the quilt. "There's nobody going to adopt me, Tommy Zimmer. Not with this face."

"Your face ain't so bad," said Tommy, studying her the same way he studied his sister's breasts when he thought no one was looking. "It's the way you act."

She swung at him with both fists but he ducked before she could get him. "You take that back!"

"Will not."

"Will."

"Will not."

She threw herself at him like a mad dog after a bone. "You take that back!" she screamed, sinking her teeth into his shoulder.

"You better stop right now, Corey." Tommy's voice was squeaky and scared sounding. "I'll tell Pop to take the strap to you."

"I'll hit him back," Corey said fiercely as she pummeled his chest with her balled-up fists. "He better never do that to me or I'll do something awful."

Tommy's eyes were wide as he broke away from her. "You gone crazy, girl. Not even my ma ever hits him back."

"Maybe she should," Corey shot back. "Maybe then he wouldn't be so all-fired mean to everyone."

Tommy opened his mouth to speak but his mother's bellow drowned him out. "You get yourself down here before I count three, Corey, or I'll know the reason why!"

Mrs. Zimmer grabbed her by the arm as soon as Corey got to the landing.

"Look at you!" She brushed the dust from Corey's dress with hard and ugly hands. "They're going to think I don't take care of you like I should."

"You don't," Corey said. "You only care about me when you think somebody might adopt me."

Mrs. Zimmer pinched her upper arm but Corey didn't so much as blink. "Listen to that," she said in a snakey kind of voice. "I do for her for six months and don't get so much as a thank you from the little brat." She pinched Corey again for good measure.

Corey's heart was pounding so fast she thought it would burst right through her rumpled dress. Mrs. Zimmer had been mean from the start but she'd never hurt her before. If she'd do something like that right before strangers came to visit, what would she do when they were all alone? She'd seen Tommy with his eyes all black and blue. And Dana's arm had been in a cast for weeks and weeks. They'd said she fell off a swing at the playground but Corey's eyes were sharp. She'd seen the way Dana cringed every time her pop walked into the room.

She'd lived with families like that before, families where the father spoke with his fists and everyone scurried around like scared little mice. She'd lie awake at night, listening to the sounds shivering through the walls and wonder why nobody ever fought back. If anyone ever came near her like that she would kick and scream and make sure she gave as good as she got.

She'd be happy just to get away from the Zimmers before something really awful happened. All of a sudden she wished she hadn't got her dress all wrinkled up or her hair mussed. She was too smart to think anyone would want to make her part of a forever family but it was time to leave the Zimmers.

"I don't like them," Millicent said as she ran a finger across the sticky countertop. "What kind of people make company wait in the kitchen?"

"Don't even offer a body a cup of coffee," Jack said, shaking his head. He put a real store on things like that, always had. "They're not our kind, Millie."

Millicent nodded. "Now we don't want to be rude to the little girl, but after we talk to her for a bit, I'll say I have one of my headaches and we'll say goodbye."

Jack looked toward the back door like a dog itching for his freedom. "Wouldn't mind if we left right now," he said, jingling the car keys in his pocket.

Millicent opened up her mouth to say something when the kitchen door swung open and Mrs. Zimmer poked her head inside. Her smile was as fake as Millicent's hair color. "Didn't mean to keep ya'll waiting so long but the girl wasn't ready." She rolled her eyes and her smile widened, exposing a jumble of horse teeth.

Millicent refused to smile back. "We'd like to meet the child," she said in an even tone of voice. The kitchen smelled just awful, like spoiled chicken and backed-up drains. Hadn't the woman ever heard of Mr. Clean? She wouldn't keep a cat in a house like this, much less a little girl.

Mrs. Zimmer disappeared. "Get yourself in there," Millicent heard her say in a threatening voice. "Don't you go running for that door! It's not like you get a whole lot of chances...."

Good Lord, what kind of life was the poor little thing leading? Millicent's heart was pounding so hard she could scarcely breathe. *Run, Millicent! You don't want to be here and you know it.* She was in way over her head. All she had to do was turn around and walk right back out the door. Nobody, not even Mrs. Zimmer, could stop her.

She'd been dreaming about a baby, all soft and sweet and smelling of powder and formula, not a six-year-old with a scarred face and a bad start in life. She and Jack were happy together. They'd managed to build a good life without children, hadn't they? Maybe the time had finally come to accept the way things were and stop wishing for things that couldn't be.

"Millie?" Jack's face was creased with concern. That little vein at the side of his neck was pumping like a Texas oil well. "You're white as a sheet."

"Let's go," she said, grabbing for his hand.

"We haven't met the girl."

"I don't want to meet her. I want to leave." Her words tumbled over themselves as she pulled him toward the door. "We shouldn't have come here, Jack. We had no business making that poor little girl think we might adopt her." Tears filled her eyes. "We should never have listened to Reverend Evans," she said fiercely. "Never!"

"You better sit down, Millie," Jack said. "You look like you're about to keel over."

He didn't understand what was happening. Fate was backing them into a corner, a terrible corner, and if they didn't get out of that house right that minute they'd find themselves saddled with more troubles than they could shake a stick at. Millicent was a sucker for unfortunates, a pushover for a hard luck story. But parents weren't supposed to pity their children; they were supposed to love them. A child deserved more from her parents than pity and pity was all Millicent felt in her heart.

"You stay here if you want to," she said to Jack. "I'll wait for you in the car." She took a step toward the door, then another one and another one. Her hand wrapped around the doorknob and she threw open the door and that was when fate swooped down and grabbed her in its clutches.

There on the top step sat a small child with the most beautiful deep blue eyes Millicent had ever seen. *Sapphire*, she thought as she took in the brilliant color and the thick, curling lashes. The child's skin was creamy with a soft pink wash highlighting her cheeks. Millicent's eyes danced over the scars, erasing them as she went. The child had a straight nose, a pointed little cat's chin, and an alarmingly determined jaw. She had trouble written all over her, as surely as if the Lord had written it in ink, but somehow Millicent knew she was meant to belong to her and Jack.

My child, she thought as her heart turned over inside her chest. *My daughter.*

"You're Corey, aren't you?" she asked, bending down beside the child.

The girl nodded. "Who are you?"

Millicent turned slightly and looked at her husband. His own eyes were wet with tears and he nodded his head. "I'm Millicent," she said, her voice cracking with emotion. "Your new mama."

"Yeah," said the child. "I've had lots of new mamas."

This wasn't the way it happened on Millicent's beloved TV shows. She swallowed hard and plastered a smile on her face. "That may be so, honey, but I'm the last one you'll ever have. We'd like to adopt you."

"How do you know that?" Corey asked, sounding much older than her six years. "Maybe you won't like me. Most people don't like me because I'm ugly."

"I love you," Millicent said, meaning it to her great surprise. "You're the daughter I've waited for my whole life."

The child looked over at Jack who was standing in the doorway, arms folded across his chest. "What if he doesn't like me?"

"He's your daddy," Millicent said proudly. "He'll love you as much as I do."

The child considered her words for what seemed a lifetime to Millicent. "Maybe," she said after a long moment, "but I wouldn't bet on it."

Jack cleared his throat. "You go and get your things, Corey."

The child nodded then disappeared into the house.

"I can't leave her here, Jack," Millicent said by way of explanation. "I know it's crazy but it feels right."

Jack dragged a shaky hand through his thinning hair. "I hope we're not making a mistake. That little girl needs more than we can give her." He touched the side of his face, tracing the pattern of the child's scars. "Parents who can afford a good doctor, for starters."

"She needs love," Millicent said fiercely, "not a doctor. There's nothing wrong with her that a home and family can't cure."

"She's mad at the world," Jack went on. "She's going to be a handful."

"Give her time," Millicent said. "Once she realizes she has a family of her own, she'll come around."

And if Corey didn't, what did it matter? Millicent was sure she had enough love for both of them.

7

Cincinnati, 1973

"We're at our wits' ends, Mrs. Banning," said the principal of the Hillman Grade School. "This is the third time we've caught Catherine stealing from the other children."

"I understand, Mrs. Lucas." Millicent struggled to sound calmer than she felt. "I'm sure there's some misunderstanding."

"Misunderstanding?" Mrs. Lucas laughed hollowly. "She was found with her hand in her classmate's coat pocket in the cloakroom. Certainly there was no misunderstanding."

Millicent sighed. She knew there hadn't been a misunderstanding. There never was, not when it came to Corey. "She'll be punished for this," she assured the prim young woman who sat behind the sturdy wooden desk.

Mrs. Lucas nodded but Millicent saw no compassion in her dark grey eyes. "That is all well and good, Mrs. Banning, but the fact remains that we simply can't keep on allowing the child to disrupt classes this way."

Millicent could hear her pulse beating in her ears. Jack would just hit the roof if Corey was expelled from a second school. The last thing on earth she wanted was to see that I-told-you-so look on his face. She remembered how Vanessa on "Love of Life" handled it the time Barbara got into trouble with her teacher and lifted her chin proudly.

"I understand," she said to Mrs. Lucas. "What do you suggest?"

Mrs. Lucas leaned back in her chair. "A suspension."

"No!" The word exploded from Millicent's throat. "Absolutely not!"

"Do you have a better idea?" the principal countered.

"Detention," Millicent said. "Extra chores at home." Things they'd already tried but to no avail—but Mrs. Lucas didn't need to know that.

"I think perhaps Corey needs a new environment. Someplace more structured." There was a private school on the outskirts of town that specialized in difficult girls.

To her horror, Millicent began to cry. "Please don't do that," she begged, her pride forgotten. "We can't afford special schools. You're our only hope."

Mrs. Lucas's stern face softened. She pushed a box of tissues across the desk toward Millicent. "Corey is an intelligent girl, Mrs. Banning, and underneath it all a nice one as well. But there are some problems inherent in her character that need to be addressed. She doesn't fit in with the other children and that makes her angry and difficult to handle."

"The scars don't bother her," Millicent retorted. "Why should they bother anyone else?" Her girl was beautiful, inside and out. It wasn't Corey's fault if they were too blind to see it.

"Children this age can be terribly cruel." Mrs. Lucas went on as if Millicent hadn't spoken a word. "They are not tolerant of differences."

"We can't afford fancy surgery if that's what you're driving at."

"It begins with the way she looks, Mrs. Banning, but what I'm talking about is the way she acts. Her anger keeps the children from getting close to her in friendship."

"That's their loss," Millicent snapped. "If they can't see beyond their own noses, that isn't my girl's problem."

"You're really gonna get it, Corey Banning." Rosemary Hogan glared at her from the other side of the hallway. "This time they're gonna tan your hide but good."

"Oh, shut up!" Corey wadded up a piece of loose-leaf paper and lobbed it at the dumb girl sitting on the bench opposite her. "Just because we got caught doesn't mean we're gonna get punished."

"Shows how much you know. Your mama's in there right now with the principal." Rosemary's fat lips parted in a nasty smile. "I'll just bet they're gonna send you to jail."

"They don't send kids to jail," Corey said, wishing she'd given some thought to that possibility before she'd stuck her hand in old Ginny Albright's slicker.

"Oh yes, they do," Rosemary declared. "They sent my brother Donnie to jail and he didn't come home until he was twenty-one."

Corey's stomach lurched with fear but she refused to let Rosemary know her words had found their mark. "If I go to jail, you go to jail too," she said in what she hoped was a grown-up voice. "You're just as much to blame as I am, you dumb cow."

"I'll tell them you made me do it."

Corey grinned in triumph. "And I'll tell them the cloakroom was your idea."

Rosemary paled beneath her red freckles. "They won't believe you. Everyone knows you're the biggest liar in the class."

"I have your note."

Rosemary let out a shriek and leaped up from the bench. "You give me that note!"

"Make me."

Rosemary threw herself at Corey but Corey ducked and the girl rushed headlong into the wall. Rosemary's wail of anguish brought Mrs. Lucas and Millicent hurrying from the office to see what was wrong.

"Catherine!" the women cried in unison. Nobody ever called her Catherine except when they were furious. Sometimes she even forgot that was the name the nurses at the hospital had given her when she was a baby.

"She did it," Corey said, pointing at the sobbing girl who sat on the floor by the bench. "She wanted to beat me up."

"Take her home," Mrs. Lucas said to Millicent. "She's on suspension for the rest of the week."

Millicent's face fell. "Mrs. Lucas, please, just let me—"

"No." The principal's angry expression made Corey squirm. "I think it's best for all concerned if you took her home immediately and gave me a chance to rethink my position when I'm feeling more charitable."

Before she knew what was happening, Corey found herself in the front seat of the family station wagon. Millicent slammed the passenger door the minute Corey was inside then walked around the front and climbed behind the wheel. She slammed the driver's door so hard it made Corey's teeth rattle.

She'd never seen Millicent so mad before. Her hands actually shook as she tried to stick the key in the ignition. Usually Millicent took Corey's side but it was pretty darned clear that this time Corey was on her own.

"Mom."

Millicent ignored her as the engine sputtered to life.

"Can we go to McDonald's, Mom?"

Millicent threw the station wagon into Reverse and backed out of the parking spot. She wasn't a real good driver and Corey winced as she barely missed rear-ending the car in front of her. "We're going straight home, missy."

"But I didn't have lunch."

"And you won't be having supper either. Not once your father hears what you've done."

"I didn't do anything!" Corey protested. "It was that Rosemary Hogan. She's the one who started it."

"Don't lie to me, Catherine Banning. I know exactly who started it and she's sitting next to me right this very minute."

"You can't believe everything that old bat Mrs. Lucas says. She'd say anything to get me out of her dumb school."

"And I don't blame her."

Corey's mouth fell open. "Mom!"

Millicent pulled the car over to the side of the road. Her hands shook, her chin trembled, and to Corey's amazement, big tears rolled down her cheeks. "Why are you so unhappy, honey?" she asked in a broken voice. "What have we done to make you want to hurt us this way?"

Corey felt as if someone had hit her in the chest with a brick. "I—I don't want to hurt you."

"But you do, honey. Every time you do something like this, you hurt your daddy and me right to the quick."

She wanted to say that she was sorry but the words just wouldn't come. They were locked away deep inside and no matter how hard she tried she couldn't get them to break free. She looked out the window at the passing cars.

"Don't you have anything to say to me?" Millicent asked as the minutes ticked by.

Corey shrugged her shoulders. "You wouldn't believe me if I did."

"No," said Millicently sadly. "I wouldn't at that."

It was even worse than Corey had imagined it would be. Jack didn't yell at her the way he sometimes did when she sassed him. Instead he looked at her with the saddest eyes she'd ever seen and said he was too hurt to even talk to her. He sent her up to her room without supper and Millicent didn't even try to talk him out of it. Instead she sat by the window, her knitting on her lap, and looked out at the backyard.

Corey lay sprawled across the bed in her room and stared up at the ceiling. The plaster was beginning to crack and she wondered if one day the whole thing would just drop down on her while she was sleeping and crush her like a bug. She supposed she should be scared at the thought of such a thing but tonight it didn't sound half bad. She'd brought nothing but trouble to the Bannings in the four years she'd been with them and she knew it was only a matter of time before they realized it.

The only thing that surprised her was that it was taking them this long. Most other families had it figured out before the first year was over. "She's more than we can handle," they'd tell the social worker and Corey would find herself back in the system, waiting for another family to give her a try.

But not the Bannings. No matter what she did, they found a way to forgive her. Even the time she'd burned down the next-door neighbor's tool shed, Jack had said, "Kids will be kids," and handed over a check. Sure, he hadn't been real happy with her for that stunt, but after he yelled at her for a few minutes, his bad mood blew away like a thunderstorm and all was forgotten.

They said they loved her but Corey wasn't buying it. If she was so lovable, her real mother wouldn't have given her away like a sack of old clothes. If Millicent and Jack had been lucky enough to have their own little girl, Corey knew darn well not even God Himself would have been able to tear her away from their arms. Even dumb old Rosemary Hogan's parents had kept her, even though Rosemary had carrottop hair and a nose that looked like a squash blossom. Somehow they had found something about Rosemary to love, some invisible thing that made her worth keeping.

No, the problem was Corey. She was too ugly and too mean and sooner or later even the Bannings would get tired of her and ship her back where she came from.

All this thinking about her real mother made her feel sad. Hot tears burned against her eyelids and she buried her face against her pillow to stem the tide. She didn't want to cry. Only babies cried when their feelings got hurt and she wasn't a baby anymore. Maybe if she hadn't had the dream last night, she wouldn't be feeling so sorry for herself but the dream had seemed so real that when she woke up that morning she almost believed her mother had come to claim her little girl.

"Dope," she whispered, pinching the inside of her wrist to keep from crying. Her mother couldn't find her even if she wanted to. Who would ever think to look in Cincinnati? It was just a stupid dream that was never, ever going to come true, no matter how hard she wished it would.

If only she knew something about the woman who'd carried her in her very own body for nine long months. Was that where Corey got her blue eyes and black hair? Sometimes she wondered about her father, too, but mostly it was her mother who came to her in her dreams, all shadowy and mysterious and beautiful. Why had she given up her baby to strangers? Did she ever wonder what had happened to Corey? Did she know about the car accident? Did she think about her and love her even though she didn't want her?

"Corey."

She jumped at the sound of Millicent's voice.

"Corey, honey, I have some supper for you."

"Go away," Corey mumbled. "I'm not hungry."

The door creaked open and she pulled the pillow over her face.

"Some nice tomato soup and crackers," Millicent said, stepping into the room. "And a big glass of milk."

"I hate milk."

"That's the first I've heard of that."

"And I hate you."

She heard the sound of a tray being set down on her nightstand then felt the mattress shift beneath her as Millicent sat down. She waited for Millicent to tell her that she didn't really mean it, that good girls didn't tell their mothers they hated them, but Millicent surprised her when she said, "I'm sorry you feel that way."

But I don't really feel that way, she thought, wishing she knew why she said and did such terrible things when she didn't really mean them. It was as if she wanted to lash out and hurt Millicent so the other shoe would finally drop. So they would send her away before she believed she'd found a forever home.

"You're not very happy, are you, honey?" Millicent stroked her hair beneath the pillow.

"I'm happy," Corey muttered.

"Happy girls don't do the things you do."

Those awful tears were back again, running down her cheeks and wetting the pillowcase.

"We love you, Corey." Millicent's voice broke and she cleared her throat noisily. "But we don't want you to stay with us if you're this unhappy."

There it was. The awful words she'd known she'd hear sooner or later.

"So get rid of me," she said, pushing the pillow off the bed and sitting up. "It doesn't bother me."

"But it would bother me," Millicent said, reaching for her hand.

"Then why do you want to get rid of me?"

"Because love means putting the other person's needs ahead of your own and if you would have a happier life somewhere else, I need to know that."

"I don't understand."

Millicent smiled sadly. "I know you don't, honey. That's one of the problems."

"Why did you adopt me if you're willing to give me away?"

"We adopted you because we wanted you to be part of our family." She patted Corey's hand. "So far you don't seem too pleased with that idea."

Corey wanted to pull her hand away and tell Millicent that she didn't need to be part of any stupid family, much less a dumb family like theirs, but she didn't. There was something comforting about being touched like that, as if Millicent were really her mother and she was really their little girl. It was fun to pretend that she was just like Rosemary Hogan and all the other girls at school who didn't know how lucky they were.

She looked at Millicent. "Why did my other mom give me away?"

"To give you a better life, honey."

"How do you know that?"

"Why else would she give you away?"

Corey knew double-talk when she heard it. "Maybe she gave me away because I was a nuisance."

"You couldn't possibly be a nuisance."

"Or because I'm ugly."

"Ugly?" Millicent sounded genuinely outraged. "Why, you're beautiful, honey."

"I'm ugly," Corey persisted. "Everyone says so."

"You tell me the name of one person who said you were ugly and I'll give them a tongue-lashing they won't soon forget."

"Rosemary Hogan's mother said it's a sin I didn't have surgery when I was a baby. She said now I'll never be normal."

"Bess Hogan is a mean-spirited shrew who hasn't set foot inside a church for twenty years. She's a fine one to talk about normal."

"That's why my mom gave me away," Corey went on. "I know it is and I don't blame her. I was ugly and awful and nobody wanted me."

"That's not true, honey. Somebody wanted you very much."

"Who?" Corey demanded, feeling the way she did when the teacher made her sit in the corner for sassing her. "Nobody ever wanted me." *Except you.*

"Stay right there," Millicent said, rising to her feet. "I'm going to show you something."

She was back beside Corey in a flash and handed her a newspaper clipping that had been sealed in plastic. "What's this?" Corey asked suspiciously.

"I think it might answer some of your questions."

Corey began to read:

Tennessee Intelligencer-Sentinel,
March 16, 1963: Page 6

LOCAL COUPLE KILLED IN CRASH— BABY INJURED

Raleigh, North Carolina (AP) —Mr. and Mrs. Blake Dumas of Nashville were killed yesterday evening in a traffic accident near Raleigh, North Carolina. The car Mr. Dumas was driving was hit head-on at the intersection of Corey and Main by a truck driven by Lucas Dunwoodie. Mr. Dunwoodie, 77, had apparently suffered a heart attack seconds prior to the accident and was trying to steer his vehicle toward the shoulder. Mr. Dunwoodie died two hours later at Community General Hospital. Both Mr. and Mrs. Dumas were pronounced dead at the scene. A baby girl, who was riding in the Dumas car, was badly injured.

"[It's a] miracle she's still alive," an unnamed eyewitness said. "I never saw so much blood before in my life." "That little baby flew out the back window like a rock from a slingshot," said Marjorie Spencer, another eyewitness. "Just makes me want to go home and hug my own little ones."

Mr. Dumas owned a chain of stores in the Nashville area. His wife was involved in charity work and served on the board of several foundations. It was believed Mr. and Mrs. Dumas were on their way home from a trip to Atlanta.

Community General Hospital declined comment on the infant girl's condition, pending notification of her family.

Tears streamed down Corey's face and she could barely read the last sentence. "They were almost my parents," she said in a voice of wonder. Once upon a time she'd been a beautiful baby girl with a family to love her, just like everyone else.

"They wanted to be," Millicent said gently. "They were going to adopt you but the accident . . ." Her voice trailed off.

She read the last sentence over again. "Did they find my real family? Did they tell my real mom what had happened?"

Millicent's eyes filled with tears and Corey felt the last of her hopes vanish. "The name on the birth certificate was false, honey. They were never able to find your birth mom."

"They didn't try hard enough!" Her voice was so high it sounded like chalk on a blackboard. "They should've looked harder—"

Millicent hugged her close, so close Corey could barely catch her breath. "Maybe she didn't want to be found, honey. Maybe she believed she was doing what was best for you, for your future. She'd found a wonderful family for you. She never expected something so terrible would happen. I'm sure she thinks about you all the time and loves you the same as if things had been different."

But Corey knew better. Somehow she knew her real mom was out there and she never thought about Corey at all.

BOOK THREE

The Wife

8

Las Vegas, 1976

Meg Cormier slipped off her spike heels and rubbed her feet. "So when are you going to put him out of his misery, Lilly? The poor man's been staring at you for almost a week and you won't even smile at him."

Lilly Ann peeled off her skintight showgirl costume and stepped out of it. The boning in the bodice had left angry red marks on her breasts and along her rib cage. The thought of donning a bra made her wince. Wearing only bikini panties, fishnet stockings and heels, she reached for her pale pink terry cloth robe.

"You're ignoring me, Lilly," Meg said, stifling a yawn. "If I weren't so damn tired I'd be offended."

"I'm not ignoring you," Lilly Ann replied, tying the belt smartly around her waist. "I just have nothing to say."

"I'm an old married woman with two kids. If I can't live vicariously, what hope is there for me?"

Lilly Ann plucked a cigarette from the pack on the side table then lit it. Settling down opposite Meg, she kicked off her shoes and sighed with relief. "God, that feels good." She leaned back in her chair and filled her lungs with the rich tobacco smoke.

"He's crazy about you," Meg said. "The least you could do is have dinner with him."

Lilly Ann ignored the shiver of excitement dancing up her spine. She'd long ago learned that sexual chemistry had damn little to do with happiness. "I don't want to have dinner with him."

"Every girl in the place is trying to get his attention and he only has eyes for you."

"He's attractive," Lilly Ann conceded in a matter-of-fact tone of voice that belied her emotions, "but he's not my type."

"He's so gorgeous he's probably my husband's type."

Lilly Ann threw back her head and laughed. "You're wasting your time serving drinks, Meg. You should be doing stand-up in the lounge." Tony Cormier was as macho as they came and was totally smitten with his wife.

Meg reached into her cleavage and withdrew a business card. "He asked me to give this to you."

Lilly Ann arched a brow. "Why didn't he give it to me himself?"

Meg grinned. "Let's just say he thought he might need a little help from a friend."

"Don't play matchmaker," Lilly Ann warned. "I'm not looking for a man." She'd had more than her share and, for the most part, preferred her own company.

"Yes, but if the man who's looking for you is one of the richest men in the country, you might want to reconsider."

A funny prickling sensation moved up Lilly Ann's spine as Meg handed her the business card, as if she were moving toward a destiny she hadn't realized was there. The name Carter Spaulding II was engraved in the top left-hand corner in bold letters. She knew that name. What American woman didn't? He owned the second most successful cosmetics company in the country and spent almost as much time in the society pages as Jackie O.

What are you waiting for, girl? Opportunities like this don't come along every day.

Lilly Ann ran her thumb across the letters then caught herself.

Meg was watching her. "Admit it, Lilly. You're impressed."

"It's a nice card."

"It's a nice card," Meg mimicked. "Any other woman in this place would be in his bed by now."

"I'm not any other woman."

"Tell me about it," Meg said, rolling her eyes. "I swear you're the most secretive girl in town. We've been working together for ages and I still don't know the first thing about you."

"There's nothing to know, Meg." *Except that once upon a time I had a beautiful little girl.* "I'm about to turn thirty." *I was seventeen when she was born.* "And I've never been married." *No home, no family, no friends.*

Meg chatted on about her kids and how they expected her to be up bright and early to see them off to school. Lilly Ann smiled politely but her mind was wandering. She couldn't imagine getting home after the second show then having to get up again three hours later to take care of a husband and family. No, her dreams were bigger than that. If she ever found someone to marry, she'd never work again. She'd stay home and raise a big family, lavishing all of her time and attention on her husband and children, the way it was supposed to be.

The way it should have been . . .

She glanced over at Carter Spaulding's business card. It wasn't the first time she'd been pursued by a wealthy man. It came with the territory on the Strip. Rich men got off on showering expensive trinkets on showgirls, everything from diamond bracelets to luxe apartments on the penthouse floor. She had her share of tribute tucked away in her lingerie drawer, insurance against the time when her boobs sagged and her thighs weren't as shapely as they were today.

She'd been praised, flattered, wined, dined and bedded with various degrees of success but she'd never once been proposed to. You fucked showgirls; you didn't marry them. You saved the wedding ring for the skinny society girl back home who would give you a pair of blue-blooded children to carry on your unsullied name.

All in all, Las Vegas was an awful lot like Euless. There was the right side of the tracks and the wrong side. As usual, Lilly Ann knew where she belonged.

Carter Spaulding sent Lilly Ann flowers the next night and champagne the night after that.

"You have to stop this," she told him when he came backstage after the second show. "I don't want your presents."

"Go ahead," he said, flashing a winning smile. "Encourage me."

She pointed toward another showgirl across the room. "She looks like the champagne-and-roses type."

"But she isn't you," he said in a low voice that thrilled her to her toes.

"Good night, Mr. Spaulding," she said, turning away from him. "And thanks for the roses."

Her knees trembled as he walked out the door. He was only a man. Why did he have such an effect on her equilibrium?

"This is like watching a train wreck," Meg said, looking up from her makeup mirror. "Sleep with him, you fool. What can it hurt?"

Lilly Ann ignored the question. Of course, sleeping with him couldn't hurt anything at all. She wasn't married and neither was he, if the gossip columns were right. The problem was, sex didn't seem worth the effort. All of that spine-tingling buildup that led to absolutely nothing. Why bother? Besides, she no longer believed Prince Charming was about to ride in on his white horse and save the day.

However, Carter Spaulding was not easily dissuaded. Over the next week, he filled the dressing room with roses and gardenias, freesia and lilies of every size and color. She sent armloads of flowers home with Meg and the other girls and still the place smelled like a florist shop. He sent candy, the fancy Belgian kind with chocolate so dark and silky it felt sinful to eat it. Meg's kids had a field day with it. And there were the magnums of expensive champagne that Lilly Ann could scarcely lift.

Lilly Ann felt her defenses beginning to topple.

"Like you have something better to do?" Meg asked during a break. "Maybe you're studying for your bar exam or entertaining Paul Newman between shows?"

"Oh, shut up," Lilly Ann snapped. "This is none of your business, Meg."

The truth was she didn't know why he made her feel the way she did and she didn't particularly want to find out. Still, his attentions were immensely flattering.

The flowers and champagne and candy stopped three nights later. Between shows, she scanned the casino for Carter

Spaulding, but he was nowhere in sight. A well-to-do matron from San Francisco had taken his spot at the baccarat table.

"I'm heartbroken," Meg said a few days later after the second show. Spaulding had been absent for five nights. "If I thought I could get away with it, I'd find him and date him myself."

Lilly Ann started to laugh the way she always did at Meg's outrageous statements but the laugh died in her throat. She wouldn't admit it to Meg, but she was disappointed that he'd given up so easily. *You're a quitter, Mr. Spaulding,* she thought as she began to remove her makeup. *One more night and I would have said yes.*

Well, no sense thinking about it. He was gone. She was there. And that was that.

She leaned forward and removed the double strips of false lashes. She looked younger without them on. The heavy stage makeup, while it camouflaged from a distance, was harsh and unforgiving up close. Foundation caked in the starburst lines at the corners of her eyes and hinted at the smile lines on either side of her mouth.

It was beginning, she thought, the whole sad decline into middle age. Next week she'd turn thirty and the only things she had to show for it were a handful of credits at UNLV and the realization that life never turned out the way you planned. She'd wanted to get away from Euless and she'd succeeded. She'd wanted independence and she had achieved that. She had her own apartment, a small bank account, a life that belonged to no one but her. Grandma Hattie was six years dead and with her had gone the last of Lilly's ties with her old hometown. Not even the Franklins were still in Euless; they'd moved to Houston not long after Lilly had the baby.

Thinking about Euless made her feel strangely unsettled, almost melancholy. What had happened to all those dreams she'd had back when she was growing up? Where had they gone? Sometimes she wondered if she'd given up her right to dream along with her baby daughter. She'd always had the sense that life had something special in store for her, some wonderful surprise it was going to spring on her when she least expected it.

Little Miss High-and-Mighty, Grandma Hattie had called her. *You're no better than the rest of us.*

But she *was* better than the rest of them even if right now it didn't quite look that way. She was meant to be more than what she was. She'd known it since she was a little girl, back when she'd sit on the front porch and dream about the places she would go and the people she would meet when she was grown up and famous. She'd never quite figured out how she was going to manage it but she knew it just the same.

Years ago she'd thought Cliff was the answer to her prayers. When she'd found out she was pregnant with his baby, she'd thought her future was secure. His death had put an end to that dream.

"See you tomorrow," Meg called over her shoulder as she left for the night.

"Meg, wait!" Lilly spun around to face her friend. "I—I thought maybe we could have a cup of coffee or something before you went home. Your kids don't have school tomorrow and I—"

"I wish I could, hon," said Meg, "but Tony Junior has a Cub Scout meeting first thing in the morning and guess who has to drive him." She waggled her fingers in farewell. "Maybe next week!"

It sounded like something from a television show, Lilly thought. Meg drove carpool and went to Cub Scout meetings and sewed fairy princess costumes for her daughters to wear on Halloween. All the things American mothers were supposed to do for their kids. Try as she might, Lilly couldn't imagine herself living that life. Not without a husband to share it with.

Those first years on her own had been both bleak and terrifying as she struggled to keep a roof over her head and food in her stomach. New York had seemed like another planet to her, a loud and angry planet, and when someone suggested she was wasting her time working as a cigarette girl at the Copa, Lilly had jumped at the opportunity to go west to Las Vegas. Anything had to be better than Manhattan.

She'd made more than her share of mistakes along the way but at least she hadn't made a mistake when she gave up her baby. In New York she'd been barely able to keep body and soul together for just herself. If she'd added the baby into the mix—well, it didn't bear thinking about.

A baby needed care twenty-four hours a day. She never would have been able to afford a baby-sitter, not on her salary. And if she'd told her bosses she was somebody's mother, they would have fired her so fast her head would spin. Cigarette girls sold more than smokes, they sold an image of glamour and availability. Motherhood didn't fit the ideal. She would have ended up unemployed and on relief, with each day melting into the next until she was too old and worn out to care.

Just thinking about it made her stomach clench into an icy cold knot of fear. *You're a bad one, Lilly Ann, thinking about yourself instead of your baby. A real mother would hang onto her little one for dear life....*

Lilly closed her eyes and tried to conjure up a picture of her daughter. Even as a newborn she'd had the nurses oohing and aahing over her big blue eyes and soft wreath of black hair. At thirteen she'd be a lovely little thing, teetering on the edge of adolescence. She'd be the apple of her daddy's eye, cosseted and spoiled and loved just as if she'd been born to them. And her mother adored her, bragging about her every chance she got at her fancy ladies' lunches at the country club. She couldn't quite remember what Blake and Candy looked like but she did remember that they were rich.

Her beautiful daughter would have a frilly canopy bed with lots of pink satin and white lace where she would curl up against a mountain of fluffy pillows and scribble her most secret thoughts into her velvet-covered diary. They'd have a special savings account for her college education and an even more special one for her wedding. She'd have everything a little girl could ever want: a fancy home, two parents who adored her and a future without limits.

Lilly wished she could say the same thing about herself.

In some ways Grandma Hattie had been right. Maybe Lilly was more like her mama than she knew. Euless hadn't been big enough to hold her mama's dreams and it hadn't been big enough for Lilly's either. Sometimes she daydreamed about going back there in a fancy limousine and making all those mean-spirited hags eat their words with Sunday supper but the truth was she never wanted to see Euless again as long as she lived. Ambition wasn't a crime. Wanting to make something of your life wasn't against the law. If she couldn't go back there a success, she'd never go back there at all.

She unpinned her hair from the elaborate uptwist of Grecian curls they favored at Caesar's. She swore she could hear her scalp sigh with relief as the thick dark waves tumbled down around her shoulders. Parts of her scalp were sore from the pins and the pressure and she winced as she drew a brush through her hair then loosely tied it back with a piece of black velvet ribbon. Carefully she removed the theatrical makeup that was part of the uniform, then soothed her skin with a rich emollient cream.

She started to laugh as she put the jar back in her locker with the rest of her gear. Carter Spaulding II's company made the skin cream, along with the mascara, blusher and lipstick. Maybe Meg had been right after all. If she'd played her cards right and gone to dinner with the man, she might have ended up with a year's supply of cosmetics.

She was still chuckling at the thought as she made her way through the passage that led from the dressing rooms to the employee exit.

"Glad to see you smiling, Lilly." Buzz, the night watchman, greeted her as she clocked out. "You're too young and pretty to be so serious all the time."

She pinched his cheek then stepped outside into the cool Las Vegas night. She was getting too serious. She couldn't remember the last time she'd enjoyed herself. Was it last month? Last year? Another lifetime ago? Was she going to wake up one morning and find out she was eighty years old and there was nothing to look forward to except dying alone?

The heavy metal door clanged shut behind her. She stood perfectly still and let her head drop back, breathing in the clean spring air, drinking in the blessed silence. There was something magical about the desert at night. It made her feel that all things were possible, all the things that daytime held just beyond her reach. She lifted her arms overhead and stretched, surprised she couldn't touch the sky.

The Big Dipper winked at her. She settled on a star halfway up the handle and made herself a wish. A selfish, private wish that didn't stand a snowball's chance in hell of coming true but she made it anyway. Then wished again for good measure.

She heard footsteps behind her.

"I made a wish too." The man's voice was smooth as fine brandy, rich and full-bodied. She knew that voice. Maybe she'd always known it. Lush vowels, sharp consonants. He sounded the way champagne tasted. Her heart pushed up against her rib cage.

He came closer, stopping a few feet away from her. He smelled like the crisp night air, only more so.

"Don't you want to know what I wished for?"

Her breath caught. "Don't tell me," she said, not turning around. "It won't come true if you do."

Carter Spaulding II reached for her hand. "I'll take my chances," he said.

His touch electrified her. Heat sizzled through her body, sending her blood racing to pulse points she hadn't thought about in years.

"Is anybody waiting at home for you?" he asked.

She shook her head. "No one." She paused a moment, then added, "Is anyone waiting for you?"

"Only my accountant."

She looked at him then laughed. "And he'll wait?"

Carter grinned at her. "As long as I pay him."

He led her toward a sleek black Jaguar idling near the curb.

"I thought you'd have a limo," she said, trailing a finger along the lacquered surface of the right front fender.

"Not tonight."

His words resonated inside her chest. Her survival instincts had been sharpened over the years. She had one chance to break the spell she was falling under, one chance to run for the safety of her everyday life.

But, damn it, she didn't want to run. She was almost thirty years old and time was running out. She wanted to throw herself headlong into an adventure before it was too late.

One night, she told herself, as they drove toward Lake Mead. One night in the arms of a handsome, powerful man. She wouldn't be beautiful forever. Why not give in to the magic? She hadn't been with anyone for a very long time and she ached with the need to be held.

They drove toward Lake Mead, leaving the lights and noise of Las Vegas behind. He wasn't much of a gambler, he told her. He liked winning too much to get hooked on a game of chance. She knew there was more to his words than the obvious.

They parked near a marina and walked barefoot along the water's edge. She told him about being a showgirl and made him laugh at her description of descending a staircase while balancing the Statue of Liberty on your head. It felt easy and natural yet there was an almost visible electric charge lighting up the sky every time she looked into his beautiful green eyes.

He didn't say very much. He held her hand while she talked, brushed her hair from her cheek when a cool breeze off the lake turned it into a tangle of waves. He made her feel like the most important woman in the world—the universe!—and she never wanted the night to end.

In silence they watched the sun rise. Lilly Ann had the sense that there was something special about that moment, almost holy, as if the act of nature were somehow tying them together.

And she knew he felt it too. He drew her into his arms and brought his mouth down on hers, stealing her soul. Sealing their fate.

Carter Spaulding II and Lilly Ann Barnett were married three days later at the Little Chapel of Dreams across the boulevard from Caesar's Palace. Meg Cormier and Carter's accountant stood up for them and when it was over Lilly Ann dissolved into happy tears.

"You'll never regret this," she said to Carter as they ducked a hailstorm of rice. "I'll be the best wife in the world to you."

She hadn't slept with him yet, a fact that had both frustrated and delighted him. If he'd wanted to win her heart, he couldn't have found a better way to do it. He was gallant, patient, infinitely tender. Everything she could have asked for in a man. Lilly Ann fell hard for him but not so hard that she didn't realize she had a problem.

He thought he knew all about her, about Euless and New York and her dreams of glory, but he didn't know the most important thing.

He didn't know about her daughter.

Of course she had to tell him sometime. Husbands and wives didn't keep secrets like that from each other, not even in his world. Sooner or later she'd have to open up about Clifford and the accident and the baby she'd given up to Blake and Candy but not now. Not yet. She'd waited so long for this moment that she wanted to savor it for as long as she possibly could.

She stole a look at her left hand. Her ring finger was encircled with emerald-cut diamonds set in platinum. She still couldn't believe they were real.

Carter saw what she was doing. He took her hand and raised it to his lips, pressing a kiss against the palm.

"I owe you an engagement ring," he said as she shivered at the touch of his mouth on her skin.

"You don't owe me anything. I have everything I could possibly need right now."

He whispered something in her ear, something dark and enticing and unknowable, and she could think of nothing else.

Hawaii

"My shy young bride." Carter's voice was as silky as the ocean breeze wafting through the open window of their suite. "You are a feast for the eyes."

Lilly hesitated in the doorway to the bedroom. She'd lingered in the bathroom as long as she dared. The poor man had to be wondering if he'd married an eternal virgin. It was their wedding night. It was time.

Carter lifted the bottle of champagne from the ice bucket and eased the cork out with a satisfying pop. Lilly Ann laughed as the bubbly wine spilled over his hands. She grabbed two crystal flutes and held them out to Carter to be filled.

"To us," he said, touching his glass to hers. "We're going to have a good life."

Backlit by the moon he was a beautiful sight. At forty-five years of age, Carter Spaulding was a man in his prime. Standing a shade under six feet tall, he owed his vigor and strength to a daily exercise regime that included strenuous workouts on the tennis court and in the gym. His dark brown hair was graying slightly at the temples but, as with most men, instead of aging him it only added to his appeal. He exuded both confidence and power and Lilly Ann had the sense that she had finally come home.

She sipped the champagne slowly while he told her of the New York apartment that would soon be her home. He named the East Side building but it meant nothing to her. He might as well have been talking about Mars. The New York she'd known was nothing like that.

"It's the penthouse, of course," he said, pouring himself some more wine. "Two stories, the usual layout." He topped off Lilly Ann's glass then placed the bottle back in the ice bucket. "You might find the decor a little early bachelor. You can change anything you want."

"I'm sure I won't want to change a thing," Lilly Ann said. A pleasant champagne buzz resonated inside her head. Hot and cold running servants, he'd said. And she would be in charge of everything. She wondered if there was a school you could go to that taught you how to be rich.

They watched the lights of Honolulu dance along the ocean in silence while they finished the champagne. Finally Carter took her glass and put it down on the sideboard next to his.

"I want to love you," he said in a low and thrilling voice.

She nodded, not trusting herself to speak. He slid one nightgown strap off her shoulder, trailing a finger along her collarbone. Desire rocked her to the core. He did the same with the other strap and the nightgown slid gently over her breasts, baring her to the waist.

She didn't move. She scarcely breathed. She didn't need oxygen. The way his eyes caressed her was enough to sustain her. She had always accepted her beauty as a gift, like a talent for piano or for drawing. Being beautiful opened doors and closed a few of them as well. It was part and parcel of who she was, as familiar as the sound of her heart beating inside her chest.

But suddenly it was all different. She saw herself in his eyes, felt what he was feeling. Fierce longing. Admiration. A touch of awe. *Yes,* she thought in triumph. *Yes!*

He bent his head to her left breast and drew warm, moist circles around her nipple with his tongue. Coils of heat sprang from breast to belly... and beyond. She threaded her fingers through his hair as he moved to her other breast, then moaned as he drew her nipple into his mouth and sucked. Her legs grew weak and she sagged against him. *This is enough,* she thought. *I don't need any more than this.* If the ultimate pleasure continued to elude her, that was all right. She already had more than she'd ever dreamed.

9

"We can't!" Lilly Ann whispered, placing her hands on her husband's chest. They were in the lavatory of a 747 bound for New York.

"Of course we can."

"What if someone sees us?"

"No one will see us."

"The stewardess knows we're in here."

"She won't say a word."

"You can't be sure of that."

"I'm sure," Carter said. "Trust me, darling."

She did trust him. She trusted him with her life. Why else would she even think about making love in the teeny-tiny bathroom of a jumbo jet 35,000 feet above the ground?

She wriggled against him as he snaked his hands under her skirt and tore off her panties. The sound of lace ripping seemed to echo in the tiny room. "There's not enough room in here to do that."

He gripped her by the waist and lifted her onto the narrow sink. She barely stifled a wild giggle. The stainless steel was cold against the bare skin of her buttocks and thighs. He took her hand and placed it against his erect penis and she shuddered. She wanted him inside her, wanted to be filled by him.

"You're a wicked man," she whispered, unzipping his fly and releasing him. "We'll burn in hell."

He grinned at her. "That's what I'm aiming for."

He spread her thighs and drove into her, short, hard strokes meant to inflame. She started to cry out with the sheer joy of being taken that way but he captured her cries with his mouth. Instinctively she wrapped her legs tightly around his waist, pulling him more deeply inside her body. A low guttural groan escaped his control and she threw back her head and laughed out loud at the wondrous power she had over him, power she'd never even realized existed until now.

He pulled out until the tip of his penis teased the swollen lips of her vagina. Their eyes met. She had the feeling she was seeing him for the very first time, this stranger...her husband. He was everything she'd ever wanted, all the dreams she'd never believed would come true.

"You're going to come this time, Lilly."

Her body jerked with surprise. "Wh-what?"

"You heard me. This time you're going to come." He thrust part of the way into her. "You've been faking it. I don't want you to fake it any longer. Not with me."

"I didn't—I mean . . ." Her face burned with embarrassment. She wanted to run away, hide someplace where he wouldn't be able to find her. She trembled as her body accepted more of his length. "H-how did you know?"

"You're part of me," he said as he moved his hips in an intoxicating rhythm. "You can't hide anything from me."

She froze, thoughts of the baby washing over her. But then he moved again, slowly teasing her until she was whimpering for him, begging for him to take her the one place she'd never gone before.

"Tell me what you want," he urged as she bucked wildly against him. "Tell me, Lilly . . . tell me!"

She cried out then as wave after wave of violent, pure sensation rippled through her. It was pleasure and it was pain and it was everything in between and she prayed it would never end.

A few hours later the limousine rolled to a stop in front of 1040 Fifth Avenue. Lilly reached for her compact to check her makeup but Carter laughed and snatched it away from her.

"You look beautiful," he said. "Well fucked."

She felt a warm rush of heat between her thighs as visions of their interlude in the airplane's lavatory filled her brain. "Shh!" She gestured toward the driver. "He'll hear you."

"What if he does?" Carter said, laughing. "He's an employee. Does it matter what he hears?"

She didn't know how to answer that. Carter had an entirely different way of looking at things, a way she still didn't understand. She had the feeling it had to do with being wildly, obscenely rich. She'd learned a lot on that subject these last few days. If there was a line, he expected to move to the head of it. If there was a problem, he expected a solution. If there was an obstacle, he expected it to vanish just because it was in his way. He believed he was beyond reproach, above embarrassment, and he expected his wife to feel the same way.

Lilly didn't. Not yet. Probably not ever. She could still see the knowing grin on the stewardess's face when they exited the bathroom. Carter acted as if nothing had happened while Lilly Ann wished she could vanish into thin air. She'd read Fitzgerald when she was at UNLV. He'd said the rich were different and she'd snickered along with everybody else. Of course they were different. They had more money.

But now she knew it was much more than that. Rich people played by different rules . . . if they played by the rules at all. And, what was most surprising, they got away with it.

"We'll have dinner alone tonight," Carter was saying as the driver got out to open the door for them. "Tomorrow's soon enough to start introducing you to everyone."

The thought of meeting his friends made her sick to her stomach. She couldn't imagine herself mingling with the people she read about in the society columns. If only they'd had time for a proper honeymoon. Six or seven months would have been nice. Time for the bride to learn how to live with the man she married.

The last few days had been magical. Alone with Carter in a Hawaiian paradise, she'd actually forgotten that sooner or later they would have to reenter the real world. A world that might not be as kind to her as she hoped.

You have to tell him about the baby, she thought as he led her into the lobby and toward the bank of private elevators. Sooner or later somebody would discover her secret and she would lose him.

Her ears popped as they glided up to the sixty-fourth floor. She could tell him tonight. After dinner while the glow of champagne was still on them both. Or after making love while he was still inside her, sated and happy. But it would be tonight. That much she was sure of.

The elevator doors opened into a hallway as big as the lobby of the movie theatre back in Euless and twice as opulent. She had a quick impression of thick ivory carpeting, silk wallpaper in cream and rose and soft blue, a cherrywood table with a gilt-framed mirror suspended on the wall above it.

"They'll bring our bags up in the service elevator," Carter said as he led her down the hallway. "Mimi will unpack for you."

"Mimi?" she asked.

"She takes care of personal needs. Gretchen oversees the kitchens and general housekeeping chores."

"You have more than one kitchen?"

"One upstairs, one down." He stopped just before the doorway to the living room and drew her into his arms. "You'll get used to it, Lilly," he said, kissing her. "I promise."

She peered over his shoulder and gasped at her first sight of the living room. The far wall wasn't a wall at all, it was floor-to-ceiling windows that overlooked Central Park and, beyond that, the Hudson River.

"Oh, Carter!" she breathed. "This is so beautiful. I never—"

She stopped in midsentence as the lanky form of a teenage boy unfolded itself from a couch facing a window. He was taller than Carter, all long arms and legs, with a head of curly blond hair that seemed to capture the light and throw it right back at you. He was breathtakingly beautiful, like a painting of a fallen angel come to life.

"Surprised?" the boy asked. His voice was in the process of changing. It was the only thing about him that was less than perfect.

"Very," said Carter. He didn't sound like himself. There was a hard edge to his words, a coldness Lilly hadn't heard before. "What are you doing here?"

"Spring break," the boy said, eyeing Lilly with open curiosity. "Don't worry. I go back up to school tonight."

"You can stay an extra day," Carter said with little warmth. "So we can spend some time together."

"Spend time together?" The boy laughed bitterly. "I waited at school for you to pick me up. After three days I figured you were either dead or—" he looked Lilly up and down "—busy."

"How did you get here?" Carter asked.

The boy shrugged. "Hitched."

Carter's jaw tightened. "I forbade you to hitch."

"Yeah, well, you also said you'd pick me up at school."

"This wasn't deliberate, Grant. Circumstances were beyond my control."

The boy sauntered toward them. He stopped a few feet away from Lilly. "I wouldn't unpack if I were you," he said, a mocking light in his clear green eyes. "You probably won't be staying long. None of his girlfriends ever do."

"Apologize to my wife," Carter snapped.

The boy's face crumpled with surprise. Lilly's heart went out to the boy, despite the fact she felt as off-balance and uneasy as he obviously did.

"Your wife?" The boy's voice broke on the last word.

Carter held up her left hand. She curled her fingers toward her palm, uncomfortable with his grandstanding gesture but it was no use. Her wedding ring glittered in the unfiltered sunlight.

"My wife," Carter repeated. It sounded like a challenge.

The boy looked at them and laughed out loud, as if that were the funniest thing he'd heard in years. Lilly knew it wasn't a real laugh, though. The pain in his eyes gave him away.

"My apologies, Lilly," said Carter, placing a protective arm around her shoulders. "I'm afraid my son has a lot to learn about good manners."

"Your son?" Carter hadn't even hinted at the boy's existence. Not so much as a whisper.

The boy snorted. "Figures he didn't tell you. Why mention somebody you never see?"

"Go to your room, Grant," Carter ordered. "We'll deal with this later."

"Carter," Lilly began, "maybe we should deal with it now." It was bad enough she and his son had to meet under these circumstances. If Carter sent him away in anger, Lilly Ann wouldn't stand a chance with the boy.

"Save your breath," Grant said to Lilly. "I was leaving anyway. Jake's old man is driving us back up to school."

Lilly placed a hand on his forearm. "Please," she said softly. "I'd like you to stay."

The silence in the room was thick with tension. Lilly had the feeling she'd made a terrible mistake but she didn't back down. There was something about the boy that touched her heart.

"You're kidding, right?" Grant asked, searching her face with his eyes. "This is a joke."

She shook her head. *He's lonely,* she thought. *As lonely as I was.* "We're family now," she said, meaning it. "I think we should get to know each other."

The boy looked at his father. Carter forced a tight smile. "If Lilly feels that way, so do I."

She half expected the boy to tell them both to go to hell but he surprised her. "Just one night," he said but she sensed a grudging pleasure in his words, "then I gotta go back to school."

"Tell your friend that you're staying," Carter ordered brusquely.

Moments later they heard the sound of the elevator doors sliding open then shut again.

Lilly drew in a deep breath. Apparently she wasn't the only one who'd been keeping secrets.

Carter sank into a mushroom-colored leather chair facing the window. "Pour me a drink, would you, Lilly?" He gestured toward the bar on the side wall.

She poured him a drink then handed it to him. "I hope this is what you want."

He looked at the glass then up at her. "You know what I want."

Heat suffused her body but she willed herself to ignore it. She had to keep her wits about her. She moved toward the window and leaned against the sill. "How many other children do you have, Carter? Are five or six more going to pop up and surprise me?"

He winced at her tone. "Just the one," he said.

"You should have told me about him."

"Would it have changed things?"

She hesitated a beat too long. Marrying Carter Spaulding II had been a crazy, impulsive, reckless act. If anything as real and important as a child had been thrown into the mix, she would never have gone through with it. In the storybooks, Cinderella only had to worry about the clock tolling twelve, not being stepmother to Prince Charming's children.

"That's what I thought," he said. "I wasn't going to risk losing you, Lilly."

"I had the right to know I was becoming a stepmother."

He dismissed her words with a wave of his hand. "Grant is in boarding school. You won't be seeing much of him."

He doesn't mean that the way it sounds, Lilly Ann. He's trying to put a good face on it for you. Certainly he loved his son more than his tone of voice would indicate.

"Did you see the way he looked at me?" she persisted. The pity in the boy's eyes had been unmistakable. "How could you just spring me on him that way?"

"This isn't the way I had it planned, Lilly. He was supposed to be in school." He drew in a breath and she noted the way the veins in his temples pulsed angrily. "We were going to drive up to New Hampshire next weekend and break the news to him."

"And when were you planning to break the news to me? I had no idea you had a son, Carter. Not a clue."

He placed the tumbler on the floor next to his chair and stood up. "We've had a few other things to think about this past week."

"I know but—"

"I didn't go to Vegas expecting to bring back a wife." His tone was lighthearted but there was something darker beneath the surface. Something Lilly wasn't certain she wanted to explore. "You know that as well as I do."

"Of course I do, but—"

He pressed her back against the window. That fragile pane of glass was all that stood between her and the ground sixty-four stories below. "We happened hot and fast, Lilly. There wasn't time to think."

He cupped her buttocks in his hands, kneading her flesh through the silky fabric of her dress. He had servants. People who could walk in on them at any moment. Even, God forbid, his own son.

"Carter, maybe you shouldn't—"

He lifted her left hand to his mouth and kissed the band of diamonds on her ring finger. "I should and I will." He pressed his mouth to the inside of her palm. She felt herself melting against him.

"It will work out," he said as he inched her dress up over her thighs. "Lean back against the window."

She was helpless to refuse. She arched her back, thrusting her pelvis forward.

"Spread your legs, Lilly."

"Carter, I—"

"Spread your legs."

She did, feeling naked and exposed in the bright sun that streamed through the wall of windows. Quickly he unzipped his trousers, freeing his erection, then drove himself into her again and again with no apparent thought to her satisfaction. Anger boiled up through her and for a second she wondered what he would do if she reached down and grabbed him by the testicles but then he slowed his rhythm, slowed it until it matched hers, slowed it until her anger shifted into desire and they came together in a loud and messy climax.

"You're good for me," he said as she pressed a cocktail napkin between her legs and let her dress slip back down over her thighs. "You make me feel like a new man."

Which only seemed fair, Lilly thought as her bridegroom zipped up the fly of his expensive Italian slacks. She certainly didn't recognize the new woman she'd become.

Grant didn't show up for dinner. Carter was mildly irritated but he didn't seem to miss the boy's presence at all. He made it clear to Lilly that he didn't want to share her with anyone, not even his son. "You belong to me," he said, "not to anyone else."

She and Carter made love again later on, then jet lag finally hit him and he fell deeply asleep. Lilly was also feeling jet-lagged but the strangeness of her surroundings made it impossible for her to relax. She walked from room to room, staring at the priceless antique vases, the opulent rugs, the furniture that had been handed down from generation to generation. If someone had told her she'd landed on another planet, she wouldn't have doubted it for an instant because nothing in her experience had prepared her for this new life of hers.

She used to sit in the Rialto Theater back in Euless, eating popcorn and watching Doris Day movies. The stories were silly but Doris's beautiful clothes and her wonderful apartments stole her breath away. Doris acted as if it were nothing special to have plush white wall-to-wall carpets and canopy beds and a maid who kept the whole thing neat as a pin, but Lilly was beginning to suspect that being rich was a lot trickier than it looked.

She was curled up in a chair in the living room, staring out over Central Park, when Grant finally came home.

"Come sit down," she said, motioning for him to join her. "The view is beautiful."

He stood in the archway to the living room, hands jammed into the pockets of his khaki trousers. He looked defiant and uncertain and her heart turned over at the sight of him. He reminded her of a younger, more vulnerable version of his father. Grant couldn't be more than fourteen or fifteen yet there was something terribly old about him . . . and terribly sad.

"Central Park," he said, shrugging his bony shoulders. "Big deal."

Lilly smiled at him. "Maybe it's not a big deal to you, but it's a huge deal to me. I've never seen anything like it before." She turned back to the window and leaned forward. "All those twinkling white lights over there—do you have any idea what they are?"

He didn't answer her. She hadn't really expected him to. Still she wasn't discouraged. "They almost look like Christmas lights," she went on. "Maybe it's the zoo."

"It's not the zoo," he said, crossing the room toward the window. "It's Tavern on the Green."

He stood about five feet away from her, leaning casually against the sill. *You're lonely,* she thought. *I know all about being lonely.*

"And what about that?" She pointed toward a tall building with many brightly lit windows.

"The Plaza."

They gazed out the window in companionable silence for a few minutes then Lilly said, "I guess we were both pretty surprised this afternoon."

He grunted something that sounded like agreement. "He probably forgot all about me. That'd be just like him."

"No," she said quickly. "It was nothing like that at all. Your father wasn't sure how I would feel about becoming a stepmother."

"So he lied."

"He didn't lie," she said carefully, "but he didn't tell the whole truth either."

"You mad at him?"

"I was," she said, "but I'm not any longer."

"Figures," Grant said. "I'd get grounded for life if I did something like that."

"I'm glad he didn't tell me," she went on. "If he had, I might have made the biggest mistake of my life and not married him."

"You'd be better off," Grant said. "My dad's not a very good husband."

"I think it will be different this time."

The boy snorted. "Yeah," he said. "Sure it will."

She refused to be put off by his attitude. "I think you're going to be pleasantly surprised."

"He's going to hurt you," the boy blurted out. "He hurts everyone."

Her eyes filled with tears. He was too young to carry so much anger. She wondered where it came from. "Has he hurt you?"

Grant's adam's apple bobbed. "He can't hurt me. Nothing he does can bother me."

She started to say something vaguely comforting but stopped herself. Carter was a difficult man. Even she could see that and she'd known him only a few weeks. She had no business telling his son what to think or how to feel. All she could do was offer him her friendship and hope for the best.

"I'm sorry you and your father are having problems, Grant, but I hope that won't get in the way of us becoming friends."

His smirk faded. "You want to be friends?"

She nodded. "I think that's a good place to start, don't you?"

"His other wives wanted me to get lost, same as him."

"I'm not any of his other wives," she reminded him gently. "And I don't want you to get lost."

"You'll change your mind."

A wellspring of maternal feelings rose up from nowhere and it was all she could do to keep from forcing a hug on the poor kid. "We're family now and I'd like us to get to know each other."

Grant considered her for a few moments then gave one of his shrugs. "Maybe," he said. "That is, if you're still here when the semester's over."

"I'll be here," she said. "From now on you can count on me."

10

Carter was gone when Lilly woke up the next morning but Grant wasn't. She slipped on a blue cotton dress and a pair of flats and joined him on the terrace.

"Coffee?" she said, raising an eyebrow. "Shouldn't you be drinking milk or something?"

He laughed out loud but it wasn't an unpleasant laugh. "I'm not a kid anymore."

She poured herself a cup and sat down opposite him. If anything, the view of the park was even more beautiful in the early morning light. "Anyone under thirty is a kid."

"How old are you?" he asked. It was the first sign of curiosity he'd shown.

"Thirty," she said with a self-mocking laugh.

"Really?" He sounded surprised which flattered her.

"I can't believe it either. I don't feel any different than I did when I was your age."

"You're a lot younger than Carter."

"You call your father by his first name?"

"Yeah," said Grant. "What else would I call him?"

"The important question here," she said lightly, "is what are you going to call me?"

He grinned and her heart did a dance inside her chest. *You could be mine,* she thought suddenly. He was only a few years older than her baby girl. This beautiful golden-haired boy could have been her own child.

"How about Mrs. Spaulding?"

"How about Lilly?"

"Yeah," he said after a moment's thought. "Lilly's good."

It is good, she thought. *For now.*

He gulped down the last of his coffee then pushed back his chair. "Gotta go," he said. "My train leaves at ten-thirty."

"I'll take you to the station."

"I've been going to the station alone since I was eight," he said, not unkindly. "I can manage."

"I'm glad you stayed the night, Grant."

"Yeah," he said, seeming sheepish and painfully young. "Me, too."

"Do you have enough money?"

He looked down, obviously embarrassed. "Enough for cab fare but . . ." His voice trailed off.

"Wait a second!" She leaped up and ran into the bedroom. Carter had left her a fistful of money and credit cards. She quickly withdrew a pair of hundred dollar bills while Grant stood in the doorway, watching. She extended the bills toward him. "Take this," she said. "In case any emergencies pop up."

Grant hesitated.

"Really," she urged him. "You never know when you might need something."

"You're great, Lilly." He gave her a quick, unexpected peck on the cheek. "Really great!"

"You're pretty great yourself," she said, meaning it.

He kissed her again. "Maybe this whole family thing is gonna work out after all."

"Yes," she said, hugging him. "Maybe it is at that."

It was the easiest two hundred dollars Grant Spaulding had ever scored. He'd expected maybe fifty dollars at most. When she handed him the two C notes he almost shit himself with surprise.

You did good this time, old man, he thought as the door-man flagged down a cab. For once his father hadn't fucked up.

His last two wives had been tight-assed bitches. Not only did the new wife look like a walking wet dream, she was a soft touch for the lost boy routine. All he'd had to do was train the baby greens on her and she was done for. She couldn't get to her wallet fast enough.

The doorman waved him over.

"It was good to see you, Master Spaulding," he said as Grant slid into the back seat of a cab.

"Yeah," said Grant. "You, too." He pulled the door closed after him. If the doorman expected a tip for doing his job, he was in for a surprise. Grant didn't go around giving his money away to pissants. He'd rather use it on something important, like Maui Gold. If he turned up the charm with stepmom, he might even be able to afford some Colombian snow this summer, the kind that made you feel you could rule the world.

He reached into his book bag and pulled out a flask. Unscrewing the cap he took a long pull of bourbon. "To you, Mom and Dad," he said.

Things were finally looking up.

"Carter did *what?*" Whitman Paley barked at his assistant Elaine. "Tell me you're joking."

"I'm not joking, Whit," said Elaine. "He got married."

Whit slammed his fist down on his desktop. The silver inkwell skidded toward the edge of the desk but Elaine caught it before it fell. "What the hell was he thinking of?"

"I think I can hazard a guess," Elaine said dryly. "She's a Vegas showgirl."

Whit groaned in disgust. "I've told him a thousand times tits and ass were going to be his downfall. I hope the stupid son of a bitch got himself a prenup."

"Why do I have the feeling that was the last thing on his mind?" Elaine asked.

Easy for her to joke about it. Whit was the one who had to go in and clean up his old friend's messes. By virtue of friendship and position, it inevitably fell to Whit to disentangle Carter from his romantic intrigues with as little personal and professional damage as possible. He should have known things had been too quiet this past year.

"Didn't he learn anything after the last time?" Whit groused as he slid his arms into his suit jacket. "He said he was swearing off marriage permanently."

"Do you expect an answer to that?" Elaine asked. "You've known him longer than I have."

The Mayfair executive offices were on Park and 58th, an easy walk to Carter's apartment. He strode up the street, fueled by anger, just in time to see a cab peel out from the stand in front of the building. He thought he saw a familiar face in the back seat.

"Was that who I think it was?" he asked.

Jimmy the doorman muttered something better left unheard. "Mr. Spaulding's boy," he said through clenched teeth. "Back to school and not a minute too soon."

Whit was glad he'd missed Grant. He knew the boy and his father had their problems and he knew it couldn't be easy not having a mother around to smooth things out but still there was something about the kid that didn't sit right with him. He had the face of a choirboy but Whit had the illogical suspicion that something a lot more sinister lurked beneath that golden surface.

But the kid wasn't the problem today. The old man was. And whoever it was he'd married.

He tried to picture the new Mrs. Spaulding as the elevator glided up to the sixty-fourth floor. Big hair. Too much makeup. Bright red fingernails out to there. The kind of woman who gave gold diggers a bad name.

Damn it, Carter. What in hell were you thinking?

The elevator doors slid open. He stepped into the foyer and found himself face-to-face with a tall dark-haired woman with the most beautiful blue eyes he'd ever seen. They were a dark blue, almost sapphire, framed with thick, curly dark lashes. And her face—sweet Jesus, her face! A perfect oval with high cheekbones and a catlike chin, a small straight nose and a lush mouth made for all manner of erotic delights. She wore a plain blue cotton dress, flat shoes, and no makeup and still she put most works of art to shame.

"Hi," she said in a soft, vaguely southern, voice. "Can I help you?"

"I'm here to see Mrs. Spaulding."

"*I'm* Mrs. Spaulding."

"No," Whit said. "That's impossible." He knew exactly what the new Mrs. Spaulding looked like and she wasn't it. "You can't be."

"I can and I am," said the improbable new bride. "Who are *you?*"

"Whit Paley."

There wasn't so much as a glimmer of recognition on her lovely face. "Are you selling something?"

"Carter hasn't told you about me?"

"Should he have?"

"One would hope so." He held out his hand. "We've been friends a long time." Her hand disappeared into his. "I heard that the old man had taken a bride and I wanted to see for my-self."

She lifted her chin. "Do I pass muster?" There was more than a hint of challenge in her eyes.

He couldn't help but admire her.

"He's my oldest friend," Whit offered by way of apology. "You can't blame me for being curious."

"Well, come on in," she said. Definitely southern, he thought. A native New Yorker would have kicked him out on his ass. "Carter went out for a little while but you're welcome to wait."

"I don't want to interrupt your day."

"Interrupt my day?" She laughed out loud. "Are you *sure* you're a friend of Carter's? We seem to have help to do just about everything except take naps for us."

She was complaining about having too much help? Carter had really struck gold this time. "I wouldn't mind a cup of coffee."

"As long as we get the kitchen back to rights before Gretchen comes home." She shivered in mock fear. "That woman terri-fies me!"

"You don't have to be afraid of Gretchen," he said as he followed her into the apartment. "You're the one in charge."

She threw him a look over her shoulder. "Tell her, Whit Paley. I don't think Gretchen would believe it from me."

"You've never had help before?"

"I've *been* the help," she said easily, "but I've never had help."

She grinned and set about warming up the coffee. He was surprised to find out he liked her. Hell, he *more* than liked her.

She placed two cups of coffee on the table. "Do you know where Gretchen keeps the sugar?" she asked.

He shrugged. "Try the cabinet by the phone."

She raised up on tiptoe to reach the sugar bowl. You could bounce a quarter off her nicely rounded ass. Large firm breasts, long shapely legs. The face of an angel. He felt a stirring in his gut. *Off-limits, old man,* he told himself. There were still some rules.

She took her seat at the table. "So how long have you known my husband?"

"How old are you?" he countered.

"Thirty."

He winced. "Just about that long. We were in prep school together."

Her eyes grew soft. "So you knew him when he was a boy. I can't even imagine it!" She leaned forward. "What was he like?"

"Impulsive," said Whit. "Driven. Intense."

"He hasn't changed much, has he?"

"He's taller and older, but that's about it."

They both laughed.

"You two are very different," she said. "You seem a lot more easygoing than Carter is."

"That's probably why we've been friends so long."

"Am I what you expected?" she asked over a second cup of coffee.

"Not exactly." He knew appearances could be deceiving but somehow she'd managed to touch his heart and his libido in record time. This woman was the real thing.

"What were his other wives like, if you don't mind me asking?"

"Denise was a sweetheart," Whit said. "Too damn young to die."

"How did it happen?"

"She and Carter were on vacation. They got a call that Grant was sick. Carter said the boy was in good hands, but Denise was worried. They had words. She flew back to New York. Only thing was the plane never made it. It crashed into Jamaica Bay.'' He cleared his throat, wishing he had a Scotch. "No survivors.''

Her big blue eyes swam with tears. "How sad. Poor Carter and Grant.''

"Poor Grant,'' Whit said. "He lost both his mother and his father. Grant had no use for the kid after that.''

"He couldn't possibly blame Grant for the accident.''

"Unfortunately he did. By the time he got his head back on straight, it was too late. I don't know if he can ever make it right with the kid.''

"What about his other wives?''

He paused. "The other two...'' His voice trailed off.

"Please tell me,'' she urged. "I can't ask Carter and I don't know anybody besides you who can tell me.''

"He wasn't a great husband.'' It just fell short of being a warning. "It's something we have in common.''

"He cheated on them?'' There was no beating around the bush with the new Mrs. Spaulding.

"Let's say he had a notoriously short attention span.''

"That's all going to change, Whit,'' she vowed. "I promise you I'm the last wife he's going to have.''

She believes that, he thought. She was filled with hearts and flowers, rosy dreams of happily ever after. He tried to think of something to say but the only thing that came to mind would probably end up with him getting slapped then tossed out of the apartment.

They heard footsteps in the hallway. Lilly Ann leaped to her feet. "Oh, no, it's Gretchen!'' She grabbed for the cups and saucers. "She'll kill me!'' Whit was about to stop her when Carter walked into the room.

If she'd been beautiful before, she was radiant now.

"I'm so glad you're home!'' She threw herself into his arms.

Carter met Whit's eyes over his bride's head. His old pal looked triumphant and more than a little in love.

Damn you, Whit thought. *Damn you for finding her first.*

It didn't take Lilly Ann long to realize that she was a living, breathing "before'' picture. Her makeup was too Las Vegas.

Her taste in clothes was unsophisticated, at best, and her hair, too long and juvenile. Every time she walked down the street, construction workers burst into loud whistles and applause. Last month she would have taken that as a compliment but last month she hadn't been Mrs. Carter Spaulding.

Dressing rich seemed to have something to do with understatement, a concept that didn't come naturally to her. She'd seen the looks the other Mayfair wives had exchanged over lunch at Tavern on the Green last week. Carter said they'd invited her so they could welcome her to the fold, but she knew better than that. They'd wanted to get a good look at the showgirl who'd managed to snare the boss. She'd dressed carefully for the occasion. She wore her hair in a tousled topknot and left her false eyelashes at home. Her fatal mistake was the turquoise sundress with a halter neckline and short flippy skirt, which was perfect for a summer lunch everywhere in the world except Manhattan.

Lunch with Martians would have been easier and more fun. The good wives' jaws dropped open simultaneously. It would have been funny if Lilly hadn't been so mortified. Not only did the wives talk in code, but there seemed to be a uniform that rich women wore, silky wrap dresses and sleek suits with buttoned jackets that barely grazed the hips. The colors were always muted; the fabrics, obscenely expensive. Lilly thought they looked dull as dishwater but what did she know? She'd only been a Mayfair wife for three weeks.

Walking home from Tavern on the Green, Lilly pondered the question. As far as she could tell, rich women didn't dress for men, they dressed for each other. She couldn't imagine anything more boring or counterproductive but whoever said the rich made sense? Certainly not Lilly.

She pondered the question a while longer then broached the subject with her husband.

"Compared to your friends' wives, I dress like a tramp," she announced to Carter that night in bed.

"I like the way you dress."

"You're a man," she said. "You'd probably like it if I wore my showgirl costume complete with fishnet stockings."

He gave her a friendly swat on the rump. "I wouldn't mind if you put them on right now."

She squirmed out of his reach. "*They* wouldn't wear fishnet stockings."

"Who'd want them to?" he countered.

"My skirts are too short, my makeup's too heavy, everything about me is—"

"Fuckable."

"What?"

"You're wonderfully, eminently fuckable," he said, pulling her back near him, "and they're jealous."

"It's not that simple, Carter."

"It's that simple."

She looked down at his rock hard penis. "Again?" She started to laugh. They'd made love not an hour ago. "You're amazing."

He slid two fingers into her body then brought them to her lips. "That's how we taste," he said in a hoarse whisper. "Both of us, together."

The taste was musky and sweet, intoxicating and forbidden.

"I don't want to share you with anyone." He licked his way down her torso, over her belly, then between her legs. "Not with anyone."

He was fierce in his lovemaking, demanding responses from her when she thought she had nothing left to give. He encircled her clitoris with his lips, flicking his tongue against the tender flesh until she was sure she would explode from the ferocity of sensation. He drank her in, all of her, as she lay quivering and exposed and ravenous against the rumpled sheets.

"Oh God, Carter..." Her voice was weak, a whisper of itself. It was pleasure on the knife edge of pain and she was losing what was left of her mind.

She raised her hips, begging him to enter her, to fill her with his hardness, to ease the emptiness inside that had been there for so long.

"Carter?" He rolled off her and was reaching toward the nightstand on his side of the bed. "Is something—"

A pool of light fell across the bed, illuminating their bodies. Reality hit her like a splash of ice cold water. She grabbed for the top sheet but Carter pulled it away from her.

"I want to see you," he said, kneeling again between her legs.

She squirmed, trying to find a way to cover herself. "You've seen me before."

"Not like this." He drew his tongue across her labia with a voluptuously carnal movement while his hands moved along her belly. His fingers came to rest along the two silvery lines.

Please, God, no!

She knew she should do something, some wildly sensual thing, to distract him but she couldn't move. For years she'd been running as fast as she could and suddenly she couldn't run anymore. In a way she didn't even want to. Tears welled up and she closed her eyes.

"Stretch marks," he said, in a flat tone of voice.

"I wanted to tell you," she managed, "but I was afraid."

He didn't move a muscle as he watched her. His expression gave away nothing. "So tell me now."

At first the words wouldn't come. She stumbled badly, trying to tell him about the boy she'd loved, about the wedding they'd planned, about Cliff's accident and Maisie and Eileen Fontaine.

The more she told him, the greater the distance between them grew. It was as if her words were invisible wedges, pushing them apart. She'd never claimed to be a virgin. She'd never claimed she didn't have a past. If Carter couldn't handle the fact that there had been other men, then there was no hope for them.

She was about to say exactly that when the truth hit her right between the eyes. Clifford wasn't the problem and neither was her pregnancy. It was the baby.

Suddenly she understood him in a way she'd never understood another human being. *He's afraid,* she thought in amazement. Afraid that there was someone who held a prior claim to her heart. A little girl who could take her away from him, the way Grant had taken Denise.

Didn't he realize he had nothing to worry about? It was so long ago that sometimes it seemed to Lilly as if it had happened to someone else, in some other life. The relentless pain of labor. The triumph of hearing that first cry. The last look she'd had of that perfect little face. Gone, all of it, almost as if it had never happened.

"And the baby?" His voice broke the silence, chipping it like chunks of ice. "What happened to the baby?"

There was only one thing she could do, only one right answer. Only one way to ensure the happy ending she'd always dreamed of.

"Dead," she whispered, as she finally let go of the past. "My baby is dead."

11

The Franklin-Daye Preparatory School

"Jesus, Spaulding, you really like to live dangerously, don't you?" Chandler Moore Davenport III leaned out of the open window and stared down at his roommate. "They're gonna catch you out there."

"Gimme a hand, goddammit!" Grant snarled. Security was already watching him like a hawk. If they caught him hanging from the building like a bat, he'd be up to his bony ass in trouble. "This trellis is creaking like a son of a bitch."

"You're nuts!" Chandler grabbed Grant by the forearms. "Bed check was two hours ago. I risked my ass covering for you again. Next time—"

Grant hoisted himself over the windowsill and into the room. "Shut up, will you?" He brushed some snow off his jeans then gestured behind him. "And close the window. It's cold as hell in here."

Chan was a pussy but he was rich and he usually did what he was told which made him primo roommate material. Grant grinned at the sound of the window slamming shut.

"Lock it," he added over his shoulder. "Gotta keep the townies outside where they belong."

"Bastard," Chan muttered, tossing himself onto his bed. "Someday someone's gonna knock you on your butt."

"Take your best shot, buddy," Grant replied. "You don't scare me."

"I know," Chan said glumly. "I don't scare anyone. It's the story of my life."

"Get over it." Grant sank onto the edge of his bed and tugged at one of his pricey leather boots. "Gimme a hand, will you?"

"Go to hell."

Grant laughed. "Tell me that after you see what I scored down in Boston."

Chan propped himself up on one elbow. "Better than grass?"

"So much better it'll blow your fucking head from here to Connecticut and back."

"Show me."

"Get your ass over here and help me with these boots and I'll do better than that."

He and Chan had met in freshman year and before the first semester was halfway over, Grant had the kid from Greenwich completely under his thumb. It hadn't even required physical violence. Not that Grant had anything against physical violence, it was just that he'd learned a long time ago that the best way to manipulate your enemies was to find out what they wanted more than anything on earth, the one thing they'd sell their balls for. Once you had that figured out, you owned them.

At the moment he owned three quarters of the student body and a surprising number of faculty members. The way he figured it, by spring break he'd rule the universe. Too bad Christmas vacation started two weeks from today. He could've made a killing with the holiday trade. Still, it wasn't a total loss. His old crowd in Manhattan still hadn't caught on to that magical white powder. Maybe he'd play Santa Claus and dole out a few free samples while he was in town, stir up a little new business. You had to give in order to get and he was more than willing to play the odds.

Give the people what they want and they'll beat a path to your dorm room. Right now the people wanted cocaine and Grant's third-floor room was the best supermarket in town.

New York City

"Over there...a little to the right...lower...yes! That's it!" Lilly clasped her hands together in delight. "Admit it, Carter. That's the most spectacular tree in all of Manhattan."

Carter picked a strand of tinsel from the sleeve of his heavy sweater and made a show of inspecting the twelve-foot tall pine tree that held the place of honor in front of the living room window. Hundreds of white lights twinkled from the branches, reflecting the jewellike colors of the Austrian glass ornaments. "Trees like this belong in the foyer, darling. It's blocking our view of the park."

"The foyer?" Lilly wrinkled her nose at the thought. "What's the point of having a beautiful Christmas tree if you can't enjoy it? We can look at the park anytime but Christmas comes just once a year." Where she came from people put their Christmas trees right in the middle of the living room so everybody could see them.

Carter reached for the tumbler of Scotch on the windowsill. "You are a revelation, Mrs. Spaulding. The thought wouldn't have occurred to me."

"That's exactly what's wrong with you, Carter. You've forgotten how to have fun."

He offered her a sip of his Scotch but she shook her head. She was flying high enough on sheer excitement.

"That's why I married you," he said, drawing her into his arms. "For fun."

That familiar hum began inside her body, deep and thrilling. There was something dangerous about Carter, the kind of danger you didn't expect to find with the man who lay in bed beside you every night. She never quite knew where she stood with her husband. Sometimes he looked at her as if she were the center of his universe; other times he didn't seem to see her at all. She'd thought marriage to a wealthy older man would be safe and comfortable. So far it had proved to be anything but. She wouldn't have it any other way.

She snaked her arms around his neck and looked up into his eyes. "The staff has the night off."

"You should have given them the week off."

She could feel his heat right through her clothes. "We have the party tomorrow night," she said as he cupped her buttocks and drew her closer. "What would we do without help?"

He was hard. Beautifully, wondrously hard. "Cancel the party," he growled into her ear. "I'll call the airport. We could be in Aruba by morning." He told her about how it would feel to make love on a secluded strip of beach with the hot sun caressing their naked bodies and the sound of the waves urging them on.

"We can't," she whispered. "Grant will be coming home and—"

"Let him stay at school."

"It's Christmas."

"He can stay with one of his friends."

"Carter, he's your son. His place is here with us."

"His place is where I tell him it is."

She pulled away from him. "I wish you wouldn't say things like that."

"Don't go getting sentimental about him, Lilly. He's been trouble since the day he was born."

"Is it any wonder?" she said, leaping to the boy's defense. "I'm not blaming you, Carter, but he hasn't had much of a home life since he lost his mom."

Carter ran a hand through his thick silver hair then reached once again for the tumbler of Scotch. "You see what you want to see. You don't know the whole story."

"Then *tell* me," she demanded. "I'm his stepmother. How can I help him if I don't know what he needs?"

"He needs discipline."

"He needs a family."

"He has a family."

She touched his forearm. "Why don't you take him out of that boarding school and let him live here with us? We're surrounded by schools and, God knows, we have the room. I think—"

"Don't think," he said. "Let's finish what we started."

He made to pull her close again but Lilly was like a dog with a bone. "Really, Carter, think about it. We have an enormous place here." She struggled to find the right words. "Real families live together. They don't send their children away and—" She stopped, her own words echoing inside her head.

"You're all the family I want," he said, sliding his hands under her skirt.

A thought came to her. A forbidden, dangerous thought. "Make love to me, Carter," she whispered. "Let's make a baby together." How could he resist a sweet little baby? She'd show him how wonderful it could be to have a family.

He was stroking her, long deep strokes with his elegant, amazing fingers. "No baby," he said, his mouth pressed against the base of her throat.

"A beautiful child," she went on as if he hadn't spoken. "Our very own family."

"No, Lilly."

"Maybe not now," she said quickly, "with the holidays and all. Maybe after New Year's."

"There isn't going to be a baby, Lilly." He spoke slowly and carefully, the way you would to a foreigner who didn't quite understand the language. "Not now. Not after the holidays."

"You want us to enjoy being newlyweds," she said, not believing her own words for a minute. Something was wrong. She could see it in his eyes.

"Lilly." He sounded so serious, so stern that her stomach knotted up.

"We don't have to talk about this right now," she said, insinuating her body against his. She'd make him forget this terrible conversation. It would be as if it had never happened. "I'm still young. We have all the time in the world to have children."

He met her eyes. The truth was right there between them and it wouldn't go away.

"No, we don't," he said at last. "I had a vasectomy."

For days Lili grieved in a way she hadn't grieved when she gave up her own child. With those simple words, "I had a vasectomy," Carter had stripped her of the dream that had sustained her for the almost fourteen years since she gave up her baby for adoption.

You thought you were going to have it all, didn't you, girl? Grandma Hattie's mocking voice followed her everywhere. *You should've known the Almighty would have the last laugh.*

Giving up her baby girl to strangers had been a wicked, evil thing to do and now she was being punished for it.

Nothing's ever going to be enough for you, Lilly Ann. Never was, never will be.

She had a rich and powerful husband who thought she was the sexiest, most exciting woman on earth. All she had to do was snap her fingers and whatever she wanted materialized at her feet like magic. But all the money in the world couldn't give her the one thing she wanted more than anything else: it could never give her a baby.

Lilly went through the motions of preparing for Christmas. She spent more on gifts than she'd earned in her entire lifetime and two full afternoons addressing cards to people she'd never met. There were three and four parties per night—elegant, formal affairs where nothing as common as a Christmas tree marred the snooty decor.

This is what you wanted, isn't it? taunted Grandma Hattie as Lilly mingled with her husband's friends and colleagues. *You wanted to be rich. You wanted to be safe. Never heard you say you wanted a family too....*

What did Grandma Hattie know anyway? She'd lived in the old woman's house for almost seventeen years but she might as well have lived alone for all Hattie Barnett had learned about her granddaughter. Lilly would never deny the fact that she'd wanted the good things in life. Only a crazy person wanted to worry about where her next meal was coming from or if she'd have a roof over her head come tomorrow. Just because you wanted enough money to make life go down easier didn't mean you didn't know what else was important.

She wasn't the one who'd left Clifford Franklin in the lurch. He'd up and died on her. She'd wanted nothing more than to be married to him and have his babies. And she'd never have given up their child if she'd believed for even an instant that the day would come when she didn't have to worry about money any longer. She and Clifford and their beautiful little girl would have been a family, the kind she'd dreamed about.

But she couldn't change the past. Right or wrong, she'd made her choices and she was willing to live with them. Was it possible Carter felt the same way? He'd made his decision to have a vasectomy years before he met her. He'd been bitter, sleeping with lots of different women, positive he'd never marry again. Children had been the last thing on his mind and a va-

sectomy was the perfect way to protect himself from both unwanted children and unwanted lawsuits.

She told herself that it would have been different if she'd met
him years ago. There would have been no vasectomy. There
would have been no need. When two people loved each other,
they wanted to start a family together and she knew, deep in her
heart, that she and Carter would have been no exception.

*If you ask me, the fella ain't much in the father department.
Looks to me like he made the right choice, not having any
more.*

Carter and Grant were oil and water on the surface but Lilly
sensed that their similarities were the real problem between
them. Grant professed enormous disdain for the family business but Lilly had caught him scanning Mayfair's latest stock
report when he was home for Thanksgiving. Carter only saw his
son's shortcomings. Lilly was determined to make him see his
assets, as well.

She'd fallen in love with the boy the moment she saw him.
Something about Grant had touched her heart in a way she
wouldn't have believed possible. Oh, she had experienced a
tidal wave of maternal love and pride when her daughter was
born but she'd been young then and naive, unaware of how
fleeting a thing happiness truly was. She was older now and she
knew better. Happiness was elusive and when you found it, you
had to hold on to it as if your life depended on it.

Maybe this wasn't exactly what she'd been praying for but it
was a thousand times more than she'd ever thought she'd find
back in Euless a thousand lifetimes ago.

Grant was due home on the twenty-third. She made sure
Gretchen stocked his favorite foods and soft drinks and took
advantage of the woman's day off to make a huge batch of
Christmas cookies for the boy. He was probably way too sophisticated to appreciate a sappy, sentimental gesture like that
but baking those cookies made her feel like part of a family and
that was exactly what she needed.

She'd just put the last cinnamon dot on a gingerbread man
when Carter strode into the kitchen. He sniffed the air then
noticed the array of cookies spread out on racks to cool. One
eyebrow arched.

"You made these?"

She pushed her hair off her face with the back of a hand. "You sound surprised."

"I am surprised. I didn't know you could cook."

"I can't," she said honestly, "but I can bake with the best of them."

He broke off the leg from a gingerbread man then popped it in his mouth. "Damn good."

She inclined her head. "Thank you."

"I've missed you, Lilly."

She gathered up her bowls and utensils and began loading them in the dishwasher. "I don't know why," she said lightly. "I've been right here."

"You're many things, my beautiful wife, but you are not a good liar."

She sighed. Life would be a lot easier if she'd learned how.

"You've been far away," he said.

"I suppose it must seem that way."

"How can I convince you to come back?"

Her eyes welled with tears. "You don't have to convince me to come back, Carter. I never really left."

But she had and they both knew it. She was, after all, a lousy liar.

The radio car dropped Grant off in front of his old man's building just before eight-thirty on the night before Christmas Eve. Grudgingly he reached into his pocket for a pair of singles and shoved them at the driver. Bad enough he drove a limo for a living. You'd think he'd have more pride than to go begging for a tip.

"Mr. Spaulding took care of everything," the driver said, waving away the dollar bills. "Merry Christmas."

Grant shrugged and stuffed the money back into his pocket. "Yeah," he mumbled. "Back at you."

Like he gave a shit if the guy had a merry Christmas. Hell, he didn't care if he had one himself. He'd called his old man last night, trying to back out on this bullshit exercise in family unity but Carter wasn't buying it. "Be here by eight-thirty tomorrow night," he said, "or you won't see daylight until New Year's."

It wasn't as if Christmas were any big deal to them. One of the maids usually decorated a stupid-looking fake tree and propped it up on the hall table opposite the door so people would think the Spauldings gave a damn about the holidays. Every year Carter took off the day after Christmas to go skiing in Vail, leaving Grant alone with the housekeeper and a skeleton staff.

He wondered about Lilly's take on Christmas cheer. His old man's last wife hadn't been big on yuletide spirit, except when it came to raking in the presents. He'd only met Lilly twice. Both times she'd been a soft touch for the lost boy routine and forked over some bills. But that didn't mean she wanted to spend Christmas with him.

"Merry Christmas, Master Spaulding." The night doorman tipped his hat as Grant pushed by him. "You're looking well."

"Yeah," he said. "You, too."

Same routine with the elevator operator. Like Grant even noticed how they looked. He glanced at his watch. Three minutes early. He pointed to the time. "It's 8:27," he said to the guy as the doors slid open. "Remember that."

The first thing he noticed when he stepped into the foyer was the absence of a Christmas tree. *Good going, Pop,* he thought, tossing his backpack down and shrugging out of his jacket. He wouldn't have thought Christmases at Happy House could get any lousier but it looked as if he'd underestimated his old man.

He moved through the hallway, getting more pissed by the second. He could've gone to Connecticut with Chandler and checked out the Greenwich action or bummed a ride into Boston and done a few deals. If the old man thought he was going to keep him locked up until New Year's, he was crazy. He'd hang around until the day after Christmas; when Carter and the new wife took off for Vail, Grant would blast out of there.

"Grant!" His stepmother's low, sweet voice stopped him in his tracks. "I thought I heard you come in." You'd almost think she was happy to see him.

"Yeah," he said, slowly turning around. "And I'm on time, too."

She frowned slightly, as if she didn't know what he was talking about. "Of course you're on time. You knew we couldn't wait for you to join us."

What the hell was she smoking? She had a lot to learn about life at Chez Spaulding. She linked her arm through his and a weird kind of warmth spread through his chest. He'd never had anyone on his side before. It was a good feeling.

"Come on," she said. "Your father's in the living room. We held dinner for you."

"This is a joke, right?" His old man hadn't even waited around for him to be born. He remembered his grandmother telling him how Carter had gone out golfing, leaving his mother alone in the hospital.

Lilly's smile widened as they reached the archway to the living room. "Judge for yourself."

A huge Christmas tree blocked the view of Central Park. And it wasn't one of those fake trees either. The smell of pine filled his head and, despite himself, he grinned. White lights twinkled from every branch along with ornaments of all shapes and sizes. Shimmery tinsel caught the light. He hadn't seen tinsel since he was a kid. Brightly wrapped packages were stacked under the lowest branches and if he didn't know better he'd think a real family lived there.

Hell, he thought, looking over at Lilly. It wouldn't kill him to pretend.

BOOK FOUR

The Daughter

12

Cincinnati, 1980

Corey leaned forward and stared intently at her reflection in the mirror. It was the same face she'd had for seventeen years. Wouldn't you think she'd be used to it by now? She tilted back the shade on her desk lamp and angled the light toward the right side of her face. Her breath caught. She adjusted the lamp again.

"Ohh!" The sound escaped before she could stop it. She turned her face the tiniest bit more to the left, then dipped her chin the way Patti Hansen had on the cover of last month's *Vogue*. The bad side of her face was hidden by shadows and if you didn't know better, you might not even realize the scars were there.

The girl looking back at her was pretty. Better than pretty. She could be one of the girls in *Seventeen* or *Glamour,* laughing for the camera so the whole world could admire her. She had a good mouth, fine bones, big wide-set eyes the color of sapphires. Her dark hair was glossy and thick. The girl looking back at her could have any boy she wanted just by snapping her fingers.

Too bad the girl in the mirror wasn't real.

Corey leaned back in her chair and brushed away tears of frustration. Nothing had changed. She'd been stupid to pretend they had. The scars were still there, red and angry, tugging at the side of her mouth like a puppet master's strings. No matter how hard she tried, she couldn't wish them away. Why did she even care about things like hairstyles and makeup? There wasn't enough hair spray and eye shadow in the world to turn her into the girl she wanted to be.

She switched off her desk lamp and sat in her darkened bedroom. Sometimes she wondered if maybe Millicent and Jack were crazy. All these years she'd been waiting for them to notice what everyone else in the entire world saw the second Corey walked into a room. Were they dumb? Blind? Just plain stupid? They told her how smart she was and how loving but they never, not once, seemed to realize she was ugly. Those fire-engine red scars that sent little kids running for cover were invisible to her adoptive parents, as if somebody had waved a magic wand and made the scars disappear.

How could they not know the way she felt each time she met someone new and had to endure that awful moment when they zeroed in on her scars? It wasn't as if plastic surgery were a new invention or something. If they really loved her, wouldn't they do something to help her?

Really, she didn't even have to be beautiful. All she wanted was to like the face that looked back at her in the mirror. That didn't seem like so much to ask when other kids were praying for brand-new cars and dates to the prom. Sometimes it scared her to think that maybe she looked the way she did because there was something really wrong with her, some terrible black mark on her soul that made her different from everybody else, something that had made God want to single her out from the pack and make her pay.

When she first came to live there with the Bannings, she used to stand by the front gate and watch the neighborhood girls strolling down the street toward the pond. They'd look at Corey and Corey would hold her breath, praying that this time it would be different, this time they'd ask her to be one of them, but it never happened. Not even once. She could still hear the sound of their laughter as they turned the corner, heads pressed together, part of something Corey could only imagine.

Reading was her escape. She devoured both Kafka and *Glamour*, Dostoyevsky and *Vogue*. She could rattle off the names of the elements and the last twelve *Harper's Bazaar* cover girls and, deep in her heart of hearts, she knew she'd rather be Cheryl Tiegs than Jonas Salk any day.

She wanted someone to hold her close, someone who would dance with her in the moonlight and press his mouth to hers and—

Her breath caught as she ran her hands up her rib cage then lightly, sweetly, over her breasts. She wanted to be touched, to know how it felt when a boy pressed his body against yours. Sometimes she couldn't sleep for the hunger that seemed to be gnawing its way out through her rib cage. Lying in bed at night, she thought about things that scared and tantalized her, things she could never tell another living soul. Dark, unknowable things that were just beyond reach.

What if nobody ever touched her that way? What if she lived her whole life without discovering the magic that happened between a man and a woman? That could happen. People died every day of the week without knowing how it felt to be held and loved. Sometimes when she and Peter from next door were studying, the unfamiliar heat grabbed hold of her and it took all of her willpower to keep her mind on her work.

For weeks now she'd teetered on the verge of doing something crazy, something so dangerous and thrilling just the thought of it made her blush from head to foot. She and Peter had been friends since freshman year. He wasn't much of a student—football players usually weren't—but he had to keep up his grades in order to stay on the team. Mr. Forsythe had asked Corey if she'd be willing to help Peter with English and history and, not knowing how to say no, she'd agreed.

"Just don't tell anybody," Peter had said, giving her one of the off-center grins that turned the other girls to mush. "I don't want them to think I'm stupid."

And so for the last three and a half years she'd helped him with American history and written most of his English term papers and she'd never once let on to anyone that the great Peter Macmillan wasn't quite as great as he wanted people to think.

He was always kind to her. He didn't ignore her in the cafeteria or snicker when she walked past his locker. He greeted her with a friendly hello when they bumped into each other and even remembered her at Christmas with a box of candy.

She knew for a fact that he hadn't dated anyone since Cheryl Kurkowski dumped him for Steve Waverly three weeks ago. Three weeks was a long time for a seventeen-year-old guy to go without doing it. After three weeks, even someone like Corey could look good.

"You're so lucky." Francine Glass smiled at Millicent from under the plastic bonnet of the hairdryer at Pam's Hair Palace.

Millicent smiled back from under her own plastic bonnet. "Lucky?"

Francine's laugh was girlish. "Corey's such a good student. Study, study, study! At least you know where she is on Saturday night. My Annette has so many boyfriends that I said I'd name my gray hairs after each one of them!" Francine launched into a story about Annette's high school conquests that made Millicent want to turn the hairdryer switch up to fry.

"Mil?"

Millicent blinked. Didn't the woman ever stop talking? "Yes, Francine?"

"I asked if Corey was going to the senior prom?"

Millicent felt as if someone had plunged a knife into her heart. "No," she said evenly. "Corey's been way too busy with her studies to even think about going to the prom."

Francine's red lips pursed in a phony smile. "You must be so proud of her."

Millicent was, but a woman like Francine would never understand how she felt. "Our girl has a scholarship," she said, trying not to sound too uppity or full of herself. It wasn't anybody's business that it wasn't a full scholarship. Three years ago they hadn't been sure their girl would even graduate.

It did her heart good to see Francine go green with envy. The woman didn't have much else to say after that. Her dopey cow of a daughter couldn't win a scholarship to beauty school. Francine settled back under the dryer and pretended to read last month's *Good Housekeeping,* the one with Deborah Raffin on the cover. The last thing Millie wanted was for Francine to know how much her words had hurt her.

Proud as she was of her girl's accomplishments, Millicent would have traded those scholarships just to see one real smile on Corey's face. She couldn't remember the last time Corey had looked really and truly happy. She worked part-time at the local grocery store three afternoons a week and studied on Fridays with that nice boy from next door. Every now and then she'd go fishing with Jack or to a movie but mostly she worked. Millie was proud as punch about the scholarship but she knew there had to be more to a girl's life than SAT scores and grade point averages.

Millicent sighed as she thought about the stack of magazines stuffed under Corey's bed. She hadn't meant to snoop but it had been a dog's age since the mattress had been turned and it had seemed as good a time as any to do it. There, poking out from under the dust ruffle, was the corner of last month's *Vogue*. Mumbling about her bum knees, Millicent had bent down to retrieve it, only to find a dozen more where that came from. *Harper's Bazaar. Glamour. Mademoiselle.* Splashy magazines with lots of color pictures of beautiful girls wearing beautiful clothes while they did exciting things no real person ever did.

At first she'd laughed. The apple really didn't fall very far from the tree. Millicent loved her magazines, too, everything from *Ladies Home Journal* to *People* to *Family Circle.* She knew what Cher's house looked like from the inside, what Suzanne Somers cooked for company dinner, how many cars Wayne Newton had in his collection. She supposed it was silly, a grown woman knowing so much about people she'd never meet, but Millicent had been born curious and probably always would be.

She started to slide the magazines back under the bed when she noticed how many pages had been marked. Curious, she flipped through *Harper's Bazaar.*

It seemed as if the corner of every other page had been neatly turned down. The margins were filled with notes, all written in Corey's precise hand. How to find your best hairstyle. How to look five pounds thinner. How to make your eyes bigger, your lips fuller, your cheekbones more striking. How to make a sad-eyed girl just like everybody else.

It had come close to breaking Millicent's heart. Somehow it was worse than if she'd read her daughter's diary. She sat on the floor next to Corey's bed and worked her way through every single magazine. How could she have been so blind, not to see how much the girl was hurting?

Maybe people only saw what they wanted to see. She and Jack had been so darned proud of their girl that they hadn't bothered to look past the good grades and fancy scholarships to see what it was Corey really wanted. Millicent looked down at the perfect faces that smiled out at her from the pages of all those magazines. Was this what Corey wanted—to be beautiful?

Lord knew, she'd been a real handful when she was little. Those first few years hadn't been easy, what with Corey getting into fights every time Millicent turned her back. Kids had built-in radar when it came to the best ways to hurt each other and Corey had suffered through more than her share of ugly taunts and cruel jokes. Of course, Corey had usually managed to give back as good as she got, but still those childhood hurts never really went away.

Somehow Millicent had let herself believe that everything was wonderful, that because she was so happy Corey was too.

"How're we doing under there?" Pam, owner of the beauty parlor, rapped on the bonnet of the dryer.

"Could use something to drink, Pammy. It's hot as the dickens."

Pam smiled at her and bustled off to get Millicent her usual plastic cup of lemonade. Millicent had to be real careful, what with her diabetes and all, but Pam always had a special batch of lemonade made with Sweet 'n Low for when Millicent came in.

She cast a look at Francine whose nose was still buried in her magazine. Francine was getting that stringy look around her throat that all the makeup in the world couldn't hide. Bette Mullen said that Francine had gone to a doctor in Chicago and had the bags under her eyes removed but Millicent didn't believe it. Why would anyone have surgery if it wasn't a matter of life or death?

Corey would. The voice was so clear she almost jumped out of her seat. It was as if someone were sitting inside her head, talking to her. A few years ago the girl had told them about some hotshot doctor who did wonderful things for people who'd been in accidents. Millicent hadn't paid much attention at the time. Oh, she remembered that they'd argued and that Jack had gotten real upset but she'd figured it was a phase Corey was going through. Most teenage girls complained endlessly about their faces and figures and Corey was no exception.

Later on Millicent couldn't say exactly why she did it but suddenly she leaned over and plucked a copy of *People* from the stack on the table next to her. There was a big color picture of John Travolta on the cover, looking like every mother's nightmare in tight jeans and a black leather jacket. She'd liked him so much more when he wore that nice white suit in that dance movie. She flipped past the letters to the editor, the index and the movie reviews. It was as if her fingers had a life of their own. She didn't even stop to read a story about that pretty little Olivia Newton-John and the store she was opening up in Hollywood. No, Millicent kept on turning those pages like a woman possessed until she reached the next-to-last article.

THE MOGUL AND THE SHOWGIRL
And They Said It Wouldn't Last!

Mayfair cosmetics owner Carter Spaulding and his wife Lili flew two hundred of their nearest and dearest to Caesar's Palace in Las Vegas last weekend to celebrate four years of wedded bliss. "Meeting Lili was the luckiest thing that's ever happened to me," Carter Spaulding, 49, said after they renewed their vows at the Little Chapel of Dreams. "It's time she had the wedding she deserves." Lili Spaulding, 34, wore a shimmering, silver gown by designer Calvin Klein. "Mrs. Spaulding's gown has over 30,000 beads hand-sewn to the bodice and skirt," said a Klein representative. Lili Spaulding is known for—

It was exactly the kind of story Millicent loved best. Private jets, beautiful people, fancy clothes, and big parties. And, as if that wasn't enough, a love story to boot. This was even better than Cinderella because it was true. Four years ago Lili Spaulding had been a run-of-the-mill showgirl at Caesar's Palace, dancing by night and going to school by day. Then

Carter Spaulding came along and bingo! She was the wife of a millionaire, hobnobbing with presidents and movie stars and even the Prince of Wales. Millicent sighed contentedly. It wasn't that she had any desire to be anyone but Jack's wife and Corey's mother. She loved her life as fiercely as she loved her God and wouldn't trade it for anything in the world. But how she loved to read about people like the Spauldings.

She wished she had her magnifying glass with her so she could study the color photo of Lili Spaulding. The young woman was as beautiful as a movie star with her glossy black hair and deep blue eyes. No wonder Carter Spaulding fell in love with her!

"Here's your lemonade, Mil." Pam handed her a red plastic cup filled to the brim.

"Thanks, Pammy."

Pam reached under the bonnet and touched Millicent's head. "I think you're done. Why don't we move over to the mirror and see what's what?"

Millicent gathered up her purse and her cup of lemonade and made to follow Pam when she noticed *People* lying on the floor at her feet. She hesitated a second—she'd really scanned most of it already—then bent down and picked it up. Maybe she'd read that Olivia Newton-John article after supper tonight.

Millicent got home around six. She set the potatoes to boil on the stove. She usually made spaghetti sauce on Fridays but her hair appointment took longer than usual and Food King was closed by the time she got there. Jack would probably be disappointed at having leftover meat loaf but she'd make it up to him. There wasn't much in this world that mashed potatoes and gravy couldn't cure. At least not with her husband.

Things were perking along quite nicely, she decided. Maybe she could sit down in the living room for a few minutes and finish her magazine. The Olivia Newton-John story had been a real disappointment but the John Travolta article hinted at some juicy gossip. He was dating that redheaded gal from "Taxi" but Millicent was sure it would never last. Why buy the cow when the milk pitcher's always filled? These modern, up-to-date girls still didn't understand that sometimes the old ways were the best ways.

She was walking past the dining room when she caught sight of Corey bent over her homework. That nice young man from next door was there with her. Millicent kept hoping their friendship might turn into a romance but so far that hadn't happened and even Millicent had to admit it probably never would.

High school was such a special time. The memories you built up then lasted an entire lifetime. How she wished there was some way Corey could have those memories, too.

She stopped in her tracks and looked at her beloved daughter. From that angle, you'd never think Corey's face was anything but perfect. Her shiny dark hair swung over her cheek like a curtain of silk. Her long lashes cast a shadow on her cheek while she nibbled on the eraser end of her pencil with her perfect white teeth. She was so beautiful she could be in a magazine, just like the models she admired so much. Just like that Lili Spaulding—

Millicent's heart seemed to stop beating. She leaned against the doorjamb for a second while a wave of dizziness washed over her. No, she thought, forcing herself to take deep, steadying breaths. It was too silly to even think about.

Still, she pulled the magazine from the deep pocket of her apron and flipped to the page with the article about Carter Spaulding and his ex-showgirl wife. She looked from the photograph of the smiling woman to her own studious daughter. The same straight nose. The same strong chin. Even the eyes were—

She shoved the magazine back in her pocket, furious with herself for being so foolish.

Imagine thinking her Corey could be the natural daughter of Carter Spaulding's wife! Didn't that just beat all? They even said in the article that Mrs. Spaulding couldn't have children. She could just hear Jack when she told him about her silly flight of fancy tonight during pillow talk. "You should be a writer, Millie," he'd say with that booming laugh of his. "With that imagination of yours, we could be millionaires."

If only, she thought with a sigh. If they were millionaires, they could give Corey the world. As it was, they couldn't even make her happy.

13

Millicent had a long-standing Friday afternoon hair appointment at Pam's Hair Palace, which meant that from one o'clock until almost five-thirty, the Banning house was empty. Corey had the time and the place, now all she had to find was the nerve.

Thinking about sleeping with Peter was easy; actually making it happen was another story entirely. Maybe if he'd been the one doing the asking it wouldn't have been so scary but every time she was about to proposition him, her mouth got dry, her hands began to shake, and she wished she was Catholic so she could become a nun.

She told herself that the worst thing he could do to her was say no and that was true. *No* wouldn't kill her. At least she didn't think it would. But that deep, aching need inside her heart was another story.

Time was running out. It was the end of April. School would be over in less than two months and their Friday study afternoons would be history.

Her last class that Friday was English. Mr. Forsythe was pretty much of a pushover when it came to Corey. He was the first one to recognize the fact that she had a brain and it was his encouragement that had inspired her to push toward a scholarship.

When she thought about the time she'd wasted she wanted to scream. A partial scholarship wasn't going to cut it. The way she figured it she'd have to aim for sixteen to eighteen credits per semester in order to get through in four years and she'd have to take a part-time job besides.

Her parents had said they would pick up the rest of her bills but she knew that would be a lot tougher for them than they let on. Pop had been laid off from the factory and was working odd jobs wherever he could find them and even Mom was beginning to glance at the Help Wanted ads on Sunday morning.

Still and all, thanks to Mr. Forsythe she had a future now and she felt rotten for lying to him this way but that didn't stop her. When she told him she needed to skip class to get a handle on the presentation she was writing for the debating team, her mentor waved her off with a smile.

She raced home, threw off her clothes, and leaped into the shower. She scrubbed herself all over with scented soap, creamed her arms and legs, then dusted herself with bath powder. If only she had something special and glamorous, like Chanel No. 5 or Shalimar, instead of her old standby Jean Naté but there was no point daydreaming over what she couldn't have.

Besides, Peter would be there any minute. She quickly slipped into clean underwear and a simple cotton dress that matched the deep blue of her eyes. She usually wore baggy jeans and a cotton sweater that hid her body and the dress felt particularly daring as it brushed against her bare legs. She studied her face in the mirror, wincing as always at the scars. Her everyday ponytail wasn't good enough. Not today. She parted her hair on the side and let it fall like a dark curtain over the bad side of her face.

And then the front doorbell rang.

Heart thundering, she raced down the stairs and flung open the door.

"Hey, Corey," Peter said, heading toward the dining room where they usually worked. If he noticed the change in her appearance, he didn't let on. "This Shakespeare is a bitch and a half."

She wasn't oblivious to his appearance. He looked so...so *beautiful* in his tight jeans and patterned shirt that her breath caught. His chestnut brown hair was thick and full, just grazing the back of his collar. Her fingers itched to touch the silky strands as if her very skin hungered for the feel of him. The sight of him made her heart ache the way a beautiful sunset did or a night sky full of stars.

She cleared her throat. "How about something to eat?"

"Sounds great," he said, spreading his papers out on the table. He was all business.

She stood in the doorway, unable to move. He seemed so comfortable within his own body, as if he didn't know or care

142   *Barbara Bretton*

that he was perfect. She couldn't imagine how it felt to coexist with yourself in such harmony.

She shifted her weight from her right foot to her left. He took no notice. She'd hoped he would immediately know what she had in mind, but he barely seemed to register her presence in the room. Okay, so maybe he wasn't perfect. He didn't read minds. She'd have to actually say something.

"Peter," she began, sounding more like Minnie Mouse than a budding femme fatale, "there's something we need to talk about."

He grinned up at her, his golden brown eyes twinkling with amusement. "I know, I know. I didn't forget. I'll have the reference outline finished tonight. I swear it."

She made a nervous gesture with her hands. "It's—it's something personal."

The light in his eyes dimmed and her heart lurched dangerously. "Personal?"

She nodded, letting her hair swing over the bad side of her face. "My mom won't be home until six."

"I know," he said. "This is her hair day, right?"

She nodded again. "And my dad is working evenings at the gas station."

He didn't say anything, just looked at her with a puzzled expression.

She stepped closer. The dress swished around her thighs. "I—uh, I thought maybe we could work on the presentation later."

"Later? Corey, we're running out of time. We—"

"Peter," she said softly, "we're *alone*." She paused, praying he would understand what she was saying without her having to tell him.

"You don't look so good," he said, peering at her. "Maybe you should sit down."

"Oh God," she said, as a hysterical laugh threatened to escape. "Don't you know what I'm saying, Peter? We're *alone*."

His eyes widened then two patches of bright red appeared on his angular cheeks. "You're kidding, right?"

"No, I'm not." She took a step closer to him. She'd have to come right out with it. "I'm on the pill so you wouldn't have to use a rubber."

His gaze darted from her breasts to the window to the hidden place between her legs. "You want to do it?"

"Yes." She wanted to be kissed and held. She wanted to know how it felt to be just like everyone else.

His silence was deafening. Was that a paradox or an oxymoron? She could almost see the words throbbing behind his adam's apple. Finally he spoke.

"I like you a lot but I don't love you." *And I don't really want you.* He didn't say those words but she heard them just the same.

"I don't love you either." She kept her gaze level, direct. She'd never let him know how much his hesitation hurt. "So, forget it," she said, as if it didn't matter, as if her pride weren't hanging in the balance. "It was just an idea. Let's get to work."

"Wait a minute." He pushed back his chair and stood up. Her breath caught at the sight of his bulging fly. "Actually it's a good idea."

She ducked her head so he wouldn't see the look of triumph she knew was in her eyes. "I don't want you to do something you don't want to do, Peter."

"You're sure you're on the pill?"

"Trust me," she said, more harshly than she'd intended. "I'm not looking to get pregnant." No way would she make her real mother's mistakes. When she got pregnant—*if* she ever got pregnant—it would be on her terms and in her own good time.

"So, now what?"

"So, now we do it."

"Here?"

She hadn't thought about exactly where the great event would take place. "My room," she said.

He flashed his most-likely-to-succeed grin. "Lead the way."

He followed her upstairs to her bedroom. They didn't say a word to each other. They didn't hold hands but then they'd never held hands before. Why should today be any different?

Bright April sunshine streamed through her open window and spilled across her twin bed. Somehow she'd always imagined it would be dark the first time. How could she stand there and take off her clothes in broad daylight? Nobody had ever seen her naked, at least not since she was a little girl.

Why hadn't she thought about that? Was she supposed to undress herself or would he slowly strip her of her clothes the way it happened in the movies? A horrible thought occurred to her: what if he was waiting for her to unzip his pants? If he was, he'd be waiting a long time because she could never touch him there, not in a million years.

Suddenly the whole thing didn't seem like such a good idea anymore. She opened her mouth to say so just as Peter pushed her down on her bed and shoved his hand under her skirt. The touch of his fingers against her bare skin was like a jolt of electricity, painful and unexpected.

"Peter!" She tried to push him off her. "What are you doing?"

"What do you think?" He didn't sound like himself. His voice was thicker, edgier, and she had the feeling he didn't really see her at all.

Shouldn't he be kissing her? She'd imagined there would be kissing, lots of it, long slow wet kisses that would make her tingle from her toes to the top of her head but his face was pressed against the side of her neck and all she felt was his moist breath on her skin.

He snaked his fingers inside her panties. His fingertips scraped against her tender flesh and she cried out. He took the sound as encouragement and the next instant he jammed a finger inside her body.

She struggled to pull away from him but he held her fast. She'd wanted warmth and tenderness, not this horrible invasion of her very self.

You asked for this. This is what you wanted—

But it wasn't. She'd wanted to feel cherished and safe, as if she were the most important girl in the whole world. As if she were beautiful—

"Touch me," he urged. "Help me put it in."

Put it in? He must be crazy. If his finger hurt that badly, what would it feel like if he—she didn't even want to think about it, much less do it. But he kept talking to her, urging her on, stroking her with his finger, faster and faster, until she arched against him, clinging to his shoulders as if they were a lifeline.

He inched her panties down over her hips and thighs and knees, trapping her ankles. He was blind to her, as if she were an inflatable doll and not a living, breathing human being. She didn't want it to be this way, not her first time. She had to do something to make him see her, to make him realize it was Corey Banning he held in his arms. Corey Banning and not some stranger he'd picked up at a dance.

"Wait!" She pushed against his chest with all of her strength. "Not this way!"

"What the—"

She reached behind her and unzipped the dress. Warm spring air caressed her back and she shivered. *Don't lose your nerve, Corey! Do it now!* With one swift gesture she pulled the dress over her head and tossed it to the floor, then kicked off her panties the rest of the way. *Look at me, Peter. Forget about my face and really look at me.*

His low moan was music to her ears and she experienced a surge of power unlike anything she'd ever known. He saw her, he finally *saw* her the way she needed to be seen. Naked she was beautiful. Naked she was every bit as beautiful as the other girls. He didn't tell her in so many words but she knew by the way he devoured her breasts with his eyes, the way his hands moved up and down the length of her body as if he couldn't get enough of her.

When she was a little girl she'd known that being ugly gave her power over people. Just by walking into a room she could stop a conversation cold. Smiles would freeze in place. Laughter would die away. All eyes would be on her. The pretty little girls with their blond curls and rosebud mouths would fade into the wallpaper as all eyes zeroed in on Corey. She hated being different but in that moment she understood her own power and gloried in it.

And it was the same this time. The moment she stripped off her clothes, the balance shifted and all of the power she'd given to Peter came rushing back to her, filling her with strength and confidence. He positioned himself between her thighs and she closed her eyes as his erection pressed against the opening to her body. She started to shake but he gentled her with his hands, whispering things to her that made her tremble even more fiercely.

Everyone said the first time was all pain and no pleasure but Corey didn't care. Someone wanted her at last. Pain seemed a small enough price to pay.

14

It was a foolish idea, thinking Lili Spaulding was Corey's birth mother, but for some reason Millicent couldn't quite let it go. Weeks passed and still she thought about the resemblance between the woman and her Corey. She'd clipped the article about Mrs. Spaulding from the newspaper and stashed it in the drawer of her nightstand, along with the magazine photo and everything else she could accumulate about the woman.

One May afternoon while Corey was at school and Jack was out looking for work, she took down the old photo albums from the hall closet and laid them out on the living room floor. Then she fetched the packet of papers from the nightstand and spread them out in neat rows so she could compare Corey's pictures to those of the beautiful Lili.

There was no denying the resemblance. Putting aside the scars, Corey's features were remarkably like Lili's. Enough so that Millicent went out to the library the next morning and spent three hours poring over old newspaper and magazine clippings about Lili Spaulding.

There were a lot more photographs of Lili than there were articles but to Millicent they all were gold. Apparently she couldn't have children—at least that's what the stories said— but that didn't mean seventeen years ago she hadn't given birth to a little girl. The only real information about Lili began four years ago when she married Carter Spaulding and took New York society by storm. Everything before that was vague and shadowy, as if her life hadn't even started until she fell in love.

When Corey first came to live with them they'd been prepared to answer questions about her birth parents and why her mother had given her up for adoption. They'd waited, armed with Dr. Spock and "Sesame Street" and anything else that might help them deal with a ticklish subject, but she never asked. Once Millicent had even brought up the topic herself but Corey had shrugged off her questions then run out to climb her favorite tree in the backyard.

"We better thank our lucky stars," Jack had said as they watched their girl reach the highest branch. "We won't have to share her with anybody."

But Millicent couldn't help but wonder about the woman who had given birth to their daughter. Did she ever think about Corey? Did she know about the car accident or did she think her child was growing up rich and beautiful in Memphis, Tennessee?

Millicent wished with her entire heart and soul that they'd tried harder to find out more. Back then it had seemed the less they knew about Corey's birth parents, the better off they were. The last thing they wanted was for someone to pop up on their doorstep one day, looking to take their darling girl away from them.

But something was wrong with Corey these days and it was more than the anger that was as much a part of her makeup as her sharp tongue and quick wit. Corey's grades were slipping, her attention span was the size of a mayfly's, and suddenly she was going out on school nights and getting home way past midnight looking guilty as sin. And the boys—just thinking about them made Millicent's blood run cold. They were calling all the time, asking for Corey and doing God knows what with her once they found her.

Doctor DeSimone had put Corey on the pill two years ago to help regulate her periods. Millicent had tried her best to ignore the other, obvious benefit and prayed Corey would, as well. She'd never shown the slightest interest in boys which was just fine by Millicent. She didn't care what anybody said, seventeen was just too darned young to be thinking about sex.

You don't have to do that to be popular, honey. You're worth a thousand of those boys.

But she knew Corey would never believe her, not as long as those scars were the first thing she saw when she looked in the mirror each morning.

Millicent had been doing a lot of thinking lately about doctors. They really did perform miracles these days with their fancy laser beams and such. She'd read a magazine article with pictures of magical transformations where accident victims were made whole again by what seemed like wizardry. But it wasn't wizardry. Modern technology had made miracles possible—as long as you knew where to look.

She had it all planned out. Corey could have the surgery the moment school ended and be recovered and ready for college at the end of August. Millicent had gone to see a surgeon in town last week, so she could show him pictures of Corey and find out if there was anything he could do.

"Absolutely," he'd said without a moment's hesitation. "The only crime is that you've waited this long." He described what he would do and how Corey would look when he'd finished. Millicent's heart soared with joy.

And then he told her what it would cost.

She sat in her car and wept for an hour after that. Insurance wouldn't cover half of the doctor's fee and she didn't dare think about the hospital bills.

After all these years the answer to her prayers was staring her right in the face and there wasn't a darn thing she could do about it. How could she have been so blind? Her own happiness at being someone's mother had overshadowed everything, including her beloved daughter's pain.

Corey was funny and bright and ambitious but that terrible scarring on her face would hold her back. Not everybody could see beyond the externals to what lay beneath the skin. Corey had the brains to take the world by storm but without plastic surgery Millicent knew her girl would never stand a chance.

"Yeah...that's it, baby...that's it." The boy's narrow hips bucked once, then twice, and he fell across her body like a dead weight.

Corey winced as her back pressed against the door handle of the beat-up car. "I've got to get home," she said after a few moments. She poked the boy in the shoulder. "Keith?" No response. "My parents think I'm still at work."

He muttered something unintelligible.

"Don't you dare go to sleep!" She poked him harder and he grumbled loudly. "I want to go home."

He rolled off her and sat up. "Okay."

She buttoned her sweater and adjusted her ponytail. Once again she'd been disappointed. Keith hadn't kissed her or held her close, the things she craved more than air and water.

Don't cry, Corey. If you cry he'll know how much it matters.

He started the car and gunned the engine. "Tomorrow night?" he asked as he guided the car down the densely wooded path.

"Sure," she said after a moment. Maybe tomorrow would be different.

She was quiet on the drive home. It wasn't as if they had a whole lot to talk about. She knew it would never occur to Keith to ask her if she wanted to stop someplace for a burger and fries, hang out with his friends. No, she knew her place. Peter had made sure to let her know the score that fateful afternoon back in April.

"You're going so soon?" Corey had asked as Peter gathered up his books from the dining room table. They'd managed to have sex and outline his study sheets for next week and it wasn't even four o'clock yet. Somehow this wasn't the way she'd imagined it would be at all.

"Didn't I tell you?" He tossed some papers into an envelope then tucked the envelope into a folder. "Dad needs some help with the lawn. I promised I'd give him a hand before dinner."

"You didn't mention it before."

"Guess I forgot." He flashed her his best grin. "That's not a problem, is it?"

He was looking right through her, all the way to the front door. She was invisible again. Somehow she'd managed to vanish as neatly as if a magician had murmured "Abracadabra" and made her disappear. For a couple of precious minutes upstairs in her bedroom she had been the center of his world but now he couldn't wait to get away.

"It's not a problem," she said. Sex had hurt but that was nothing compared to how much it hurt to stand next to someone who had been inside your body and now couldn't even manage to meet your eyes.

"See you at school Monday," he said, reaching for the doorknob.

"Wait a minute." She sounded too eager, too needy. "I—uh, I wanted to ask you about the prom."

"What about it?"

She supposed she should be grateful he didn't have the faintest idea what she was about to ask him but somehow it hurt. "I . . . well, I—I was wondering if maybe you'd go with me."

He started to laugh. Politely at first, then louder and louder until he was leaning against the doorjamb, his muscular shoulders rocking with the effort.

"You scared the shit out of me, Corey!" His words were interspersed with howls of laughter. "For a minute I thought you were serious."

He couldn't have hurt her more deeply if he had stabbed her through the heart, but she would rather die than let him know it. "Serious?" Her voice was high and brittle with pain. "You've got to be kidding."

His big wide smile flickered for a moment. "You *were* kidding, weren't you?"

She pictured him dead, his body crumpled beneath the weight of her hatred. "I'm not into proms." She fixed him with a steady look. "You know that, don't you, Peter?"

"Yeah, well, I thought I did but—" He stopped, his handsome face flushing bright red. "Like I said, you scared the shit out of me."

He means it, she thought. Screwing her was okay. The prom was another story. "Who are you taking?" she asked, forcing herself to stay cool and calm.

"I figure there's a chance Viv Conway might break up with Trace Wendell. If she does I'll move in for the kill."

Corey nodded, as if it all made terrific sense. "What if they don't break up?"

"Then I'll probably stay home." He was his old relaxed self now that he knew he wasn't in any real danger. "Hey, if you don't go either, why don't we find some place . . ." His words trailed off, heavy with meaning.

She knew exactly what he meant. They could find someplace where it was dark and deserted and he could screw her brains out without anyone knowing the great Peter Macmillan was scraping rock bottom.

* * *

Corey got home a little after midnight. She let herself in the front door quietly, praying her parents wouldn't hear her. It was getting harder and harder to explain away her late nights. On tiptoe she started for the stairs.

"How was work, honey?" The familiar voice floated toward her through the darkness.

"Mom?" She peered into the living room, heart thumping in surprise. "You're still up?"

Her mother switched on the table lamp next to the sofa and Corey grimaced at the assault of light. "Where have you been?"

"I—" She hesitated, suddenly aware of her wrinkled clothing, the smells on her skin. "There was a problem with a shipment at the store. I had to stay and help."

"Sit with me," her mother said, patting the cushion next to her.

Corey shook her head. "I'm bushed," she said, feigning a yawn. "I'm going to take a shower and go to bed."

"This won't take long, honey. I just want to talk to you."

Corey perched on the arm of the sofa. Her mother couldn't possibly know what she'd been doing. She'd been careful to cover her tracks. "Is everything okay?"

"I just don't know, honey. I was hoping you'd tell me."

"You're talking about school, aren't you?" she said quickly. "I know my grades are down but I'm working on them. I guess I let up once we got word about the scholarship. I'll still graduate near the top of the class, if that's what you're worried about."

"You know better than that," Millicent said, her expression serious. "I'm worried about you, honey, not your grades."

"Me?" Corey laughed out loud. "You don't have to worry about me. I'm fine."

"I don't think you are."

"I haven't had a cold or a cavity in years." She rapped the top of her head with the knuckle of her right hand. "See? I'm solid as a rock."

"I haven't mentioned any of this to your father," Millicent said slowly. "I wanted to talk to you first."

"And now you've talked to me," she said brightly. "It's late, Mom. You should get some sleep."

"You don't have to do it, honey."

A dull pain grabbed Corey by the chest. "I don't know what you're talking about."

"Those boys aren't good enough to shine your shoes," Millicent said. "When are you going to realize it?"

"You're imagining things, Mom. You know there aren't any boys. Who'd want to date someone like me?"

"People are talking, honey. They're saying things, terrible things, about you."

"I don't believe you."

"Francine told me she saw you down near the river with Joe Boyle."

Oh God, no. The last thing she'd wanted to do was to hurt her parents. "Mrs. Glass must have me confused with someone else."

Millicent raised her hand. "Don't do that, honey. Not now."

"But, Mom, I—"

Her mother's eyes flooded with tears. "Those boys don't love you. They're using you, honey, using you to get what they want."

"I don't care."

"Of course you care. You're worth more than all of them put together and it's high time you realized it."

Millicent watched as her beautiful girl turned and ran up the stairs. She slammed her bedroom door behind her and the pitiful sound of her sobs tore at Millicent's heart. Thank the good Lord Jack had taken one of those pills the doctor had prescribed to help him sleep. She didn't want him to know about any of this, not while there was breath left in her body.

Jack had enough to worry about, what with losing his job and all. His blood pressure was up and those chest pains scared the daylights out of her. No, it was best if Jack knew nothing about the fact that his daughter was sleeping with any boy who asked her and a few who didn't.

It was a different world out there, one that Millicent couldn't understand. Young people did things that she and Jack still hadn't gotten around to doing. Dating and sex seemed to go hand in hand. Maybe that she could understand if she set her mind to it but her girl wasn't dating anybody. There was nobody to take her to a double feature at the Trylon Theater in town, nobody to take her for a hamburger or invite her to the senior prom. Corey didn't even have herself some nice girl-friends to talk to on the phone or go shopping with on a Saturday afternoon.

She was always on the outside looking in, just like when she was a little girl moving from foster home to foster home looking for someone to love her. The thought hit Millicent like a runaway truck. That was the trouble with growing older, the years tended to dull the pain of adolescence, until you could no longer remember the way it really was.

Last week Millicent had watched Dr. Joyce Brothers on the "Mike Douglas Show." Dr. Brothers had said that low self-esteem was the cause of most teenage problems and her words had touched a nerve in Millicent. Corey loved herself so little that she made it impossible for anyone to realize how worthy of love she truly was.

Of course her mother knew the truth but what seventeen-year-old girl believed a single word her mother said? Millicent knew in her heart of hearts that there could be no happiness for Corey until she was able to love herself and that wouldn't happen until she learned to love the face in the mirror.

People said money wasn't everything but it sure seemed like it was when you didn't have enough to help someone you loved.

She'd filched grocery money and pawned her dead mama's charm bracelet to hire a private detective to snoop around Lili Spaulding's past, trying to find some link between the former Lilly Ann Barnett and Corey. Most of the people who'd known Lilly Ann were dead or had moved, but the few that remembered all were of the same mind when it came to one fact: Lilly Ann was pregnant when she left Euless, Florida at the end of 1962.

Millicent's heart went out to the dirt-poor teenage girl who was pregnant by her dead boyfriend and shunned by his family. She could only imagine how alone Lilly Ann must have felt up there in Atlanta while she waited for her baby to be born. She had no schooling, nobody to turn to—was it any wonder she'd given up her baby so the child could find a better life?

But Millicent knew, deep in her heart, that no woman would ever forget her own child. Late at night in her fancy house, Lili

Spaulding would remember that little girl and wonder what happened to her. And she would want to help.

Millicent sat for a long time. Her cup of tea grew cold but she didn't notice. A plan began to form, a crazy plan but she knew it was their only hope. She made another cup of tea, added milk and sugar, then gulped it down. She fetched her writing paper and pen from the desk in the hall then hurried to the kitchen table.

The words poured from her even faster than she could write. Her pen scratched across her good stationery as she filled page after page. She didn't even bother to reread the letter. She didn't dare. If she reread it she'd see it for what it was, a mother's last-ditch effort to save her daughter from herself.

15

Corey left for college near the end of August. Millicent and Jack wanted to drive her to the campus but that was the last thing she needed. She was terrified at the thought of leaving home but knew that she no longer had any other options. If her parents delivered her to the dorm she was afraid she would throw herself into her mother's arms and cry like the forgotten six-year-old she'd been when they first took her into their hearts.

"Greyhound runs right past the school," she said, praying they'd see the wisdom of her words. "Why should you go to the trouble?"

"Trouble?" Her father sounded as if he couldn't believe his ears. "You're our girl. How could you be any trouble?"

Oh, Pop, she thought a week later as the old car rumbled toward Columbus, *let me count the ways.*

She'd made so many mistakes these past few months, mistakes that made her want to die every time she thought about them. She had to get as far away from home as possible, someplace where she could forget the foolish, dangerous things she'd done.

Don't play hard to get, Corey…it's not like this is your first time….

It would be different at school, she told herself. It had to be. She'd discovered it was better to be lonely than to let yourself be used.

C'mon, baby, what's the matter? They told me you were a good lay….

A reputation was a funny thing. She'd never thought too much about her own until it was gone. Corey had spent most of her life on the outside looking in so it was only natural she hadn't heard the whispers when they first started. Millicent had tried to tell her but Corey had convinced herself that her over-protective, doting mother was imagining things.

You put out for the other guys. Don't start saying no now….

To Corey's horror, Millicent had been right. Suddenly she became aware of the looks aimed her way in the grocery store, the snickers in the halls at school. Everything she'd done, every boy she'd been with, every embarrassing detail was common knowledge. She might as well have taken out an ad in the local paper.

In the front seat Millicent and Jack bickered companionably about which radio station to switch on. Corey closed her eyes and rested her forehead against the window. She'd told herself she wasn't going to be one of those weak-willed girls who got homesick the second the car backed down the driveway but they'd barely cleared the city limits before hot tears burned her lids.

Her parents loved each other so much that there were times Corey forgot they were two separate people with separate identities. Even as an angry little girl she'd recognized that there was something special between her parents and that realization had made her even lonelier than before.

She wasn't good for Millicent and Jack. She'd already caused them untold embarrassment. God only knew what other misfortunes she could bring down on them before she was on her own.

Still a part of her wanted to stay with them, to burrow beneath her familiar blankets in the safety of her room and never leave.

Although Millicent wouldn't admit it to another living soul, this was the happiest day of her life. They'd packed Corey's duds into the trunk that morning and Millicent felt as if they'd packed away all of Corey's problems along with them. The girl needed a fresh start. She needed to go far away from home, someplace where she could leave the past behind and begin all over again. College was a special place, a place where smart and funny girls like Corey could make their mark.

They stopped for lunch at a little roadside hot-dog stand south of Columbus and while Jack went to fetch them all some rootbeers, Millicent searched for a way to tell Corey everything that was in her heart.

"You're the first one in our family to go to college, honey," she said. "You've really made us proud."

Corey said nothing, just ducked her head and let her mane of dark hair swing out over her face. Millicent reached forward to push the glossy strands away but Corey jumped back as if burned. *Have I lost you already?* she wondered. Was the connection between them so fragile that leaving for school was all it took to break it forever?

The thought made her heart ache but she knew that was something she would have to risk if Corey was to have a chance to live up to her potential.

The campus looked exactly the way Millicent had always imagined a campus should look, lots of big old trees and grassy fields and scores of happy, laughing students racing about. Impulsively she squeezed Corey's hand. "You're going to be so happy here," she said, her eyes filling with tears. "I just know it!" Millicent grabbed herself a pair of suitcases while Corey lugged a box of books upstairs to her third-floor room. Jack, muttering something about feeling like a pack mule, tried to corral a red-haired young man into helping him carry the rest.

The door to room 312 was open. Millicent poked her head inside. "Hello?" she called out as Corey caught up with her. "Don't mean to intrude but—"

"Well, hi there!" A pretty little gal with long blond hair leaped from the bed by the window and hurried toward them. "I'm Sarah Bennett. Real pleased to meet y'all."

"I'm Millicent Banning and—" she pushed Corey forward "—this is my daughter Catherine, but we all call her Corey."

Sarah's eyes widened slightly as she noticed the scars on Corey's face but her mama would be real proud of the way the girl didn't let her gaze linger there.

"I'm just plain Sarah," she said directly to Corey. "I have three sisters so I'm used to sharin' a room. I know we'll be good friends."

Sarah hailed from Charleston. She had a friendly, easygoing personality and she tried her best to draw Corey into conversation but to Millicent's embarrassment, her girl refused to cooperate.

"Now I know not everybody is partial to country, so I promise not to wake you up each mornin' with Tammy Wynette!" Sarah gestured toward a stereo set up under the bookshelves. "You're welcome to play anything you want, Corey, just so long as it isn't opera."

"Don't worry. I don't like opera," Corey said in a real snippy tone of voice then turned toward the suitcase that lay open on her bed.

Don't do this to yourself, Millicent pleaded silently. *First impressions are everything.* She could see Sarah's smile settle into the strained lines of disappointment and she knew Corey had an uphill battle ahead of her.

"We're going out for pizza," Millicent said after they had Corey settled in. "Why don't you join us, Sarah?"

"No!" They both turned toward Corey whose cheeks flushed bright red as she looked away. "I mean, Sarah probably has something better to do."

Sarah, who had been arranging her own belongings in her bureau, looked from Millicent to Jack to Corey then shook her head. "I appreciate the offer, Mrs. Banning, but Corey's right. I do have something else to do." Murmuring her goodbyes, the girl from Charleston excused herself and left the dorm room.

"Why did you do that, honey?" Millicent asked her daughter. "You're going to be living with that gal. The least you could do is make friends with her."

"I'm not here to make friends," Corey said. "I'm here to go to school."

Jack had said it was time for Corey to spread her wings but suddenly Millicent was afraid those wings were too damaged for her girl to fly.

"Your parents are nice," Sarah said after Millicent and Jack left for home. "They really love you a lot."

Corey looked up from the stack of books she was lining up on the shelves near her bed. The girl's expression was perfectly pleasant but Corey was sure she wasn't imagining the note of surprise in her lilting voice.

"No accounting for taste," she said lightly, shoving *Catcher in the Rye* between *A Moveable Feast* and *Atlas Shrugged*.

"You don't like me very much, do you?" Sarah was sitting on the window seat, her slender legs curled up beneath her. A can of soda rested on the sill, next to a half-empty bag of barbecue potato chips. She looked like a magazine ad promoting college life in America. Corey envied her so much it felt as if someone was pouring hot lead into her chest.

"I don't know you," Corey said, reaching for *Gone With the Wind*.

"You don't like what you know."

"So what?" Corey retorted. "I doubt if you'll lose any sleep over it."

Sarah's brows knit together in a scowl and she turned away. Corey wanted to tell the girl she was sorry, that it was only her own nervousness and fear talking but the words wouldn't come. She'd never lived with another girl her own age before. It was like being trapped on the other side of the looking glass.

Sarah was everything Corey wasn't, everything Corey had always dreamed of being. Her corn silk hair fell to her shoulders like satiny ribbons. Her skin was porcelain smooth, a faint peachy color that made her clear blue eyes seem even larger and more luminous than they were. Tiny diamond studs dotted each ear lobe, drawing the eye to the perfection of her face. She was small-boned but curvy and she wore the simple college uniform of cutoffs and T-shirt with the self-confidence of a woman wearing a designer gown. In her presence Corey felt like Frankenstein's monster, too big and ugly to mingle with the rest of humankind.

Besides, what difference did it make if Corey Banning liked Sarah Bennett or not? As the weeks passed, it became clear that everyone else in the dorm knew and loved little Sarah from Charleston. Corey was constantly fielding messages for the girl. *Tell her we're going to grab some pizza at Kong's then take in*

*a movie. Tell her we're going dancing at Stanton's near town.
Tell her—*

They pretended it was nice to meet Corey and said they were
sure they were going to be just supergreat friends but she knew
it was a crock. They never asked her to join them for pizza and
a movie. They never asked her anything at all. Their perfectly
made-up eyes zeroed right in on Corey's face, taking in the
railroad track scars, measuring her imperfections. She'd watch
as their smiles faltered then shifted into something jittery and
insincere and she knew they couldn't wait to get back to their
rooms so they could talk about poor Sarah who was stuck
rooming with a freak.

November was there before Millicent knew it. She missed her
girl with all of her heart but it helped to know that Corey was
no longer the center of gossip and speculation in town. Even the
worst of the busybodies had moved onto greener pastures and
were eagerly whispering about some other poor soul's misfor-
tune.

She wrote to Corey twice a week, long chatty letters about her
garden and Jack's latest attempt to build a toolshed in the
backyard. Corey didn't write back very often and when she did
her letters were quick, distracted affairs that were more like
notes you'd send to a total stranger. Millicent told herself there
was nothing to worry about, that it was normal for a college girl
to be so busy she didn't have time to keep in touch with the
folks back home, but that didn't make her miss her daughter
any the less.

Every time she sat down at the kitchen table with her pen and
stationery, she remembered the night she'd poured out her heart
to Lili Spaulding. Three months had passed since she mailed
that letter and still there was no answer. The mail arrived each
morning 9:30 and she was halfway down the driveway before
the truck made it to the Macmillan house next door.

"What gives, Millie?" Jack asked over breakfast a few days
before Thanksgiving. "The way you've been haunting the
mailbox makes me think you're expectin' a love letter or
something."

Millicent poured him some more decaf then helped herself to another slice of toast. "Wouldn't you like to know," she said, trying to sound lighthearted and flirtatious.

"Seriously," Jack persisted, adding two sugars to his cup. "You don't have to hide the bills from me, Millie. This old heart of mine can take the truth."

"I'm not hiding the bills from you, honey." She made a production of slathering butter on her toast. "I just ordered something special from a catalog for Christmas and I guess I'm just worse than a kid when it comes to waiting."

"Don't you go ordering anything expensive for me," he warned, a frown darkening his beloved face. "We have to tighten our belts this year."

"Don't worry," she said, feeling more guilty by the second. "I won't do anything foolish."

She almost choked on that lie. She'd already done something so foolish even she couldn't believe it. Writing that letter to Lili Spaulding had been a ridiculous, crazy thing to do. Whatever had possessed her? Why, she hadn't even known where to send the letter. Mayfair had offices all over the place, in New York City and London, in Paris and Milan and who knew where else. And it seemed that the Spauldings had houses and fancy apartments in just as many different cities, if not more. Finally she'd just crossed her fingers and picked the New York City office.

She could just imagine how some mailroom clerk must have laughed over her cheap stationery and awkward handwriting. She'd written Personal on the envelope but not much was personal these days. The letter had probably been read by a score of people already, not one of them Lili Spaulding.

I had to do it, she thought, sipping her coffee while Jack read his sports section. She knew the odds were a million-to-one that Lili was Corey's birth mother but she had had to take the chance.

"They're playin' your song," Jack said as the familiar whine of the mail truck sounded outside.

Millicent leaped to her feet. "You stay right here," she said, her heart pounding in anticipation. "I'll be right back."

If Jack knew what she'd done, he'd up and leave her. The thought that his wife had gone begging to a stranger would break his spirit. She might as well have taken out an ad in the Sunday paper that Jack Banning couldn't take care of his own.

"Not much today, Mrs. B.," Billy the mail carrier said as he handed her the water bill and the new *Good Housekeeping*.

She smiled as her disappointment faded. "You make sure you give that new baby of yours a kiss from me, you hear?"

She watched from the foot of the driveway as the little mail truck disappeared around the curve.

This has to stop, Millicent. You can't keep on this way.

She was never going to hear from Lili Spaulding, not in this or any other lifetime. The Bannings of the world were invisible to rich people. Their problems were as insignificant as choosing what dessert to serve with supper.

In every fiber of her being, Millicent believed that if there was even the slightest chance that Corey was Lili's natural daughter, the other woman would have risked heaven and hell to help her own flesh and blood.

Millicent would have and there was no reason to expect any less from Lili.

So that was that. All of her carefully figured out clues were nothing more than a string of coincidences that brought her right back where she'd started from. There would be no help from Lili Spaulding. Publishers Clearing House wasn't going to show up on her doorstep and give her a big, fat check. And that pot of gold at the end of the rainbow remained as far away as ever.

"I'll find another way," she whispered as she tucked the mail under her arm and started back up the driveway to the house. If it took her until her dying day, she would see to it that her girl got everything she deserved and more.

BOOK FIVE

The Woman

16

New York City

Some people said the Russian Tea Room had become a cliché, but Whit Paley wasn't among them. He loved everything about the elegant old restaurant: the shining samovars on the side tables, the waiters in their bright red cossack uniforms, and the fact that if you sat there long enough you'd see everyone in New York pass through its portals.

He'd already counted two senators, Mayor Koch, Mike Nichols, and Ronald Reagan's painfully slim wife, Nancy. Nancy had swept in with Betsy Bloomingdale and Babe Paley, looking for all the world like a First Lady in waiting. The election was over and he found himself experiencing an odd sense of relief that Jimmy Carter would be saying goodbye to the Oval Office and hello again to Plains.

Not long ago that thought would have sent him into a loud and angry tailspin but his growing sense that America had lost its will to survive had begun to erode his liberal sensibilities. Besides, conventional wisdom said Republican administrations were good for business and God knew something sure as hell had better be good for business and soon if Mayfair was going to make it through the eighties. Right now he would say there was only a fifty-fifty chance.

"Your drink, Mr. Paley." His favorite waiter appeared at his side.

"Thank you, Albert."

"Would you care to order now?"

Whit glanced at his watch. "No," he said, "I'll wait awhile longer."

"As you wish, sir." Albert left him alone with his martini.

It wasn't like Lili to be late. He'd give her another ten minutes then he would start phoning around town. She treated Manhattan as if it were her own personal garden party, a place where nothing bad could possibly happen. He'd tried to tell her to be more cautious, to consider hiring a bodyguard to accompany her on her rounds, but she always laughed and told him he was being an old fool. The woman was fearless. He supposed she would have to be, being married to Carter.

The martini was dry, with just the right blend of bitters and vermouth. A good martini was a rare thing these days. Oenophiles were putting mixologists out of business. Whit appreciated a good martini, a fine cigar . . . a good woman.

He chuckled hollowly. There hadn't been many women, either good or bad. He supposed he could blame it on age but that would be a cop-out as the kids liked to say. Fifty wasn't old these days. He liked to tell himself that it was barely middleaged. He kept himself in shape with regular squash games and putting in time on his treadmill when he was in town.

He motioned for Albert to bring him another drink. It wasn't as if he didn't occasionally indulge in the old pas de deux. On rare occasions, when the mood was right and the moment, he would take a lady to bed but the exercise, while enjoyable, was always less than memorable. He'd even married one of those women, a comely socialite from Boston who was not unlike his first wife Emmaline, only to find himself divorced six months later. "You're a nice man, Whit," wife number two had said as they signed the papers. "Too nice to go around marrying women you don't love."

Truth was, he had been dealt a blow almost five years ago, one from which he most likely would never recover. Nobody came close to touching his heart the way one very special woman did.

"Have I kept you waiting long?" That familiar voice, soft and quick and endlessly enticing.

He rose to kiss Lili Spaulding on the cheek. Her familiar scent enveloped him. "Another ten minutes and I would have called out the dogs."

"You worry too much, Whitman Paley." She took her seat in a fragrant cloud of perfume. "You need a hobby, my friend. Maybe then you wouldn't worry so much."

I need you, Lili. But, of course, he couldn't say those words. She was, after all, his best friend's wife.

Whit seemed a tad distant to Lili. She tried to make him laugh with a story about her morning meeting with a women's group from Paramus but he didn't so much as crack a smile.

Finally she lit a cigarette, leaned against the plush seat back, and waited for him to realize she'd stopped talking.

"Lil?"

"Ah," she said, drawing out the sound. "At last I have your attention."

He had the good grace to look embarrassed, but that didn't surprise her. Whit Paley rarely put a foot wrong. When he did, it was worth noting.

"My apologies," he said, inclining his head. "My mind wandered."

She brought the cigarette to her lips and inhaled. "Wonderful," she said, resting the cigarette on the lip of the ashtray. "Americans haven't the faintest idea how to produce a decent cigarette."

Whit scowled at the plume of smoke wreathing her head. "You should quit."

She gestured toward his empty martini glass. "So should you."

"Martinis don't come with a warning from the Surgeon General."

"Perhaps they should," she said pointedly. "You've been drinking a great deal lately, Whit. I'm concerned."

"Emmaline and I divorced over remarks like that."

"You and Emmaline divorced because she finally decided to marry Sid Zuckerman."

"Many thanks for the reminder."

"I'm not trying to be difficult. I'm your friend. I'm worried about you."

"You shouldn't be. I'm strictly a social drinker."

"I hope so."

He met her gaze across the table. Dark circles ringed his eyes
and her heart ached. *You're getting older, Whit,* she realized.
So was Carter...so was she. *Why didn't anyone warn you about
how quickly it happened?*

The last four years had vanished in the blink of an eye. There
were times when she was hard-pressed to remember that she'd
had a life before Carter Spaulding. She could never repay Whit
for all he had done to make her transition from Las Vegas
showgirl to pillar of New York society possible. It was Whit
who had taught her the difference between a salad fork and a
shrimp fork; Whit who had taken her under his wing and protected her from the sly whispers and cruel laughter that had almost sent her running back to her old life.

He took her to the Plaza for tea where, instead of talking, she
would sit there and listen to the high-toned accents of the other
women as they chatted about people and places she knew
nothing about. He took her to the New York Public Library,
past the two stone lions who guarded the entrance, and showed
her the world.

Every morning she would breakfast with Carter, then dress
carefully in one of her perfect Chanel suits and head down to
the library where she would surround herself with books and
papers and magazines, wishing she could absorb the precious
information through her fingertips. That led her to NYU, where
she quietly audited classes in sociology and business. With
knowledge came confidence and by the end of her third year as
Carter's wife, she felt she'd finally come home at last.

Whit was her closest friend. He had made her happiness with
Carter and Grant possible and she owed him a debt of gratitude she knew she could never repay.

Whit's dear, familiar voice broke into her thoughts. "We
have to talk, Lil."

"We are talking," she said, trying to lighten his suddenly
somber mood. "I've been talking nonstop since I arrived."

He refused to smile back at her. "You know what I mean."

"Yes," she said, stubbing out her cigarette. "As a matter of
fact I do."

"Carter is being a horse's ass," Whit said. "Mayfair is in serious trouble and he refuses to address the issues that can turn things around."

"Like the issue of women in the workforce."

She saw the light of approval in his eyes. "You're on the advisory board, Lil. Talk to him. Tell him about what needs to be done."

"He's heard the arguments, Whit. He simply doesn't see it that way."

"He damn well better see it that way and soon or our competition will eat us for lunch."

Lili listened as he spun one terrifying scenario after another, all of which ended up with the demise of Mayfair. "This isn't World War II with the boys coming home, looking to take their jobs back," she said slowly, as an idea began to take shape. "Women are in the workplace to stay. We seem to be the last company to acknowledge that fact." Elaborate makeup rituals were fine for nights on the town but the modern working woman needed to get out the door in record time each morning, looking polished, professional . . . and beautiful.

Whit leaned across the table. She could sense his excitement. "Can you write that up for me?"

She frowned. "I can't even write a decent letter, Whit. You know that."

"Then how about you present that idea to R and D this afternoon?"

"You really think I'm on to something?"

"I *know* you're on to something, Lil." His enthusiasm was catching. Lili's pulse beat accelerated. "Remember the time you pinpointed what was wrong with the Island Dreams promotion?"

Lili nodded. "I don't know how they missed that problem with the hinge on the blusher compact. Women don't want to break their nails while doing their makeup." A mistake so basic that it sailed right past the noses of top-level designers.

"Let's face it, Lil. Somehow you're plugged into what makes this business work. You're a natural resource. Why don't we use you?"

The idea excited her but she had to consider all the angles. "I'm not certain Carter would approve."

"Speaking for Mayfair, I don't much give a damn."

Whit went off to make a telephone call to Lew Paxton in R and D. If he had his way, Lili would be pitching her ideas about working women to the entire staff that very afternoon. She felt like letting out a whoop of excitement but Mrs. Carter Spaulding would never allow herself such a vulgar display of enthusiasm. But deep inside, Lilly Ann Barnett was jumping up and down.

Although she couldn't admit it to anyone, Lili was sick to death of the social circuit, bored beyond reason with the endless round of charity lunches, political dinners, balls and parties and country weekends. At first it had been heady stuff. Little Lilly Ann Barnett from Euless, Florida hobnobbing with Rockefellers and Kennedys and Forbeses.

Funny thing though, it had taken surprisingly little time for that whole mad whirl to become routine. There had never been any question that certain people supported certain charities and social causes with huge sums of money. The parties and lunches only existed to give rich men's wives something to do with their time.

Once Lili caught on to that fact, a great deal of the glamour lost its lustre.

To her surprise, she discovered she needed a reason to get up in the morning. For the first few years, Carter had supplied that for her. Their sex life had been the stuff of dreams. Urgent. Frequent. Downright wild. With him she discovered a part of herself she'd never known existed, a sensual side with appetites that would not be denied. Sometimes she felt like Dorothy in the *Wizard of Oz,* leaving black-and-white Kansas for the technicolor world of the Emerald City.

But even the sex, incredible as it was, had cooled. Carter worked around the clock, getting home late at night and leaving early the next morning. She understood hard work and admired his dedication to the company his father had built, but more and more she had the awful feeling that he'd lost the ability to lead.

At first she'd blamed it on some midlife crisis, the kind pop psychologists made their bread and butter talking about on television, but she had the feeling there was more to it. It wasn't anything she could put her finger on, more a vague sense of unease, as if things were changing just beneath the surface and before too long those changes would be impossible to ignore.

She sighed softly and toyed with her glass. A baby would have made everything different. Whenever she broached the subject of adoption with Carter, he told her that he wanted nothing to come between them. But that argument no longer rang true. Many things had come between them, from his work to her own charitable obligations. A baby would only bond them together.

Carter pointed to his son Grant as a perfect example of the kind of trouble a child could bring to a marriage but that argument didn't hold water with Lili. A child could never harm you. Only the loss of that child had the power to break your heart. The truth was, she'd fallen in love with the boy the day she met him and nothing that had happened since had changed her mind. Grant was starved for attention and Lili was more than happy to provide it. Especially since Carter acted as if the boy didn't exist.

She told herself that Carter had lost Grant's mother to death; maybe the boy reminded him of the woman he'd once loved and lost. Or maybe Grant reminded Carter of himself although Lili wasn't entirely sure the answer was that simple. All she knew was that the boy needed a champion, someone who would love him the way a son deserved to be loved, and it fell to Lili to be the one to provide that love and support.

Grant was the absolute joy of her life. If he wanted tickets to see the Giants play, she found him a pair on the fifty-yard line. If he and his pals needed reservations at Le Cirque, she knew what strings to pull. Party invitations, speeding tickets fixed, whatever the boy needed Lili was happy to provide.

Grant was eighteen years old now. Carter had warned his son that much was expected from him. "Keep your nose clean," he'd warned Grant, "or you'll be looking for work with Estée after you graduate." There had been a few nasty bits of business along the way, none of which were Grant's fault. Grant couldn't be blamed for the fact that he had matured into a stunningly handsome young man and, as such, had garnered more than his share of female attention. When you added the Spaulding name to the mix—well, you had a dangerous combination.

One enterprising young woman had had the gall to file an attempted rape suit against Grant. The suit was settled out of court, much to Lili's relief. She had wanted to file a counter-suit against the woman, claiming defamation of character, but Lili's personal attorney, Patrick deRossier, convinced her that would only exacerbate matters. Still, she hated injustice and it struck her that no one should play God with another person's life, not unless they had the proof to back up their claims. Her blood ran cold at the thought of how close they'd come to see-ing Grant's brilliant future derailed by a baseless, groundless complaint.

"Should I be jealous?" Carter had asked once, his light tone at odds with the dark look in his eyes. "I'm beginning to think you married me for my son."

Lili had laughed and pointed out the fact that she hadn't known about Grant's existence when she became Carter's wife, but they both knew that the bond between stepmother and son was deep and strong. When it came to Grant, Lili was a mother lioness defending her young. All of the love and caring and fierce protectiveness she would have showered on her own child belonged to him and there wasn't anything on earth she wouldn't do to make sure he got what he deserved in life and more.

Which made the issue of Mayfair's financial future all the more disturbing. Carter's control seemed less masterful than it once had. She'd heard the whispers about some of his more unpopular decisions. Some people hinted about drugs. Once Whit had even asked her if there were problems within the marriage that might be having an impact on the company. She would have slapped anyone else who'd dared to suggest such a thing but she knew Whit had spoken only out of a real con-cern for his friend and for his own future at Mayfair.

She adored Whit but he wasn't family. There were some things you just didn't talk about with strangers, no matter how dear they were to you. Maybe it was the shadow of Euless rearing its ugly head, but everyone knew that family secrets were meant to stay exactly that—secrets. Come hell or high water, you protected your own. Sooner or later Carter's zest for business would return and there'd be no need for all the whis-pers and conjecture. Until then, she would do whatever was

necessary to keep Mayfair on solid ground. The company was
Grant's birthright and nothing would take that away from him,
not while there was breath in her body.

She was magnificent, as Whit had known she would be. She
carried herself with style and confidence and projected the right
amount of warmth without even trying. He'd expected that.
What he hadn't expected was brilliance.

Whit watched as Lili wrapped the R and D staff around her
beautiful little finger. For fifteen minutes she'd spoken pas-
sionately about Mayfair, about her very real devotion to Carter, about where they were going wrong—all from the
perspective of a woman whose vision hadn't been clouded by
corporate think. She was funny, a touch acerbic, and right on
the money.

"This isn't 1950," she told a group of stunned marketing
types. "Women don't stay home making brownies anymore.
It's a two-paycheck world out there and the American woman
is in the work-force to stay this time." The Mayfair campaigns
were geared toward a woman who no longer existed, a woman
who had the time and inclination to spend endless hours on
beauty rituals that had gone the way of the Edsel.

The brains from Wharton and Harvard Business tried to
dazzle her with their academic prowess but she didn't bat a
perfectly mascaraed eye. She knew what she was talking about
because she'd lived it and that gave her an edge no master's
degree could compete with.

Whit had asked his assistant Elaine to call Carter and let him
know his wife was knocking them dead in the conference room
but Carter was tied up on a transatlantic call and said he'd join
them as soon as possible.

"Wow," said Elaine. "Beauty and brains. I hate her."

He wished he could. Hating Lili would make his life a hell of
a lot easier. Maybe if he hated her he could go out and take
advantage of one of those twenty-something types who flirted
with him in hotel bars and at cocktail parties.

As it was, he could only lean against the back wall of the
conference room with his heart on his sleeve and watch as the
woman he loved took another step away from him.

17

The impromptu presentation before the R and D department led to another one for marketing and a third for advertising. When was the last time she'd heard applause meant just for her? Lili stood there, basking in the approval as if the podium were a stage and she'd just given the performance of her life. Over the years she'd grown accustomed to being moon wife to Carter's sun. It was exciting to do a little shining on her own for a change.

"Carter doesn't know what he missed," said Ron Von Heemstra, one of the VPs from the creative side.

"Damn right," said Frederick Stadtler, a board member. "The question is, why has he been letting you waste your time on charity luncheons when you could be working here? He should have been here to see what you can do."

Lili felt some of her sparkle dim but she willed herself to keep a smile on her face and a twinkle in her eye. Obviously he didn't realize that Carter had made a brief appearance near the end of her second presentation. Her back had been to the door but she'd known the minute he walked into the room. Her husband came with his own magnetic field and her entire body registered his presence.

She'd spun around, expecting to see a man beaming with pride, but had been brought up short by the look of utter indifference on his face. His eyes roamed the crowd restlessly, as if he were looking for something he couldn't find, then he turned and left the room as quickly as he'd come into it. Lili recovered her poise and continued speaking to her audience as if she'd been doing so every day of her life but she sensed that a tiny part of her heart had died.

She fielded compliments for at least an hour then the last of the astonished executives went off to do whatever it was they did behind the closed doors of their high-priced corner offices.

It was nearly half past six when Whit said, "The limo's downstairs waiting for you, Lil."

"Thanks," she said. "Tell Fleming I won't be a minute."

"Will do."

There was something about the look in his eyes that brought her up short. She touched his forearm. "Whit, is something wrong?"

"Wrong?" His dear familiar chuckle warmed her heart. "I just watched you perform a miracle, Lil. What could be wrong?"

She squeezed his arm affectionately. "I don't really know," she admitted, "but for a second you looked terribly sad."

"Tired," he corrected her. "I'm getting old."

"Old? Not you, darling. Maybe it's all your late nights."

"My late nights are highly exaggerated."

She clapped her hands over her ears. "Please! Leave me my illusions. I'd like to think there's one real man-about-town left in this city."

"Far be it from me to shatter your illusions, Lil." He executed a courtly, slightly mocking bow. "Go find your husband. I'll tell Fleming you're delayed."

She watched as he strode away from her. In many ways he and Carter were cut from the same pricey bolt of cloth. Self-confident, wealthy, accustomed to a certain deference from mere mortals. But where Carter approached life as a battle to be won, Whit saw it as an endless cocktail party meant to be enjoyed.

She pressed the button for the private elevator that would take her to Carter's suite on the forty-fifth floor. She'd met Whit's first wife Emmaline once at a charity luncheon and had found her pleasant and easy to talk to. She seemed exactly the sort of woman Lili could imagine as her good friend's wife but, according to Carter, the marriage had been doomed from the moment Whit and Emmaline said I do.

Who knew what made any marriage tick—or stop ticking entirely. Marriage was like an enormous Chinese puzzle. As soon as you were about to fit the last part of the picture into the whole, some joker would come along and turn the table up-side down and you were back where you started from, scrambling for the pieces and praying you remembered how to put them together.

This afternoon was a perfect example. Things had gone so well for her. Carter couldn't possibly be displeased in any way. She'd been a bona fide smash with the other executives. There'd been no mistaking their very genuine enthusiasm for both her and her ideas. Who could have imagined some plain old horse sense, as Grandma Hattie used to call it, would be greeted with cheers of approval? It wasn't as if she were trying to be something she wasn't. She enjoyed being Mrs. Carter Spaulding just fine. Wives were supposed to help their husbands, weren't they? This was no different than being a shopkeeper's wife who pitched in behind the counter.

The elevator doors slid open and she stepped out into the foyer. A stunning Persian carpet in muted shades of rose, ivory and blue, served as a pricey counterpoint to the thick midnight blue carpeting that stretched from wall to wall. The walls were papered with heavy cream-colored silk that was blind-embossed in the fleur-de-lis pattern Carter's great-grandfather had adopted as the family's crest shortly after the turn of the century. The rococo mirror that hung above a mahogany side table had belonged to his grandmother Claire who had brought it with her from England when she married into the Spaulding family.

Everywhere she looked she saw evidence of her husband's privileged upbringing. Sometimes she wondered if rich people ever went out and just bought furniture or knickknacks. Everything seemed to have come from somewhere else, from some*one* else, woven tightly into the family chain by history and privilege.

It was the same way at home. Table linens, duvets, drinking glasses, even the ashtrays in the library—every single item had a longer pedigree than she had. She tried to imagine one of Carter's illustrious forebears hopping off to the January white sale at Bloomie's but they wouldn't cooperate, not even in her fantasies.

Once, early in their marriage, Carter had asked her about Euless, about Grandma Hattie and the mother who had run off when Lilly Ann was a little girl. She'd tried to tell him about the swampy, primitive smell of the Everglades, about not wearing shoes from May to September, about feeling trapped in a place that had nothing to do with who she really was inside or who she wanted to be. She'd told him about cents-off coupons and retrieving pop bottles from the side of the road for deposit money and dresses made from used tablecloths Grandma got at the church jumble sale.

He listened to her but she knew he didn't hear her. She could see his mind skittering off in more comfortable, familiar directions and she didn't blame him. It wasn't as if she spent much time reminiscing about the old days but still it bothered her that the events that had formed her character were so far beyond his comprehension.

The outer offices were as quiet as a chapel. Both Carter's receptionist and his secretary had left for the night. She noticed that the door to his sanctum sanctorum was slightly ajar. The pale yellow glow of lamplight spilled out onto the dark carpet.

"Darling?" She modulated her voice to the low pitch he admired. "The car is waiting. I thought perhaps we could—" She pushed open the door and stepped inside. "Carter?" The lamp on his antique cherrywood credenza was on. Music played softly from the sound system she'd surprised him with on their fourth anniversary. His chair was pushed back from his desk as if he'd gone off to do something but would return any moment. His Mont Blanc fountain pen, cap partly off, was angled near the edge of his desk blotter.

Carter was meticulous about details. When he left his office for the night, his desk was clean, his chair in the proper position, his beloved pen tucked into his attaché case. She had long ago learned that he expected his home to be run the same way. It had taken her awhile to get used to maintaining the degree of perfection he required, but it was a small price to pay for the miracle of being his wife.

She'd discovered that she was stronger, smarter, more adaptable than she would have believed possible. How else could you explain the fact that Lilly Ann Barnett had just spent the afternoon telling millionaire businessmen how to do their jobs?

You're gettin' above yourself, girl. It ain't gonna last.

Wouldn't you know it? Grandma Hattie's voice, plain as day, doing her level best to rain on Lilly Ann's parade.

"Go away," Lili murmured, glancing over her shoulder as if she expected to see the mean-tempered old woman glaring at her from across the room. "You don't know anything about my life."

She paced the office restlessly. Where had Carter disappeared to? She'd entertained visions of a cozy ride in the limo, maybe across the river to one of those New Jersey restaurants whose main claim to fame was a heart-stopping view of the Manhattan skyline, glittering against the night sky. It had been ages since they'd done anything spontaneous and romantic and she found she missed those carefree days more than she cared to admit.

The telephone trilled and she leaped to answer it. Carter, she thought, lifting the receiver to her ear. Who else could it possibly be?

"You might as well call it a night, Lil," Whit said in lieu of a greeting. "There's a problem out at factory number one. Carter's going to be tied up for hours."

"He's at the factory?" she asked, surprised.

"Dominguez said he left over two hours ago with a contingent from marketing and R and D."

"Tell Fleming I'll be right down," she said then hung up the phone. *Two hours ago.* Maybe that could explain his sudden departure during her presentation. She gathered up her bag then her eye was caught by the stack of mail in his leather inbox. She wasn't a snoop—God knew she would never open his mail—but occasionally the urge to peek into the work side of his life was irresistible and how better than to take a peek at the kinds of things that passed across his desk these days. Two slick trade journals from organizations she didn't recognize. Invitations from various political types to donate money, donate time, donate the Spaulding name. Contracts to be signed...or not. Everything was neatly typed on expensive stationery with watermarks and engraved letterheads.

Everything, that was, except for the letter on the bottom of the stack. She held the thick pink envelope between her thumb and forefinger. The paper was smooth, like the cheap stock she'd used back in high school typing class. No tooth. No subtlety. She was about to dismiss it as too uninteresting to bother with when she noted that the envelope had been addressed in a looping, childish hand to Mrs. Carter Spaulding.

Startled, she looked at it more closely. No doubt about it; it was meant for her. Carter's secretary must have meant to attach a note, asking that he deliver it to her. The bright blue ballpoint ink had smudged over the *U* in Spaulding, leaving a diagonal smear across the right-hand side. She turned it over, an odd feeling of dread tapping between her shoulder blades and along her rib cage. The flap had been neatly tucked into the envelope itself and written on the upper left hand corner was the return address:

Mrs. John Banning
26 Patterson Place
Cincinnati, Ohio

Banning. She racked her brain but couldn't think of anyone they knew by that name. Certainly anyone in Carter's circle would have infinitely better taste in stationery. Was it possible one of her old friends from Euless had married and moved to Ohio and suddenly decided to drop her a line?

She slid a nail under the flap then withdrew the letter. Three pages, all written in the same earnest, round hand. What on earth was the matter with her? She was having trouble focusing on the words. She was only thirty-four. She couldn't possibly need glasses already.

She took a deep breath then tried again.

Dear Mrs. Spaulding,
*   I'm writing to you because my girl needs help and I'm hoping you can be the answer to our prayers....*

18

The driver looked at his watch for the third time. "You sure she said she was coming right down?"

Whit nodded. "That's what she said."

"It's been almost fifteen minutes."

Whit checked his own watch. Eighteen minutes was more like it. At least a half dozen explanations occurred to him, most of which included death, dismemberment or kidnapping. "You stay here," he told Fleming. "I'll go upstairs and see what's keeping her."

The building had decent security but nothing was perfect. In Whit's opinion Lili didn't pay half enough attention to her own personal safety. She seemed to think that marrying Carter had provided her with a protective bubble that would keep her from harm.

He pressed for the elevator, waited a moment, then pressed again. What in hell was taking so long? The damn building had all but emptied out over an hour ago. She could be lying dead somewhere, murdered by a crazed felon who preyed on innocent women.

Minutes later he burst into the foyer of the executive suite. He could smell the faint scent of her perfume in the air.

"Lil?" He pushed open the door to Carter's office. "Where are—"

"I'm over here, Whit." She stood in the shadows near the window.

"You had me worried, Lil."

A quick smile drifted across her lovely face then disappeared. What if she asked about Carter and his latest paramour? He'd always believed the truth was vastly overrated, as likely to destroy a marriage as save it. But this was Lili he was talking about and there were his own selfish motives to consider.

She turned toward him and he caught the shimmer of tears. *I'd never make you cry, Lil.* The thought made him deeply sad, as if he'd somehow seen into his future and found himself alone.

"Talk to me, Lil." He crossed the room to where she stood.

She shook her head and he was suddenly reminded of the young woman he'd first met, the one who'd believed in happy endings.

"Not this time." Her husky voice trembled with emotion. "Not even you can help me with this one."

"Don't underestimate the master." He fell short of the light, cynical tone he'd been aiming for. "I spent three years in the diplomatic corps."

She hesitated, her long slender fingers toying with a thick pink envelope. "This came today."

"Bad news?"

"I don't know."

"Let me see."

"It's personal, Whit."

"You have a priest you can turn to?"

She laughed, even though it was obviously the last thing she wanted to do.

"Use me, Lil," he said, sounding like a teenage boy begging the prom queen for a date. "What are friends for?"

She handed him the letter. "You may not be my friend after this."

He checked the return address. "Cincinnati? Who do you know there?"

"Just read it, Whit."

Dear Mrs. Spaulding,

I'm writing to you because my girl needs help and I'm hoping you can be the answer to our prayers. My daughter Catherine has herself a bad problem and I don't know where to turn. Now I know you don't have any idea what I'm ~~talking about~~, trying to say, at least not yet, but I read a story about you and your hubby in People Magazine *two three years ago and this real strong feel-*

*ing came to me and I haven't been able to forget it
since.*

*Now you may call me crazy, Mrs. Spaulding but
every time I look at my girl I see your face and . . .*

"A nut," he said, meeting Lili's eyes. "You've had letters
like this before. It's part of being in the public eye."

"Keep reading."

The *New York Times Book Review* would savage the prose
but Whit had to admit Mrs. Banning's words carried a violent
emotional punch. Her adopted daughter had been badly injured in an automobile accident as a baby and needed recon-
structive surgery, had needed the surgery for seventeen years.
He tried to imagine his own beautiful daughters scarred and
then tried to imagine his own anguish if he couldn't do anything to help make them whole. Lili was right: this wasn't your
normal pleading letter. This was more personal, more heartbreaking. The woman laid her heart bare for the world to see,
and it was beginning to scare the hell out of him.

"Lil, what's the point? You can't take on the problems of
every poor soul who picks up a pen. Carter gives a considerable amount to charity every year. Your conscience should be
clear." There would always be another Mrs. Banning with another terrible story to tell.

"You didn't finish reading the letter, did you?"

"No, but—"

"She thinks the girl is mine."

"Say that again."

"She believes I'm the girl's biological mother. She hired a
second-rate detective who traced me back to Florida and—"
Lili waved her hands in a gesture of helplessness.

He threw back his head and started to laugh. "That proves
she's certifiable." His sympathy vanished. Folding the letter he
stuffed it back into the envelope. "I told you there was nothing to worry about, Lil. It's public record that you grew up in
Florida as Lilly Ann Barnett. But the fact remains that you
never—" He stopped at the look of unutterable sadness on her
lovely face. "You're kidding."

She shook her head. "Seventeen years ago."

Her words hit him like a punch to the gut, swift and hard. "Does Carter know?"

"Yes." Her voice was little more than a whisper. "I told him the child was dead."

"Is she?"

The tears that had been poised on the tips of her lashes fell freely down her cheeks. She made no move to wipe them away. He'd never loved her more than he did at that moment. "I don't know."

"Could this girl be your daughter?"

"No!" The word seemed to tear from her throat like a gunshot. "My daughter was adopted by a rich family from Tennessee." Years ago she'd scraped together money to hire a private detective. She hadn't wanted to disrupt the child's life but she'd longed for some proof that the decision she'd made at seventeen had been a good one. "He couldn't find her," she said, her voice breaking on the last word. "He said that there were no birth certificates registered with my name as the mother. But she's out there, I know she is, with Blake and Candy in Tennessee."

She told him how it had happened, about Eileen Fontaine, about her own terror and confusion. She'd been little more than a child herself when she'd given birth and there had been no one for her to turn to, no place where she could go for help.

"My daughter was perfect," she said, wiping her cheek with the back of her hand. "She couldn't possibly need the help that Banning woman described." A beautiful, blue-eyed baby girl with silky dark hair and skin like roses and cream.

He'd read enough of the letter to know that Mrs. Banning hadn't been describing congenital abnormalities but the traumatic results of an accident. Lili had read the letter. Hell, she probably had it memorized. "Things happen," he said carefully. "You said it's been seventeen years."

"You don't understand!" She grabbed his hands in hers and held them tight, crushing the letter between them. "I wanted her to have a *better* life than the one I had. Eileen's friends were beautiful and rich and kind. I knew they'd give her all the things I could never ever afford." Music lessons, ponies, beautiful dresses with ruffles and lace. Everything a perfect little girl deserved. Everything he'd given to his own daughters so easily and with so damn little thought. "This isn't how my child would have ended up. I don't know many things in this life, Whit, but I know that for sure."

Her carefully cultured tones were slipping away. The lazy drawl of Euless stretched out her impassioned words, calling to mind the girl she'd been almost twenty years ago. The girl he hadn't really known until now.

He drew her into his arms and she came willingly. She rested her head on his shoulder as he held her close and she cried as if her heart would break. The sweet smell of her hair filled his senses with dark pleasure. Her body was soft and yielding against his and years of banked emotion broke free and pushed him over the edge.

"Lil."

She looked up at him, eyes wet with tears. He cupped her face with his hands. Her skin was as dewy and soft as a girl's against his roughened fingertips. The proud curve of her jaw, the aristocratic cheekbones, the full, lush mouth—he memorized them all against the time when she turned him away for this.

Her lips parted to say something but before she had the chance he did what he'd wanted to do from the first moment he saw her. His mouth brushed hers, gently at first, then with more pressure until he was kissing her the way he'd dreamed of kissing her, drinking in her spirit and her sweetness and the utter hopelessness of it all.

Whit hadn't been aroused that totally, that artlessly, since he was a teenager. He was as hard as iron and she gasped as he pulled her closer to him but she didn't pull away. Instead she wrapped her long, slender arms around his neck and stood utterly still. The only sounds in the room were her breathing and the ferocious pounding of his blood.

She tasted vaguely of wine and chocolate. The inside of her mouth was slick and warm, so erotically inviting he wanted to take her right there, standing up, with no preamble, no apologies. He wanted to see her eyes widen as he filled her, wanted her to wrap those showgirl legs around his waist and ride him hard and fast.

Their tongues met and mated, long voluptuous strokes that excited but didn't satisfy. He wanted more. He wanted her to love him, full out, unconditional, till-death-do-us-part *love* him. She was lonely, whether she wanted to admit it or not. And she was vulnerable. Unfortunately, she was also Carter's wife. What a damn shame it was that things like that still mattered to him.

Ending the kiss was the hardest thing he'd ever done.

"My apologies," he said, bowing slightly. "I overstepped my bounds."

Her color was high. He wanted to believe it was from more than embarrassment. "I was upset," she said, running a visibly shaky hand through her hair. Tears balanced on the ends of her lashes. "You were comforting me."

"It was more than that, Lil."

"A friend helping a friend."

"I love you."

She flinched as if he'd struck her a blow. "Don't say that."

"I love you," he repeated, astonished by the simple power of those very simple words. "I have for a long time, Lil." From the first day, the first moment.

She turned away from him.

"I wasn't going to tell you but..." His words trailed off. What good were words anyway when the emotions inside his heart were dangerous enough to destroy them both.

"You shouldn't have told me," she whispered. "I didn't need to hear it. We could have gone on this way forever."

"I couldn't, Lil."

She met his eyes.

"I'm going to take a sabbatical."

"A sabbatical?" Her beautiful sapphire eyes glittered with tears. "Does Carter know?"

"You're the first."

"You don't have to leave because of this." She made a graceful, sweeping gesture with her hands. "It's all forgotten."

The soft southern accent was being replaced by the careful, old money tones she'd cultivated over the years. Piece by piece she was donning the armor of wealth and position. It was as if the entire interlude hadn't even happened. As if he hadn't handed her his heart. "About the letter," she said after a moment.

"The letter." Lili had switched gears effortlessly, but it took him a moment. "We can find out where your daughter is, Lil," he said. "We'll put our own private investigators on this. You'll get your answers."

"You misunderstand me, Whit. I can't do that. Carter believes my child is dead."

"So tell him the truth."

"You know Carter better than anyone, Whit. He doesn't even want to share me with Grant. If I find my daughter, I'll lose my husband." She met his eyes and he saw what she wanted him to see. "That's not a trade-off I'm willing to make."

"You're sure of that?"

"Absolutely." She reached into his breast pocket and removed the square of white linen. "Damn this Banning woman anyway. You know it's not like me to get all weepy."

"She touched a nerve."

"Of course she did. I can't imagine how it would feel to have a child who needed help that I couldn't provide." She smoothed down her hair with a sharp gesture then adjusted the sleeves of her expensive suit. "What's the best way to deal with Mrs. Banning?"

"Deal with her?" *You're moving too fast, Lil. What if the girl really is your child?* She should know better than most people how many twists and turns a life could take. Just because she had signed over her baby to a wealthy family from Tennessee was no reason to believe that was where the child had ended up.

"That's not my child," she said firmly, as if she'd read his mind. "There's nothing I can do to help her. I have my own responsibilities to Carter and Grant." She gestured wide. "I don't want anything—or *anyone*—interfering with that."

"Not even your child?"

"I'll pretend you didn't say that, Whit." Her tone was dismissive.

"A letter from an attorney is usually all it takes to dissuade most of the beggars."

She winced. "A harsh term."

He said nothing. She didn't seem to notice.

"I'll take it to Patrick deRossier," she said. "He's the right one to handle this."

"We have three dozen of the finest lawyers in-house, Lil. Any one of them would be glad to handle it for you."

"No." She softened her tone. "This is my problem. I think I should use my own attorney. I don't want to press my luck."

She didn't want the Banning letter to make its way through the company to Carter. She wouldn't risk anything that could shatter her fairy-tale existence.

"This is just between us, Whit," she said, as if reading his mind. "There's no reason for Carter to be worried by any of this nonsense."

"Right now, it isn't Carter I'm worried about."

"I'm fine. Wherever my daughter is, I'm sure she's happy. I made my decision years ago and I'm going to stand by it."

"If I felt that way, Emmaline and I would still be together."

"Irreverent, as always." She smiled and touched his cheek. "That's the Whit I know and love. What on earth would I do without you?"

"I don't know, Lil," he said, reaching for a bottle of her husband's whiskey. But the day was coming when she would have to find out.

19

Whit accompanied Lili downstairs to her car.

"It's been a long day," she said, brushing his cheek with hers. "We'll talk."

"Of course," he said as Fleming opened the passenger door. "Take care, Lil."

There was something about his tone of voice that brought her up short. "You won't do anything foolish, will you?"

"Nothing foolish," he said, a half smile lifting the corner of his mouth.

"Promise?"

"Go home to your husband, Lil." He turned and walked back toward the building.

"Whit! Please—" She caught herself. Fleming was looking at her with open curiosity, as were a number of passersby. Thank God she'd stopped herself in time. You never knew when a reporter or photographer would leap from behind a parked car and secure a place for you on page one of the *New York Post*.

"Mrs. Spaulding."

She drew in a deep breath then turned toward Fleming, who was holding open the door to the Rolls. "I'm sorry I kept you waiting, Fleming."

"No problem, Mrs. Spaulding." He held her elbow as she lowered herself into the car. "I hear you knocked them dead today. Congratulations."

"Congratulations?" What on earth was the man talking about?

"Your big speech," Fleming said as he closed the door. "Everyone's talking about it."

She nodded her thanks. The events of the past few hours had completely obliterated her triumphant afternoon at Mayfair.

Fleming walked around to the other side of the car then climbed behind the wheel. "The bar is stocked, Mrs. Spaulding," he said through the intercom. "Traffic is light. We should be in Greenwich within the hour."

Another thing she'd forgotten. Renovations on their penthouse apartment had started that afternoon and would continue well into the new year. She couldn't imagine Christmas anywhere but in their home overlooking Central Park. Grant had an invitation to spend the holidays in Aspen and she was afraid the appeal of Christmas *en famille* in bucolic Greenwich wouldn't be able to compete.

"Thank you, Fleming," she said. "If I need anything else, I'll ring."

The connection crackled and died. She slipped off her handmade lizard pumps then curled up in the corner of the cushy rear seat with her legs tucked underneath her. What was it Grandma Hattie used to say? *Sit up straight, girl! Don't you go lazing around like poor white trash with your skirt bunched up around your hips.*

Grandma Hattie didn't hold any power over her, not any more. Lili Spaulding didn't wait at the corner of Church and

Main for a rickety old county bus to take her into town when she needed to go shopping. Lili Spaulding had a chauffeur-driven Rolls and a smart little Mercedes 450 for those times when she felt like antiquing in Connecticut or New Jersey. And that didn't count the Land Rover they kept at the Amagansett cottage or Carter's pair of vintage Jags or even Grant's pride and joy, a Maserati that was almost as beautiful as he was.

Lili Spaulding had everything Lilly Ann Barnett had ever wanted: jewelry, cars, designer clothes and a man who loved her. Too bad that man wasn't her husband.

I love you. Whit's voice echoed inside her head. What she wouldn't give to hear her husband say those words. Carter said he adored her, doted on her, wanted her, and occasionally even needed her. But love her? That was the one thing he'd never said.

She closed her eyes and let her head fall back against the thick leather upholstery. How hard could it be to say those words? Whit had no business saying them and yet he hadn't been able to hold them back any longer. Carter had every right and it never occurred to him.

Not once.

She'd known about Carter's women for a long time. He went to great pains to be discreet about his liaisons but ultimately it was impossible to hide the signs from a wife who still loved her husband. And Lili did love him. The sexual heat of the early years had ripened into something deeper, more lasting. She loved him for his strength and determination. She loved him for all the things he was and even for the things he'd never be.

He was her home, the center of her life. Take away the penthouse and the mansion, the diamonds and the private jets, and she was still Mrs. Carter Spaulding. Still Carter's wife and Grant's stepmother. Still part of a family that meant more to her than anything on earth, a family that she would fight to protect. She overlooked Carter's other women and mopped up after Grant's accidents. She threw dinner parties for people she hated, made excuses to people whose company she enjoyed. Everything she did, she did for the greater good of the man she loved, the family she needed.

She'd never expected the biggest threat to her happiness would come from out of her own past.

*Still trying to run away, are you, girl? Not even you can run
fast enough this time.*

Lili's eyes popped open and she flipped the switch on the
console next to her. A small, buttery pool of light illuminated
her hands as she opened her purse and withdrew the pale pink
envelope. She had no respect for this Banning woman. No respect at all. Obviously the woman didn't have any pride. Why
else would she try to beg money from a total stranger? Mrs.
Banning couldn't possibly believe her daughter Catherine was
Lili's biological child. It was too confusing and implausible to
waste even a moment of her time thinking about.

*So why did she pick you, Miss High-and-Mighty? There are
lots of other rich gals out there she could've written that letter
to.*

"I don't know," Lili muttered, stuffing the letter back into
her purse. Her hands shook as she fastened the clasp. Strange
things happened when you were in the public eye. Celebrities
found themselves besieged with letters filled with pleas for
everything from autographed photos to free cars to beach
houses on the Côte d'Azur. It came with the territory.

Lili had received her share of peculiar letters before. In the
beginning she'd wanted to help everyone who asked. She had
called Carter heartless and cold, too isolated in his ivory tower
to understand how it felt to be poor. It had taken her years to
come to grips with her new reality.

But then came a letter like this one from Mrs. Millicent
Banning of Cincinnati, Ohio and everything she thought she
understood about human nature went out the window as raw,
naked fear obliterated reason. The details in the letter struck
fear in her heart. It was all there, every last bit of it, right down
to Grandma Hattie and the Franklins.

She wasn't ashamed of her background but she certainly
didn't go around bragging about her old life in Euless. That was
another lifetime. The things that happened had happened to an
entirely different person. A girl who had no bearing on the
woman Lili had become.

What if Carter had seen the letter? The idea made her physically ill. If he hadn't been called away suddenly, he very well
might have plucked the pink envelope from the pile and opened
it. The fact that it was addressed to Lili wouldn't have deterred

him. He was the kind of man who believed he owned his family the way he owned his corporation: totally and absolutely. There was no room for weakness, no room for human frailty.

No room for the child she'd left behind.

Don't much matter what your hubby thinks if that Banning gal ain't yours.

Of course the Banning girl wasn't hers. She'd have to be an utter fool to even consider such nonsense. But she knew·Carter. They hadn't discussed the child since that night more than four years ago when he first noticed the faint, silvery marks on her belly. To have the spectre of her past rise up between them now—

I need a drink, Lili thought, reaching for a glass and the Dewar's. She wasn't thinking clearly. Too much had happened today, too many disparate incidents that refused to blend together into a cohesive whole.

Her heady success at Mayfair.

Mrs. Banning's disturbing letter.

Whit.

She knew she would have to think about him some time when she wasn't feeling so fractured and upset. Whit Paley loved her as a friend, the same way she loved him. It must have been the martinis speaking and not his heart at all.

But he'd kissed her and, God help her, she'd kissed him back. She hadn't meant to. Kissing him had been the last thing on her mind. But he'd felt so solid, so strong, and she'd been in need of strength—more so than she had realized. He didn't mean that nonsense about taking a sabbatical. The problems with Mayfair had taken a toll on him, that's all it was. What he needed was a week of margaritas and a pink casita at Las Brisas to bring him back to center. She would speak to Carter about it tonight, maybe arrange for the Spaulding jet to fly Whit and a companion to Acapulco.

She took a long swallow of Scotch and shuddered. She felt like she had after Clifford Earle Franklin died and left her all alone with his baby growing inside her belly. She took another swallow and shuddered a little less.

Actually it was almost funny. Whit loved her and Carter didn't. The stuff of English drawing room humor and Hollywood romantic comedies. So why wasn't she laughing? Why did she feel as if her entire life had been turned upside down in the space of a single day and there was nothing she could do to right it?

Nothing you can do? Where's your backbone, girl! All that rich living has made you soft.

She'd learned about problem solving back at UNLV. She knew how to prioritize. The first thing she had to do was take care of Mrs. Banning and she didn't dare put it off until tomorrow. She had to make certain no more letters popped up on Carter's desk. Someone had to put the fear of God into the woman.

She buzzed the intercom.

"Yes, Mrs. Spaulding?" Fleming said.

"Has the mobile phone been repaired?"

"Yes, ma'am. It's up and running."

She breathed a sigh of relief. "Pull over, Fleming. There might be a change of plans."

It was after midnight when she finally reached Greenwich. The car turned off the main road and began the slow, winding climb to the house on top of the hill. The driveway alone was longer than Main Street back in Euless.

Lili had been dozing in the back seat of the Rolls, soothed by the Scotch and the fact that her attorney Patrick deRossier would see to it that Mrs. Banning never bothered her again. Truth was, Mrs. Banning would probably never bother anyone again once Patrick finished with her. He was a hard-nosed man, one whose sensibilities lay with his client, right or wrong. The Mayfair lawyers Whit favored would have been more concerned with corporate image.

"Home sweet home, Mrs. Spaulding."

Fleming brought the car to a halt at the front door.

She hid a yawn with the back of her hand. "Thank you, Fleming," she said as he helped her from the car. "You've had a long day. Why don't you take tomorrow off?"

"Sounds good to me, ma'am." He walked her to the door. "Thank you."

She said good-night then let herself inside. The house was dark but a puddle of light spilled out into the hallway from beneath the closed library door. Her chest tightened. Carter was home. She slipped off her shoes and draped her coat over the banister then padded quietly across the foyer toward the library.

"Carter." She pushed open the door. "I'm sorry I'm so late but—" She stopped dead in her tracks. Her husband was bent over his desk snorting cocaine from the bowl of a sterling demitasse spoon that had belonged to his grandmother. "Oh my God . . ."

He brushed away the white powdery residue with the back of his hand then beckoned to her. "Join me," he said, flashing her the seductive smile she hadn't seen in ages. "Coke makes you fuck like a teenager."

Disgust filled her and she took an involuntary step back. "I'd rather make love like an adult."

"Try it, Lili. The rush is incredible."

"How long have you been doing this?"

"Since Christmas."

"Christmas?" She couldn't keep the shock from her voice. "That's almost a year." He hadn't touched her in nearly as long.

"Coke makes you forget you're getting older. I can get by on three hours sleep a night."

"You realize what you're doing is illegal, don't you?"

"Are you going to call the authorities?"

"People talk, Carter. What if I'd been one of the maids?"

"They're paid to keep their mouths closed."

"What if somebody paid them more to talk?"

He grabbed her by the waist and pulled her close.

"I'm hard as a rock already."

"Good for you," she said, trying to pull away.

He started tugging at her clothes. The pearl buttons from her jacket flew across the room.

"Carter, for God's sake, this is a Chanel! Stop it—"

She knew she sounded ridiculous but it didn't matter. He wasn't listening to her. She wasn't entirely certain he even saw her. His hands were everywhere—on her thighs, her waist, her breasts. The silky fabric of her ivory camisole tore as he tried to yank it over her head. She felt vulnerable, exposed, standing there topless in front of her husband.

"Touch yourself," he said in a voice she didn't recognize.

"Go to hell," she snapped, straightening her spine.

"Do it!"

His tone terrified her. Tears filled her eyes as she cupped her breasts, let them settle into her palms.

"Good girl," her husband said.

"Carter, I—"

He placed his fingers against her mouth. "Suck me."

He drew his thumb across her lips again and again until she parted them and he thrust two fingers into her mouth. His skin tasted salty and sweet, forbidden and familiar. She pushed him away. "I don't want to do this, Carter."

"You don't know what you want, Lili," he said, his grip on her tightening, "but I do."

He didn't care that she was terrified. He didn't care that sex was the last thing on her mind. He intended to ram himself into her whether she wanted him to or not. They'd played sex games before but always, *always,* she'd been an eager and willing participant. That had been an implicit part of the bargain. The fact that her consent no longer mattered made something inside her snap and she slapped him hard across the face.

"Damn you," he said, releasing her from his grasp.

"Congratulations," she said quietly as she turned to leave the room. "I do believe you got your wish."

Lili lay motionless in the bed she shared with her husband and listened to the sound of the front door slamming shut behind him.

That should be you walking out that door, girl, after what he did to you....

She rolled onto her side and clutched her pillow close to her chest. She'd suspected that he was experimenting with drugs but had managed to convince herself that what she didn't know couldn't harm her. The clues had been there for ages: his reliance on booze and sleeping pills, the mood swings that had his staff buzzing about manic-depressive or flat-out schizophrenia.

Carter was doing cocaine. At least that's what she assumed the white powder was. She wasn't totally blind to the fact that many of Manhattan's high-powered executives were spending a lot of time behind the bathroom doors at society parties and fancy restaurants. They were all risk-takers, pirates at heart, and a walk on the wild side of the law got their juices flowing.

She didn't have to like that fact to understand it, but somehow deep in her heart she knew it was different for Carter. He was using coke the same way he used sex: to fill the empty place inside him that nothing, not even Lili, had been able to fill.

Damn that Banning woman. If it hadn't been for that pathetic letter, Lili would have been there waiting for Carter when he returned home and none of this would have happened. Maybe Carter didn't love her the way she'd dreamed of being loved when she was a girl back in Euless, but he needed her and in many ways that was even more important.

God had been watching out for her today. If Carter had read that letter, she would have been powerless to do anything but tell him everything about the baby. That simple lie she'd told when they were first married would have opened wounds she feared would never heal. Carter trusted her the way he trusted no one else on earth and she would sell her soul, if necessary, to keep it that way.

She leaned over and plucked cigarettes and a lighter from her nightstand. Carter hated it when she smoked in bed but he wasn't there to complain. She inhaled deeply, letting the rich cigarette smoke steady her nerves. Carter was slated to speak before some executives in London the first week of December. Lili had intended to pass on the trip and concentrate on Christmas shopping while her husband was out of town. Perhaps it was time to rethink that decision.

Mayfair kept a pied-à-terre near Kensington Palace, a charming flat where she and Carter had shared some blissful interludes. She remembered long nights saturated with the scents and sounds of their lovemaking. They couldn't get enough of each other back then. Carter had been insatiable, as demanding and powerful in bed as he was in business and she'd wondered what she'd done to deserve such deep, amazing happiness.

She pulled the duvet up over her shoulders and closed her eyes as exhaustion washed over her. Sleep…she needed a good night's sleep. Tomorrow morning she'd be able to figure out where they'd gone wrong and what she could do to make it right.

She had made it happen once. She had no doubt she could make it happen again and, unless she missed her guess, London would be the perfect place to start.

"Mama!" The child's cry cut through the still night. "Mama, help!"

Lilly stood at the edge of the lake as the sound bounced off the water. She cupped her hands around her mouth. "Where are you?" she shouted.

"Help me, Mama!" The cry grew more desperate. "I can't swim any more. I can't swim—"

Lilly dived into the lake, gasping as the icy water tried to pull her down. "Talk to me," she called. "If you don't keep talking, I won't be able to find you."

"My arms hurt!" the child sputtered. "I can't do this no more."

Lilly had never been much of a swimmer. Her strokes were shallow, not half as powerful as she needed to make her way across the lake. She struck out from the shore, praying she was headed in the right direction.

"Help me, Mama! Please..."

The little girl's terrified cries were behind her, in front of her, to her left and to her right.

Suddenly the lake erupted in waves, huge swells that lifted Lilly high above the surface then tossed her down like a discarded toy. Brackish water washed over her, around her, filling her throat. Her chest burned as she tried to drag air into her lungs. The child's cries seemed to be everywhere, growing louder and more desperate with each second, but she couldn't concentrate any longer. Air... she needed air. If she stayed in the water any longer she would die and, God forgive her, she didn't want to die.

"I'm sorry," she whispered as she turned back toward shore. "So sorry—"

Lili awoke with a start. The bedcovers were tangled around her legs and hips. She struggled to free herself, heart pounding as if she'd just finished running a race. Hands trembling, she fumbled around on the nightstand for her cigarettes and lighter. It took three tries to light a cigarette.

You didn't need Freud to figure out the meaning of that dream. It was so real she could still hear the child's cry, feel the icy water closing over her head, dragging her down—

She shivered and stubbed out the cigarette in a crystal ashtray. This was ridiculous. She had no reason to feel guilty because Millicent Banning's daughter needed surgery her family couldn't afford. The woman had a hell of a nerve to insinuate herself into Lili's life. You had to earn what you got in this world; you couldn't go around throwing yourself on the mercy of total strangers.

Maybe she'd been too hasty, calling out the legal dogs the way she had. Desperation wasn't a crime. God knew she'd been desperate a time or two in her life. But it was too late. She'd unburdened herself to Patrick deRossier and put the matter into his hands. She would lose face if she changed her mind now.

She lit another cigarette. What on earth was the matter with her? Her marriage was teetering on the verge of collapse and she was obsessing over a woman she didn't know, a child she would never meet. She should be thinking about her own family. . . about the husband who still wasn't home.

What if he decided to divorce her? She tried to imagine her life without Carter there at the center of it but the idea was too terrifying to contemplate. Even more terrifying was the thought that she could lose Grant. He was her child as surely as if she'd given him life. Her blood didn't run through his veins but her strength and her ambition did. Their connection was deeper than flesh and bone; it was one of spirit.

Her breath caught. Could that be the way Millicent Banning felt about her daughter? That deep, almost religious sense that something even more elemental than sex had brought this child into her life. Millicent Banning was willing to beg for her Catherine. Lili was willing to kill for her Grant. Their lives were nothing alike but in some ways they were sisters under the skin.

Lili had been exactly where Millicent Banning was. She knew how it felt to pray for a miracle that wasn't going to happen. Those few days after her baby's birth had been the worst days of her life, alone with a helpless infant she couldn't afford to feed, much less clothe or educate.

She tried not to think about those days and most of the time she was fairly successful. Millicent Banning's letter had brought it all back to her, the confusion and guilt and the terrible rush of relief she'd felt when she climbed aboard that bus for New York and left her baby girl behind. She'd always supposed it was unnatural to feel that way, as if some terrible burden had been lifted from her shoulders as the doors closed behind her.

"You've had a good life," she whispered. "Everything a girl could ever want." She'd always imagined that somewhere her daughter was living a life much like Grant's, one of privilege and boundless opportunity.

But what if—

She refused to even finish that thought. That was the sound of guilt and she had nothing whatsoever to feel guilty about. If she thought there was even a chance her daughter had ended up in difficult circumstances, she would move heaven and earth to lend her a helping hand but she knew that wasn't the case. When Grant was in trouble she knew it by the sharp pain that settled right in the center of her abdomen like a built-in alarm system. Surely it would be the same with her biological child.

Lili rested her cigarette on the edge of the crystal ashtray then fiddled with the ornate gold-and-diamond ring on her left hand. She had more rings than there were days in the month to wear them, more bracelets and necklaces than there were days in the year. Carter had showered her with all of the visible signs of affection and wealth she could possibly desire, the kinds of things a woman like Millicent Banning couldn't even imagine.

Who would believe that sometimes the worst thing that could happen to a woman was for all her dreams to come true?

20

Cincinnati

Jack Banning stared at the letter as if it were a shark dangling from the end of his fishing line. "What in holy hell were you thinking of, Millie?"

Millicent flinched. In almost forty years of marriage, she'd never heard him roar with anger before and it scared the daylights out of her. "It's just a letter," she said, trying to soothe his temper. "I thought maybe—"

"You've lost your marbles, woman!" He waved the letter from Lili Spaulding's lawyer in front of her nose as his beloved face seemed to crumble before her very eyes. "Why, Millie?" His voice broke. "Why?"

Millicent couldn't hold back the tears. "For Corey," she said, wiping her eyes with the back of her hand. "I knew it was a one in a million chance, but I had to try."

"You actually thought this Spaulding woman was Corey's mother?"

Millicent couldn't lie to him. That fancy lawyer had even returned her letter, all neatly folded, in the same envelope as his response. "Yes," she said miserably. "The more I looked at Mrs. Spaulding's pictures, the more sure I got."

"That's crazy," Jack exploded as he paced the room. "Why would a rich woman give away her baby?"

"She wasn't always rich. She was a showgirl in Las Vegas when Carter Spaulding married her."

"That doesn't mean she's Corey's mother."

"I know it's crazy, but one afternoon I was watching our girl doing her homework and she looked so much like Mrs. Spaulding that I—" She stopped abruptly. How could she explain something she didn't understand herself? All she knew was that she'd seen a chance to help Corey and she wanted to grab it, no matter how silly or far-fetched it might be. "I was thinking about Corey, that's all."

"What if that woman really was our girl's mother?" Jack was shaking so hard he grabbed the back of the kitchen chair for support. The letter fluttered under the table. "What if she took her away from us? What then, Millie? What would happen to us then?" He started to cry then, big ugly rasping sobs that filled the room.

"Oh, honey!" Millicent ran to his side and threw her arms around him. All she'd wanted was to help Corey and now see what she'd caused. "It's just a letter from a lawyer. There's nothing so scary about that, now, is there?"

"Don't let them do it, Millie," he begged, clutching her arm. His forehead was wet with sweat and his upper lip seemed oddly pale. "Swear to me you won't let them do it."

"Do what, honey? I don't know what you mean."

"What they're going to do." He bent down and retrieved the letter then pushed it under her nose. "Didn't you read this? They're going to try to take her away from us, they're going to—"

She grabbed him by the shoulders. "Nobody's going to take our girl away from us. That fancy lawyer just wants me to leave Mrs. Spaulding alone." She couldn't let him know that she was terrified of a lawsuit, terrified that everything they'd worked so hard for would be taken away because of her one, foolish act of desperation. Terrified that she'd stumbled onto the truth and it would destroy them all.

"There's more to it," he insisted, his voice growing shrill. "Swear to me they won't take our girl." His breathing sounded funny, as if he'd climbed a flight of stairs too fast.

"Of course they won't take our girl. Mrs. Spaulding isn't her mother. She doesn't have the right." Terror had her by the throat. What on earth was the matter with Jack? The letter was plain as day, even if she didn't believe it for a minute. ... *Mrs. Spaulding states unequivocally that Catherine Banning is not her biological daughter. Any and all further attempt on your part to promote that untruth or to contact Mrs. Spaulding with regard to the minor child will be dealt with to the fullest extent of the law.*

"This is my family!" His pain ripped at her heart. "I'd give my life to keep us together. No stranger is going to take my daughter away from me."

"Please, Jack! Stop saying that." He was scaring her more than the lawyer's letter. "Aren't you listening to me? They don't *want* Corey. They just want us to stay away." They might try to take their house or their savings, but Corey was safe. Why couldn't he see that?

"Don't let them do it, Millie!" The veins in his temples throbbed like twin purple grapes ready to pop. "Swear to me you won't let them take her."

"They won't take her," she said, starting to cry. "I promise you—" She stared in horror as he clutched his left shoulder.

"What's wrong?" He took a step forward then staggered. "Jack!"

He crumpled to the floor in front of the stove. Millicent's scream bounced off the walls of the small kitchen.

"Oh, God, honey!" She cradled his head in her lap. "What's wrong? What's happening? You have to tell me what's wrong, Jack. Please!"

She had to get to the phone and call 911. His heart, his poor battered heart, had finally given out and it was all her fault. Every last bit of it. She'd done something terrible, something crazy, and now she was going to pay for it.

She grabbed for the wall phone and, balancing the receiver between her ear and shoulder, knelt down next to her beloved husband. "We need an ambulance!" she cried as she held his hand tightly in hers. "Hurry!"

"Millicent." Jack's eyes opened and she saw the fear in them and she saw the love and she saw that she was going to lose him. "I—"

"Don't talk," she whispered fiercely. "Save your strength."

"—love you."

"The ambulance is coming, honey. You're going to be fine."

Oh, please, God, don't take him, she prayed as the faint wail of a siren sounded in the distance. He was the only man she'd ever loved, her dearest friend in the world. They had so many years ahead of them—God wouldn't take him now. Not when she needed him so much.

It should be raining, Corey thought as the funeral procession made its way toward the cemetery at the edge of town. There was something obscene about bright golden sunshine and cobalt blue skies on the day Jack Banning was buried, as if not even God cared that a good man had died.

Next to her Millicent cried quietly, almost apologetically. She'd been crying for days, it seemed, soft sobs that set Corey's teeth on edge and made her want to grab her mother by the shoulders and shake her. There was nothing quiet or polite about death, nothing gentle or forgiving. Millicent should be beating her breast, berating God for allowing this to happen. She shouldn't be huddled into the corner of the funeral parlor limousine, fading away before Corey's very eyes.

I wish I could cry for you, Pop, she thought, holding Millicent's hand in hers. She wished she could feel something but it was as if part of her heart had died right along with him.

She closed her eyes. Vivid, terrible images of the past four days came back to her. She'd been called out of her dorm room to meet with her advisor at his office. "Don't you have a class?" the dorm monitor had asked, a puzzled look on her face. Corey had shrugged and muttered something about nursing a bad cold.

She'd pulled on a pair of jeans and a sweatshirt then made her way to the administration building. Mr. Clift's office was on the first floor. Usually there was a crowd of kids lined up in the hall, waiting to see him. That day the hall was empty and Mr. Clift was waiting in the doorway to his office. The second she saw his face, forehead pleated with lines of concern, she knew.

"Who?" she managed, struggling to keep her voice from shaking. "My mother?"

Mr. Clift shook his head. "Your father, Corey. I'm so sorry."

She hadn't cried. He'd offered her tissues and a place to sit down but she'd refused both. And she didn't cry when she saw Millicent. Her mother had seemed so small, so racked with grief, that Corey couldn't add her own sorrow to the burden. She moved through the days of viewing at Walton's Funeral Home like a sleepwalker, staying one step ahead of her grief.

Everyone marveled at her strength, but they hadn't a clue. It wasn't strength they were seeing. It was just another wall that had been erected around Corey's heart.

"I thank God every day that Millicent has you," Reverend Evans had told Corey just before the services started. "You're everything to her now."

Everything. The thought terrified her. She didn't know how to be everything to someone, not even to herself. She was a failure in almost every way that mattered. She had no friends. She'd screwed up her reputation. She'd cut more classes at school than she'd attended because the simple act of walking into a room of strangers was more than she could bear. She was smarter than two thirds of the kids who were pulling down Bs and soft As but what good was being smart when you didn't have the guts to do anything with it?

She'd spent her whole life on the outside looking in. Why had she ever believed things would change just because she was in college? She was still the same outcast she'd always been, searching for a way to fill the empty space inside her heart that her real mother had left behind when she abandoned her.

Millicent reached over and patted Corey's hand. The simple, loving gesture came close to pushing Corey over the edge. Tears burned her eyelids and she struggled to contain the sudden rush of emotion building inside her chest.

I miss you, Pop, she thought. She missed his quiet strength, his unconditional love, his unwavering belief that she could be anything she wanted to be if she put her mind to it. Who would ever believe in her so totally again? What other man would ever see past her damaged face and love her for her imperfect heart?

Thanksgiving came and went but Millicent scarcely noticed. Corey made a small turkey with all the trimmings. She set the table in the kitchen with the best dishes and even lit candles but Millicent couldn't manage more than a mouthful.

What was there to be thankful about with the man she loved dead and buried in his grave? She knew she should get down on her knees and thank God for a daughter like Corey but Millicent's heart had died with Jack and not even her beloved girl could bring it back again.

Mornings were what she hated most, that moment before she opened her eyes and realized her Jack was dead and gone. "Wake up, sleepyhead," she'd say, stifling a yawn of her own. "Time to rise and shine!" She'd wait a second, eyes closed, then scoot over to his side of the bed to kiss his cheek.

But he wasn't there. His side of the bed was cold and empty, the covers as neatly tucked in as they'd been the night before. Her eyes would spring open and the truth would grab her by the shoulders and shake her until her teeth rattled.

He's gone, you old fool. Can't you get it through your head?

But she couldn't get it through her head, not by a long shot. Maybe this was some terrible dream she was having. Maybe she was sick with a fever and that fever was causing all sorts of strange delusions to take control of her brain. She just knew that Jack was going to walk through the door any minute. "Sorry I've been gone so long, Millie. Hope I didn't worry you any." And she would leap to her feet and run right into his arms where she belonged and she'd never go against his wishes ever again.

Corey took to doing the food shopping late in the afternoon when most of the neighbor women were home cooking supper for their husbands and children. She liked pushing the cart through the empty aisles, checking the prices on canned corn and green beans, planning elaborate meals she wouldn't dare try to cook.

The truth was, it felt good to get out of the house. Her mother's grief filled every corner of the home she'd shared with Jack. It seemed to suck the oxygen from the air and leave Corey gasping for breath. She shopped and cleaned and cooked the best meals she could but her mother had no interest in any of it. She'd pat Corey on the hand then fade away again into a dreamworld where nothing bad ever happened, certainly not to someone she loved.

It broke Corey's heart to see her that way, looking so lost and fragile and alone. She would give anything to be able to ease her mother's pain but, short of being able to bring her father back from the grave, there was nothing she could do.

"Corey!" Pammy's voice rang out over the display of potatoes in the produce department. "How's our Millicent?"

"Just fine," Corey said, wishing she hadn't wasted time comparing prices on ground meat. She could have been through the checkout line by now and on her way home.

Pammy peered into Corey's shopping then looked back up and smiled. "You tell your mom I'll hold her Friday afternoon appointment as long as necessary."

"I'll tell her," Corey said, inching away from the well-meaning woman.

"And you too, honey. I know you're not much for beauty parlors but you're welcome any time. Cynthia is doing makeovers these days and I know she could do something wonderful for you."

Pammy meant well but her words stung. There weren't any makeovers or miracles in her future. Her brief college stay hadn't been a total waste: at least it had taught her that much. The pattern of her days was set in stone.

* * *

It snowed the first week of December, one of those light snows that lay across the ground like sugar frosting on a wedding cake. Millicent woke up at dawn and pushed back the covers. She swung her feet to the floor, feeling around with her toes for the fuzzy slippers Jack had given to her two Christmases ago before he lost his job. She'd oohed and aahed over those slippers, rubbing the soft pink fluff against her cheek until Jack laughed and said he didn't want to see what she'd do if he'd given her diamonds. "I don't need diamonds, honey," she'd said, meaning every word. "I've got you."

Funny thing, this time the memory didn't make her sad the way it would have just a few days ago. Somehow it made her feel closer to Jack, as if he were in the other room, watching TV. She sat there, waiting for the crushing pain of loss to spread across her chest, but it never did. The sorrow was still there, and the loneliness, but somewhere buried deep inside her heart the seeds of acceptance were beginning to grow.

She went downstairs to make a cup of tea. Her movements were awkward and clumsy. She felt light-headed, as if she'd been bedridden with the flu for a very long time and was only now getting back on her feet. It felt strange to make only one cup of tea and even stranger to sit alone at the kitchen table.

Being out of work had been hard on Jack but although she'd never mentioned it to him, she had enjoyed having him home with her. She loved setting the kitchen table with two place mats and two soup bowls and two glasses of milk from Krauszer's Dairy on the other side of town. Jack wasn't much of a talker so they listened to the radio, commenting on whatever the story of the day might be.

Their last months had been good ones, she thought as she sipped her tea. She wouldn't have traded them for the world but now it was time to face up to the way things were now. She'd managed to keep the bills from Corey, stashing them away in a brown manila envelope when the girl wasn't looking. It wasn't right that her daughter should have to worry about money.

Millicent laughed hollowly. Not that there was much money to worry about. Jack's pension was minuscule and his insurance policy had barely covered the funeral. They already had two mortgages on the house and Millicent didn't have the slightest idea how she was going to manage to pay either one of them. And Corey—what was going to happen to their girl? Millicent could see the change in her since her daddy died, the way Corey was pulling away from life like a turtle retreating into its shell.

You can't run before you walk, Millicent, she told herself. They said you could eat an elephant if you did it bite by bite. Maybe she'd find a way out of this mess if she took it one bite at a time.

That feeling carried her all the way through the day and the one after that, as well. She called the bank and spoke to the manager. He expressed his condolences over Jack's death and arranged a payment plan that would make the next six months easier. The electric company was just as kind, which more than made up for the telephone company's flat-out refusal to hear her story. She'd managed to buy a little time and she was grateful for it.

Bite by bite, she told herself. Bite by bite.

She was still moving slowly through her days but it seemed to Millicent that she grew a little stronger, a little more sure of herself, with each passing day. If only she could say the same for Corey. Before she knew it, it was six days before Christmas. Goodwill was due that afternoon to pick up the clothing she'd promised them the week before Jack died. She woke up with the sun that morning, knowing what she had to do.

Jack's closet.

Millicent hadn't been near it since he died. Her hand shook as she grasped the knob and opened the door. His smell of tobacco and bay rum filled her head and she bit back a cry of pain. His good gray trousers...his red Christmas sweater...his favorite bedroom slippers, the ones with the scuffed leather toes.

You'll always be with me, honey, she thought as she lovingly folded the items. She didn't need a pair of trousers to keep his memory alive. Clothes were meant to be worn, not stored away in some kind of shrine. She liked to think that her beloved husband's things would help warm someone's winter.

She was emptying his sock drawer, smiling over the fancy dress socks he'd never worn, when her hand brushed against an envelope. Jack had always been real fussy about his things.

Millicent used to stack his clean laundry on the bed and he would neatly put things away just the way he liked them. She withdrew the large brown envelope and turned it over. There was her name on the front in Jack's sturdy handwriting. Curious, she slid one nail under the flap and withdrew a thick, legal-size document and looked at it.

She had to be dreaming. This was a gift, that's what it was, a gift from heaven!

Jack had an insurance policy she hadn't known about. A wonderful, amazing insurance policy that took her breath away. She drew in a series of breaths, struggling to steady her racing heart. It was enough to pay off their mortgages, enough to provide a cushion against her old age.

Or maybe enough to make a miracle.

Jack had always said every time God closed a window, He opened a door and Jack was right. But this time it was her beloved husband who had swung the door wide-open.

"Oh, honey," she whispered as tears filled her eyes. "Our girl's going to be all right."

BOOK SIX

The Family

21

New York, March, 1995

"Better ditch the coat," said Ed, Lili's limo driver. "The nuts are out in full force today."

Lili peered out the tinted window and suppressed a groan. Not only was an early spring snow falling, but a dozen or so women, brandishing picket signs, were lined up on either side of the entrance to Le Cirque. The handmade signs were an embarrassment. Real Women Don't Wear Animals. "And when was the last time you went to McDonald's for a burger?" Lili murmured sotto voce.

Ed laughed. "You're right on the money, Mrs. Spaulding, but I'd still ditch the coat if I were you. These folks mean business."

"I'm not about to be intimidated by a group of lunatics," she said, drawing her mink more closely around her. "If they could afford it, they'd be wearing fur, too."

It was getting so a woman had to reinvent herself every time she left the house. Fur was verboten. Cigarette smoking was akin to committing mass murder. If the activists had their way, a woman would face criminal charges for using lipstick or mascara.

Ed got out and walked around to open her door and, moments later, she strode toward the front door of the restaurant.

"Mrs. Spaulding?" A woman in jeans and a black raincoat stepped in front of Lili as she was about to enter Le Cirque.

"Do we know each other?" she asked, a slightly forbidding smile on her face.

"I'm with the Committee for Humane Treatment of Animals. Do you realize your company is in violation of every principle of respect for living—"

"I have a reservation," she said, turning away. "If you'll excuse me . . ."

The woman grabbed her by the forearm. "Not so fast, Mrs. Spaulding. We're tired of getting the runaround from your public relations people. Your company's policies on animal testing are barbaric. If you don't—"

"Is this woman bothering you, Mrs. Spaulding?" The doorman from Le Cirque elbowed his way between them, effectively shielding Lili.

"Thank you, George," Lili said in a calm and measured voice. "If you'll both excuse me . . ." She turned on her heel and darted into the restaurant, ignoring the woman's shouted complaints. She'd bowed to pressure and begun carrying a handgun last year and for the first time she was glad.

The restaurant's manager greeted her in the lobby. "We apologize for that incident, Mrs. Spaulding. Yesterday they spray painted Angela Bourdette's fur wrap as she was stepping into her car."

"Fools," Lili murmured, regaining her composure. "We've been dealing with them for weeks now. Apparently they're against both fur coats and carnivores."

"And cosmetics companies, though God only knows how we figure in this." She aimed a smile at the man. "It's wonderful to see you again, Nicholas. How long has it been?"

"Almost four years," he said.

"I'm delighted you came back to us, although I'm surprised you could bring yourself to say goodbye to Paris."

"I was sorry to hear about Mr. Spaulding's passing."

"Thank you." To her surprise, her voice broke and she glanced away. Carter had died three years ago but she still found it difficult to talk about it. The doctors had called it a stroke, as random and unpreventable as lightning on a hot summer's day, but that was a lie. Carter had killed himself with coke and everyone who had known him those last few years knew the truth. Hit by hit, he'd signed his own death warrant and there had been nothing Lili could do to stop him.

She had tried everything. She'd flushed thousands of dollars' worth of the white powder down commodes from New York to Tokyo. She'd threatened, cajoled, begged, even tried an intervention. Carter had agreed to go to Betty Ford but at the last minute he ordered his pilot to land in San Francisco where he went on a two-week coke spree that almost landed him behind bars.

Watching the man she loved systematically destroy himself had toughened Lili in ways not even giving up her baby had managed to achieve. She grew more wary, more distrustful of people, as she realized the day would soon come when she would once again be responsible for her own future. Unfortunately, she'd been all too right.

Nicholas was a perceptive man and instantly he picked up on her change of mood. Instead of waiting for her to resume the conversation, he launched into an amusing anecdote about life in Paris as he showed her to her favorite table.

"I'll have Rene bring you a glass of white wine."

Lili was grateful for the chance to recover her poise. First that obnoxious woman on the street and then the unexpected reminder of Carter. She hoped that wasn't an omen of things to come. She had so been looking forward to her weekly lunch with Grant.

A waiter set down a glass of wine at her place then disappeared. She was grateful to have something to do while she waited. Sipping the Chablis, she watched as the other tables began to fill with the rich and powerful. Fortunately Le Cirque attracted an eclectic mix that went far beyond the usual ladies who lunched. Movie moguls, business execs and publishing types all found their way to one of the most elegant watering holes in Manhattan.

Caroline Kennedy Schlossberg was seated three tables away, talking with her cousin Maria Shriver. Lili tried hard not to stare at the Kennedy cousins but failed miserably. Strange how some families maintained their mystique despite the harsh glare of publicity. She'd seen Caroline's mother around town many times before Mrs. Onassis's death—so had everyone in Manhattan—but she'd never actually met her. If she had the nerve she'd go over and introduce herself to Caroline, but not even Lili had the guts for that.

Lili had been working as a hatcheck girl at the Copa when President Kennedy was assassinated. She could remember how alone she'd felt, watching the funeral on her tiny TV, wishing she had someone to share her sorrow with. She'd watched the way Jackie moved through those dark days with dignity and class and she wished some of that polish could be absorbed right through the screen. Almost thirty-two years ago, she thought. It just didn't seem possible.

She forced herself to look away. How must it feel to be reminded of your late father's faults everywhere you turned? It seemed as if stories about JFK's philandering popped up every other week. The infamous Judith Exner stories, the conjecture about Marilyn Monroe—how could time heal old wounds when people kept ripping off the bandage?

At least Grant didn't have that to contend with. Carter had been discreet. Neither his cocaine abuse nor his dalliances had ever made it into Liz Smith's column or Page Six and for that Lili would be forever grateful. There was something to be said for illusions.

When he died she'd wanted to die with him. Night after night she would lie awake in the enormous bed, waiting to hear the hushed sound of his footsteps as he made his way down the hall to the room they'd shared. *Just tell me what you want me to do,* she would have said to him if she had the chance. *Tell me who you want me to be and I'll be her.*

Looking back, it seemed that everything had changed on that fateful day when she made the impromptu presentations for the R and D team. For the first time in her life she'd felt as if she'd found her niche and she'd wanted Carter to share her excitement. She knew it wasn't her native brilliance that had dazzled everybody; it was a question of being the right person in the right place at the right moment in time. Mayfair had needed a glamorous diversion to draw the media's eye from falling revenues. Who better than the owner's wife—even if the owner himself couldn't quite bring himself to see it.

Carter had been downright meek the morning after she'd first caught him using cocaine...the morning after he'd tried to rape her. He'd apologized profusely and when she couldn't bring herself to forgive him, he'd filled the penthouse apartment with lilies of every variety, flown there from the four corners of the globe. It was the type of grand gesture he did so well and, despite herself, Lili had been charmed.

"You had your moment yesterday when you talked to the board," he'd said as they lay together in their big wide bed after making love. "Now settle back down and be my wife."

But she couldn't. She was enough of a survivor to know that when things were going wrong you couldn't turn away from the solution—especially not when that solution was you.

She had been swept up into a whirlwind of coast-to-coast PR junkets, print and television interviews, speeches made to women's groups from Alabama to Wyoming. They called her a natural, an Estée for the eighties. She spent three weeks out of each month on the road and after a while she wondered if her husband even noticed she was gone.

I'm doing it for you, Carter, she had thought at first. *For Grant's future.* And then, to her surprise, one day she realized she was doing it for herself.

No one seemed to realize she was learning on the fly, substituting ambition for fear, and sheer grit for knowledge. The best thing she had going for her was the one thing no one at Mayfair was willing to admit: she understood the average working woman because she'd been one of them.

"Forget Harvard Business School," *Vanity Fair* had trumpeted in their Women To Watch issue back in 1984. "Lili Spaulding has a manicured finger on the pulse of the American woman and may just help resuscitate a flat-lining cosmetics giant."

Lili. She couldn't remember when she started spelling her name that way but it wasn't long after her marriage. The name Lilly Ann carried the swampy smell of Euless with it and, as far as she was concerned, Euless had ceased to exist.

Two years ago their corporate identity had changed from Mayfair to Lili! International, a strategic move calculated to aggressively enter the global marketplace with none of the baggage from the past to slow them down. There was even talk of marketing her image in the women's slicks, an idea that thrilled Lili to her core.

Power was intoxicating. Anyone who denied that fact was lying. Lili enjoyed striding into a boardroom, knowing that she held the futures of the men assembled around the polished cherry wood table in the palm of her perfectly manicured hand. Those years of watching and listening, the NYU classes and the hours spent in the library had paid off in spades. She might not have found happiness in her forty-nine years on this earth but she'd found power and that was more than most women could say after a lifetime.

She nursed her wine, trying not to glance at her watch. Grant was not known for his punctuality. As it was, she needn't have worried. He was only fifteen minutes late which, for her son, was tantamount to an early arrival. Her eye was drawn to him the second he entered the restaurant and so were the eyes of every other woman in the place. Thirty-three-year-old Grant Spaulding had been blessed by the gods. The promise inherent in the boy she'd first met had been fulfilled in the man and the results were impressive.

Charisma, Lili thought as he made his way to their table. An overused word but one for which there was no substitute. Grant glowed from within, as if a spotlight had been installed in his sternum at birth. He commanded attention simply by virtue of his existence. It was both his greatest gift and greatest liability.

"Looking beautiful as always." He kissed her warmly on each cheek.

"You need a haircut, darling. That shaggy look is painfully outdated."

"Point well taken. I'll see Ambrose after lunch." He claimed the chair next to her.

"How charming you are when you're being agreeable." She patted his hand. "There's hope for you yet."

He motioned for the waiter with a casual gesture that tugged at Lili's heart. It was his father's gesture, both offhand and imperious, to the manner born.

Grant ordered an intricately specific martini while Lili opted for another glass of white wine. The waiter hurried off.

"Martini?" she asked, eyebrows raised. "I thought you were strictly beer and tequila."

"I took your advice to heart."

"Martini advice?"

"On life, sweet stepmother." He took her hand in his then raised it to his lips. "On growing up."

"What is that for?" she asked, charmed to her toes by the courtly gesture. If the boy could bottle that charm, he could rule the world.

"For saving my sorry ass."

Relief washed over her like a spring shower. "You'll stop seeing Felicia Weatherly." Felicia was the only daughter of Mr. and Mrs. Paul Weatherly of the Newport Weatherlys. She was sweet, agreeable, and all wrong for Lili's boy.

"Actually I thought I'd marry her."

Lili stared at him for a second then burst into hearty laughter. "Felicia wouldn't survive a year with you, my wild child. She would be seriously overmatched."

A wicked twinkle danced in his bright blue eyes. "Felicia is helping me change my evil ways."

"If I have enjoyed only limited success in that endeavor, the poor girl doesn't stand a chance."

"I think we're a good match."

Her relief was rapidly evaporating. Was there any possibility that the boy was serious? "She's not for you, darling. You need more of a challenge." A strong woman who would keep him on a short lead.

He met her eyes. "She's pregnant."

"Oh, God. . . ." She felt as if he'd knocked the breath from her body with his words. His expression remained frustratingly blank as she forced air back into her lungs. "Fine. This isn't the end of the world. You made a mistake. We can deal with this."

"She won't have an abortion."

"Nobody is asking her to have an abortion." Was it possible he loved the girl? She had to tread carefully. "There are other alternatives."

"Forget it."

She raised a hand. "Hear me out."

"No," he said. "*You* hear *me* out. This is what I want."

"Ridiculous." She made a dismissive gesture. "You can't possibly know what you want."

"That's where you're wrong, my darling Lili. I've always known exactly what I've wanted."

"Yes, and much of what you've wanted over the years has been illegal." She thanked God he had turned away from drugs not long after graduating college. She would walk through fire to make certain that Grant didn't end up the way his father had.

"Past history."

"Perhaps." She loved him but she wasn't blind to his weaknesses. "Unfortunately past history has a way of popping up when you least expect it."

"Take a look at Ted Kennedy," he countered. "Chappaquiddick didn't stop him for long, did it?"

"A singularly poor example."

"Like hell. Rose's youngest is a role model for resurrection."

She lit a cigarette and deliberately refrained from offering one to her stepson. "Perhaps it's time for you to rethink your choice of role models, darling. Teddy can be a charming man but I wouldn't recommend you follow his example."

Grant leaned back in his seat and motioned for another martini. "I intend to learn from his mistakes."

"Pray God you never make a mistake of that magnitude."

"Hell, I don't plan on making *any* mistakes."

"What do you call getting Felicia Weatherly pregnant?"

His swashbuckling smile returned. "I call it, Step One."

For two hours Grant laid his life plan on the table for his stepmother along with their arugula salads and poached chicken breasts.

"We both know I'm not cut out for corporate life," he said flatly. He needed more excitement than that. He needed to walk the tightrope on a daily basis and what better way than to throw his hat in the political ring.

"You're too young to run for office," Lili said. "Aren't you?"

"I'm thirty-four. Next year I could run for president."

"Good God," she said, rolling her eyes. "I wouldn't wish that on my worst enemy."

"Don't worry. I'm willing to start small." A seat in the House would be a nice jumping-off spot. "Felicia and I will buy a house in Westchester, establish residency and a base of operations for the '96 election." With some careful planning, no one would see the shadows of his checkered past peeking through the brand new paint job. He'd managed to dodge more than his share of bullets, from his days in the juvenile drug trade at prep school to his adult sexual escapades. Over the years he'd learned how to cover his tracks and he had no reason to believe his luck wouldn't hold.

"What about the company?"

"I'll stay on until the election." Voters held rich men's sons to a high standard. They actually expected them to hold down jobs.

He had it all figured out, right down to what politically correct social issue he would embrace as his own.

"Please don't make it animal rights," she said wryly.

"And put us all out of business? Not bloody likely." Better to blind a rabbit than a woman with a good lawyer.

She told him about her encounter with a protester in front of the restaurant. "Have there been any more incidents out at the plant?"

He gestured for another round of drinks. "A lot of threats from PETA imitators, but only a few break-ins with moderate damage. We've upped security at Somerset and Holbrook but now that we have FDA approval, I expect things will ease up."

Lili outlined her plans for the launch of Night-Way while his mind wandered.

Marrying Lili was the smartest thing his old man had ever done. If it weren't for her, the family company would have died along with his father.

Dying was the second smartest thing his old man had ever done, at least as far as Grant's future was concerned. The day after Carter's funeral, Grant had petitioned Lili for a chance to prove himself and she'd let him take over the R and D department.

For the most part R and D ran itself, which suited him just fine. He'd caught on quickly to the overkill mentality of the tech types. If one round of tests was good, ten rounds of tests were even better. Hell, if you kept looking, you could probably find something wrong with breast milk. He made sure their testing procedures followed government regulations to the letter but he'd be damned if he pissed away the company's assets, hunting for problems that weren't there.

Political campaigns were costly and this was his last chance to skim a little profit off the top before the company went public and he had the SEC breathing down his neck.

At least he didn't have to worry about any greedy siblings crawling out of the woodwork to grab a piece of the pie. Carter had never managed to get Lili pregnant and, as far as Grant knew, he hadn't managed to get any one else pregnant either before he died. Being an only child had some definite advantages—

"Darling." Lili's voice broke into his thoughts. "Enough of this pleasant chitchat. We have business to attend to."

"I thought that's what we were doing," he said. "Attending to business."

Her smile lit up her eyes. "For once I don't mean Lili! We have a wedding to plan."

"You'll support my decision?" She'd made her opinion of Felicia painfully clear.

"Did you ever believe I wouldn't, darling? I told you years ago that I'd never let you down and that promise still holds."

He lifted his glass in salute. "To the best stepmother a man ever had."

Rich, loyal and sterile. It just didn't get any better than that.

22

Five hundred and thirty of Lili's nearest and dearest friends attended the wedding of her son Grant Landon Spaulding to Felicia Weatherly on the first Saturday in April. The ceremony was performed by Reverend Doctor Terhune at Saint James Episcopal Church and when it was over the happy couple, and their five hundred and thirty friends, repaired to the Waldorf-Astoria for a reception that Lili intended to be the talk of the city for years to come.

The Weatherlys had wanted the wedding to be held in Newport but Lili would hear none of it. Manhattan was the center of the universe, she'd insisted. At the very least it was the center of the only part of the universe that mattered.

Although Lili had been reluctant to accept the fact that Grant was marrying a woman she hadn't handpicked for him, she had to admit he'd done well for himself. Felicia was a pretty little thing. She looked positively angelic in her Priscilla of Boston wedding gown with the Juliet sleeves and full, billowing skirts that masked her pregnancy. And, even more important, discreet sleuthing proved that the baby she carried could belong only to Grant.

There was nothing dangerous about Felicia. No dark secrets to leap out and destroy a husband's career. She would be content to live by Grant's side, to raise his children and look at him adoringly as he climbed the ladder of political success. And if she didn't have the strength to keep him in line, that was no problem because Lili would be more than happy to do it for her.

All in all, Lili was relieved. One year ago Grant had been heading toward utter disaster. His hedonistic ways had gotten him into one scrape after another and it was only a matter of time before he ruined his reputation so thoroughly that no amount of laundering could wash away the stains. Without the veneer of a wife and child, Grant would never be seen as more than a rich man's son and they both wanted a great deal more for him than that.

Music and laughter swirled around Lili as she sat at her place of honor at the head table. Correction, she thought. As she sat *alone*. Carter was dead. Grant was starting his new life. Whit was sunning himself on some Caribbean beach. And there she was, the mother of the groom and keeper of the checkbook, and she didn't even have an escort for the wedding.

Across the ballroom Grant caught her eye. She lifted her glass in salute. He grinned, said something to Felicia, then started across the crowded ballroom toward Lili. Everything about her son was larger than life. He occupied more space than other men, both literally and figuratively, and he commanded more attention. There was a sense of destiny about him that not even his loudest detractors could deny.

"This is our dance, Mother," he said. He smiled and his even white teeth gleamed in the glow of the candles that lit the room.

Lili's happiness knew no bounds. She took his hand and followed him onto the floor.

"You look beautiful tonight," he said as he swept her up into the rhythm of the waltz.

"I wanted to do you proud."

"You succeeded."

Suddenly she found herself catapulted back in time to those first heady days with Carter. "You have your father's smile, darling." She touched his cheek affectionately. Time had softened much of the disappointment she'd felt during her marriage. "I wish he were here to share this day with us."

"Felicia's father has his eye on you." As always, Grant bypassed talk of his own. "He said it wasn't often that the mother of the groom gave the bride a run for her money."

"Take care with Paul," she warned, pushing down memories of the past. "Behind that hail-fellow-well-met exterior lies a man who will be watching everything you do from this point on. You don't dare put a foot wrong."

"And when was the last time that happened?"

Lili couldn't help but laugh. "I only know the last time you were caught."

"Sylvie Rothman," he said, "It won't happen again."

"It *can't* happen again. Not if our plans for your future are going to succeed."

"You worry too much," he said, spinning her around in a dizzying turn. "Nothing's going to stop me now, Lili. I'm on my way to the top."

Whitman Paley stood in the archway to the ballroom and surveyed the scene. From the champagne to the squab to the soft glow of candlelight at each table, every last detail had been accounted for by a master. He almost pitied Mrs. Weatherly. The mother of the bride hadn't stood a chance against that elegant juggernaut named Lili Spaulding. The room resonated with a certain high-gloss glamour that fell just to the right side of being vulgar.

It was something the woman had in common with the room.

He watched as Lili laughed with Dayton Fox, one of the Mayfair money men. Somewhere beneath all that polished perfection was the girl he'd met nineteen years ago but he'd be damned if he could find her.

"Sir?" A white-jacketed waiter appeared at his elbow.

Whit helped himself to a flute of champagne then nodded his thanks. The Weatherlys were an old Newport family, which meant they were long on pedigree and short on cash. He was certain Lili had not only orchestrated her stepson's wedding reception but paid for it as well. He'd learned a long time ago that there was nothing she wouldn't do for Grant, a fact that Whit found disturbing on a professional as well as personal level.

While Carter was alive, Grant had been held accountable for at least a small percentage of his actions. No saint himself, Carter had still expected a certain degree of responsibility from his only child. Not so Lili. The sun rose and set on the son of a bitch and, short of mass murder, Whit had no doubt Lili would forgive her stepson any transgression.

Nodding toward an acquaintance whose name he couldn't remember, he made his way across the crowded dance floor toward Lili. She was in the arms of a Revlon exec, looking up at him as if the sun rose and set above his graying head. Whit knew she was determined to woo her dance partner over to the fold and, from the way the guy was beaming at Lili, she'd probably have him signed, sealed, and delivered before Grant's new bride cut the cake.

He tapped the exec on the shoulder. "May I cut in?"

"Whit!" Lili was in his arms an instant later. "I didn't think you were going to be here."

"Neither did I," he said as she embraced him. "It was a last minute thing."

"Your timing left a lot to be desired. Aronson was teetering on the brink of saying goodbye to Revlon." She pressed a kiss to his cheek. It wasn't close to being enough but it was more than he'd dared to dream about. "Still, I'm glad you're here."

"So am I," he said, drawing her into his arms. She was all gentle curves and taut muscle, as paradoxical in flesh as she was in personality.

"Sorry," she murmured as they started off on the wrong beat. "I think we're a bit rusty."

"It's been a long time," he said, adjusting his rhythm to match hers.

"I know," she said softly. "I've missed you."

He met her eyes. "Have you, Lil?"

"What a question!" Her laughter held a note of surprise. "Of course, I've missed you."

"I wasn't sure you'd notice I was gone."

"Fishing for compliments, are you? That's not like you."

"I've been gone for six months, Lil. A man likes to know someone noticed."

"How much champagne have you had? You sound downright maudlin."

"Weddings bring out the best in me. I'm sure Grant will be a model husband."

"If you're going to criticize my son, I don't want to hear it."

"Why would I criticize him?" Whit asked, unable to curb his temper. "He's a paragon of virtue."

"For God's sake—" She tried to pull away but he wouldn't let her. "If you can't be happy for him today, you have no business being here."

"I didn't come here to toast the happy couple," he said. "I came here to see you."

He heard her inhale sharply.

He lifted a brow. "That can't be a big surprise to you, Lil."

"Of course it's a big surprise. I haven't heard a word from you since you said you were taking a sabbatical."

"I said everything that needed to be said before I left."

"That isn't how I remember it." Her voice held the edge of anger he'd heard her use in the boardroom.

"I asked you to marry me, Lil, and you said no."

"We both know that wasn't a legitimate proposal."

"I'm too old to get down on one knee," he said, "if that's what you mean, but it was legitimate. Don't think otherwise."

She didn't crack a smile. "You knew I was still mourning Carter."

"I know that's what you said."

"What's that supposed to mean?"

"Don't pretend with me, Lil. We both know the truth about Carter."

"I'm not going to have this conversation. I'm here to celebrate my son's marriage."

He inclined his head. People were beginning to notice and what he had to say wasn't for public consumption. "As you wish, Mrs. Spaulding."

"What *is* the matter with you?" she snapped. "You're not acting like yourself at all."

"That's what a sabbatical can do for you," he said as they applauded the orchestra. "My tolerance for bullshit is at an all-time low."

She met his eyes and to his surprise she started to laugh. Full, throaty, the kind of woman's laugh he hadn't heard in a very long time. "We'll talk later," she said as the mayor walked toward them. She hadn't moved a muscle but he could sense that she'd left him behind. "After the reception."

"The Presidential Suite," he said softly. "I'll be waiting for you."

Same as he'd been doing for the last nineteen years.

Grant's bride of six hours was busy working the room, kissing maiden aunts and flattering aging uncles, making sure everyone felt appreciated. He'd been right about her all along. Not only was she endowed with a spectacular trust fund, she had a well-developed sense of noblesse oblige that would make her an invaluable asset in political circles. People really didn't want their leaders to be one of the guys. Jimmy Carter's and Gerald Ford's execrable presidencies should have proved that beyond a reasonable doubt. Somewhere deep in the collective unconscious, the unwashed masses recognized their basic inadequacy and turned toward the elite to guide them. An altogether admirable tradition in Grant's opinion.

Felicia reminded Grant of a young Jacqueline Kennedy Onassis. She didn't possess the woman's leonine dark beauty but she did share that mysterious serenity that drew people to her, even as it kept them at arm's length.

And she was fertile.

All in all, he'd done damn well for himself. This time next year he'd be a legitimate family man, with the house in Westchester, the pedigree wife, and a child to link him with the next generation.

His master plan was right on schedule. Now if he could just shake the feeling something was lurking in the shadows, ready to bite him in the ass, he would actually be downright happy. Frank DeVito, from the R and D department at Lili! had paid him another visit on Wednesday, armed with facts and figures meant to put the fear of God and lawsuits into Grant's black heart. DeVito was dead certain that CG-47, the key ingredient in the new Night-Way line, had the potential to cause irreversible chromosomal damage to fetuses.

"The testing process hasn't turned up any problems," Grant said, his cool demeanor masking his unease. "We expect full FDA approval by the end of the year."

DeVito spewed a frightening stream of facts and figures but Grant turned a selectively deaf ear. If he encouraged the man, he would never be rid of him.

After DeVito left, Grant had picked up the phone and called Dan Jarreau, his political image consultant, and laid the whole mess out for him.

"Quit worrying," Jarreau advised. "The launch date is after the election. If there's a problem with Night-Way, we'll take care of it during the campaign and get some mileage out of it while we're at it."

Grant would be the knight on a white charger, putting consumers' health over the crass concerns of business and profit. He could see himself now, shutting down production in order to save innocent women and children from harm. It was almost enough to make Grant hope Frank DeVito was right about his suspicions.

Someone tapped him on the shoulder. He turned around to see Felicia's maid of honor Nina smiling up at him. They'd been enjoying an ongoing flirtation for months now, the kind that usually led to great sex sooner or later.

"Lili told me to tell you they'll be wheeling in the cake in fifteen minutes."

Her dress dipped low at the bodice, exposing the tops of her ripe young breasts and impressive cleavage. His blood flow shifted south. "Fifteen minutes isn't a long time," he said.

Her gaze traveled down the length of his body. "It's long enough if you do it right."

He motioned for her to follow him then walked casually toward an exit at the far corner of the room. From there, the corridor led through the back of the Waldorf's service kitchen and into a storage room.

"It's awfully dark back here," she said, giggling. "I can barely see you."

Grant pulled her up against him, his hands cupping her buttocks through the billows of satin and lace. "You don't have to see me, Nina. Just feel me."

She giggled again. He wouldn't have pegged her as the type. She had the icy blond good looks that usually came with a sangfroid that matched his own.

"I can't believe we're doing this," she said, her eager little hands groping for the zipper on his trousers. "The last thing I want to do is hurt Felicia."

He ignored the comment. If she was so concerned about Felicia, what was she doing with her hand in his pants?

He pressed Nina up against the wall and covered her mouth with his. Her lips parted eagerly. A bit too eagerly for his taste. He usually preferred a struggle, a show of resistance that made the taking sweeter. This time the element of risk would have to be enough to push him over the top.

The inside of her mouth tasted like hot champagne as he stroked the silky cavern with his tongue. He would have preferred burying his face between her legs but there wasn't time for preliminaries. His bride was expecting him to be by her side in less than ten minutes for the cutting of the cake and he wouldn't disappoint.

He lifted her skirts and drew his hand up the length of her thigh. She wasn't wearing panties. Another disappointment. The sound of ripping lace had an aphrodisiac effect on him.

Still, Nina had other attractions. Fair-skinned blondes usually had a childlike nest of gentle curls, but not this girl. The curls covering her mound were thick and soft, like a down pillow. They tickled his palm as he parted her lips then entered her with his middle finger. She was tight and throbbing and ready. It was good, but still not good enough.

"C'mon, baby," he said, breaking the kiss. "Open wide and let me in."

Using the wall behind her for support, he held her by the waist as she wrapped her long slender legs around his hips then lowered herself onto him. In the semi-darkness he watched as her head dropped back, eyes closed in ecstasy. A low, rolling moan built inside his throat as she tightened her muscles around him, quick bursts of powerful sensation that made him feel as if the top of his head were going to explode. Apparently Felicia's best friend had picked up a few party tricks along the way.

Suddenly she stopped moving. "What was that?" she whispered.

His fingers gripped her buttocks more tightly and he arched upward like a heat-seeking missile.

"Grant!" She placed her hands against his chest. "I hear someone."

"I don't."

"Listen."

A woman's voice sounded on the other side of the wall. "...and you *must* serve the coffee *precisely* at nine-fifteen..."

"That's your mother!" The girl struggled against him but her body clutched him tighter. "Oh, my God, what if she sees us?"

He thought about Lili watching as he slid in and out of his wife's best friend. The image didn't do much for him. He'd rather think about the time he saw her down on her knees for his old man. That came close to doing it for him but it wasn't enough.

"...I'm sure he'll be here any second, Mrs. Spaulding. Grant wouldn't disappoint me." His bride's voice floated toward him, not fifty feet from where he stood fucking her best friend.

That was all he needed. Nina gasped as he drove into her but she matched him stroke for stroke.

All things considered, his wedding night was off to a great start.

23

It was nearly midnight by the time the last wedding guest said goodbye.

Lili sat in the darkened, empty ballroom and nursed her champagne. She'd reached her limit three glasses ago but this was a special occasion and you always celebrated special occasions with an excess of champagne.

Grant and Felicia were long gone, on their way to Belize or Saint Martin or whatever romantic Caribbean destination he'd chosen for their honeymoon, vanished in a hail of rice and rose petals and wishes for a long and happy lifetime together. It was enough to make her weep.

Weddings had a way of making you take stock of your life and Lili discovered she was not immune. She'd found herself thinking about Grandma Hattie and the people in Euless who'd never believed she'd make anything of herself, but instead of feeling triumphant about her success, she felt strangely deflated, as if someone had taken away a vital part of her soul.

Five hundred and thirty close friends and nobody there beside her when she turned off the light. She was forty-nine years old. In a few months she would be fifty. Her life was half over—and that was being generous. She longed for someone to touch her, to hold her close. Someone who would tell her it was going to be all right.

Whit. She knew she hadn't imagined the look in his eyes. He wanted her. He'd wanted her for ages but the timing between them had never been right. Was it possible that the moment had finally arrived?

She reached for someone else's half-empty glass of champagne then polished it off before she could consider to whom it had belonged. She needed something to give her courage because if her dearest friend didn't want her anymore she didn't know where she would turn.

"Lil." Whit stood in the doorway to his suite of rooms. He wore one of the hotel's luxurious terry-cloth robes that hit him midcalf. His graying hair was damp, curling around his ears and along the nape of his neck. "I was expecting room service."

Lili, almost prostrate with nerves, smiled up at him. "Disappointed?"

"Surprised."

Her smile began to falter. "May I come in?"

He stepped back as if she'd poked him with a cattle prod. "My apologies," he said, opening the door wide. "Please."

She hesitated then silently chided herself for being such a fool. What on earth was she so afraid of? This was Whit, after all. Just Whit.

She swept into the room, dangling her strappy pumps from her fingertips. "No music?" she asked, tilting her head to the side. "I think you still owe me a dance."

He closed the door then followed her into the living room.

"You smell divine," she said, angling her smile into something sharper, more powerful. "What is it?"

"Something new, Lil," he said, crossing the room to the window. "It's called soap and water."

Her merry laugh rang out. "We've been looking for a new men's scent. Maybe we should bottle you, darling."

He offered up a polite smile then poured himself a drink. "Would you like something, Lil?"

"Do you have champagne?"

"Scotch, vodka or rum. Take your pick."

You, she thought but didn't say. *I'll take you.* "Whichever goes best with the bubbly."

"Water," he said, reaching for a bottle of Perrier. "That's what goes best with the bubbly. I think you've had enough."

Take it down a notch, she warned herself. *Don't push so hard.* She wasn't Lilly Ann Barnett anymore and he wasn't Carter Spaulding. This was Whit, after all. He knew her, warts and all. He even knew about the baby she'd given away all those years ago. She didn't have to impress him. He already loved her. Hadn't he told her so? Six months on a Caribbean beach couldn't change that.

He handed her a tumbler of mineral water. "Not terribly exciting," she remarked, wrinkling her nose at the slightly metallic aftertaste.

"It's not meant to be."

She settled herself down on one of the sofas and crossed her legs. Gravity was having its way with her in other areas but her showgirl legs were still worth displaying. "So what did you order from room service?"

He said nothing, just stood near the window, looking down at his whiskey or whatever it was he had in his tumbler. A terrible thought occurred to her and she glanced toward the closed bedroom door.

"Oh, my God," she said. "Have I interrupted something?"

"Why are you here, Lil?" His tone was weary and she was reminded of those last miserable scenes in *Gone with the Wind,* where Rhett Butler tells Scarlett it's too late.

"Am I mistaken, darling, or didn't you invite me to join you?"

"That's not what I mean."

She took another sip of that miserable water. "No, I don't suppose it is."

The silence between them was as wide and deep as the ocean. She wanted to tell him that she was so lonely she thought her heart would break but her pride wouldn't let her say the words. *Don't you know why I'm here, Whit? After all these years, do I really have to tell you?*

He spoke first. "So the wedding's over, is it?"

"Everything except paying for it."

"That shouldn't prove to be a problem."

"You're right," she said. "Thank God, it isn't."

"How do you think you'll like being a grandmother?"

"You know about Felicia?"

He looked at her and chuckled. "Lil, everyone knows about Felicia."

"Not that it matters," she said quickly. "Half the brides in this country are pregnant on their wedding day."

"Grant looked pleased with himself."

"He's very much in love," she said, daring Whit to challenge her statement. "I'm sure he's on top of the world."

Whit polished off his whiskey then poured himself another one. "And now what?"

Lili shrugged her shoulders. This certainly wasn't going quite the way she'd expected it to. "I assume they'll enjoy a wonderful honeymoon."

"That isn't what I meant."

"I didn't think so." She sighed, a long slow exhalation of breath that seemed to use up the last of her energy. "I think I should leave." She reached down and retrieved her shoes, struggling to fasten the fragile straps. "Oh, damn," she said as tears filled her eyes. "Damn."

He bent down in front of her, that beautiful elegant man, and encircled her right ankle with his fingers, causing a tremor to move through her body. She placed her hand atop his head; his hair was silky and damp against her fingertips. Her mind seemed to empty of everything but sheer physical sensation. It had been so long since anyone had touched her—she and Carter had stopped sleeping together five years before he died and there hadn't been another man since.

Whit pressed his lips against the rise of her instep and arrows of sensation pierced her skin. He moved from the instep to the ankle, from the ankle to the firm muscle of her calf, and she bit down hard on the inside of her cheek to keep from crying out with a terrifying combination of fear and pleasure. He slid a hand under the hem of her skirt, skimming his fingers along her silk-clad thighs, his fingers teasing...probing... gently toying with one of her satin garters.

She prayed he wouldn't speak. Words would destroy the magic and she was in sore need of magic, hungry in both body and soul for something she hadn't realized she needed until it was long gone. She sat there motionless, afraid that movement would break the spell. There were so few perfect moments in a woman's lifetime and this was so close to being perfect that she thought her poor battered heart would crash through her chest and fly away.

He touched. He stroked. He caressed. He didn't remove her clothes or his. She was a trembling, whimpering mass of nerve endings by the time he took her hand and led her into the bedroom.

She cried openly when he began to undress her. Her gown dropped to the floor, leaving her nearly naked and exposed in her stockings and garter belt and demicup bra. She wasn't a girl any longer or even a young woman. Where once she'd been firm and beautiful, she was now soft and imperfect. She felt the loss deep in her soul, for both of them, for all the years that had slipped through her fingers while she mourned the death of her marriage.

He stripped off his robe and let it drop to the floor next to her dress and moments later they were both naked.

"I wish I were young again," she whispered, her mouth open and hungry against his shoulder. "I wish I could be the woman I was."

There were no words of praise from Whit. He made no attempt to convince her she was beautiful. Instead he swept her up into his arms and carried her to the bed. His body was strong and well-proportioned. Late middle-age had softened his belly and widened his waist but he was wonderful to look at and even more wonderful to touch. Her skin was hungry for him as she ran her hands across his furry, graying chest, palms skimming his flat male nipples, tracing the swell of muscle at his shoulders. How glorious he must have been when he was in his prime.

She smelled his neck, his chest. She dipped her tongue into the well of his navel and tickled her cheek against the tapering mat of hair angling down his belly. He moved against her, then, gripping her by the shoulders, he rolled her onto her back.

"I wasn't finished," she said, teasing him as he knelt between her thighs.

"If you kept doing that, I would have been."

She closed her eyes as he entered her body, overwhelmed by the knowledge that for the first time in years she wasn't alone.

Few experiences in a man's life live up to expectations. For Whit Paley, however, this was one of them. The texture of her skin, her smell, the sounds she made, the suppleness of her shapely limbs—she was all he'd dreamed about and more. Almost twenty years had gone by since the day he first saw her in her blue cotton dress and she was more beautiful to him now, more womanly . . . and maybe she was finally his.

They hadn't reinvented the wheel or discovered new and exotic ways for a man and a woman to come together. They'd been clumsy sometimes and hasty at others, but they'd never once lost sight of the miracle they'd found in each other's arms. He was in his sixties and the future suddenly seemed as bright as it had when he was twenty-one.

She murmured something in her sleep and burrowed her nose deeper into his armpit. He pulled the covers up over her shoulders and cradled her closer. Her hair smelled faintly of gardenias. Years ago he'd given a date a corsage of gardenias and helped her pin it to the bodice of her dance dress. The back of his hand had brushed the curve of her soft breasts and a shock had rippled through his body that he remembered to this day.

Nothing he had ever done with a woman since had had a greater, more memorable effect on him.

Until tonight.

Holding Lili while she slept touched something in him that not even the act of making love had been able to do. Real emotion sometimes got overwhelmed in the excitement of new tastes and scents and sounds. But when you could hold a sleeping woman and feel as if you'd hung the moon—that's when a man knew he'd stumbled onto something very special.

A few hours earlier he'd thought it was over. He'd called the airlines and booked a flight back to Barbados. She'd been brittle and aloof, more interested in doing business than welcoming home an old friend. He'd watched her closely enough over the years to recognize when she was in overdrive, pushing toward another goal that only a powerhouse like Lili could possibly attain. He wanted to tell her to slow down, that she'd brought Mayfair back from the dead and that should be enough for one lifetime but she hadn't given him the chance.

In typical fashion, she showed up on his doorstep and changed his life forever.

Lili was fastening the strap on her right shoe when Whit woke up. She'd hoped to make a graceful exit without having to face him, but apparently that wasn't to be.

"Lil?" He sounded sleepy, his voice husky and quite appealing. "What are you doing?"

She walked over to his side of the bed and brushed a lock of hair back from his forehead. "I don't want to overstay my welcome," she said lightly, praying he wouldn't press the issue.

He encircled her wrist with his fingers and drew her closer. "It's still dark outside. Come back to bed."

"I wish I could but I must get home." She didn't mean to sound so formal but she was struggling to find a way to steel herself against temptation.

He leaned up on one elbow. "There's no one there waiting for you, Lil."

"I have a meeting tomorrow morning. I have to shower, change my clothes—"

"Tomorrow's Sunday."

"Whit, I—"

"Marry me, Lil."

"Please." Her voice was a whisper. "Don't say that."

"Marry me," he repeated. "That's where this is going, Lil. Why wait?"

"Good Lord, Whit. Aren't you moving too fast?"

"Nineteen years," he reminded her. "We're not kids anymore. There's nothing to stop us from packing our bags and moving to Barbados permanently."

"Barbados?" She stood up and began pacing the room. "You can't be serious."

"Damn right I'm serious." He leaned back against the pillows, his eyes never leaving hers. "It's a different world down there, Lil. I have a villa not too far from Sandy Lane that opens onto the most beautiful stretch of beach you've ever seen."

"That sounds like a wonderful vacation place," she said carefully.

"It can be more than that. We could make a life there."

She drew in a deep breath. "I have a life, darling, right here in Manhattan."

"Chuck it."

"Now, you're being ridiculous."

"The hell I am." He swung his legs from the bed, draping the top sheet over his midsection in a display of modesty she found affecting. "It's time to move on, Lil. Sell your share of the company and start over with me. I'll sign a prenup. You can live off my money."

"I couldn't possibly do that," she managed. "You know about the changes in store for the company next year. Going public, the launch of Night-Way—how could I possibly walk away?"

"One foot in front of the other, Lil. The same way I'm going to do it."

She stopped near the window and turned to face him. "I had hoped your sabbatical was over." She'd hated these last six months without his shoulder to lean on.

"It is," he said. "I'm turning in my resignation first thing Monday morning."

She crossed her arms over her chest. "I don't appreciate the threat."

"It's not a threat, Lil." She heard nothing but sadness in his voice and a knot of fear formed in the pit of her stomach. "It's something I've spent a hell of a lot of time thinking about."

"You can't leave us."

"I have to."

"New York is your home. You'd be miserable anywhere else."

"You're wrong, Lil."

"What if I won't let you quit? It's my company. I can make things difficult for you." She wasn't above pulling rank. Not when it came to keeping her dearest friend by her side.

"I'll leave anyway."

"You're serious, aren't you?"

"Dead serious, Lil."

"Do it for me," she urged. She knew she wasn't playing fair but fairness was out of her range at the moment. "I need you here, Whit."

"In your bed or in your life?"

"I'm not going to answer that." How could she tell him that what she'd found with him scared her senseless? She hated feeling vulnerable and suddenly it was as if every nerve ending in her body were exposed.

"I'm leaving this afternoon. Come with me."

"I can't, darling Whit." Her voice broke on the words. "You're asking too much of me. I have responsibilities here."

"Don't lie to yourself, Lil," he said in a harsh tone of voice she'd never heard before, "and don't lie to me."

Her back stiffened. "You, of all people, should know what's involved in running the company. I can't turn away."

"You don't want to turn away."

"I have responsibilities."

"To Grant?" He laughed out loud. "He's a bastard, Lil. Everyone knows it but you."

"Don't go any further," she warned. "Grant is my son."

"He's your *step*son."

"A distinction I don't choose to make."

"A distinction you should make. He has no loyalty to you, Lil. He had none toward his father and he has none to the company. He's conning you and you're too blind to see it."

"I'm not going to listen to this." She scooped up her purse from the nightstand. "You have no right to insult my family."

"Goddamit, he's not your family. Haven't you heard a word I've said?"

"He's as much my son as if I'd given birth to him," she snapped, "and I won't allow you to say terrible things about him."

"I'm not talking about blood, Lil, I'm talking about honor and integrity. He doesn't give a damn about you or the company and he never will."

"I've had enough, Whit. Call me when you can speak to me in a civil fashion." She started for the door again.

"I won't be calling you."

Lili hesitated. He couldn't possibly mean that. "Of course you'll call me. We'll talk tomorrow."

"No, Lil."

She turned back to face him. There was no lightness in his expression, only a terrible sense of sadness and resolve. "We need time to think." She gestured toward the rumpled bed. "What happened took us both by surprise."

"If you believe that, Lil, then we never had a chance." He stood up, knotting the top sheet around his waist. "You'll have my resignation in the morning."

His words hit her like a blow but her pride wouldn't let her show it. If his commitment to the company meant so little to him, then good riddance.

"Fine," she said at last, smoothing her skirt with the palm of her hand. She didn't need Whit Paley or anyone else telling her how to live her life. She gave the orders now and it was time everyone realized it. "Someone from Personnel will contact you about your pension."

"Have a nice life, Lil," he said as she turned once again to leave.

She didn't break stride. "I will," she replied with conviction. "Can you say the same thing?"

She didn't wait for an answer. She already knew the answer and it broke her heart.

24

Cincinnati, late September

Corey parked her rented car in front of Millicent's house. The driveway was blocked by an enormous red-and-white moving van loaded with crates of furniture bound for her mother's new home.

The end of an era, she thought as she tried to imagine the small frame house belonging to someone else. By this time tomorrow morning, Millicent would be ensconced in her retirement cottage overlooking the river, a sunny place with twenty-four hour security and doctors on call.

"It's the right thing to do," she murmured as she gathered up her belongings and swung open the driver's side door. The *only* thing to do. For the past three years Millicent had been in failing health and it was clear to everyone but Corey's mother that the time had come when she could no longer live alone. The broken hip from 1989 hadn't healed properly and now her diabetes had caused severe vision problems. Millicent was a proud woman and she'd refused all offers of help from Corey, who had volunteered to take over bill-paying chores and to arrange for someone to keep house. "I'm old but I'm not senile," Millicent had said in an out-of-character display of temper. "You mind your business, missy, and I'll mind mine."

Corey had even tried to convince Millicent to pull up stakes and move to Boston to be near her, but Millicent was having none of that, either.

"This is my home," she said stubbornly. "The only way I'll leave is in a pine box."

It took a foreclosure notice from the town to force the issue.

"I thought the house was mortgage-free," Corey had said to the bank president. "There must be some mistake." Her father had left a windfall in insurance, enough to pay off the house and change Corey's life. At least, that was what Millicent had told her. So why were there two mortgages outstanding and enough unpaid bills to choke Donald Trump?

"There's been no mistake, Ms. Banning." He went on to explain about the two mortgages that were in arrears, the taxes that had gone unpaid for almost four years. "We've given your mother every opportunity to straighten this out and she's refused us at every turn. I'm afraid it's out of our hands now."

Corey was doing extremely well at Baker, Boxford and Deane Advertising, but not well enough to pay off two mortgages and back taxes laden with penalties. Millicent had fallen behind every year since Jack's death. The bills had multiplied while Jack's tiny pension shrank in relation to escalating prices. Corey had had no choice but to allow the bank to foreclose on the house and then she used the opportunity to force Millicent into safer, more secure surroundings for which Corey would be financially responsible. It wasn't a perfect solution to the problem but it was certainly an improvement, even if her mother vehemently disagreed. She would do everything in her power to see that Millicent lived the rest of her life in comfort.

Is that your guilty conscience speaking? The last few years in Boston had been exciting ones and she was ashamed to admit that occasionally days went by when she didn't think about Millicent at all. Then she'd be overcome with remorse and would call her mother long-distance or send her a bouquet of flowers to assuage her own guilt.

And yet somehow Millicent understood. Corey had her own life now. She had a fabulous job and a beautiful place. Her social life wasn't the stuff of dreams but that was the way she wanted it. She knew from experience that she had lousy judgment when it came to men. Her three-month grad school marriage to Professor Henry Prescott was a perfect case in point. Henry was a good man and a great teacher, but even he would admit he was rotten husband material. She had simply been swayed by the amazing fact that someone had actually wanted her enough to marry her. Everyone had a fatal flaw; neediness was hers.

She longed for home and family. She wanted the comfort of dailiness, of knowing when she woke up in the morning the same familiar face would smile at her from the pillow next to hers. She wanted to raise a child to know the world was hers for the taking. Those dreams hadn't come true with Henry Prescott and as the years went on, she began to wonder whether they would ever come true.

Her marriage hadn't worked out but at least her career was going great guns. She poured all of her energies and intellect into what she did and BB and D rewarded her in kind. Maybe it couldn't fill the empty spot inside her heart but, then, she didn't really expect it to. That empty spot was part of who and what she was and she wouldn't know how to be Corey without it.

She gathered up her purse and briefcase and climbed from the car. Millicent had refused to take her calls these past few days and Corey knew she was about to walk into the eye of a particularly upsetting storm. Mentally she lined up her arguments designed to convince her mother of the wisdom of moving: the neighborhood was going downhill, there'd been three robberies across the street in the past six months—why, that small kitchen fire Millicent had started when she forgot the pot of rice on the stove was only a harbinger of worse things to come. She'd plead to her mother's common sense and, if all else failed, she'd stomp her feet and cry. No matter what, however, Millicent would be sleeping in her new home tonight.

"How is it going?" she called to one of the moving men as he jumped down from the truck.

His back was to her as he brushed dust from his shaggy blond hair. "Figure another two or three hours."

"Great," she said, heading up the driveway to the front door.

"Uh, wait a minute!" the mover called out as she stepped past him. "Are you Mrs. Banning's daughter?"

"Yes, I am."

He let out a low whistle. There was no denying the look of male interest in his eyes. "You're even prettier than your pictures." Millicent papered the house with photographs of Corey.

"Thanks," she said lightly. Blue-collar men were a great deal more direct than their white-collar counterparts. "I'd better not tell the photographer."

"Like I said, we'll be done before too long. What would you say to grabbing a beer later on?"

"I—uh, thanks for asking but I flew in to spend time with my mother." She had a degree from Ohio State and a Master's from Harvard Business. Wouldn't you think she'd have learned how to field a compliment somewhere along the way?

He looked her up and down in a blatantly sexual manner then grinned. "Hey, you can't blame a guy for asking."

"No," she said, grinning back despite herself. "You can't."

She walked slowly into the house, her body painfully, wonderfully alive to sensation. It was the same every time. Men flirted with her on line for the ATM, at the grocery store, from their cars when she was stuck in Boston traffic. Her female peers at BB and D complained loudly about what they called street harassment but Corey loved every single politically incorrect moment of it and always would.

For them it was an annoyance, but for Corey it was a miracle.

Hard to believe that nearly fifteen years had gone by since Millicent had surprised her with the money for plastic surgery. "Daddy had insurance I didn't know about," her mother had explained, barely able to conceal her excitement, "and I know exactly what we should do with it." Millicent said she owned the house free and clear and this insurance money was a windfall earmarked just for Corey.

She'd spent her entire life praying for a miracle and now that there was one within reach she discovered she was terrified. What if the surgery didn't work and she ended up worse off than before? What if the doctor took a look at her and said there was nothing he could do to help her? Or, the scariest possibility of all, what if the surgery was a success and nothing else changed? What if she was meant to stay on the outside looking in for the rest of her life and no amount of tempting fate could change it?

They fought for six months over it while Millicent dragged her from surgeon to surgeon, each of whom told Corey the same thing: "I can help you." She wanted to believe them. They took photographs and drew pictures and showed her before-and-after shots of patients whose faces had been even more

badly scarred than Corey's. Wonderful faces that were now so
normal and everyday average that you'd never look twice at
them in a crowd.

How amazing that had sounded to Corey. How far beyond
her reach.

It took three years and many operations, but Dr. Mario
Coscia had performed a miracle. "I haven't changed a thing,"
he told Corey. "All I did was restore the beauty that was always there."

But she hadn't been able to believe it. Every time she looked
in the mirror, a stranger looked back at her. The doctor had
warned her about this phenomenon but she never thought it
would happen to her. A period of mourning for the "old" Corey? The one she'd been so anxious to leave behind? She'd
known that crazy-quilt face so well, had been so totally defined by it, that without it she was as exposed and vulnerable
as a newborn baby.

"Give it time," Dr. Coscia had said as she cried in his office
every afternoon for the first month after the last procedure.
"You're the same woman you were before, Corey. Only the
packaging is different."

But that wasn't true. That change of packaging had created
a whole new person, one she didn't recognize either inside or
out. Life became easier for her. The process of getting through
each day carried fewer roadblocks, less ugliness. She went back
to school and threw herself into her studies, determined to
make up for twenty years of lost time. A new confidence filled
her; it was like being on a permanent adrenaline rush. And if
the new improved Corey still found it hard to make friends, at
least she knew they weren't laughing at her anymore.

She paused in the hallway and glanced around. How empty
it seemed without the telephone table near the foot of the
staircase and the big oak hat rack that had stood by the door for
as long as she could remember. She wrinkled her nose. The
place even smelled different, as if the sense memories of
Thanksgiving dinners and gingerbread men and thousands of
apple pies had been loaded on the truck along with the sofa and
chairs.

She closed her eyes and tried to conjure up the booming sound of her father's voice as he came through the front door after work. "Where are my girls?" he'd call out as he hung up his hat and coat. And she and Millicent would race out from the kitchen to hug him and welcome him home. Had any parents ever loved a child the way Millicent and Jack loved her?

Those had been good days. If only she hadn't been so angry and defensive, so unable to accept love when it was offered. She'd wasted so much time daydreaming about her birth mother, waiting for some fairy godmotherlike creature to swoop down into her life and make everything all right that she hadn't seen that in most of the ways that counted, her life was all right indeed. Millicent and Jack had handed her unconditional love on a silver platter that she had been somehow convinced was really tin.

"'Scuse me, miss." Two moving men lumbered through the hallway, carrying the Bannings' big pine kitchen table.

Corey quickly turned away. She'd never been very good at endings.

"Mom!" she called out from the foot of the staircase. She waited a moment and when there was no answer she hurried up to the second floor. Knowing her mother's feelings about moving, she guessed Millicent was in her bedroom, refusing to acknowledge what was going on around her. She was probably sitting in the rocking chair by the window, looking out at the yard Jack had been so very proud of.

Corey felt a combination of guilt and annoyance as she hurried down the hall. She should have seen to it that Millicent moved years ago. Ghosts were everywhere in that familiar house. It would do her mother good to move someplace where Jack's memory wasn't so vivid.

As she suspected, Millicent was in her bedroom. What she hadn't counted on was the fact that her mother was in bed with the covers pulled up under her chin.

"Mom?" Corey's heart thudded against her rib cage. "Are you asleep?" She looked so small and pale against the white sheets. Corey placed a hand on her mother's forearm. "Mom."

Millicent stirred slightly then opened her eyes. Corey had never seen an expression like that before. Millicent looked as if she had traveled back from a far place, a place where she wanted to return.

A terrible chill spread through Corey's chest.

"I'm glad you're here," Millicent said. Her voice was soft but her words were clearly spoken.

"So am I," Corey said breezily. "Now you'd better get up and get dressed or the moving men will load you and your bed on the truck."

"I'm not going."

"We've been through this before, Mom. You have no choice. As of tomorrow, the house belongs to the bank."

"This is my house and this is where I'm staying."

"This is the bank's house," Corey repeated, praying Millicent didn't know how frightened she was. "Your place is at Riverview Knolls."

"Honey, I know you mean well but I'm not going to Riverview Knolls. I'm not leaving this house ever again."

"Stop talking like that," Corey snapped. "This is absolutely ridiculous." She picked up the housedress that lay across the rocker by the window. "Now put this on, please, before the moving men catch you in your nightdress."

"Sit down, Catherine."

"Catherine?" she said, her voice catching on the familiar name. "I must be in big trouble if you're calling me Catherine." Millicent patted the side of the bed and, reluctantly, Corey sat down. "Mom, we really don't have time for girl talk right now. Can't it wait until we get you settled in your new place?"

"I love you, honey."

Corey started in surprise. "Wh-what?"

"I said, I love you."

"Of course you love me," she said, trying to make light of it. "I'm a very lovable person."

Millicent reached up and touched Corey's face with a sense of joy that almost brought her to tears. "So much like her," her mother said, more to herself than Corey.

"Like who?" Corey asked.

"So much to tell you—" Millicent's eyelids appeared to grow heavy and an instant later she drifted off into a deep sleep.

Corey heard a tap on the door.

"Miss?" The blond moving man stood in the doorway. "Can we start in here yet?" His glance moved from Corey to the sleeping woman and the twinkle in his eye quickly vanished.

"Very soon," she said. "I promise you."

He lingered a moment, as if he wanted to say something more, then turned and walked away.

Corey sat on the edge of the bed, holding her mother's hand, as the fear inside her threatened to break free. This couldn't be happening. People didn't climb into bed one day and decide to die. Millicent had seen the doctor only last week and he had confirmed that she was doing well on all counts. Corey's mother had her problems, it was true, but things seemed to be under control.

She glanced around the room. Nothing had changed in almost twenty-five years. The same rose print wallpaper. The same white chenille spread and pillow shams. She tried to find comfort in that but all she found was the growing certainty that her mother was slipping away from her and there wasn't a thing she could do to stop her.

She didn't know how long she sat there—it could have been minutes or hours. Finally Millicent's eyes fluttered open again and she looked at Corey.

"I don't want you to be sad," Millicent said, sounding almost cheerful. "I'm going to be with your daddy and that's a good thing."

"Sure you're going to be with Pop," Corey said, "but not this minute."

"Ah, honey." Millicent patted her hand. "You're doing fine now. I don't have to worry about you anymore."

But I'm not doing fine, she wanted to say. *I'm scared and lonely and I can't imagine how I'll manage without you.*

"I'm going to call the doctor," Corey said. "Maybe you're having some kind of reaction to your medications. There's probably something he can do to make you feel more chipper."

"In my nightstand," Millicent said. "All the papers you'll need."

"We packed them already, Mom. I won't let you forget anything." She stubbornly chose to misunderstand her mother's words. She'd seen the papers before, they had to do with burial plots and funeral arrangements, things she refused to let Millicent talk about.

"Un-under the bed," Millicent continued, her voice growing weaker. "A box..."

Corey lifted the corner of the spread and saw a large white box. It was tied with brown string and labeled For Corey in black marker.

"What is this?" Corey asked, forcing a smile. "Your wedding dress? I know I disappointed you when I eloped with Henry, but I promise you one day I'll—"

She stopped short. Millicent's eyes were closed. Corey felt a stabbing pain in her chest as she placed her fingers alongside her mother's throat. "Thank God," she whispered. A pulse, thready but there. She reached for the telephone on the nightstand but there was no dial tone. Service had already been disconnected. Sweat formed at the back of her neck and along her temples. She ran to the window and called down to the moving men. "I need help! Go next door and call for an ambulance!"

She raced back to Millicent's side. If possible, her mother's hand felt lighter, more insubstantial than it had moments ago. Corey rubbed it between her two hands, willing her own strength into her mother's body, though she knew it was a lost cause.

"Please, Mom, please... you have to hang on for me..." *I know I haven't been the kind of daughter you deserve but I can make it up to you if you'll give me the chance.*

Millicent stirred and Corey's heart leaped. There was still hope—there had to be.

"Mom, I called for an ambulance. You probably need to have your medication adjusted. If you feel this strongly about Riverview, we'll—"

"Hush, honey." Her mother's voice was as soft as a kiss. Corey had to lean close in order to make out her words. "You're... best... to me..."

Tears spilled down Corey's cheeks. *Please don't leave me, Mom. I'm so afraid of being alone.* "I'm going to remember all this at Christmas,'' she said, trying to make her mother laugh. "My stocking better be filled to bursting with goodies.''

Millicent smiled but it was a distant kind of smile, as if she'd moved beyond things like Christmas and silly stocking stuffers. As if she'd seen the place she wanted to be. "So... beautiful... like her.''

"Like who, Mom?''

Millicent moaned slightly and closed her eyes. In the distance Corey heard the wail of an ambulance. *Hurry,* she prayed. *Please hurry!*

"Mom!'' She shook Millicent gently by the shoulder. "Don't fall asleep on me.''

"... Lili... you shouldn't be alone—''

"Lily?'' Corey frowned. "What do you want with lilies?''

Millicent's breathing slowed.

"Mom!'' Corey shook her again. "Talk to me, please.''

Millicent didn't stir. Her mouth was curved in a gentle smile and the worry lines on her forehead seemed to have disappeared as if by magic.

"Oh, God, no!'' Suddenly she was the little girl nobody wanted, the little girl who'd wanted a family more than anything in the world. The little girl who'd been lucky enough to be loved by Millicent Banning.

She gathered Millicent's soft familiar body to her breast, cradling her mother the way she herself had been cradled all those years ago, and wished she'd found the words to tell her how much she loved her.

25

Boston

"We were sorry to hear about your loss,'' Charles Boxford said on Corey's first day back.

"Thank you, Charles." It wasn't often Boxford said anything to anyone. She supposed she should be flattered he would acknowledge her mother's death. "She'll be greatly missed."

"If you need more time to handle your mother's estate, just ask, Corey. We understand what a difficult time this is for you."

Corey thanked him again. She'd known her first day back after Millicent's death that things would be difficult and she was right. Still it was better to be back at work than home, surrounded by memories. The last thing she wanted was an expanse of endless hours waiting to be filled with guilt, recriminations, and sorrow. No, she'd had a bellyful of that back in Cincinnati, enough to last a lifetime. She hadn't even managed to get through all of Millicent's personal belongings. She'd shipped three boxes back home to deal with when she had the emotional strength.

What she really needed now was to throw herself headlong into work and begin the slow and painful process of healing.

"I'm so sorry to hear about your mom." Linda, the office manager, was waiting at the door to Corey's office. She handed Corey an envelope. "We took up a collection. You can give it to your Mom's favorite charity or pay her bills or whatever."

Corey's eyes filled with tears as she mumbled her thanks. Her emotions were embarrassingly close to the surface these days. Everything from trash bag commercials to the nightly news had the power to bring her to tears.

"I put your mail on your desk," Linda said. "All of your accounts sent flowers. We donated them to the hospital the way you asked us to, but the cards are with your mail."

"I appreciate it, Linda." If she saw one more flower, she would scream. After much puzzling about her mother's last words to her, she'd decided Millicent had been requesting lilies for her funeral and Corey had seen to it that the funeral parlor was filled to bursting with the flower in every color she could find. If her mother had meant anything else by the whispered word, she'd taken the secret with her to her grave. "I'll let you know if I need anything, Linda. Thanks."

Linda closed the door behind her when she left. Corey sank onto her plush leather chair and exhaled softly. The stack of mail piled up on her desk blotter was impressive, nearly as thick as the stack of condolences. Every one of her accounts, from the French restaurant in Cambridge to Estée Lauder to AT&T, had said how sorry they were about Millicent's death and how proud they were sure she had been of her daughter's success.

They were right, Corey thought. Millicent *had* been proud of Corey's success, "button-busting proud," she used to tell Pam at the hair salon. Pam must have gotten real tired of hearing Millicent brag on her daughter, but Pam knew how long Millicent had waited for the chance and she always listened as if she were hearing it for the very fist time.

In a little over five years Corey had worked her way up from local account executive to national account executive to vice president. She'd moved past planning the specific campaigns to orchestrating the entire image. She specialized in what she called revisionist advertising, or spin control: that peculiar art of changing the public's perception of a negative event until only a positive memory remained. She'd gained recognition while in Harvard Business when she did some apprenticeship work with a major pharmaceutical company that had suffered credibility problems after a disgruntled employee tampered with a half-dozen capsules of a popular painkiller. Corey had spun that incident until the only perception left clinging to the public's gray cells was that of a caring, compassionate company looking to protect their customers from harm no matter the cost. She'd been writing her own ticket at BB and D ever since.

She was popular with her co-workers but she held herself aloof from their afterwork activities. No matter how hard she tried she couldn't lower her defenses enough to be "one of the gang." The old Corey was never far from the surface, waiting to show her face. Her *real* face. The one not even the doctor's scalpel had been able to erase.

The one nobody would ever love.

Corey got home a little after six to discover that the boxes she'd shipped up from Cincinnati had arrived. She tried to ignore them but a sense of unfinished business nagged at her. So instead of an evening spent vegging out in front of the television, she changed into jeans and a T-shirt and reluctantly dragged the big flat box marked For Corey out of the hall closet.

Somehow she knew this was going to be harder than packing away Millicent's clothing for charity. She wasn't much of a drinker but there were times when nothing but a stiff Scotch could get you over a rough patch. She poured two fingers' worth into a juice glass then sat down on the floor in front of the television to open the box.

Peter Jennings droned on about the situation in the Middle East since the Rabin assassination while she sifted through old report cards, crayon drawings. Her whole life was in that box, all of her hopes and dreams and small triumphs. The photographs were hardest of all. She hated looking at the angry, damaged little girl she'd been. She took a generous swallow of Scotch. *Tell the truth, Corey,* she challenged herself. *Things haven't changed that much.*

Dr. Coscia had been painfully right. Although the packaging was different and she'd acquired some polish along the way, the girl inside was still the same. Angry, defiant, afraid to let anyone get too close to her in case they'd find out she wasn't perfect.

"To hell with it," she muttered, stacking the photographs facedown on her thick white carpet. She didn't have to look at pictures if she didn't want to. Just because her mother had attached great sentimental value to them didn't mean Corey had to share the same opinion.

She reached into the box again. This time she found handwritten letters from World War II, heartbreaking love letters Millicent and Jack had exchanged while he was stationed in Europe. Corey cried as she read them, feeling as if she were invading their privacy but finding it impossible to stop until she'd all but memorized each and every one. They'd loved each other so much. Their trust and loyalty and rock solid commitment to their marriage was evident in every line, every word. The paragraphs where they talked about the children they would have one day all but broke Corey's heart. They'd asked for so little from life: a roof over their heads, good health, children to love. Why had God chosen to withhold the most basic joy from them, a child of their own?

Not that she'd ever heard either one of them complain. From the first second she met them on that rickety porch in Tennessee, they'd treated Corey as if she were their own biological child. They'd taken her into their home, into their family, into their *hearts,* and if even once they'd regretted their choice they'd never let on. And, oh, how she'd gone out of her way to make them regret loving her. Even now, years later, she could hear the angry, hurtful words she'd hurled at them only to find waves of love flowing back to her.

And the awful thing of it was that she was still angry. She'd worked so hard to bury that rage the way she'd buried the memory of the scars that had marked her life for so long, but she'd failed on both counts.

"I can't do this," she said, finishing the Scotch. The wounds were too new, the guilt too fresh. Whatever else was in here would have to wait. She scooped up the pictures and letters piled on the floor next to her and was about to toss them all back into the box when her eye was caught by a large, square scrapbook peeking out from beneath a copy of *Life* magazine dated the week President Kennedy died.

She hadn't noticed any photos of Millicent and Jack's wedding or early life. Maybe her mother had neatly placed them in a scrapbook for safekeeping. Corey flipped open the padded cover and steeled herself for the sight of her parents' happy young faces beaming up at her, filled with love and optimism for the future.

"What in the world—?" Her high school graduation picture, the one where the photographer had played with the angles and the lighting and managed to minimize her scarring. It was the only photograph of herself she'd ever liked. Taped next to Corey's picture was a magazine clipping of a beautiful dark-haired woman dressed in a designer gown. The woman's face was angled slightly away from the camera, much like Corey's in the graduation photograph. If you didn't know better, you would almost think the pictures were of the same woman some twenty years apart.

The caption read, "Lili Spaulding enjoying a dance with New York's mayor."

Lili.

Millicent's last word to her. Corey rested her head on her knees and tried to take a deep, steadying breath. It was the Scotch, she told herself, that's all it was making her so dizzy. She'd gulped down the booze on an empty stomach and now she was paying the price. Next thing you knew she'd be watching a parade of pink elephants dancing through her living room.

She sat perfectly still for what seemed like ages, then, drawing in another deep breath, looked again. Nothing had changed. The word *Lili* seemed to rise up from the page and hang suspended in front of her eyes. The scrapbook was filled to bursting with clippings of Lili Spaulding at charity functions, behind her desk at Mayfair, celebrating her son's wedding at the Waldorf-Astoria a few months ago. Corey remembered seeing the wedding photos the first time they were published in *People*.

Lili.

Millicent had obviously followed Lili Spaulding's career with great interest . . . and for a long time. It just didn't make any sense. Millicent had always been a fan of movie stars and television personalities but Corey had never once heard her mother display the slightest interest in the cosmetics tycoon. And she'd certainly never associated herself with Lili Spaulding. She'd known a number of publicity types who'd worked for the company and barely escaped with their sanity. The woman was hard-hearted and demanding and everyone knew that not even the bottom line was more important than her stepson Grant.

So why on earth had Millicent kept a scrapbook of clippings about the woman? A thick manila envelope caught Corey's eye. It was probably filled with clippings her mother hadn't had time to paste into her book. A sick feeling settled itself in the pit of her stomach as she slid her index finger under the flap and withdrew a sheaf of papers and a business-size envelope with the name Patrick deRossier, Esq. engraved in the upper left-hand corner. Millicent's address was typed dead center and it was postmarked November 2, 1980. Her father had died on November 5 of that same year. A coincidence, more than likely, but her apprehension went up a notch.

"Oh, God—" The words were almost a moan. There were two letters inside, one from her mother and one from the attorney. Millicent's letter was dated August 14, 1980, that terrible lost summer when Corey had given herself to any boy who asked. She tried to comprehend her mother's words but a rushing sound inside her brain made it hard for her to think. Millicent had been too proud to come to Corey when she fell behind in mortgage taxes. But somehow she'd managed to beg help from a total stranger for Corey. The daughter who had never known how to tell Millicent all that was in her heart.

The reply from Lili Spaulding's attorney made Corey wince. The threat to Millicent and Jack had been couched in legalese but the meaning was crystal clear: back off or else.

> ...Mrs. Spaulding states unequivocally that Catherine Banning is not her biological daughter. The information you have provided, while interesting, has no bearing on the situation. Any and all further attempts on your part to contact Mrs. Spaulding with regard to the minor child will be dealt with to the fullest extent of the law.

Corey had dealt with this type of thing before. Celebrities received letters like Millicent's all the time, desperate letters pleading for help from total strangers. She'd drafted her share of strongly worded replies designed to scare off the great unwashed. The thought that Millicent had loved her enough to swallow her pride and beg made Corey wish she could reach back through time and spare her mother the humiliation... and maybe even save her father's life. Had Jack seen these letters? Had Millicent's desperate act cost her the man she loved? And still her mother had carried her burden without complaint—

But where on earth had Millicent gotten the crazy idea that Lili Spaulding was Corey's birth mother? Of all the women on earth, *why* Lili Spaulding? It just didn't make any sense. Sure, Corey could see the resemblance when their photos were laid side by side, but that didn't mean they were related. It didn't mean anything at all.

Her hands shook as she flipped through a paper-clipped stack of receipts from a private detective in Cincinnati named Glen Leeson. They were clipped together, all of them dated late summer and early autumn 1980. Most of the receipts were in the two and three hundred dollar range. For Millicent and Jack, it might as well have been two or three million.

Attached to the receipts was a typed page of notes from Glen Leeson, detailing the whereabouts of one Lilly Ann Barnett.

> NAME: Lilly Ann Barnett
> DOB: October 15, 1946
> PLACE: Euless FL
> FAMILY: None living

Subject lived with grandmother Hattie Barnett until moving in with Franklin family after death of fiancé Clifford Earle Franklin Junior. Last seen in Euless late December 1962. Of twenty people questioned who remember her, fifteen believe subject was pregnant with Franklin's baby and was sent to Atlanta to give birth. Grandmother died in 1968. Mother and father dead. Franklin family moved to Texas in 1963. Checked Atlanta records for 1962-1963 but no Lilly Ann Barnett listed as giving birth. Believed alias was used and child given up for adoption through baby broker. Subject now known by name Lili Spaulding.

Corey pushed the papers away from her. This was crazy. Lili Spaulding had nothing to do with her. Absolutely nothing. There must have been a thousand babies born in Atlanta that month to a thousand unmarried mothers.

But you were born in Atlanta, weren't you?

That didn't prove anything. Another coincidence in a line of idiotic, meaningless coincidences.

And didn't Millicent tell you the name under Birth Mother on your birth certificate was false?

Of course the name was false. Thirty years ago, an unwed mother's reputation depended upon maintaining her anonymity.

Lily. Millicent's last words. Lili.

Lilly Ann Barnett had given up her baby for adoption but it was Lili Spaulding who had turned her back on her child.

She saw Jack in his casket, his life quite probably ended by the shock of that letter from Lili's lawyer. And she saw Millicent, drowning in a sea of bills but too proud and loving to come to Corey for help. Millicent would have owned her house free and clear if she'd used the insurance money for its original purpose, but she'd sacrificed her own security so the child of her heart could have a chance for a better life.

The pain was so ferocious Corey thought she would die from it. She prayed her heart would stop beating so she wouldn't have to face the truth another second. All the years of wondering about her birth mother, fantasizing about some wonderful selfless woman who'd cared only for her baby's happiness—

Bile filled her throat and she barely made it into the bathroom in time. She crouched over the toilet until dry heaves racked her body. Finally she lay on the floor, her hot cheek pressed against the cold white tiles, as a plan began to form.

Millicent had left a paper trail for Corey that a blind woman could follow. Her heart had been filled with optimism right up until the end, an unflagging belief in the goodness of people. This was her last gift to Corey. She had wanted her daughter to know she wasn't alone in the world, that the woman who'd given birth to her was alive and well and living the good life in New York City.

Millicent believed in happily-ever-after endings and pots of gold at the end of the rainbow. Millicent would have wanted Corey to meet Lili Spaulding, to talk to her, to become part of her life.

She would do that for Millicent. She would go to New York and meet Lili Spaulding.

And then Corey would do something for herself.

She would find a way to take Lili Spaulding down.

26

"This is beyond comprehension!" Lili tossed down the memorandum and glared up at her assistant Devon. "What does he mean, abandoning us at such a critical time?"

"It's all there in black and white," said Devon. "Blake Morrow told you to take his job and shove it."

"He's been with us for over twenty years. In all that time we've been nothing but generous with him. What on *earth* is his problem?"

"Maybe BB and D offered him more money."

"Nonsense!" Lili poured herself a mineral water. "He's fifty-six years old. His peak earning years are all behind him. There's nothing cutting edge about him anymore. This simply doesn't make sense."

"Maybe he doesn't think you're cutting edge anymore either."

"You're being insubordinate."

Devon planted her hands on her size-22 hips. "So?"

"Check your dictionary, darling. Insubordination is a bad thing."

"If you're in the army, maybe. Last I heard, this was a free country, boss. I'm entitled to my opinion."

"Of course you are, but must you share it with me every chance you get?"

The world really was going to hell in a handbasket, Lili thought as the door closed behind her assistant. Why else would she be forced to accept such treatment from a paid employee? No other sane person would accept it. However, even Lili had to admit Devon served a unique purpose in her professional life. Not only were the woman's skills top drawer, she served as a reality check for what was really happening at Lili! International.

Lili hated being taken by surprise and Morrow's resignation had done exactly that. With the trouble they'd been having with the animal rights groups, the last thing she needed was to have her public relations captain jump ship. Her competitors would have a field day with that knowledge and it might even affect stock prices when they went public after the new year. Thanksgiving was only days away and a month after that, Christmas would be on top of them and then—

She drew in a deep steadying breath. It didn't bear thinking about. If only she'd seen the signs of unrest in Blake Morrow. Maybe then she could have done something to convince him to stay on. She'd told Devon that he was no longer cutting edge, but he still had a few good years left before the quickly changing times left him behind for good.

"Damn it." She tossed a pencil across the room. She was angry and nothing good ever came from anger. What was it her massage therapist had told her last week as he pounded the knots of tension from her shoulders? Something about getting in touch with her inner child or realigning her chakras—some such nonsense. She wasn't about to start communing with her six-year-old self, but there was something to be said for regaining her composure before she did anything she might regret.

Maybe Morrow did her a favor, quitting the way he had. The term *wake up call* was badly overused but in this case it was right on target. She reached for the telephone.

"Get me the head of personnel," she ordered Devon. "Tell her to drop whatever she's doing and get up here or her head will roll."

"*Sieg heil,*" Devon drawled.

Lili would have a new spin control expert in place by Friday or know the reason why.

Grant didn't share Lili's anger over Blake Morrow's defection. One public relations whiz was the same as the next and so long as it didn't affect his political plans, Mickey Mouse could be running the show for all he cared.

"You have time for everyone but me," Felicia had complained the other night when he told her he had to cancel out on their last Lamaze class.

"You'll thank me later," he'd said, trying to ignore her painfully swollen belly as he kissed her goodbye. He couldn't imagine wanting to bed her again. "This is for our future."

Even at the congressional level, campaigns began long before you announced your candidacy. Dan Jarreau, his image consultant, had already opened doors that might have remained closed without Jarreau's long and impressive track record of success. So far, Jarreau's advice to ignore Frank DeVito's warnings about Night-Way had been dead on. The FDA had given its approval a few weeks ago and now it was clear sailing toward a launch late next summer.

That was why he made it a point to surround himself with the best people in their fields. He had no problem delegating authority to experts. Why waste time trying to learn everything there was to know about every subject that came up? You could always find someone who had the answers you needed, *when* you needed them.

What you couldn't find was someone like Grant Spaulding. He had the breeding, the looks, the sheer star power a candidate needed to make his mark on the national scene. With the renewed success of Lili! International behind him, a seat in the House was practically a sure thing.

He ducked Lili's meeting with Blake Morrow's remaining staff in public relations. He wasn't in the mood to hear another post mortem of the situation. There were plenty of great PR people out there. One of them would end up at Lili!

Friday

Corey felt a modicum of guilt over disrupting Blake Morrow's life but the sum settled on him by the corporate headhunters would ease his transition quite handsomely. Mr. Morrow didn't know it yet but he was about to be offered her old position at BB and D and if he was as smart as she'd heard he was, he wouldn't let it get away.

The morning after Thanksgiving, she stepped off the elevator on the twenty-third floor of the Lili! International building. The reception area was wide and spacious, a sleek mix of marble, antiques, and fresh flowers.

"Wow," the receptionist said in a voice that screamed Flatbush. She was the one incongruous element in the quietly elegant room. "Are you a model or the spinner?"

"I'm Corey Prescott. I have a 10:00 a.m. appointment with Mrs. Spaulding."

"The spinner," said the woman, nodding. "Take a seat. I'll tell the boss you're here."

Corey's adrenaline was flowing too fast for her to sit down. She made a show of flipping through her Filofax while she willed her heartbeat down to something approaching a normal rate. Those childhood dreams about finding her mother, dreams about seeing a face that looked like hers, hearing a laugh that sounded like her own laugh—they had all come back full force since she'd learned Lili Spaulding was her biological mother.

Last night had been the longest of her life. Bad enough that it was her first Thanksgiving without Millicent, but the specter of finally coming face-to-face with Lili Spaulding terrified her. Her emotions veered wildly from anger to sorrow to an almost Biblical need for vengeance that sometimes threatened to obliterate everything that got in its way. There was something cleansing about having a focus for a lifetime of anger, something almost liberating.

Are you sure it's anger driving you? Maybe you're looking for a happy ending.

Ridiculous. The last thing she wanted was a happy ending with Lili Spaulding. The thought of a loving mother-daughter reunion was enough to make her laugh out loud.

She had to hand Lili one thing, however: Lili! International was a class operation. The company had provided a temporary apartment for Corey until she managed to find one of her own. She ordered in Chinese food for Thanksgiving dinner and spent the evening poring over the materials she'd amassed on the woman who'd given birth to her.

Corey knew the rags-to-riches tale by heart. Lili's rise from the Florida swampland to the top of New York society was the stuff of Hollywood movies. She knew about the years in Las Vegas, the sudden marriage to a rich and handsome Prince Charming. She knew how hard it had been for Lili to learn how to fit into Carter Spaulding's world. Rich men demanded a lot from their wives. They expected them to be wife, mistress, caretaker, social director, chatelaine and business partner, and that was just for starters. Lili Spaulding had managed all of that and found time to become a tycoon.

Corey had memorized everything that had ever been written about Lili Spaulding but not once had she ever seen mention of the daughter who'd been abandoned without a second thought. It was as if Corey had never existed. As if Lili wished she'd never been born—

"Ms. Prescott, she'll see you now."

She felt light-headed as she followed the receptionist toward Lili's inner office. It was as if everything she'd ever done, every breath she'd drawn, had led her to this place and there could be no turning back. *I'm doing this for Millicent,* she told herself and the thought gave her courage.

The receptionist rapped on Lili's door. "Mrs. S., this is Corey Prescott, the new spinner."

For the rest of her life, Corey would remember the moment when she saw her mother for the very first time. Nothing had prepared her for the violent rush of emotion at the realization that they were in the same room, breathing the same air, for the first time since Corey was born. *Did you ever think about me?* Corey wondered as she strode toward the desk by the window. *Did you ever wonder if I was even alive?*

Corey doubted it. Lili's brow was as untroubled as a girl's. Her dark hair was pulled severely off her face and looped in the back with a flat black velvet bow. She wore a Chanel suit in a vibrant raspberry and three long strands of pearls. Her forty-nine-year-old face was serene, untouched by time or trouble. Millicent had been old for years by that age, weathered by both fate and circumstance. Every minute of love and worry had been etched into her beloved face.

Lili Spaulding looked up and smiled and in that smile Corey saw the way Millicent might have been if life had dealt her a better hand, and she knew a moment of such bone-deep sorrow it almost brought her to her knees.

You really haven't a clue, Corey thought as Lili Spaulding motioned for her to take a seat. *I'm your daughter. The child you gave away without a second thought.*

"... you certainly come to us with glowing recommendations," Lili was saying. "We consider ourselves fortunate."

"I was very happy at BB and D, but I couldn't pass up this opportunity."

Lili's wide sapphire eyes glittered with satisfaction. Corey saw intelligence in those strangely familiar eyes and a formidable will, but she didn't see warmth. She would have figured the infamous Steel Magnolia had learned how to fake it along the way, but apparently even Lili Spaulding wasn't that good an actress.

You don't need a spin control doctor, she thought bitterly. *You need a trip to Oz for a heart.*

"We've run into trouble this year with the animal rights groups," Lili said. "With a new product set to debut next year, we need to keep a good spin on things."

"Night-Way," Corey said. "The entire industry knows about it."

Lili tapped a finger against her chin. Her eyes never left Corey. "I suppose you also know our key ingredient."

"CG-47. Everyone knows the name, no one knows the formula."

"And thank God for that," Lili murmured. "It will be your job to keep our name out there in a positive light *and* to keep secrets. Are you good at keeping secrets, Ms. Prescott?"

"Better than you could possibly imagine."

Lili started to say something when a silky male voice floated toward them from the doorway. "Am I interrupting anything?"

Lili rose from her seat, her lovely face aglow with delight. "Of course not. Come in, darling, and meet Corey Prescott."

Corey turned to see a tall, golden god of a man striding across the room toward them. Grant Landon Spaulding, the heir apparent. He was so gorgeous he made her teeth ache.

"You're looking particularly lovely today, Mother." He kissed Lili on both cheeks then aimed a devastatingly effective smile in Corey's direction. "Hello, Corey Prescott. Welcome aboard."

The man turned shaking hands into an erotic experience. "Thank you," she said. Not witty, but safe. She had the feeling that staying safe was vital around Grant Spaulding.

"BB and D's loss is definitely our gain." His expression didn't change a whisker but there was no denying the sexual innuendo hidden beneath the simple words.

Lili seemed oblivious to the undercurrents in the room. Her focus was one hundred percent on Grant. "I'm proud to say my son will be declaring his candidacy for the House right after New Year's."

"Interesting." Corey's stomach knotted at the look of maternal pride on Lili's face. *I went to Harvard Business, Lili, and I didn't need the Spaulding name to get me through.*

"More than interesting," said Lili. "We can't afford any gaffes between now and the election, Corey. This company is my son's birthright. Its success reflects on all of us, but most especially on Grant. We need positive press and a high profit margin between now and next November. We can't afford anything less."

"I can guarantee the press," she said. "The profit margin is up to you."

"There's no room for anything but total commitment," Grant said. "Forget having a personal life. We own you body and soul."

"I understand," she said. "That's not a problem."

Something flared in his eyes and she found herself taking an involuntary step backward. "Have you ever worked on a political campaign before?" he asked.

"Grant!" Lili's laugh held a trace of anxiety but she masked it well. "I believe Lili! International will keep our Ms. Prescott busy enough without adding to her burden."

"Just making conversation," Grant said, with a wink for Corey. "I'm not trying to steal one of your rising stars, Mother."

Lili relaxed visibly. "My resources are your resources, darling, you know that."

Corey stepped into the fray. "I'm available if you need to run something by me, Mr. Spaulding." Company secrets would be a nice place to start.

His candidate-of-the-year smile returned. "I may take you up on that."

"I hope you do. I find politics very exciting." She was careful to maintain a flat tone of voice, devoid of any inflections that could come back to haunt her later. There was something predatory about Grant Spaulding that made the hairs on the back of her neck rise in response.

Lili pressed the intercom on her desk and Devon's unmistakable voice filled the room.

"Yes, Mrs. S.?"

"Ms. Prescott is anxious to see her office."

"You got it, Mrs. S."

Corey's eyes widened. She hadn't displayed the slightest curiosity about her office.

Lili smiled up at Corey. *Stay away from him,* her look warned. *I protect my own.* "We're putting you on the fifth floor near R and D until Blake's old office is painted and recarpeted. It will take a few weeks. I hope you don't mind."

"Not at all," Corey said, returning the smile. She knew she was being punished. *You didn't protect me, Lili. You didn't give a damn if I lived or died.*

"So, darling," said Lili as she turned her attention back to Grant, "tell me how Felicia is feeling."

It was obvious that the interview was over. Corey gathered up her briefcase and shoulder bag once again, feeling as awkward as she had as a child in a room full of strangers. Lili barely acknowledged her as she left the office. She was utterly, completely absorbed by Grant's every word.

You'd do anything for him, Corey thought. *All the things you never did for me.*

Devon was waiting for her in the anteroom.

"It's not you," she said, gesturing toward Lili's inner sanctum. "When he's around, she can't think of anything else."

"So much for my poker face." A bitter anger twisted itself around Corey's heart. "She completely forgot I was there. One minute we were talking business, the next she was asking him about his wife."

"Get used to it," Devon said. "As far as she's concerned, Grant Spaulding hung the moon. A word of advice. If you want to get along with Mrs. S., make sure you never cross her baby boy."

27

"It's the next to last office on the right," Devon said, pointing down the long hallway. "Go have a look. I'll get some papers you need to sign."

The fifth floor was abuzz with activity. White-coated technicians moved between labs, carrying vials and beakers of God-knows-what while an endless parade of suits walked around like high school hall monitors. She knew full well that she belonged on the twentieth floor with the other executives but Lili had been determined to let her know from the outset who was boss. Let the new kid on the block cool her heels for a few days with the pocket protector crew. And if that also kept Corey out of Grant's line of vision, so much the better.

Her temporary office was set up with the requisite desk, credenza, computer, window without a view—and little girl. Corey stopped in the doorway. Had Devon forgotten to tell her something? A child of maybe five or six was sitting on the floor, surrounded by computer printout sheets. Her sandy blond hair was pulled back into a Pebbles Flintstone ponytail and she clutched a bouquet of crayons in each hand.

"Hello," said Corey.

The little girl looked up from her drawing. "Hello," she said warily.

"That's a very pretty picture."

The child ducked her head against her right shoulder. "I know."

"Is that your house you're drawing?"

"It's my mommy's house."

Corey tossed her briefcase and shoulder bag down onto the desk. "I'm Corey," she said. "Who are you?" No one had mentioned anything about on-site daycare. Especially not in her office.

"Jessie."

"Are you my new office assistant?"

Jessie giggled.

Corey grinned and crouched down next to her. "I bet you'd be a great assistant."

"I can make you a picture."

"Can you make me a picture of a cat?"

Jessie nodded then bent over a new section of paper. Corey stood up and walked to the doorway. "Excuse me," she said to a passing lab technician. "Is anyone missing a little girl?"

"Try Steve Gold," the woman said. "He's got a kid."

"Where can I find him?"

"Next office," she replied over her shoulder. "But he's not there right now."

"Great," Corey muttered. Her first day on the job and she'd been demoted to the techie floor and was sharing her office with a preschooler.

She went back into her office. Jessie was engrossed in her project. If the child was concerned about her father's whereabouts, it didn't show.

If you're not worried, I'm not worried, Corey thought as she took her seat behind the desk. She unpacked her personal items from her briefcase then powered up the computer. Jessie glanced up as it beeped twice but quickly returned to her drawing. She was a cute little thing, as far as kids went.

"You came to work with your daddy?" she asked.

"Uh-huh." Jessie worried her lower lip between her teeth as she colored in the cat's fur. At least Corey assumed it was a cat.

"Do you know where your daddy went?"

The little girl angled a glance at Corey. "I'm not s'posed to talk to strangers."

"And that's very good advice," Corey said, "but I'm worried. I found you all alone here in my office and I don't know where you belong."

The child's lower lip began to quiver. "I want my daddy," she whispered, her voice catching on a sob. "I want Daddy!"

Corey was surprised building security didn't storm her office. Jessie's wails were loud enough to wake the dead.

"Don't cry!" she begged the child, joining her on the carpeted floor. "I didn't mean to make you cry." She felt like a monster when all she'd wanted to do was find the kid's father.

"I want milk," Jessie said, her tears stopping as quickly as they'd started.

"Milk?"

"That's where Daddy went."

"To get you some milk?"

Jessie nodded. "A long, long time ago."

Corey bit back a smile. "I'm sure he'll be here any minute, honey. Why don't you show me how to draw a cat while we wait?"

"Damn it." Stephen Gold put the container of milk down on top of his desk and looked around. Jessie was nowhere in sight. Her crayons were gone. So was the stack of used computer paper he'd saved for her. He buzzed his office assistant. "Have you seen my kid?"

"Negative," said Drake, whose naval reserve duties colored his speech. "Want me to start a reconnaissance mission?"

"I'll let you know." Lili! International wasn't known for being sympathetic to the plight of single parents. Their housekeeper was out sick with the flu and it was either bring Jessie to work with him or stay home. Lili Spaulding might not like kids but she liked absenteeism even less.

Where would he go if he were a curious five-year-old girl who hadn't yet learned the world could be an unfriendly place? Knowing Jess, there was a good chance she was introducing herself to the Steel Magnolia herself.

A woman's voice sounded from the empty office next door. "That's a great cat, Jessie. Is it a calico?"

His little girl's unmistakable soprano rang out, "No, silly! It's Tiger."

He was at the door in a flash. Crayons and paper were scattered from one side of the room to the other. In the middle of the chaos sat his daughter and a dark-haired woman with huge sapphire-blue eyes . . . and a very short skirt.

"I told you to stay put, kiddo," he said to Jessie. "What are you doing in here?"

"This is my office," Jessie said, her little jaw set in a familiar stubborn line. "Corey said so."

The attractive woman sitting next to his daughter shrugged her shoulders and shot him a guilty smile. "Jessie said she'd share it with me."

He liked her smile. Hell, he liked almost everything about her. "I thought this was an empty office."

"I'm only temporary," she said. "Until they repaint Blake Morrow's office up on twenty."

He didn't try to hide his curiosity. "You're the new spin doctor?"

"Corey Prescott." She rose and offered him her right hand. Watching her skirt slither down over her thighs was a religious experience. "And you're . . ."

"Stephen Gold." Her grip was as direct as her manner. "Has she been any trouble?"

"Not a bit. Do you bring her to work with you every day?"

"And risk my ass on a regular basis? I'm not that big a gambler." He explained to her about his ailing housekeeper and the reality of single parenthood in the 90s.

"I don't see where you had any choice but to bring her to work with you," Corey Prescott said.

"Try telling that to the Steel Magnolia."

"The hell with the Steel Magnolia. Talk to the head of personnel. I can't believe a company of this size doesn't have some form of on-site child care available for times like this."

"You've got a lot to learn. This place is about illusion. The quicker you understand that, the quicker you'll get ahead."

"Isn't illusion what cosmetics are all about?"

"Not when it comes to ethics."

Her dark brows lifted. "Is there something I should know?"

"Stay away from the WASP prince, for starters."

He could hear her intake of breath across the room. Why the hell had he said that? She wasn't his problem and neither was Grant Spaulding.

"Care to elaborate?"

"Not really."

"You can't drop a bombshell like that and take off."

"Look, I said something I shouldn't. Forget you heard it."

"I can't forget it. You're implying something and I'd like to know what."

"Damn." He dragged a hand through his hair. If it got any longer he'd have to pull it back in a ponytail like one of those action heroes in the movies. *Super-Dad.* "You're a good-looking woman. He likes good-looking women. Good-looking women end up without their jobs. Get the picture?"

"I do," she said, "and I resent the implication."

"Hey, I'm the one who didn't want to elaborate."

"Grant Spaulding is a charming man but he's married. What makes you think I'd have anything to do with him?"

"Just playing the odds."

"Don't underestimate me, Gold. It takes more than a pretty face to win my heart."

Their gazes locked for a moment. She was the first to look away. His sister Lynn would find that meaningful. He took it as a sign it was time to leave.

He glanced down at Jessie. "C'mon, kid. Let's say goodbye to Corey Prescott and get back to work."

Before he said something else he might regret. Something like, "What *would* it take to win your heart?"

Stephen Gold helped Jessie gather up her drawings and crayons then shepherded her back to his office. There was something very touching about the sight of the craggily hand-some man holding hands with his little girl as Jessie said good-bye. He was all angles and energy, yet appealingly gentle with his child. It was obvious that fatherhood was a comfortable fit. She wondered why "husbandhood" hadn't been.

She was reminded of Jack Banning and the times he used to take her fishing in his patched-up old rowboat, just the two of them out on the river with a shoe-box of sandwiches and fruit that Millicent had prepared to tide them over until dinner. It was nice to know there was at least one good father left.

It was also nice to know that Stephen Gold saw through Grant's facade same as she did, but she didn't dare let Gold know she was anything but enamored of her new employers. She needed to get a feel for the company and the players before she aligned herself with any particular faction. To hurt Lili Spaulding, Corey would have to find the woman's Achilles heel and that wouldn't happen overnight.

After an informal getting-to-know-you meeting with her staff, Corey threw herself into trying to master the intricacies of Spaulding executive software, the link to everything and everyone in the company, and before she knew it the afternoon was half-over. Her neck was stiff from staring at the monitor and she let her head drop back and closed her eyes.

"Tired?" Grant Spaulding's voice shattered the silence.

"Mr. Spaulding, I didn't hear you come in."

"Grant."

Where had he learned to smile that way, as if he'd swallowed a klieg light whole? She wondered if it was one of those things rich people were born knowing how to do or if he'd learned it at his mother's knee. *My* mother's knee, she thought bitterly.

"I didn't hear you come in."

"Obviously." He sat on the edge of her desk, managing simultaneously to look casual, elegant and powerful.

"Can I help you with something?"

He answered her question with a question of his own. "How is your first day going?"

"Very well," she said. "I took a meeting with Morrow's staff and I think we'll be able to do business."

"Good," said Grant. "But don't think you have to adapt to their methodology. You're in charge."

"I'm aware of that," she said, bristling at the implication she was anything less than a serious professional.

"Have dinner with me."

She was rarely caught by surprise but Grant Spaulding had managed it. "That sounds wonderful but I'm afraid I have other plans."

"Cancel them."

"Sorry. I can't."

He reached for her phone and handed her the receiver. "This is business. Whoever he is, he'll understand."

The only plans Corey had entailed a hot bath and a cup of soup but she was more than happy if Grant Spaulding thought she was enjoying a fabulous social life. She replaced the receiver in its cradle. "I appreciate the invitation but no thank you."

"Listen," he said, turning up the charm another few degrees, "Mother doesn't hear the word *no* very often. Don't make me be the bearer of bad tidings." Apparently he'd missed the lesson about personal space. He had moved just close enough to make her uncomfortably aware of his presence, but not so close that she could move away without looking vaguely paranoid.

So Lili was behind this invitation. That changed things considerably. The idea of spending two hours watching Lili fawn over her stepson bothered Corey in ways she didn't want to contemplate, much less endure, but she knew this was an opportunity only a fool would pass up.

There were few things Grant Spaulding liked better than a challenge from a worthy competitor and Corey Prescott was certainly that.

Corey had been the one to break their handshake when they met in Lili's office that morning, pulling back a beat sooner than protocol dictated. At first he'd believed she'd been rocked by the obvious attraction between them; then he realized her attentions were focused solely on Lili. Most new employees hung on Lili's every word, eager to lick her pumps if that's what it took to climb the ladder. But there was nothing obsequious or fawning about Corey's interest. It was too focused, too intense for mere toadying. No, there was something else at work . . . something that felt a hell of a lot like jealousy.

"We're set for six o'clock, main lobby," he said to Lili as he walked into her office unannounced. "The lady protested but I showed her the error of her ways."

Lili was seated in her office chair, hands outstretched, while a staff manicurist painted her nails with deep red polish. "She had other plans?"

"So she said." He sank onto the sofa by the window and eyed the manicurist with open admiration. She wore the ubiquitous navy coat dress with brass buttons that had become the Lili! trademark in department stores worldwide but he had to admit she filled it out better than most. Felicia was due any day and her breasts looked like water balloons, "I think your new employee was bullshitting about being busy."

"Have you suddenly acquired second sight, darling?" Lili's tone held a considerable edge.

"Just a feeling," he said, shifting position beneath her sharp-eyed gaze.

"Margherita, would you excuse us for five minutes. My son and I need to have a brief family discussion."

Margherita screwed the cap back on the bottle of polish then left the room, affording him a great look at her nicely rounded ass.

"Off-limits, darling."

He grinned. "Why not let Margherita decide for herself?"

She waved her wet nails in a gesture of impatience he'd seen many times over the last nineteen years. "I'm talking about our Ms. Prescott."

"You wound me, mother. I'm a married man."

Lili rose to her feet and strode toward him. There was no mistaking her anger. "You are in for the fight of your life next year, Grant. Being a rich man's son isn't the ticket to Congress that it used to be. The press is watching you the way it watched Gary Hart and if you think I'm going to put the resources of Lili! International behind a doomed venture, then you don't know me half as well as you think you do." She loomed over him, her showgirl's body still taut and trim despite the fact she was staring down the barrel of the half-century mark. "I'm warning you, darling: keep your pants zipped for the next year or I'll pull the plug on your campaign right now."

He reached for her hand and kissed it. "Right as always," he said. "What would I do without you, mother?"

"I don't know," Lili said with an exaggerated sigh. "And I pray you never have to find out."

"Daddy, look!" Jessie pointed toward some people standing by the curb in front of the office building.

Stephen, who had been trying without success to stuff Malibu Barbie into his briefcase, grunted something noncommittal. It was six o'clock and he was running on empty.

"Daddy!" Jessie tugged at his sleeve and the doll tumbled to the sidewalk followed by her male counterpart. "There's Corey and her mommy."

"Have a heart, Jess," he said, bending down to retrieve the dolls before a horde of thundering New Yorkers ground them into vinyl pulp. "It's been a long day."

"Look, Daddy!" Her normally high-pitched voice was approaching dogs-only range. "It's Corey and her mommy!"

He looked where Jessie was pointing and came close to saying something that would send his daughter into therapy for the next five years. Corey Prescott was standing at the curb with Lili Spaulding and the heir apparent, Grant. "That's not her mommy, Jess. That's my boss." Seemed as if the new spin doctor hadn't wasted any time getting cozy with the power at Lili! He felt strangely disappointed, as if he'd expected better from her although he didn't know why he should even give a damn.

"But it looks like Corey's mommy."

Stephen looked again. They were both beautiful, both dark-haired, but beyond that he couldn't see any resemblance. Lili was as tough as nails. Corey still had a way to go.

"Come on, Jess." He reached down for her hand. "Let's go home."

"I want to show Corey something."

"Time to go, kiddo."

"I drew her a picture."

"I'll give it to her on Monday."

"No, I want to give it to her!"

"Your hand, Jess. Now!"

He might as well have been talking to a squirrel. His daughter took off like a shot. "Son of a bitch," he mumbled and started after her.

"Corey, I have another picture for you!" Jessie called out.

Corey spun around at the sound of Jessie's voice. So did Lili Spaulding and the aging wunderkind. On his short list of bad moments, this was *número dos.*

"Hi, honey." Corey ruffled Jessie's hair with an easy, natural gesture. "I'd love another picture."

"Daddy has it," Jessie said as he joined them.

"Isn't that Malibu Barbie?" Corey asked, tugging at a lock of blond hair poking out from his briefcase. "I always wanted one when I was a little girl."

He scowled at her and she laughed. He turned his attentions to his daughter. "I left the pictures upstairs in my desk, Jess. I promise I'll give them to Corey on Monday."

Jessie didn't start crying. He was happy about that until he realized why. She was too busy staring up at Grant Spaulding with the glazed expression most females got the first time they met him.

"She's young," Corey Prescott murmured. "She'll get over him."

Damn right, he thought. *But will you?*

Grant Spaulding was charming, attentive, and occasionally entertaining over dinner at Tavern on the Green. Lili certainly thought so. Corey found herself grinding her teeth in frustration as she watched her mother shower affection on a man who was so basically worthless as to be nonexistent. She'd only known Grant for one day and already Corey had the feeling she'd plumbed his depths.

Midway through dinner, Lili excused herself to talk to an old friend on the other side of the room. Grant poured Corey some more wine and got down to the business at hand.

"I keep a suite at the Waldorf," he said with almost admirable bluntness. "No one would have to know."

Involuntarily she glanced across the restaurant to where Lili was chatting with her cronies. Somehow it didn't surprise Corey to find Lili looking right back at her. An odd sense of triumph built inside her chest at her mother's obvious concern.

"Your mother is watching us," she said. "Would you care to tell me why she seems so concerned?"

"She loves me." He said it so matter-of-factly, as if Lili's love were as constant as the stars. "All she can think about is my campaign."

Corey took a sip of wine and considered him carefully. "Maybe you should give some thought to your campaign, as well. Believe it or not, some voters frown on adultery."

"Then we'll have to see to it they don't find out."

She was framing a suitable retort when Lili rejoined them. "You two are certainly getting on well." Her words were pleasant but Corey sensed the iron will beneath them.

Grant seized the opportunity to visit the men's room. Coward, thought Corey. Leaving her alone to defend his honor.

"Yes, we are getting along well," Corey said, meeting Lili's eyes. "Your son is a fascinating man."

"My son is a *married* man," Lili said. "A married man about to declare for public office."

"I know that, Mrs. Spaulding." Mother and son had talked of nothing else during dinner. "I'm afraid I don't understand your concern."

"If you have any romantic ideas about him, I suggest you turn your sights elsewhere."

"You might care to repeat this speech for his benefit."

"He knows my feelings on the subject."

"Perhaps he needs to be reminded."

"Just do your job, Ms. Prescott, and leave family matters to me. If you can manage that, we'll get along fine."

Lili's words found their mark in the little girl who still lived inside Corey's heart. The little girl who'd spent most of her life wondering why her mother didn't want her.

28

"Mama! Mama! Help me..."

Her baby—she had to get to her little girl before it was too late—

Lili pushed back the bedcovers and sat up. She was drenched with sweat. Her tailored pajamas clung to her body and she felt unbearably sticky and agitated. She couldn't remember the last time she'd had the dream. It had to be at least a year, maybe more.

After Carter's death the nightmare had plagued her every night for months, until she finally sought help from a hypnotherapist. She'd mastered the relaxation techniques and had reduced the occurrence of the dream from nightly to nonexistent and now, out of the blue, she was plunged back into the icy cold waters, swimming for her life while her baby drowned.

"Damn, damn, damn." She stripped off her pajamas and strode into her private bath. The sight of her naked body in the mirror filled her with a painful mixture of pride and dismay. She wasn't a girl any longer—as if she needed reminding. Her breasts hadn't sagged yet but she knew it was only a matter of time. She filled the marble sink with warm water and the prototype for Lili! Bath Gelee. Bubbles rose up like clouds of sweet-smelling lilies and freesia. She submerged a washcloth in the water then gently drew it across her chest and down to her belly where the silvery white lines shimmered in the pinkish light.

The stretchmarks. She barely noticed them anymore. There were times when she could scarcely remember how it had felt to carry a life within her body. More than thirty years had passed since the morning sickness and swollen breasts. Even the pain of childbirth had faded in memory, just as everyone had said it would.

So why couldn't she forget her daughter? There was no point to remembering the child. The perfect baby of her memory was a grown woman now, maybe even the mother of her own baby girl. Years ago Grant had filled that empty place inside her heart. He couldn't mean more to her if she'd carried him in her body for nine months.

She reached for her cigarettes and lighter. Her doctor had recommended she quit smoking but that wasn't a viable option. She'd been smoking for thirty years and, politically incorrect or not, dangerous or not, she had no intention of stopping. Certainly not in her private life. Life was all about choices, some good, some not so. You had to learn to make peace with all of them.

It had taken her a long time to learn that lesson, but she finally understood. She'd made peace with giving her child up for adoption many years ago. She made peace with it again years ago, after that dreadful letter from that woman in Cincinnati. So why had the dream returned now to haunt her? She thought back over the day, trying to figure out a possible trigger. It certainly couldn't have anything to do with Stephen Gold's little girl. She hadn't noticed much about the child except for the way she threw herself at Corey Prescott.

She inhaled deeply, letting the smoke fill her lungs for an endless moment. *Corey Prescott*. Now there was a problem in the making. She'd considered firing the young woman right on the spot at Tavern on the Green but had thought better of it. Prescott was too sharp, too savvy. She'd bring the media down on the Spaulding empire so fast Lili's head would spin with lawsuits. No, Corey Prescott wasn't the kind to take dismissal quietly.

Besides, they didn't have time to search for someone to take her place. She'd come to Lili with the most impressive credentials of anyone around and Lili couldn't allow her own personal fears to taint what should be a logical business decision.

Lili took another drag on her cigarette and began to pace the room. Still there was something about the woman that worried her, as if there were more than naked ambition driving young Ms. Prescott up the ladder. The sense that all wasn't as it should be was burning a hole beneath her rib cage. God bless her ulcer. It was like having a built-in lie detector, warning her of trouble ahead.

Still, she liked Corey Prescott's style. The young woman wasn't cowed by Lili in the slightest. In fact, she seemed to enjoy their brief confrontation at the restaurant. She was edgy and combative but Lili sensed a deep sadness hidden just beneath the glossy surface.

Why couldn't people just be exactly what they seemed? Life would be so much simpler if there was some sort of truth in advertising rule at work when it came to the human race.

Of course, that was one of the problems Grant was facing. He had already been tagged with the unfortunate label "Quayle-esque." It was going to take a lot of time and money to erase that image from the voters' minds. His physical attributes were so formidable that few believed he could count to twenty without taking off his shoes. Lili understood his frustration on that score. She couldn't count the times her own intelligence had been discounted because she'd had the good fortune to be born beautiful. Well, she'd shown them and Grant would too.

But to do that, he had to keep his trousers zipped. She knew that married life was an uncomfortable fit for him but she had no pity. He had chosen this particular road and now he would have to do his damnedest to stay the course. Same as she would do her damnedest to keep temptation—in the form of their new head of Public Relations—out of his way.

Corey spent most of Saturday familiarizing herself with mountains of data on Spaulding ventures. Because her bailiwick was public relations, much of the material dealt with the personal angle. There were reams on Lili and Carter, starting with their marriage in 1976 and continuing right up until his unexpected death in 1989. Admittedly Corey wanted to think the worst but she was left with little doubt that Lili had loved her husband very much, despite the fact that Carter had been less than faithful to her.

She'd dealt with powerful men during her years at Baker, Boxford and Deane and each time she'd been left almost weak with gratitude that she only had to work with them, not live with them. They were accustomed to wielding power in business and that autocratic attitude invariably filtered down into their private lives as well. Most of the ladies who lunched paid a high price for their gowns and bracelets. She wondered if Lili had ever regretted her choice.

"You fool," she muttered, scrolling through the material. She must be losing her mind. Lili Spaulding didn't deserve her sympathy. Lili had made choices with her own best interests in mind and whatever she got, she deserved.

Around three o'clock in the afternoon Corey realized she hadn't eaten since the night before. She rummaged around in the tiny kitchen and came up with a box of crackers, two packets of sugar, and a jar of instant coffee. Not even Julia Child could do anything with those ingredients.

She slipped a coat on over her jeans and T-shirt and went out. A brisk wind off the East River wound its way between the high-rises and reminded her that winter was on its way. Her first Christmas without Millicent. Maybe she could drink herself into an eggnog coma and wake up again on January 2nd. The notion had its appeal. Thanksgiving had been awful enough. Christmas, she had no doubt, would be a killer.

She stopped at a newsstand and picked up a copy of the *New York Times* then asked the owner if he knew where she could purchase a few groceries. He directed her to a small Korean store at Second and East 62nd where she filled her basket with lettuce, tomatoes, a quart of skim milk, a jar of mayo, two cans of tuna fish, and a crusty loaf of French bread. She tried to ignore the fact that her meager choices came to over twenty dollars.

"Get used to it," said a familiar voice from behind her. "You're in the Big Apple now." Stephen Gold, his arms piled high with groceries, was next in line at the checkout.

"Well, hi," she said, smiling. "I didn't expect to see a familiar face."

He smiled back. Some nice crinkly lines appeared on either side of his hazel eyes, softening the angles of his very masculine face. "You won't see many around here on the weekend," he said. "Just a few of us die-hard cliff dwellers."

She glanced around the store. "Where's Jessie?"

"Tap class." He dumped his groceries down on the counter. "Do you live around here?"

"Three blocks west. And you?"

"Two blocks that way." He pointed east.

"Good to see you. Maybe we'll bump into each other again."

"You in a rush?"

She hesitated. *Keep moving, Corey. A man with a kid isn't what you're looking for.* "Sort of."

"Too bad. Jess would've loved to see you."

"I'd love to see Jessie, too." *Have you lost your mind? Cut bait and run.*

"So why don't you wait a minute. We'll pick her up at dance class then we can walk you home."

She smiled despite herself. "Nobody's ever walked me home before."

"Right," he said. "You were probably the high school homecoming queen."

She let the comment pass, waiting quietly while he paid for his groceries. She wondered what he would think if he knew the truth.

They chatted awkwardly as they walked to Pavlova's Dance School across the street from Bloomingdale's. Stephen told her some funny stories about last year's Christmas party. He had an edgy, self-deprecating sense of humor that she found very appealing. It was nice to stroll down the street with a man who could make her laugh.

"Corey!" The little girl clapped her hands when Corey and Stephen arrived. "Now I can show you my picture. I drew it special for you." She wore pink tights, a tulle tutu, and ruby red tap shoes. Corey couldn't remember the last time she saw a more adorable sight.

Stephen pointed to the tap shoes. "You forgot something, kiddo."

"Please, Daddy!" Jessie looked up at her father through thick curly lashes. "Let me wear them home."

"Sneakers, Jess."

"Daddy—"

"You know the rules."

Grumbling, Jessie pulled her sneakers from a canvas tote bag then sat down on the floor. Stephen crouched down in front of

her and unknotted the grosgrain ribbons on the tap shoes. He
slipped the tap shoes off and slid the sneakers on in their place.

"Let me tie 'em, Daddy."

"Okay," he said. "Show Corey what you can do."

Corey, her eyes swimming with ridiculous tears, watched as
the child's small fingers fumbled with the cotton laces then finally managed to tie two lopsided bows.

"Look!" Jessie shrieked, leaping to her feet. "I did it! I did
it!"

"Way cool," Stephen said, grinning as he exchanged a very
low high-five with his little girl.

"I'm impressed," Corey said, meaning every word. "I bet
you're the best shoelace tier-upper in the city."

"I am," Jessie said, nodding vigorously.

Stephen ruffled his daughter's bangs. "Get your coat, Jess.
We're walking Corey home."

Jessie was back in a flash with a bright blue down jacket with
white-and-pink racing stripes on the puffy sleeves. Stephen
made to help her with it but she shook her head. "No, Daddy,"
she said firmly. "I want Corey."

"My pleasure," said Corey, holding the jacket open while
Jessie slid her arms into the sleeves. Corey saw herself at that
age, pushing away Millicent's love with both hands. Jessie was
outgoing, friendly, and self-confident—three things Corey still
struggled with on a daily basis.

Jessie entertained them with impromptu dance steps as they
walked back to Corey's apartment. The child pirouetted,
tapped and pliéed until Stephen finally asked her to concentrate on simple walking. Corey could feel her socks being
charmed right off her feet.

"You're a lucky man," she said to Stephen as they waited for
a traffic light to change. "She's a wonderful little girl."

"I know," he said. "Jess is the one good thing to come out
of a lousy marriage."

"I take it you have custody."

"Hillary's entitled to see Jess any weekend she wants . . . she
just doesn't want to very often."

"How does Jessie feel about it?"

"She seems okay with it but who knows how she'll feel ten years from now. A little girl needs her mom."

They reached her building a few moments later.

"I suppose you have a ton of leftovers," she said.

"We ate at my sister's house. She keeps all the leftovers for herself."

"I don't know how you feel about tuna salad but . . ."

Big mistake, Stephen thought as he watched his daughter pat lettuce leaves dry with a paper towel while Corey Prescott supervised. He was a sucker for domestic entanglements and this scene was already screaming danger.

"Okay," Corey said, winking at Stephen over his daughter's head, "now you put two lettuce leaves on each piece of bread."

"Two?" Jessie asked.

"That makes the sandwich crunchy."

"Did your mommy teach you that?"

He noted a slight hesitation before she answered. "Yes, my mommy taught me that."

"Does your mommy live with you?"

Another hesitation. "No, Jessie, she doesn't."

"Hey, Jess," he said, "I left the potato chips in the living room. Would you get them for me, please?

"She hit a nerve, didn't she?" he asked Corey as his daughter raced from the room. "Your mother—"

"September." She blinked back tears. "It's still pretty new."

Tears glistened at the ends of her thick dark lashes and it took a supreme act of will to keep from brushing them away with his hand. She looked different away from the office. Without her protective shield of makeup and power clothes, she seemed younger and, if possible, even more lovely.

"You feel like talking?"

She shook her head. "It just hurts so much sometimes. . . ."

"My mother died last year," he said. "I still find myself reaching for the phone to tell her about something Jess did in school."

"It doesn't get easier?"

"It gets different," he said. "I wouldn't say it gets easier."

"Damn," she said, her voice husky. "I was hoping someone would tell me it gets easier."

Their eyes met and held. Something stirred deep in his gut, a primal urge to gather her close and tell her everything would be all right. *Don't be a fool, Gold. You've gone down this road before.*

This was how it started. She looks vulnerable. You feel protective. And the whole ancient dance begins again. He had to remind himself that she made her living as a spin doctor, someone who bent the truth for a living.

Whoever came into their lives, she had to be willing to stay the course. Jessie had been hurt enough already and so had he. When Hillary walked out on them he'd made a vow that no one would ever hurt Jessie in quite that way ever again. It was a vow he intended to keep.

Jessie bounded into the room like an untamed colt. "I can't find the chips, Daddy, and I looked everywhere."

"Come on, kid," he said as Corey turned back to the tuna sandwiches. "Let an expert show you where to look."

"Good timing," Corey said softly as father and daughter left the room in search of potato chips. The mood had gotten way out of hand. She was horrified with herself for getting teary in front of a stranger. Especially one she worked with. Another minute or two of sympathy and she might have spilled her sorry guts to him and ruined everything.

Kitchens were dangerous places. It was hard to feel cool and professional when you were making tuna salad sandwiches. As a rule, she prided herself on her ability to block out emotion, to concentrate on business to the exclusion of all else, and it horrified her that she'd revealed so much . . . and so quickly.

"Come on!" she called, carrying a plate of sandwiches to the kitchen table. "Supper's ready."

Every time it seemed as if the conversation were about to veer off toward something substantive, Jessie piped up with a knock-knock joke or an impromptu tap dance recital. Corey had the feeling Stephen was every bit as relieved as she was. *Fine,* she thought. *We're in agreement.* Neither one of them was looking for anything beyond friendship.

They polished off the sandwiches in record time, demolished the bag of chips and a huge bottle of soda, then settled down to see what they could do with the carton of milk and some cookies. Jessie ate a cookie and drank half a glass of milk then fell asleep on the sofa.

"I'd better get her home," Stephen said. "It's almost her bedtime."

"Stay a little longer," Corey urged. If he left she'd be forced to think about Lili. "I'll make coffee."

She filled the pot with water, measured the coffee into the filter, then pushed the On button. Minutes later they were back at the kitchen table.

"My parents used to have coffee together every night," she said. "They'd go out for a walk after dinner then sit down at the kitchen table over a cup of coffee and talk for hours."

"My wife and I sat down over coffee every night and fought like hell."

She started to laugh. "Which explains why she's your ex-wife."

"That and the guy she was screwing every afternoon while I was at work."

"I'm sorry."

"So was I," he said. "How about you? Married, single?"

"Divorced. Henry and I had no business getting married and, thank God, we realized it before either one of us got hurt." Henry had been rebounding from a broken romance and Corey had still been struggling to figure out who the "new and improved" Corey Banning was. Marriage had seemed like a safe harbor in which to ride out the storm.

"Anyone on the horizon?" Stephen asked.

"I don't have time," she said. "Now that I'm with Lili!, I may never have time again."

"Don't knock the unexpected," he said. "Sometimes the best things pop up when you're not looking."

"I don't think that's going to happen for me, Stephen," she said quietly. "I have other plans."

29

Grant's wife delivered a healthy, seven pound baby boy on the Tuesday after Thanksgiving. Grant called Lili from the hospital to tell her the good news.

"I'm so happy for you, darling," she said. "Kiss the little one for me and give my best to Felicia." She promised to be at the hospital the next morning to meet her first grandchild.

Grandchild. The word made her shudder. She didn't feel like a grandmother. She didn't feel forty-nine years old. In some ways she was still seventeen, waiting for her life to begin.

She buzzed Devon. "Send flowers to Felicia at Mount Sinai."

"Girl or boy?"

"A boy," she said, feeling a sharp pang of something close to regret.

There was a long silence from Devon. "Does he have a name?"

"I didn't ask."

"Better find out, Grandma. The press will want to know."

An idea occurred to Lili. "Tell Ms. Prescott I want to see her immediately."

"You tell her," said Devon. "I'm calling the florist."

"Prioritize, darling. That's what I pay you to do."

Devon muttered something that Lili chose to ignore. There were times when selective deafness was the only way to deal with employees.

Corey Prescott appeared in her office five minutes later.

"You wanted to see me?"

Lili leaned back in her chair and crossed her legs. "Day care."

"Excuse me?"

"We're going to open a day care facility on prem for employees."

"You say that like it was your idea."

"It's something I've been considering for a long time."

Corey's dark blue eyes flashed with anger. "I sent you a memo about that yesterday."

"And it was a wonderful memorandum," Lili said smoothly. "It echoed my own sentiments exactly."

The young woman's jaw visibly tightened.

"You have a temper," Lili observed. "You would do well to learn to control it."

"What I have is a well-developed sense of fair play."

"Check your contract, darling, and pay particular attention to the clauses that deal with intellectual property." Corey inhaled sharply but said nothing. Lili suppressed a smile. "We'll make the announcement tomorrow morning from Mount Sinai."

"Mount Sinai?"

"My son's wife delivered a boy two hours ago. We'll have the press meet us at the hospital tomorrow morning and make the announcement *en famille*."

Corey glanced down at her hands. Lili sensed that the fight had drained out of her public relations expert. Normally that filled her with triumph but, strangely, this time she felt concerned.

"Is there a problem?"

Corey rose from her chair. "None whatsoever. I'll call Mount Sinai to secure a room for 11:00 a.m., then fax a notice to the press."

"You might want to include the major women's groups. See if there's one specifically aimed at working mothers."

"I'll get right on it."

Ms. Prescott still had a lot to learn about how things were done at Lili! International, but Lili was not displeased with the younger woman's efforts on the company's behalf. She'd quickly gauged the situation between the company and the various animal rights groups and suggested Lili host a gala for the Humane Society. In addition, Corey recommended a heavy contribution to the user-friendly North Shore Animal League, and—in a stunning display of genius—urged Lili to donate research equipment to a children's hospital in Saint Louis that specialized in treating birth defects. A not-so-subtle reminder of what could happen if a product wasn't properly tested.

Still, there was something about the young woman that un-nerved Lili, an undercurrent of anger and longing that felt strangely personal.

Suddenly Lili wanted to hear Whit's voice. She needed a touchstone, someone who knew all her secrets. Someone who would understand.

She flipped through her personal phone book and found his number in Barbados. The telephone rang six times and she was about to hang up when a woman answered.

"Whitman Paley, please."

"Who's calling?" The woman had a British accent. Lili hated British accents.

"Who's asking?" Lili countered.

"Whit isn't available right now," the woman said smoothly. "Perhaps you'd like to call back in an hour."

Not in an hour, Lili thought as she hung up the receiver. Next time he would do the calling.

"...Lili! International is committed to the welfare of the next generation same as I am committed to the welfare of my new grandson, John Carter Spaulding."

Corey watched as Lili pressed a kiss to the top of the new-born's head then looked out at the audience of hardened news types like the Madonna with the Christ child. She was almost daring them to lob a hardball her way. "The donation to the children's wing of Mount Sinai will be made in his name."

The sight of Lili Spaulding cradling her infant grandson hurt so much Corey thought she would die from it. Lili had no right to that happiness, not when the foundation for that happiness had been built on someone else's pain. It should be Millicent cooing over a beloved grandbaby, Millicent looking forward to spoiling him, Millicent with many happy years with her family still ahead of her.

Corey waited near the door while the photographers snapped pictures of the world's most glamorous grandmother. Her hands were shaking with rage and she finally laced her fingers together in an attempt to keep them still. When Lili an-nounced she would hold a press conference in the media room at Mount Sinai, Corey had found the woman's willingness to capitalize on a personal family event astonishing. She'd been accused of that same single-minded determination and seeing it in the woman who'd given her life was unsettling. She'd wanted to believe they shared nothing more than the nine months she was in Lili's womb, but maybe she was wrong.

She also realized something else this afternoon. Lili! International was only the means to an end for her birth mother. Corey had believed the corporation gave meaning to Lili's life but she'd been wrong. The day care center, the news conference, this photo op, all of it had been orchestrated with one goal in mind: to push Grant Spaulding closer to elected office. Everyone from Lili's assistant Devon to Stephen Gold to her entire public relations staff had warned her of the intense nature of the relationship between mother and stepson but Corey hadn't understood until now.

"My mother-in-law's bad enough," Devon had said over a cup of coffee yesterday afternoon. "Imagine having Mrs. S. looking over your shoulder every time you had a fight with the Golden Boy. Once that baby's born, Felicia'd better hire herself a food taster because her days are numbered."

Corey had laughed at the time but she wasn't laughing now. There wasn't room in Lili's life for anything but Grant.

Lili met her eyes from across the room then pointedly glanced at the huge clock on the far wall.

Corey stepped forward and took the podium. "Thank you for joining us, ladies and gentlemen. If you need further information, feel free to contact me at the office."

As if by magic, the door opened and Grant strode in, the conquering warrior who had come home to his family. He gave Lili a loving kiss on the cheek then scooped up his son and the three of them posed for more pictures. Didn't it occur to anyone that there was someone missing from his familial scene? Devon had hit the nail on the head. Felicia Weatherly Spaulding had done her job, now it was time to forget about her until the next blessed event.

"Ms. Prescott, we need this room immediately for another press conference." The hospital administrator sounded agitated.

Corey drew in a deep breath. "I apologize for the delay, Mr. Sweeney. Let me see what I can do."

Lili cornered her five minutes later in the hallway. Grant was with her, looking smug and unpaternal. "How dare you interrupt when we're dealing with the press. Was another ten minutes that much to ask?"

"Yes, it was. The American Cancer Society had an event scheduled for eleven o'clock. What kind of press do you think you'd get if you kept them waiting any longer?"

Lili wheeled and strode off down the hallway.

"Don't worry," said Grant, placing a hand on her shoulder. "She always does that when she's wrong."

She reached up and removed his hand. "I would have preferred an apology."

"I'm afraid that won't happen," he replied, catching her hand in his. "But she knows you're good, Corey. Your position here is safe."

Gratitude, she warned herself. *Show some humility.*

"Thank you." She managed to sound sincere, almost choking on the words. "My job with Lili! means a great deal to me."

"I'm glad to hear that," Grant said almost shyly. "That makes me feel better about what I'm about to ask you."

He was up to something. Grant Spaulding was many things, but uncertain wasn't one of them.

"What are you about to ask me?"

"To have lunch with me."

"Go have lunch with your wife," she told him. "Remember your wife? The one who just gave birth to your son."

"Whoa!" He raised his hands, palms out, to stop her tirade. "You're jumping to conclusions."

Disgusted, she started for the exit but he blocked her way.

"This is business," he stated. "I need your help planning my campaign."

"Please." She pushed past him and stepped outside into the chill November air. "Don't insult my intelligence."

"We got off on the wrong foot," he persisted, offering up an uncertain smile. "You've made your feelings clear. Trust me, Corey." He lowered his voice as two goggle-eyed nurses walked past. "This is strictly business."

She was about to tell him exactly what he could do with his business when she saw Lili watching them from the lobby with a look of naked fear on her beautiful face.

Don't do this, Lili's look said. *Stay away from him.*

That was all Corey needed to see. She answered his smile with a bright smile of her own, a smile that she hoped cut Lili Spaulding to the bone. "Fine," she said. "Let's have lunch."

Lili's stomach knotted as she watched Grant and Corey Prescott head off down the street. Carter used to say she was blind to Grant's faults but she was well aware of his failings. Carter believed Grant to be irredeemable while Lili believed wholeheartedly that one day Grant would make them all proud.

She still believed it. She'd seen the change in him these past few months. He'd truly become a family man in the best sense of the word. He'd been devoted to Felicia during her pregnancy, catering to her every whim, even accompanying her on endless trips to Rhode Island to visit with her odiously boring family. And there was no denying his joy at the birth of young John Carter.

She had some wonderful surprises in store for Grant, surprises that would boost his visibility even higher. The FDA had approved the Night-Way formula. There was no reason not to get that particular ball rolling ASAP. Under the tightest security imaginable, Lili had given the Somerset factory orders to roll out a limited quantity of product in time to grab some holiday headlines. If everything worked according to plan, Lili intended to move the launch to coincide with the primaries. Grant's nomination was far from being a shoo-in. He would need as much help as she and Lili! International could provide.

Grant wouldn't be foolish enough to risk his political future on a tumble with the new head of public relations. Even a man blinded by hormones could recognize danger when he saw it. Corey Prescott was nobody's fool. She'd probably sized up Grant's intentions within her first five minutes on the job and would know exactly how to use it against him if circumstances warranted.

She turned away from the window, feeling every one of her forty-nine years and more.

"Admit it," Grant said to Corey over blinis and caviar. "I'm not as bad as you thought."

Corey angled him a smile. "You couldn't possibly be as bad as I thought."

"I'm direct," he said. "I ask for what I want."

"I'm direct also," she countered, "and nothing has changed. I still won't go to bed with you."

"Not yet," he corrected her. "But you're weakening."

She had to laugh at the outrageousness of his statement. If he interpreted that as interest, then all the better for her. "Has anyone ever talked to you about your ego?"

"I'm a winner," he said, giving her one of those soulful looks he seemed to specialize in. "You call it ego, I call it self-confidence."

"Actually, I call it annoying."

"You're blunt," he observed. "I like that."

"I don't particularly care if you like it or not, Grant. Arrogant men don't appeal to me."

His eyes glittered with interest. "What kind of men do appeal to you?"

She thought of Stephen Gold and the way his angular face softened when he looked at his little girl. *Kind men,* she thought, taking a sip of tea. *The type of man you would never understand.*

"I like men who know what they want and how to get it."

"I want you," he said, "and I intend to have you."

By the time they said goodbye in front of the Russian Tea Room, Corey knew that the only thing worse than lunch with Grant Spaulding would be dinner with Grant Spaulding. She deserved an Oscar for making him believe he might actually have a chance with her.

"Going back to the hospital?" she asked as she dodged a goodbye kiss.

He looked at her blankly for a second then quickly dissembled. "Absolutely. John Carter's birth is the best thing that ever happened to me."

Sure it is, she thought as she made her way back to the office. She wondered if the newborn had even registered on his radar screen as anything more than a swell photo op. The thought that Lili obviously believed the earth revolved around her stepson sickened Corey in a way that went far beyond any words she had at her command.

It was a little after two-thirty when she arrived back at Lili! International. The door to Stephen Gold's office was partially open and she could hear the sound of his pen scratching across paper. She'd told herself life would be a lot simpler if she avoided Stephen and Jessie. They didn't need the complications she brought with her, but it seemed as if she somehow needed them.

So what are you going to do, Corey? Walk in there and tell him that? The poor guy would run for the hills if he knew she was that pathetic. She had to keep it light and breezy so he wouldn't realize how lonely she really was.

She knocked then walked into the room. Stephen was busy checking over some spreadsheets. He barely acknowledged her presence, not even when she perched on the edge of his desk. "Sorry I didn't make it back in time for coffee this morning. I got held up at the hospital."

He didn't look up. "No problem."

"So how's Jessie doing?"

He swiveled his chair around to face the computer monitor. "Great."

"How about some details?"

"Look," he said, glancing at her over his shoulder. "I'm swamped. Can this wait?"

His words stung. "I was just trying to be friendly."

"Save it for your pal Spaulding."

"What did you say?"

He turned back around to face her. "You heard me. I said save it for Spaulding."

"What's that supposed to mean?"

"You know damn well what it means, Prescott. You sold out to the enemy."

She whistled softly. "I'm impressed. The grapevine here is scary."

"A word of advice. If you're looking for anonymity, stay out of the Russian Tea Room."

"You were there? I didn't see you."

"I was in the bookstore across the street. I saw the two of you go inside."

"It isn't what you think, Stephen."

"You don't know what I think."

"I'm not sleeping with him."

"Not yet."

"I resent that."

"You're on the fast track, kid. Two more lunches and you're the entree."

"Go to hell," she snapped and started for the door. *Let it go, Corey. Isn't this what you want people to believe?*

"Hey," he called out. "I'm sorry. It's none of my business."

She stopped in the doorway. "You should be sorry."

"The guy gets under my skin."

"That's obvious. I was going to ask you and Jessie to go ice skating with me this weekend, but I've changed my mind."

"I suppose Grant's too busy with the wife and kid."

Their gazes locked. She felt vaguely disoriented, as if someone had changed the rules and forgotten to tell her.

"Not that it's any of your business, but he's planning a run for the House of Representatives next year and wanted to see if I was interested in moonlighting." As spinner *and* mistress, but Stephen didn't need to know everything.

"So what did you say?"

"I said I'd think about it."

Stephen muttered something unpleasant about Grant's intellectual capacity.

"You're wrong," she said, toying with a mechanical pencil. "He's far from stupid."

"How much vodka did you have, Prescott? The guy's brain is in neutral."

"Sorry to disappoint you but Grant Spaulding is nobody's fool."

"Didn't take him long to con you."

"Underestimate him at your own risk, Gold. That's one man I wouldn't want for an enemy."

"How about for a lover?"

"What do you think?"

"I think you're too damn good for him, Prescott, and you ought to bail out while you still can."

"Don't worry," she said, trying to ignore the flutter inside her chest. "I won't do anything stupid."

He looked relieved. She didn't know whether she was flattered or annoyed. She also didn't know why it mattered. She barely knew Stephen Gold and yet she had the sense she knew everything that was important.

"About that skating invitation," he said. "Does it still hold?"

Her heart did a disturbing flip inside her chest. "For Jessie it does."

"We come as a team."

"Then I guess I'll have to put up with you, too."

"Saturday morning?"

"Perfect," she said.

"You realize this will put you right up there next to Malibu Barbie on Jess's top ten list, don't you?"

"Jessie's way up there on my list too," Corey said then turned and hurried from the office before she told him so was he.

Grant returned to his office around four o'clock. Lunch at the Russian Tea Room was never a total waste. He always saw at least a few members of the Old Guard, men and women who remembered Carter with fondness and who would probably support Grant out of some antiquated sense of loyalty. He had nothing against loyalty. He didn't necessarily understand the concept, but he sure as hell had nothing against exploiting it when the occasion presented itself.

And then there was Corey Prescott. He knew the type. She'd play hard to get until she wanted something from him, then the rules would change. Which was fine with him. One way or the other he'd get her into bed. It might take a little time, but he had the feeling she'd be worth waiting for. That hot little body and candy-box face were straight out of *Playboy*. One of those Vargas paintings that had inspired more than a few teenage wet dreams. There was something about the set of her mouth that made him want to—

Her mouth. That's what had been bugging him. She was a beautiful woman, no question about that, but something about her face was off. Some little component he hadn't been able to nail down until now. Her mouth was slightly off-kilter, as if an invisible string were tugging it upward a little on the right side. She had a habit of pushing her hair off her face and once he thought he'd seen the faint white flash of scar tissue from a surgeon's scalpel just below her ear. He would have thought she was too young for a major overhaul but who knows? These days women were doing everything from pumping up their tits to sucking out their thighs. A few nips and tucks shouldn't surprise anyone.

The hell with it, he thought, leaning back in his chair and looking out the window at the traffic moving slowly in the street below. He'd find out soon enough. As long as she did her job and kept the Spaulding family looking like Manhattan's answer to the Von Trapp Family Singers, he'd be willing to wait.

"Mr. Spaulding, I need a few minutes of your time."

He looked up. Frank De Vito, the head of development for Night-Way, stood in the doorway, wearing a white lab coat and his usual hangdog expression. What was with the R and D types anyway? They were the most depressing group he'd ever encountered.

He motioned the man inside. Frank closed the door behind him and strode straight toward Grant's desk. *Copping an attitude, are you?* Grant thought, flashing a friendly smile at the man. *We'll see how long that lasts.*

"Good to see you, Frank." He gestured for the man to sit down. "What can I do for you?"

"I want to reopen testing on CG-47," Frank said without preamble. "I'm more convinced than ever that we have real potential for disaster here."

That shit again. Grant bit back a few choice phrases. He had to learn to control his temper between now and the election if he wanted to claim a seat in the House. "We've been through this before, Frank," he said in measured tones. "CG-47 passed all of our testing with flying colors."

"That's not good enough."

"Not good enough?" He arched an aristocratic brow. He knew it was an aristocratic brow because his image consultant had told him so. "The FDA thinks it's good enough."

"The old methods and procedures are outdated. Given the latest findings in genetic research, I recommend we withdraw the product and escalate to a new level of testing."

"We've met each and every requirement necessary to ensure the safety of CG-47. I see no reason to reopen the matter." They'd spent enough money getting Night-Way this close to the finish line. He wasn't about to allocate any more funds to the testing process. Especially not with his campaign gearing up.

Frank slid a thick stack of papers across the desk. "Read these and you might find one."

"Perhaps you're allowing your personal feelings to color your judgment." One of De Vito's sons had died a couple of hours after birth—mercifully, or so Grant had been told.

De Vito reddened. "You have a healthy kid, Mr. Spaulding. You should be thankful."

Direct hit, Grant thought. The guy was crumbling right before his eyes.

"Let it go, De Vito. I advise you to turn your attention toward your next project or I'll find someone else who will."

"This is important," De Vito said, standing up. "You can't blow me off like this."

"A scientist should choose his words with greater precision." Grant rose to his feet, towering over the older man. "I'm not blowing you off, De Vito. I'm telling you to get with the program the way it stands now, or find another job."

They stared at each other for a full minute then De Vito wheeled and stormed out of the office. Grant reached for the phone and dialed up Dan Jarreau.

"Storm clouds," he said when the man answered. "Big ones."

"Storm clouds have silver linings," said Jarreau after Grant finished relating the incident. "I'll take care of everything."

"So what's the story, boss?" Devon appeared in the doorway to Lili's office on Wednesday afternoon. "They're taking bets in the lunchroom about the spin doctor and your baby boy."

"What!" Lili's coffee cup clattered back into its saucer.

"Everybody's talking about it. They say you could run a computer on the sparks between the two of them."

"Don't you people have anything better to do than gossip about people's love lives?"

"Don't shoot the messenger," Devon said. "Just thought you'd like to know what the peons are saying."

"I'm not angry," Lili said, struggling to get a grip on her emotions. "I'm disgusted."

"You'll get over it." Devon leaned closer and dropped her voice. "So tell me, are they doing it or aren't they?"

"Ms. Prescott is nothing more than a business associate," Lili said with a forced laugh. "Grant and Felicia are ecstatically happy."

Devon arched an overplucked brow. "Nobody over eighteen is ecstatically happy, boss."

"My son and his wife are. They have a beautiful baby and a beautiful home—make sure you tell the lunchroom gossips that the next time you're down there."

Lili dismissed her assistant with an airy wave of her hand. Were there no secrets in this place? Devon had zeroed in on the one thing Lili didn't want to hear about: Grant and Corey Prescott. Grant was his father's son. The more Prescott said no—assuming she *had* said no to more than lunch—the more energy Grant would put into changing her mind. Energy he should be using in more important and much less dangerous ways.

She stood by the window and looked down at the bustling street below. Her old UNLV course in problem solving had

never failed her before, but this time she couldn't seem to figure her way out of the mess. Grant was a new father. She
couldn't wave a magic wand and send him to Europe or Ja-
pan. He needed to be with his wife and son, to build the image
of family for his political future. Sending him away would defeat the purpose.

But there was no reason she couldn't send Corey Prescott out
of town.

She strode over to her desk and pressed the intercom.

"When do the Christmas visits begin?" she asked Devon.
For the last few years, Lili had made trips to their biggest ven-
dors in order to hand-deliver the holiday bonuses and some
corporate good cheer.

"Monday, December 4th," her assistant responded. "Chicago, Miami—it's all there in your day book."

Lili flipped through the pages as the idea took shape. Eighteen visits to eighteen cities between now and the twenty-second
of December and then they would all scatter until after the New
Year. Propinquity and temptation went hand in hand. If she
ordered Corey Prescott to accompany her on her whirlwind
trip, she would be removing temptation from Grant's path
which was exactly what she needed to do. Besides, it had been
a difficult year with the animal rights groups. It wouldn't hurt
to have her public relations director by her side.

Corey wasn't thrilled with the prospect of spending so much
time in her mother's company. She considered mounting a
protest, pointing to the sheer volume of work that passed across
her desk as good reason to stay in Manhattan, but she quickly
realized Lili's mind was made up and nothing short of an act
of God would change it.

"The car will pick you up at your apartment Monday
morning at seven," Lili's memo read. "Pack for two nights."

Chicago. Indianapolis. Minneapolis-Saint Paul. And that
was just for starters. The schedule was more involved than the
D day invasion. Too bad they were flying on the company jet,
Corey thought. She could have racked up enough frequent flier
miles to rate a vacation in Bora Bora.

She worked late on Friday and considered calling Stephen Gold to cancel out on their plans to go ice-skating the next morning but it was after midnight by the time she got home and much too late to telephone anyone. So Saturday morning found her dressed in leggings and a bulky sweater, waiting for Stephen and Jessie in the lobby of her apartment building. She'd brought her ice skates with her from Boston and they were slung jauntily over her shoulder, as if she did casual, fun things like this every day of the week.

"Corey!" Jessie burst into the lobby like a cannonball. She threw her arms around Corey's legs and hugged her tight.

"Hi, sweetie." Corey patted her awkwardly on the shoulder. "I'm so glad to see you."

"Daddy said I had to wear a coat," Jessie said, with a sharp look in her father's direction. "Real ice-skaters don't wear coats."

"Your daddy did the right thing," Corey said. "It gets real cold on the ice. You'll be happy to have it." The coat would also cushion her tiny bottom against the inevitable tumble on the ice.

"You have your own skates?" Stephen asked.

"Doesn't everybody?"

He grinned down at his daughter. "I think we've been had, Jess."

Jessie frowned. "What does that mean?"

"Your daddy's afraid I'm going to skate rings around him, Jessie." She glanced over at Stephen. "Right?"

"Are you throwing down the gauntlet, Prescott?"

"You bet I am," she said. "First one to circle the rink pays for the hot chocolate."

The rink was already crowded by the time they got there. Children's laughter mingled with the sounds of holiday music and taxi horns blaring. The typical urban mix, it was like a shot of adrenaline to Corey.

"This place is great," Corey said as they waited in line to rent skates. "I can't believe you've never taken Jessie skating here before."

"I've got news for you. I've never taken her skating, period."

"Do you mean you don't know how to skate?"

"I don't know how to skate." He started to laugh. "You're looking at me like I just announced I'm a Martian."

"Back home, only a Martian wouldn't know how to skate."

"Where is back home?" he asked, keeping a watchful eye on Jessie who was leaning over the railing to watch the skaters as they glided by.

"Cincinnati. How about you?"

"New York City, born and bred."

"It's hard to imagine growing up in New York City."

She listened, spellbound, as he told her stories about going to Yankee Stadium as a little boy, about Radio City Music Hall, and Coney Island, and the Macy's Thanksgiving Day Parade.

"You're giving me that Martian look again, Prescott."

"I'm the Martian," she said as she thought of her own childhood. "Somehow I never believed people had childhoods in New York City."

As if on cue, Jessie tugged at her sleeve. Her eyes were big and round with excitement and she could have been the poster child for happy kids anywhere in the world. Corey doubted if she'd ever looked at anyone with such pure trust and happiness in her life.

Jessie had a million and one questions about the rink and the skaters and the Zamboni machine that kept the ice in peak condition. Corey did her best to answer them all but finally stumbled. Stephen's eyes twinkled as he watched her struggle with an explanation of artificial snow.

"Help me out, Stephen," she said. "You're the parental unit around here."

"No dice," he said. "Even parental units run out of answers now and then."

Their eyes met over Jessie's head and for a second Corey felt as if she could see into her future, a future she knew could never exist for her no matter how much she'd like to pretend.

Ankles wobbling, Jessie stepped out onto the ice. She put one foot in front of the other and, to Stephen's amazement, she skated. Not well and certainly not fast, but she stayed upright and he was so proud he wanted to shout it to the world—or at least to the other skaters. His little girl approached skating the way she approached life: full speed ahead. She took her share of spills but they didn't slow her down at all.

So far Jessie was skating rings around her old man. He had the railing in a death grip and he had no intention of letting it go without a fight. That was how Corey found him when she glided over.

"Where's Jess?" he asked, trying to act as if he meant to be draped over the handrail like a cheap suit.

"She's skating with one of the instructors." Corey did a pirouette in front of him. "I think she's in love."

"Great," Stephen said. "Maybe he'll spring for her college education."

"Are you going to hold on to the rail all day?" Corey asked.

"That was the general plan."

She held out her hand. "Come on," she said. "It's as easy as walking."

"Gimme a break, Prescott. I wasn't born yesterday."

She pointed toward Jessie who whizzed by with a uniformed instructor. "Your five-year-old is doing great."

"She doesn't have as far to fall," he explained. "The view from up here is a hell of a lot scarier than the view from down where she is."

"Wimp," said Corey, a crooked grin splitting her face.

"You'd be in big trouble if I could reach you."

"You could reach me if you weren't such a wimp."

He knew when his manhood was being impugned. "Okay," he said. "You asked for it." He let go of the railing. He didn't fall. Maybe miracles existed after all.

"See? That wasn't so hard, was it?"

"I'm just standing," he reminded her. "I haven't tried moving yet."

"Remember what I told Jessie—one foot in front of the other." Her voice bubbled with laughter.

"Easy for you to say."

"You managed a doctorate," she said. "I think you can manage ice-skating."

He took a step toward her. His feet slid out from under him and he fell flat on his butt. They probably heard the thud in Bayonne.

"The doctorate was easier," he said. He scrambled to his knees and surveyed the situation. "How do I get up?"

"Give me your hand," she said. "I'll help you."

A moment later he was flat on his back on the ice with Corey sprawled across his chest. Her perfume filled his head with the scent of spice and flowers. Maybe learning to skate wasn't such a bad idea after all.

"You didn't try very hard," she said. Her breath smelled like peppermint.

"Sure I did."

"You pulled me down." She fixed him with a fierce look.

"Okay," he said. "Maybe I did."

The fierce look softened. "Maybe?"

Her silky dark hair brushed against his cheek. He touched the side of her mouth with the tip of his index finger. Her eyes widened but she said nothing and she didn't move away. Suddenly he realized how much he wanted to kiss her.

"Stephen." Her voice was soft, as if she sensed what he was thinking. "Let me get up before we get run over."

He blinked and the skating rink came back into focus. Whizzing metal blades seemed to be everywhere—all of them too close for comfort.

She rose to her feet gracefully. He scuttled toward the railing like a soft-shell crab then pulled himself up to a standing position.

"Stay there," she ordered. "I want to see how Jessie is doing."

"Don't worry," he said. "I'm not going anywhere." He leaned against the railing and tried to strike a nonchalant pose, one that hid the fact that he and the railing were now one.

Corey skated away and caught up with Jessie on the far side of the rink. Jessie's face was aglow with excitement and he decided it was worth looking like a dope to see his daughter having such a terrific time. She darted across the ice as if she'd been born with skates on her feet and Corey was out there with her, every step of the way.

I don't get you, he thought. He'd watched Corey sucking up to Grant Spaulding as if she thought the sun rose and set over his burnished head. He'd seen her go toe-to-toe with Lili Spaulding as if she were the boss and the Steel Magnolia, the employee. She had a different personality at the office, cooler, more calculating, more forceful, and it unnerved him. His ex-wife Hillary had had that ability to compartmentalize herself and he'd never been exactly sure which wife he was dealing with at any given moment.

He'd like to think that Corey—the woman who was out there, red-cheeked and laughing with his daughter—was the genuine article but he was cynical enough to know people were rarely what they seemed to be. Too bad Jessie didn't know that too. One look at his daughter's face confirmed his worst fears. His daughter was crazy about Corey and he had the feeling it was mutual. Hell, Jessie wasn't the only one. The woman had somehow gotten under his skin in record time and he didn't know how to protect his heart or Jessie's.

It would have been better if she'd let him kiss her. Their almost-kiss was more disturbing, more provocative, more exciting than any real kiss could possibly have been.

Which, of course, made it infinitely more dangerous.

The rest of the morning was a blur of sunshine and laughter and the sweet sensation that her life had taken an unexpected detour. The fact that it couldn't last made it all the more precious.

Around noon they made their way to Serendipity for lunch, a loud and rollicking place filled with kids and parents and laughter. The kind of place Corey had never been, certainly not as an adult. She felt like an alien from another planet, set down in a strange and wondrous world she'd never known existed.

"Your daughter would love our hot cocoa," their server said to Corey. "Lots of marshmallows."

Corey felt her cheeks redden as Stephen and Jessie looked on. "She's not my daughter," she said, feeling an unexpected pang of regret. "She's my friend."

"It's still great hot cocoa," the server said. Stephen stepped in and ordered three cups with plenty of marshmallows.

Corey buried her nose in her menu. *What makes you think you'll be able to best Lili Spaulding when you can't even manage lunch?* These days she seemed to wear her heart on her sleeve. Her emotions bubbled to the surface when she least expected them . . . when she could least afford it.

Take this silliness over the server's mistake. So what if she was mistaken for Jessie's mother? She'd been mistaken for wives and girlfriends and sisters before and none of those errors had set her heart thudding inside her chest or brought a lump to her throat.

Having children wasn't on her agenda. The womb-deep baby hunger so many of her contemporaries were experiencing had never been part of her makeup. The perfect little baby everyone loved might one day become an imperfect little girl nobody wanted.

Still, she had to admit there was something about Jessie that touched her deeply. Something about that little girl that made her different from all the others, that made her special. Jessie's mother had walked out on her, same as Lili Spaulding had walked out on Corey. Corey understood the little girl's loneliness because she'd lived it herself. She had no doubt that Stephen Gold was a terrific father, but all the love in the world would never fill the empty spot in Jessie's heart that belonged to the mother who'd left her behind.

She'd spent most of her life trying to fill the empty spot in her own heart and failing miserably at it. The mistakes she'd made that terrible summer between high school and college were only the beginning of a string of mistakes that culminated in her short-lived marriage to Henry Prescott. She'd mistaken sex for love so many times that she'd finally given up on both. Still there were times, like now, when she wished she believed in happy endings.

They ordered hamburgers with all the trimmings and settled back to wait. Corey was about to comment on the hot cocoa when Jessie suddenly pointed to her face and said, "Why do you do that?"

"Do what, honey?"

"Smile like that." Jessie's mouth tilted up on the right side in perfect imitation of Corey's smile. "Like someone's pulling on your mouth and—"

"Hey, Jess," Stephen broke in. "What did I tell you about asking questions like that?"

"But, Daddy—"

Corey raised her hand. "It's okay," she said to Stephen. She met Jessie's eyes. "I had an accident a long time ago, honey. The doctors fixed me up but one side of my mouth doesn't work quite like the other."

Jessie nodded. "Maria Cangelosi's grandmother got new false teeth and now she can't talk without whistling." She turned her attention back to her marshmallow-filled hot chocolate.

"Don't be mad at her," Corey said quietly to Stephen. "It was an honest question."

"One time she asked our housekeeper if she padded her hips to make them that big and round."

Corey laughed. "I think that's what they call the wonderful honesty of kids."

"Yeah," said Stephen, "and it can get the parents into a hell of a lot of trouble." He fiddled with his spoon. "I like your smile."

"It's not perfect," she said. The old insecurities were never far from the surface.

"Maybe not," he said, "but it's yours and I like it."

She didn't know how to respond. It had never occurred to her before that anyone but Millicent and Jack could love her despite her imperfections. The idea terrified and thrilled and excited her simultaneously and the mix of emotions made her dizzy with joy. At least she thought it was joy. She wasn't certain she'd ever experienced anything like this before. Her heart seemed to beat to a new rhythm, deeper, more vibrant, more alive, as if her entire body resonated to his words.

Pull back, Corey. You're all wrong for him. For them.

Jessie knew more about love, more about being part of a family than Corey ever would. Harvard Business School had taught her how to climb the ladder of success but it hadn't taught her how to love and that suddenly struck her as a terrible shame.

For a split second Stephen thought he'd actually managed to breach the wall around Corey Prescott's heart but he'd been wrong. Whatever he'd glimpsed in her eyes, whatever momentary flash of vulnerability he'd seen hiding behind the sophisticated facade, vanished as quickly as it had come. After a while he wondered if maybe it hadn't been there at all. Maybe it was his own loneliness talking, his old battered heart looking for something that wasn't there.

She seemed as relieved as he was when they were interrupted by the server, touting the wonders of dessert.

Jessie fell sound asleep at the table after her hot fudge sundae. She'd barely made a dent in the mountain of ice cream.

"The poor kid's exhausted," Corey said.

"She's had a big day." He met her eyes. "You know Jess is crazy about you."

"I kind of thought so."

"And I don't know what to do about it."

"Why do anything?" She met his eyes over the rim of her mug. "I'm very fond of her, too."

"I don't want to see her get hurt."

"Neither do I."

"And she's going to get hurt if you become an even bigger part of her life."

"Aren't you overreacting? I've only known the two of you for eight days."

"And she's already seen more of you in eight days than she's seen of her mother in the past two years."

She tried to make light of the situation. "If this is a proposal, Mr. Gold, I'm not quite ready to walk down the aisle."

"If it was just about us, I wouldn't be saying any of this, but when it comes to Jessie, I owe her better than a parade of temporary mommies. She's hungry for a mother's touch right now and she's set her sights on you."

"Has anyone ever told you to lighten up?"

"Everyone," he said, "so don't waste your breath."

"I don't want anything permanent, Stephen," she said softly. "That's not what I'm about."

"I know," he said. "That's why it's probably better Jess doesn't see you again."

"And what about you?" she asked. "Is it better for you too?"

He tried to find the easy answer but it eluded him once again.

"That's what I thought." She pushed back her chair and rose to her feet. "Enjoy your dessert," she said. "I'll take care of the check."

"Corey, I—"

"My invitation, my check," she stated over her shoulder as she started toward the front of the restaurant. "See you around the office, Gold."

He watched her walk away and wondered if in trying to protect Jessie, he hadn't made the biggest mistake of his life.

Grant flinched as if Dan Jarreau had sucker punched him in the gut. It actually hurt to pull air into his lungs. He had a sudden powerful desire to kick out his study window and let the freezing December wind blow through the room and clear away the sense of unreality.

"Tell me this is a joke," he demanded of his advisor. "Tell me this is your idea of a practical joke."

There was no mistaking the look in the other man's eyes. Grant slammed his fist down hard on his desktop.

"Son of a fucking bitch," he roared. "How the hell could this happen?"

"It doesn't matter how it happened," Dan said. "The only thing that matters now is how you handle it."

"De Vito was right," he muttered, sinking into his leather desk chair. "He knew something was wrong with CG-47. Why the hell didn't anyone else?"

"The FDA didn't even pick up the problem," Jarreau said soothingly. He wrote the name *Frank De Vito* on a slip of notepaper and tucked it into his breast pocket.

"So how did you manage to do it?" Grant asked.

"Connections," his advisor said with a mirthless laugh. "I know people who know people who can find the answers to just about anything."

Grant stared down at the report with growing anger. "Congenital birth disorders, chromosomal damage—shit. Is there anything *good* about that fucking skin cream?"

"It works," Jarreau said. "Lili! International created an antiwrinkle cream that can turn back the hands of time."

It was Grant's turn to laugh. "It works," he repeated. "We finally manage to put the goddamn Fountain of Youth in a jar and it turns out to be lethal."

"Things aren't as bad as they seem," Jarreau said. "If you handle this right, you'll still come up smelling like a rose."

"If you can find a silver lining in this pile of shit, I'll raise your salary fifty percent."

Jarreau met his eyes. "I might hold you to that."

Grant listened as Jarreau outlined a scenario that would turn Grant from corporate screwup to folk hero.

"You're telling me that all we have to do is look the other way until the primaries, then shut down the operation just before we go into production on the test run?"

"Bingo," said Jarreau.

"We'll take a bath financially." Gearing up a factory for production cost big bucks. Slamming on the brakes cost even more.

"You'll take a bath no matter when you do it, Spaulding. Why not time it right and get the most bang for your buck where it counts—in the voting booth?" He gestured toward an imaginary marquee. "Altruistic Businessman Sacrifices Profit to Save Babies. You gotta admit it has a certain ring to it."

"What about De Vito? He could open his mouth and blow the whole thing."

"I know his type," Dan said. "Too many bills, not enough scratch. We'll make it worth his while to keep quiet."

"And if he won't keep quiet?"

"He will," Dan said. "One way or the other."

31

Sunday, December 10

Lili stepped from the shower and was reaching for her heated bath towel when the telephone rang. Who on earth would call her at home at eleven o'clock on Sunday night? *Dear God, if anything has happened to Grant or the baby, I'll—*

"Congratulations, *grandmère.*"

Her heart almost stopped beating. "Whit."

"When were you planning to tell me the good news?"

"When are you planning to come home where you belong?" she countered, struggling to contain the surge of emotion brought on by the sound of his dear voice.

"Let's start again, Lil," he said with a weary laugh. "How is the new baby?"

She drew in a deep breath. Their friendship used to be so easy, so uncomplicated. She wished with all her heart they could recover that magic again. "John Carter Spaulding is brilliant, beautiful and destined for great things." She paused a moment. "How did you find out he'd arrived?"

"Things are slower in Barbados, but sooner or later news filters down to us." It was his turn to pause. "When were you planning to tell me about him, Lil?"

"I wasn't sure you were interested."

"It's come to that, has it?"

"I don't know, Whit. You tell me."

"I wasn't the one who walked out, Lil."

She sighed. "This is old territory. Must we go over it again?"

His tone grew flinty. "So nothing's changed."

"What did you expect to change, Whit? I still have my responsibilities."

"What about your needs?"

His question took her by surprise. "My needs? Good Lord, Whit. I have everything a woman could want."

"You don't believe that."

"I certainly do believe that," she snapped. "What more could I ask for?"

This time there was no hesitation. "Happiness," Whit said.

"I'm happy."

"The hell you are."

Sudden tears filled her eyes. "Are you happy?" she whispered.

"Not without you, Lil."

"I wish you wouldn't say things like that."

"I wish you wouldn't make it necessary."

"This is getting us nowhere."

"It could get us everywhere if you'd let it."

"Whit, please—"

"Come to me, Lil. We can still have a life together."

"My life is here."

"Your life is where you make it."

His words stung. "Did your new friend tell you that?"

"What new friend?"

"I called you last week. A woman answered the phone."

"That was probably Chantelle."

"Chantelle," Lili said. "What a lovely name."

"Chantelle is my housekeeper."

She said nothing.

"You're jealous." He sounded amused. "I wouldn't have thought it possible, Lil."

She ignored the comment. There were times when the truth was vastly overrated. "You're asking the impossible of me. Come back to New York so we can talk."

"Not this time."

"Darling Whit," she said softly. "The time will never be right for us, will it?"

"The time is right," he corrected her. "Unfortunately the lady isn't willing."

A sharp pain seemed to split her heart in two. "I should go now," she said. "The Christmas visits begin tomorrow and I have a great deal to do before I leave."

"I'd hate to keep you from business, Lil."

"That's not what I meant, Whit. This conversation simply isn't getting us anywhere."

"You're right," he said. "It isn't."

"You'll come up for Christmas," she said. "We'll be at the Connecticut house. We'll talk then."

"You just don't understand, do you, Lil?"

"Whit, I—"

"I love you, Lil. Nothing is going to change that, but I'm too old to play games. If you want me, you know where to find me."

Twenty-five-thousand feet wasn't that far to jump, Corey thought as the Spaulding corporate jet flew the skies between New York and Chicago.

She glanced across the aisle at Lili who was staring out the window into space. Not more than ten words had passed between them since Corey had climbed into the limousine at seven in the morning for the ride to JFK. Lili had nodded at her then buried her nose in the *Wall Street Journal*. Corey had been doing a slow burn ever since.

No doubt about it. A free fall from five miles up would be better than this silent treatment.

She cleared her throat. "Mrs. Spaulding."

No response.

Corey upped the decibel level. "Mrs. Spaulding," she repeated.

Lili started, then turned away from the window and looked at Corey. "Yes?"

Corey was thrown for a moment by the vulnerable look in her birth mother's eyes. She drew in a breath and regathered her wits about her like a suit of armor. "If I've done something you don't like, I'd appreciate it if you told me."

Lili's brows lifted. "I'm afraid I don't know what you're talking about, darling."

"This silent treatment," Corey said without preamble. "I don't know what I've done to deserve it, but the least you can do is give me the courtesy of an explanation."

Lili's sigh could be heard above the whine of the jet engines. "My apologies," she said. "If I've made you uncomfortable, it wasn't my intention."

Corey waited for the zinger but none came. She would have rather had a direct shot right between the eyes than the sense that a real person might actually exist beneath the designer clothes and all that glossy perfection.

"Is something wrong?" It was a dangerous question but suddenly she wanted to know the answer.

Lili lit a cigarette, took a swift drag, then stubbed it out in a crystal ashtray that rested on her lap table. "Nothing that hasn't been wrong for many years."

"If it's a business matter, I might be able to help."

"If it was a business matter, it wouldn't have dragged on so long," Lili said with a mirthless laugh. "This problem is personal, painfully so."

She had to be talking about Grant. As far as Corey could tell, Lili wasn't close to anyone else. "I'm a good listener," she said.

Lili considered her for a few seconds. "Tell me, darling, have you ever been married?"

"Yes," she said, wondering where this was going. "Once and briefly."

"So you understand the dynamics between husband and wife."

"Not very well. We were better as friends than lovers."

"Unfortunately that is something you can't know until it's too late." Lili smiled and to Corey's horror, the wall around her heart cracked a tiny bit.

She understands, Corey thought. The idea terrified her. "Are you in love?" she asked.

"That's a very personal question."

"Yes, it is. You don't have to answer if you don't want to."

Lili thought for a moment. "I can't imagine my life without him in it."

"Are you in love with him?"

"I love him," Lili said carefully, "but that isn't the same thing, is it?"

Corey shook her head. "Not the same thing at all."

"He's waited almost twenty years." Lili leaned her dark head against the back of her seat. "Now he can't wait until after the election. It seems we're destined to be forever in the wrong place at the wrong time." She closed her eyes. "One of life's little ironies, I suppose."

One of life's little ironies, Corey thought as she watched Lili drift off into sleep. Like the fact that beneath the facade, Lili Spaulding was as lonely as the rest of them.

That was the last quiet moment between Corey and Lili Spaulding. From the moment the jet landed at O'Hare, it seemed to Corey as if they were in a state of perpetual motion and sound. Corey relied on caffeine and the fervent hope that nothing lasted forever, not even sheer chaos.

Lili, however, thrived on it. The original plan had been to return to New York for two days before setting out again, but Lili's adrenaline was running high and fast. To Corey's dismay, the older woman scheduled impromptu stops in Montreal and Toronto instead. The darker Corey's undereye circles grew, the more vibrant and beautiful Lili became.

They met early each morning in Lili's suite to cover the day's itinerary and Corey found herself torn between grudging admiration and white-hot rage as the woman who'd given her life barked orders at her as if she were a galley slave. Maybe *slave* was too harsh but there was nothing maternal or nurturing about the woman . . . except when she talked about her stepson Grant.

The days passed in a blur. Hourly she thought about scribbling her resignation on a piece of hotel stationery and boarding the next plane for Boston. The more she was with Lili, the less clear her own motives for being there grew and the sharper her doubts. She must have been crazy to give up her old life and go searching for some type of retribution. Nothing she did would bring Millicent back. Nothing she did could erase the years of loneliness and doubt. Those years were part of her; good or bad, they had formed the woman she was. But each time Corey was ready to throw in the towel, Lili invariably said or did something that cut straight through to her angry heart.

Lili had promised they would be back in Manhattan by Friday the 22nd so they could celebrate Christmas with their families.

"Grant is hosting an open house Christmas Day for potential campaign contributors," Lili said. "I wouldn't miss that for the world."

Of course you wouldn't, thought Corey. Lili Spaulding had a family to go home to. Corey had no one at all.

Sunday, December 17

Jess amused herself at the kitchen table with her coloring book and crayons while Stephen fixed them a light supper. They'd spent the day up in the Bronx with his family, celebrating Chanukah. They'd stuffed themselves on potato latkes and applesauce and enough chocolate coins to balance the federal budget. Soup should hold them both until breakfast—and maybe an antacid chaser for him.

Jess had been quiet since they got home. He figured she was exhausted after all the excitement. The radio was playing in the background. He had it tuned to a sports station whose main focus seemed to be ripping the New York Jets. He was getting into a major discussion of what exactly was wrong with Boomer Esiason when Jessie dropped her bombshell.

"Daddy, doesn't Corey like us anymore?"

"Sure she likes us, Jess. Why do you ask?"

"She said we were friends but she won't come to see me."

Damn it, Stephen thought. This was exactly what he'd been afraid would happen. "Corey's very busy, kiddo. She's gone away on a trip with her boss."

Jessie frowned. "The lady who looks like her mommy?"

"That's the one."

"But she didn't say goodbye to us."

"She told me to say goodbye to you but I forgot."

"Really, Daddy?"

"Really."

She looked so happy he felt like a crud for lying to her that way. The truth was, Corey had left him a note stuck to his computer monitor, telling him she'd be on the road most of the time between now and Christmas. No frills. No hello for Jessie. Strictly business. He knew he had no right expecting anything else, not after their conversation at Serendipity last week where he'd made his position clear, but somewhere deep down it seemed he'd been hoping for a miracle.

He should have known better.

"Do we light our Chanukah candles tonight, Daddy?"

Stephen glanced toward the menorah on the windowsill then back at his little girl. "You bet, Jess." At least some miracles still happened.

He tucked Jessie into bed around nine o'clock. She was so wound up from excitement it took six versions of *Cinderella* to put her to sleep. Probably from boredom, he thought as he closed her bedroom door. Storytelling wasn't his strong suit. Especially not the ones with happy endings.

He went back into the living room and flipped on the TV. The best thing on was a twenty-year-old "Mary Tyler Moore Show" rerun. He clicked off the set. He could always get some work done but that didn't sound a whole lot better. He hated Sunday nights. Sunday nights were about all the fun you didn't have on Saturday and all the work you had to do on Monday. As far as he was concerned, they could cut Sunday night out of the lineup and nobody would miss it.

"The hell with it," he muttered. Maybe he would try to knock off some work until it was a decent hour for a thirty-five-year-old man to go to sleep. He switched on the computer and went into the kitchen to pour himself a cup of coffee.

"Coward." Corey dropped the telephone receiver back into its cradle. Three times she'd dialed Stephen's number and three times she'd lost her nerve just before it began to ring. She called mayors, movie stars and assorted famous people on a regular basis. Why was she finding it so difficult to call a single father from Manhattan?

Come on, Corey. The least you can do is admit it to yourself.

"I miss him," she said out loud to her empty hotel room. She'd known him less than a month yet she already understood him better than she'd understood her husband after a year. The minute she'd seen him with Jessie, seen the way he loved that little girl, she'd known that he was the kind of man she could fall in love with.

Not that he was about to fall in love with her. He'd made his feelings on that score crystal clear the afternoon they went ice-skating at Rockefeller Center. Jessie was his first priority and he was willing to sacrifice his own happiness to ensure the happiness of his daughter. That mysterious parental connection that transcended blood ties—Millicent and Jack had known all about it.

Lili Spaulding hadn't a clue.

Corey drew in a breath and reached for the phone again. There was no reason she and Stephen couldn't be friends. She missed his slightly sardonic take on life at Lili! almost as much as she missed the fact that she had a friend.

So pick up the phone, idiot. The harsh words exchanged at Serendipity still stung. Corey left town two days later on this endless promotional trek with Lili and she and Stephen hadn't had the chance to mend fences.

She reached for the phone, hit the Redial button, and waited.

The phone rang as Stephen reached for the sugar.

"Happy Chanukah, Stephen."

He recognized her voice instantly. Low. Husky. Maybe a little lonely? "Thanks, Prescott," he said. "How goes it out there in the heartland?"

He heard an intake of breath. "It goes long," she said, then laughed. "*Very* long."

He leaned against the counter and took a gulp of coffee. "So where are you?"

"Dallas—no, scratch that. We're in Fort Worth. Lili did three presentations today before three different church groups."

"Church groups?"

"Amazing, isn't it? She managed to find a connection between religion and cosmetics."

"The Steel Magnolia could find a connection between cosmetics and nuclear fusion." He leaned against the counter and took another swig of coffee. Too bad it wasn't Scotch. "So, when do you come back?'' Not that it mattered. He was only making conversation.

"Thursday. At least that's what she said tonight. If she had her way, we'd probably share Santa's sleigh and slip a sample of bath oil into Christmas stockings from here to Taiwan.''

"You're learning,'' he said, chuckling despite himself. He didn't want to be reminded that she was funny as well as beautiful. "Nothing comes between Lili Spaulding and business. Not even her grandchild.''

"Grant does.''

"What was that?'' Her voice was so low he couldn't quite make out the words.

"I said, Grant Spaulding comes before everything.''

There was a note of longing in her tone that struck him as odd. But no odder, he supposed, than the fact that she had called him at all.

She told him a long and involved story about their stopover in Toronto that made him laugh out loud. "You could take that stuff on the road, Prescott. You'd knock 'em dead on the comedy circuit.''

"I don't think I'm cut out for the road,'' she said. "Living out of a suitcase leaves a lot to be desired.''

They were silent for a few moments and then he took the plunge. "I'm sorry about that lunch—''

"No, no! I'm the one who should be—''

"I didn't mean to come down so—''

"I'm too thin-skinned. Of course you have to—''

"It's Jessie,'' he said. "Everything I do impacts her life and—''

"I understand.'' Her tone was softer than before. "And I admire you for it.''

"For doing what's right?'' What the hell had happened in her life that she admired a man simply for taking care of his child?

"Yes,'' she said, "and for telling me right up front.''

"I made an ass of myself.''

"Maybe,'' she said with a small laugh, "but at least we know where we stand now.''

Suddenly he wasn't so sure about that. There was a softness to Corey Prescott that she did her damnedest to hide from the world. He'd seen it in the way she treated Jessie, in the way her eyes welled up with tears when she talked about her late mother—hell, he'd seen it that afternoon at the skating rink when it seemed as if they were the only two people on the island of Manhattan who understood what joy was all about.

"Stephen." Her voice broke into his thoughts. "We do know where we stand now, don't we?"

He cleared his throat. "Friends, right?"

A pause, then she said, "Of course. Friends."

Friends, Corey thought as she hung up the phone a half hour later. She'd wanted nothing more than friendship from Stephen Gold when she called him and now that she had it, she felt lonelier than ever.

He'd made her laugh with stories about Jessie lighting the menorah at his sister's house, and the latkes commentary was priceless. His wife may have walked out on him and Jessie, but he still had a large and loving family to turn to when the going got rough.

"Damn," she swore softly. Why couldn't they have met a year ago, back before Millicent died and Corey found out about Lili Spaulding? If fate had been looking for a way to play the ultimate cosmic joke on her, it had succeeded royally. She knew in her heart that she could be good for Stephen—and for Jessie, too—but she could never be part of their lives. And she had Lili to thank for that.

Stephen's telephone rang again not two minutes after he finished speaking with Corey. He'd been cursing himself roundly for forgetting to ask where she'd be staying tomorrow and he grinned as he lifted the receiver.

"Great minds," he said. "Give me the name of tomorrow's hotel and I'll—"

The voice he heard wasn't Corey's. "Sorry for calling so late," said Frank De Vito, "but we've got a problem."

* * *

The next morning Frank was waiting for Stephen at the coffee shop around the corner from Lili! International. It was a blustery, raw day thick with heavy clouds. You could smell a snowstorm in the air.

"You look like hell," Stephen said as he claimed the bench opposite the man. "How long has it been since you got some sleep?"

Frank grunted something then pushed a thick manila envelope across the table. "Read it and weep."

Stephen barely managed to suppress a groan. Frank De Vito had cried wolf so many times that nobody listened to him anymore. He'd lost his newborn son some few years ago to a congenital lung abnormality and he'd turned his anger into his work, attacking his research with almost missionary zeal. So far, no matter how hard he looked, all of the Lili! products had come up aces high.

Still, there was something about the look in Frank's eyes that made Stephen open the envelope and extract the document. "You don't expect me to read this now, do you? I'm already late for work."

"Actually, yeah, I do."

Stephen skimmed the dense columns of text and numbers. "How bad could it be?"

Frank outlined a scenario that included possible chromosomal damage.

"Do you have any conclusive proof?"

"Not yet. I spoke to Spaulding a few weeks ago about scheduling a new series of tests but he told me to pound salt."

"Does he understand the implications?"

"He doesn't understand how to tie his own shoes. All he's thinking about is how he can save money. I E-mailed Mrs. Spaulding but haven't heard back from her yet."

"You did your part," Stephen said. "You can't force them to pay attention to you."

"They're gearing up for a test run in the spring. If a pregnant woman used this shit, she—" He obviously couldn't finish his thought. Stephen didn't have to ask why. They were both fathers. They understood the miracle of a healthy child.

This isn't your fight, Stephen told himself. They'd taken him off the CG-47 Night-Way unit three years ago. He no longer had the developmental details at his fingertips. He'd have to dig back into his research notes and familiarize himself again with the entire operation before he reread De Vito's paperwork in order to do it justice.

Right now he didn't have time. They were doing a major lab push before the Lili! staff scattered to the four winds for the holidays. Maybe he'd manage to find a spare hour or two during the two-week company-wide vacation. The first batch of test product wasn't due to be jarred until April, which meant they still had four months to decide if there really was a problem.

"I'll do what I can," Stephen said, "but don't expect any miracles."

Frank's laugh was bitter. "Believe me, Gold, I'll have my miracle even if I have to blow the whistle on them myself." He told Stephen he was thinking of visiting the plants on Long Island and in Somerset, New Jersey to see what he could find out from some of the on-site technicians.

"You'd better watch your ass," Stephen said. "Spaulding has his eye on you. Make trouble and you'll probably find yourself out on the street."

"You know what?" Frank met his eyes across the table. "That might be the best thing that ever happened to me."

Corey told herself she wasn't going to call Stephen again but the next night she found herself reaching for the telephone.

"I didn't wake Jessie, did I?" she asked after he said hello. How wonderful his voice sounded. How strong and male and exciting.

"She's been asleep for over an hour," he said. "Only took three versions of *Cinderella* tonight."

"I thought there was only one version of Cinderella," she said. "The one with the happy ending."

"So where are you tonight?" he asked.

"Denver."

He whistled low. "You get around, don't you?"

"We were supposed to be heading east but the blizzard—"

"You've got a blizzard?"

"No, but you're going to get walloped with one helluva snowstorm tomorrow. Chicago's been blitzed and it's heading your way. Lili's pilot recommended we stay put another day before we begin working our way home."

"Any chance this storm will turn out to be a blizzard?"

His words sliced into her like a knife. "Thanks a lot, Gold." She tried for a flip, who-gives-a-damn tone but failed miserably. "I promise I won't drop in on you once I do get back."

"That's not what I meant, Prescott."

"Then what did you mean?" She waited but he said nothing. "Fine. Don't tell me. Believe it or not, I know how to take a hint. It's been great talking to you, Stephen, but—"

"I'm sorry."

Her eyes widened. "Really?"

"Don't sound so surprised. It's been a lousy day. I had no business taking it out on you."

"A lousy day?" She reached for her snifter of brandy. "It's my dime. If you feel like talking, I'm a fairly good listener."

"Do you know Frank De Vito?"

"From R and D, right? Tall, intense—"

"That's the one. He says there's a major glitch with CG-47."

She put down the snifter and sat up straight. "How major?"

"If he's right, it could take down Night-Way."

"What do you think?"

"I think he may be on to something."

"When will you know?"

"I'll study his findings over the Christmas break."

"What if De Vito's right and there's a real problem? Will that give you time to shut down production?"

"All it takes to shut down production is one word from Lili," he said.

Corey felt a whisper of apprehension brush across the back of her neck. "Assuming you could prove it to her before the product hits the shelves."

"There's plenty of time for that."

"I suppose there is," she allowed. "Besides, what are the chances something that important slipped past the FDA?"

"A million-to-one," he said. "Given De Vito's history, this is probably a dead end."

"What about De Vito's history?" She listened, alternately horrified and saddened, by the story. "You don't think Frank would falsify his findings, do you?"

"I hope not," Stephen said. "That's one of the things I'll have to watch out for."

"I wish I were there," she said.

"So do I."

Her heart lurched. "Really?"

"Yeah," he said. "Really."

She cradled the receiver against her cheek. "We have a lunch in Philly Friday afternoon. I'll be home by evening."

"I'll call you."

"You will?"

"I said I would, Prescott. Trust me."

She did and it scared the hell out of her.

32

Tuesday, December 19

"Daddy!" Jessie burst into the living room a little after dawn and jumped into Stephen's lap. "It's snowing outside! Can we make a snowman, please please please?"

"Whoa, Jess!" He kissed the top of her tousled head. "What about school?"

"Too much snow." She pointed toward the window. "Look!"

He swiveled his head and peered through the blinds. "Wow," he breathed. "Looks like a blizzard." The street, the cars, the garbage lining the curb, everything had been covered with a benevolent blanket of white. "You may be right about school, kiddo."

"Yeah!" Jessie threw her arms around his neck. "We can play in the snow."

"*You* can play in the snow," he corrected her. "I still have to go to work."

Her lower lip jutted forward. "Don't go to work."

"I have to go."

"No, you don't. Stay home with me."

"If I stay home with you, we won't have a home to stay in much longer." He tilted her chin with his thumb until she met his eyes. "Remember what I told you about responsibility?"

"I guess." She looked so little and vulnerable that his heart turned over.

"If you hurry up and get dressed, I bet we could sneak in one quick snowman before I leave."

Her entire face lit up. "Really?"

"Really. Go get your snowsuit. Last one out the door is a rotten egg."

Few problems in life surpassed helping a squirming six-year-old out of a wet snowsuit. By the time the housekeeper arrived, Stephen was running late. He kissed Jess goodbye, grabbed his gear, and raced out of the apartment. Normally his commute was a brisk ten-minute walk. Today it took almost half an hour which gave him time to think about the problem that had kept him up most of the night.

No matter how you cut it, Frank De Vito wasn't the guy to carry the standard into battle—assuming there would be a battle. Frank's emotions were too raw on the topic and, given past history, his arguments were likely to go unheeded. You could cry wolf just so many times before the shepherds turned a deaf ear.

They'd listen to you. The thought hit him hard. He'd been an idealist once a long time ago but he'd learned the hard way. The world was what it was; there was nothing Stephen Gold could do to make that big a difference.

He hadn't always been so cynical. When he first started working, he'd actually been shocked by the sloppy methods employed by the Mayfair research staff and tried to do something about it. He'd stormed Grant Spaulding's office, armed with facts and figures and the stink of a hundred risky chemicals, but that smug bastard had turned a blind eye to everything Stephen had to show him.

"Just do your job, Gold," the WASP prince had said, looking across a mile of marble-topped desk to where Stephen stood. "There are a hundred others who can do it as well as you can."

And when you had a little girl looking to you for support, things like that mattered.

He didn't have to save the world. All he had to do was save the part of it that would belong to his daughter and that didn't include risking the Steel Magnolia's wrath. Or his job.

Last night he'd heard genuine concern in Corey Prescott's voice. And it wasn't only concern for the future of Night-Way. He'd told her about De Vito's assumptions and her questions had zeroed in on the women and children whose lives could be irreparably harmed if those assumptions were proved right. He'd met enough spin control experts in his day to know that the bottom line was usually the first and last thing they considered when faced with a problem. The human concerns were as alien to their thought patterns as high finance was to his.

But not with Corey. She cared and that fact brought his other assumptions into sharp relief. He'd told her he didn't want her to be part of Jessie's life, that his daughter's heart had already been broken once and he didn't intend for it to happen again, but maybe he'd been lying to himself. Maybe it was his own heart he was trying to protect.

Corey called Stephen from her hotel room after dinner Wednesday night. They were in New Orleans and Lili had gone off to have drinks with some key store personnel.

"Come with us, darling," she'd said. "Francesca knows the best hideaways in the French Quarter."

"Sounds wonderful," Corey lied, "but I'm going to pass. I have a beastly headache."

Lili eyed her with curiosity. "You look perfectly well."

"I owe it all to Lili! International," she'd said, brandishing a lipstick to everyone's amusement.

She was tired of talking business morning, noon and night. She was tired of not being able to tell what city she was in unless she checked the local newspaper. And more than anything, she was tired of Lili Spaulding.

It felt wonderful to escape to her hotel room, take a long hot shower, then curl up with the telephone.

"I missed you last night," Stephen said as she leaned back against the headboard. "Why didn't you call?"

"We were in Los Angeles," she said, "at a fund-raiser. I didn't think you'd appreciate being blasted out of bed at four in the morning."

"I was awake anyway," he said. "Too bad I didn't have your number. I would have called you. Where are you now?"

"New Orleans."

"New Orleans," he repeated. "You're getting closer to home, Prescott."

An unfamiliar warmth spread through her limbs, making her feel as if she'd had a two-hour massage. "So how's the weather?" she asked, heading for safer ground. "Had enough snow?"

His laughter was low and very appealing. "Damn right but Jess thinks it's terrific."

She smiled as he told her about the snowball fight they had in the park after supper. "Sounds like fun."

"It was," he said. "Jess asked about you."

Corey's breath caught. Ridiculous that such a simple thing would bring about such an intense response. "So what did you tell her?"

"That you were on a business trip. She's worried that Santa Claus won't know where to find you."

"She believes in Santa?"

"Her mom is Catholic," Stephen said. "We cover all the religious bases around here."

"You tell Jessie that I'll be home in time for Christmas. Santa won't have any trouble finding me."

"I'm glad," he said.

"So am I," she whispered.

This is enough, she thought after they said goodbye some time later. *A friendship. Someone to talk with. Someone who cares where I am and what I'm doing. Someone who—*

She sighed and burrowed deeper under the covers. It wasn't even close to being enough.

Antoinette's was a loud, smoky jazz joint tucked between two small and pricey hotels. Lili wondered how anyone in the hotels managed to get any sleep with the music and laughter rocking the walls of the club. She thanked God and her travel agent that the hotel where she and Corey Prescott were staying was quiet, private and far from the madding crowd.

Francesca, her top east coast sales executive, leaned across the table. "Isn't this marvelous, Mrs. Spaulding? Best jazz in town."

Lili nodded and lit another cigarette. At least no one cast outraged glances her way as she drew the dark tobacco smoke into her lungs. Vices were not only ignored in New Orleans, they were encouraged. Lili had no problem with that, she only wished they could find a way to sin at a lower decibel level.

She managed to sit through two sets and six cigarettes before she pushed back her chair and rose to her feet.

Francesca frowned. "Are you leaving, Mrs. Spaulding? They say Wynton Marsalis might—"

"Ladies' room," Lili said over the din. "I'll be back."

Francesca relaxed visibly. "I'll join you."

"That's not necessary, dear." Lili forced her smile wider. "I fly solo."

She turned and cut her way through the crowd. Her head was pounding and she needed some peace and quiet, even if it was only for five minutes inside a stall.

The ladies' room was much nicer than the club would have indicated. Clean, well-lit, and blissfully quiet. Lili sank onto the padded bench facing the mirror and was calculating how much longer she needed to endure the companionship of her employees when the door swung open and a willowy blond woman of a certain age joined her.

"I don't know about you," the woman said, digging in her bag for a lipstick, "but I can't abide jazz."

Lili smiled blandly but said nothing.

"You just can't hum jazz," the woman went on, applying the bright red lipstick thick enough to caulk tile.

Lili itched to wipe her mouth with a square of paper towel and give her an impromptu lesson in makeup application. She hadn't seen such criminal misuse of cosmetics since she lived in Euless.

"Personally I think jazz is much too black for me—" she met Lili's eyes in the mirror. "Not that I'm prejudiced or anything."

"Of course not," Lili said smoothly, reaching into her own bag for her small gold compact.

"What a beautiful compact!" The woman turned around to take a better look and an odd feeling of apprehension washed over Lili.

"Thank you."

"I've never seen anything like it."

"I don't imagine you would have," Lili said. "It's one of a kind."

"Ohh." The woman's tone was reverent. She looked from the compact to Lili. "You know, it's just the strangest thing— and I promise you I'm not crazy—but I have the oddest feeling I know you from somewhere."

"I suppose that's possible," Lili said, wondering how quickly she could make it to the door and back out into the comfort of smoke and noise.

"Lili," the woman said slowly. Then, "Lilly Ann!"

The blood seemed to rush from Lili's brain as she stared at the stranger before her. "How on earth—?"

The blond woman threw back her head and laughed. "Lilly Ann, don't you recognize me? It's Teena Marie Franklin—well, it's Teena Dixon now, has been for years and years. I declare, girl, it's something to bump into you this way."

Lili thought she was going to pass out. Her blood pounded so hard she could barely hear the woman's words. Teena Marie? This nipped-and-tucked bleached blonde with the weary eyes was the same petulant teenager who'd sat across from her at Maisie's supper table all those years ago.

"It's been a long time, Teena." Lili extended her right hand. "You're looking well."

"Oh, don't you be so formal." Teena ignored Lili's outstretched hand and threw her arms around Lili. "We're family, aren't we?"

The overpowering smell of Obsession made Lili feel as if she were about to retch.

"Family?" Lili said, slipping out of the woman's grasp. "I don't think so."

"Well, of course, we're almost family." Teena's bright enthusiasm dimmed just a tiny bit. "Why, you and Clifford Earle were going to get married."

"I remember how happy that made your family." Lili couldn't quite keep the bitterness from her voice.

"Now that's all water under the bridge . . . or is it over the bridge?" Teena's laugh was as fake as her breasts. "I never can remember which one."

Lili rose to her feet. "It's been wonderful seeing you, Teena. I hope you'll remember me to your parents." *And may they rot in hell for eternity.*

"Mamma passed on two years ago this Christmas but Daddy's still with us, thank the Good Lord." Her smile widened. "So, tell me. Did you have a boy or a girl?"

Lili stared at the woman, shocked into silence by the question.

Teena patted Lili on the forearm as if they were old and dear friends. "I was there, Lilly Ann. I remember that big ol' belly of yours like it was yesterday. Was it a boy or girl?"

"A girl." Lili's voice was barely audible. She hated Teena for asking but she hated herself even more for answering.

Teena sighed. "I'll bet she's a real heartbreaker, what with how pretty you and poor old Clifford were."

I don't need this, Lili thought. Thirty-three years ago she would have sold her soul to have any of the Franklins interested in her and her baby but it was too late now. Much too late.

"Why don't you come meet my hubby?" Teena went on. "We can have a drink and talk about old times."

"No." She felt seventeen again, heavily pregnant and alone. Terrified that the life she'd dreamed about was going up in smoke right before her eyes. She drew in a breath. "I'm with some people."

"We'd love to meet your friends."

"Teena, they're not my friends. They're my employees. I'm here on business." *Can't you see who you're talking to, Teena Marie? I'm not Lilly Ann Barnett—I'm Lili Spaulding and I don't need your family anymore.*

"You always were full of yourself," Teena said, dropping the friendly facade. "Now that you're rich, you think you rule the world."

"No, Teena, I don't think I can rule the world but I'm pretty damn sure I can buy most of it. If you'll excuse me—" She brushed past the woman and escaped back into the smoke and noise. Why now, she wondered. Why after all these years did it have to happen now when she should be on top of the world?

"Are you okay, Mrs. Spaulding?" Francesca asked as Lili reclaimed her seat at the small table. "You look pale."

A bead of sweat was slowly making its way down Lili's back. "Actually, Francesca, I'm not feeling well at all. I have a dreadful headache." She pushed back her chair. "You stay here and have a good time with the others. I'm going back to the hotel."

"You can't go back there alone," Francesca said, rising to her feet. "I'll go with you."

"No!" She lowered her voice. "I'll take a cab. Stay. Have fun." She had to get out of there before she vomited up memories of Euless and Clifford Earle and the baby she'd left behind a long long time ago.

She grabbed the first taxi she saw and endured a terrifying ride back to the hotel. She was glad her handgun was tucked in her bag. New Orleans was a beautiful city but she'd always had the sense that normal rules of behavior didn't exist there and she breathed a sigh of relief when she made it to her suite and locked the door behind her. She quickly stripped off her clothes and donned a silk dressing gown. Her adrenaline had started to flow during her encounter with Teena and her heartbeat had yet to return to anything resembling normal.

There was no sound from Corey Prescott's room which was probably a good thing. Lili was tempted to call the young woman and suggest they work on her speech for the store opening in Philadelphia on Friday but employees were very touchy these days about intrusions on their personal time. She poured herself a Scotch and paced the room. The nerve of that white trash tramp to ask about the baby. Lili should have turned the tables on the bitch and asked about Teena's own illegitimate child. "Where is he, Teena Marie?" she could have asked. "How is he doing?"

She had no doubt Teena Marie couldn't answer those questions any more than Lili could. Adoption meant giving up your rights to your child, letting her become part of a real family with all of the emotional and physical ties that came with the package. It had taken her many years to come to grips with the finality of her deed but once she did, she'd never wavered. Not even for an instant.

Why would you, girl? You already know where your baby is.

Grandma Hattie's voice, as clear and mean as it had ever been.

"It's been a long time, Grandma," she whispered. "I thought you'd gone for good."

Still lyin' to yourself, missy. You've known where your baby was ever since that letter came.

She shook her head, trying to push the ugly words away. Too much Scotch, she thought. Too much noise and heat and not enough sleep. Why did it always come down to that pathetic letter from a woman whose name she no longer remembered?

Banning. Millicent Banning. Her daughter's name is Catherine. . . .

She gulped the rest of the Scotch. "I'm not going to listen to this," she said. She wasn't Lilly Ann Barnett anymore. Lilly Ann Barnett was as dead and buried as Clifford Earle Franklin and Maisie and Grandma Hattie. She was Lili Spaulding now. She had a family of her own. Carter was gone and Whit had turned his back on her but she still had Grant. She would always have Grant.

She refilled her tumbler of Scotch then reached for the phone.

New York

"Grant!" Felicia's voice was angry. "You haven't heard a word I've said."

Grant leaned back against the leather seat and looked out the window. Five more miles until the ride from hell was over. Felicia had been haranguing him since they left the Trumps' Christmas party at the Plaza.

"I've heard every word you've said, darling." He managed to keep his tone even. "You were displeased with my performance." Marriage did amazing things to sweet-tempered, shy young women. His dove had turned into a vulture.

"You embarrassed me, Grant." Her voice shook with tears. "You had no business spending so much time with Deirdre."

"Deirdre Simms and her husband will be major stockholders, Felicia." Not to mention major contributors to his political campaign. "Spending time with her *is* my business." He looked at her with what he hoped was an expression of grave disappointment. "If you had given Barry Simms at least a few minutes of your time, he might have stayed around long enough for me to get a chance to talk with him."

She looked suitably chastened. These days he found it impossible to predict her mood or her reaction to things. "You should have told me, Grant. I want to be a help to you, not a hindrance, but I'm not a mind reader."

Time for the "kindly husband" response. That was getting harder these days, too. He opened his mouth to frame a reply when the car phone buzzed.

"Oh God!" The color drained from Felicia's face as she gripped his arm. "The baby..."

He grabbed the phone. "Spaulding here."

"Darling, it's Lili."

He covered the speaker. "It's Mother," he said.

Felicia rolled her eyes. "I should have known."

"Darling!" Lili's voice demanded his full attention. "Where are you?"

"About four miles from home," he said.

"You left the Trumps' party early."

"It was winding down." He paused, glancing over at a very annoyed Felicia. "It's a little late for a chat, Mother."

Lili's laugh sounded a little reckless and he wondered if she'd been drinking. He'd never seen her anywhere approaching drunk. "I have a surprise for you, darling," she said, her voice skimming over the words. "I wasn't going to tell you about it until I got home, but life is too short to keep secrets from family. It's a wonderful Christmas present, darling, one you're going to love."

"A Christmas present?" Alarm bells went off inside his head. "Besides the cottage on Martha's Vineyard?"

Her laugh grew even more reckless, almost out of control. "Oh, this is much better than a drafty old cottage," she said. "Darling, I'm giving you Night-Way."

Dan Jarreau was at the house within the hour. His first words were, "Where's your wife?"

"Upstairs," Grant said.

"Will she stay there?"

Grant's mouth twisted in a smile. "She'll stay there." He'd forced himself to fuck her. It was the only way he could think of to allay her suspicions.

"Tell it to me again," Jarreau said. "I want to make sure I heard straight."

"She started production on Night-Way." He said the words but he couldn't bring himself to believe they were true. "Test run rolls off the assembly line in time for Christmas."

"Shit."

"My sentiments exactly."

"You've got to shut the place down," Jarreau said.

"If I could do that, you wouldn't be standing here right now," Grant retorted. "Lili's the only one who can give the order to shut down."

"And you can't tell her why."

"Exactly." The fewer people who knew the truth, the better off they were.

They sat together in silence for what seemed like aeons to Grant before Jarreau spoke.

"I was never here."

Grant looked at him. "What?"

"I was never here. We never had this conversation."

"You're bailing out on me?" If the lousy son of a bitch thought he was going to—

Jarreau silenced him with a raised hand. "Trust me," he said, standing up. "I haven't steered you wrong yet, have I?" He shrugged into his coat.

"No, but—"

"Everything's going to be fine. Just wait and see."

33

Thursday, December 21

Something was wrong with Lili.

Corey couldn't put her finger on what was different but the moment she saw the woman exit the hotel elevator that morning she knew something had changed. She waited by the concierge desk and watched as Lili made small talk with the bell captain and charmed the panty hose off a Louisiana matron.

Lili's grooming was flawless, as always. Her dark hair was brushed back from her perfect oval of a face and caught in her trademark flat Chanel bow. She wore an impeccably tailored slate blue suit with pale hose and matching pumps. Her makeup accentuated and defined but didn't call attention to anything but her natural beauty. If Corey didn't know better she would think her mother was a good fifteen years younger than she actually was.

No, Lili was her usual glamorous, put-together self. What Corey sensed was more in the way Lili was carrying herself, a certain set to her shoulders that made the woman seem more vulnerable than she had the night before.

"Good morning," Corey said as Lili joined her at the desk.

Lili's smile was automatic. "I trust you slept well."

Corey nodded. "And you?"

"Just wonderfully," she said and Corey instantly knew she was lying.

"They're bringing the car around," Corey offered. "If you'd like some coffee, they're serving—"

"No coffee," Lili broke in. "We simply don't have time. The plane is waiting for us."

"Mrs. Spaulding." The doorman appeared in full livery. "Your car is here."

Lili beamed at the man as if he'd announced a balanced federal budget and the end to world hunger. "Thank you so much, Stanley." She tucked a bill into his hand with a gesture that was neither obsequious nor condescending. "I hope you and your family have a wonderful Christmas."

Stanley beamed at Lili. "Wishing you the same, Mrs. Spaulding. Have a safe trip back home."

He helped both women into the waiting limousine then tipped his cap as they drove away.

"When was the last time you were in New Orleans?" Corey asked.

Lili thought for a moment. "Two or three years ago." She cast a sidelong glance in Corey's direction. "Why do you ask?"

"You remembered the doorman's name," Corey said, shaking her head in amazement.

"You find that remarkable?"

"Yes," Corey said. "Actually I find it quite remarkable."

There was a softness to Lili's expression that surprised Corey. "I never did read your CV, darling. Tell me—you're a Harvard Business grad, aren't you?"

Corey nodded.

"I'm afraid I didn't have the benefit of your illustrious Ivy League education. I had to rely on good manners and common sense."

"Am I being insulted?"

"It depends on how sensitive you are to the truth."

"You also married well," Corey reminded her, feeling bruised and a bit defensive.

Lili arched a brow. "Marrying well and running a corporation are two very separate things. I didn't marry Carter with the intention of running his business one day."

"Why did you marry him?" The words were out before Corey could stop them.

"Why do you think?"

"I don't know," Corey said honestly. "That's why I'm asking."

Lili met her eyes. "I loved Carter and I wanted to be a good wife to him." She straightened her shoulders and Corey watched as the woman was replaced by the Steel Magnolia. "If you have any more questions, I'd advise you to download a copy of my bio and read it."

"I'll do that," Corey said, but she doubted if she'd find a mention of the child Lilly Ann Barnett had left behind.

New York

The R and D department held their Christmas party each year at O'Leary's Pub on Third Avenue. O'Leary's was a dimly lit, raucous kind of place that specialized in great food and even greater atmosphere. It was the kind of place Frank De Vito loved, which made his absence all the stranger.

One by one Stephen had questioned his colleagues and it seemed no one had seen Frank since Monday.

"I figured it was the snow when he didn't show up on Tuesday," Amy, one of the chemists, said over a pint of ale. "But the roads have been plowed for two days and there's still no Frank."

"Did anybody call his house?"

Amy shrugged. "Beats me. Maybe Rachel would know."

Rachel didn't. Stephen polished off his pint then tried to tuck into a plate of Irish stew but his appetite flagged. Something was wrong. There was no way Frank would have missed the party without a good reason. Frank had seemed on the ragged edge when he and Stephen spoke Monday morning. Given Frank's history, he just might do anything to prove his point.

Stephen excused himself from the table and found a pay phone in the back near the kitchen and dropped a pocketful of change into the coin slot.

"Maryann, this is Stephen Gold...Merry Christmas to you, too...I don't see Frank at the party...is he... Oh." He switched the phone to his other ear. "I must have forgotten . . . no problem . . . take care, Maryann."

Maryann De Vito thought her husband was in Boston on a business trip. Fear zapped through Stephen's body. He had the feeling Maryann was either covering up for her husband or legitimately in the dark. So where the hell was Frank De Vito and, more important than that, what the hell was he doing?

Grant had three Christmas parties to drop in on that afternoon. He supposed he should be grateful that he had something to keep his mind off the disaster in the making at their New Jersey factory. Jarreau had told him to stick to his usual schedule but it was hard to get into the holiday spirit when all hell could break loose any second.

The Metropolitan Museum of Art held a classy lunch for sponsors and Grant scored points with the well-preserved women who spent their days cruising the halls for fine young talent. From there he dropped in on a soiree hosted by Condé Nast. Grant figured advertising revenue from Lili! International had funded the last ten parties. Then he stopped in at Mount Sinai for drinks with the chief of staff and his crew. It didn't hurt to come down on the right side of the health care issue. Not if he wanted to get elected next November.

He returned to the office a little after four o'clock. He wanted to check his messages and regroup for the evening round of parties. He wasn't pleased to see Stephen Gold waiting for him.

"Don't you have someplace to go?" he asked as he swept by the man and into his office. "Go home early. It's almost Christmas."

Gold ignored his attempt at humor. "I need some information," he said, following him inside.

"Most employees wait to be invited into my office." Grant tossed his cashmere coat over the back of a chair. "What kind of information?"

"Did you send Frank De Vito to Boston?"

Every nerve in Grant's body sprang to attention. "Why would I send De Vito anywhere?"

"His wife said he's in Boston on business and I know it's not R and D business."

Grant took his seat behind the desk. "What makes you think he told his wife the truth?"

"Because I know Frank De Vito."

"Maybe you don't know De Vito as well as you think you do. Men have lives separate from their families, Gold. De Vito's no exception."

"Did you send Frank to Boston?"

"No." He let the word resonate for a moment. "Does that answer your question?"

Gold wheeled and stormed out of the room. Grant waited until he heard the outer door to his office slam shut before he reached for the telephone. He began to punch in Jarreau's number then caught himself. *Forget we had this conversation,* Jarreau had said to him. *Trust me.*

Trust wasn't Grant's long suit but he'd give it his best shot. Besides, the Christmas break began tomorrow. What could happen between now and then?

Friday, December 22

To Corey's surprise, Lili took Miami's South Beach by storm on Thursday. Lili's strange mood didn't get in the way of her wowing the local crowd. They spent the night at one of the trendier hotels and Lili was once again wined and dined by her sales executives. Corey stayed behind at the hotel. She told herself it was because she was tired and needed some rest but that wasn't entirely the truth. Being around Lili was taking its toll on her emotions and she needed to carve time away whenever possible.

And then there was Stephen. She'd hoped to talk to him again that night but his machine had answered and she hung up without leaving a message.

One more stop, she told herself as the plane took off not long after dawn on Friday. One more stop and then maybe she could figure out where this had all been leading.

The steward served chilled orange juice, coffee and toast when the plane reached cruising altitude.

"Will there be anything else, ma'am?" he asked Lili.

"Nothing, John. Thank you."

He nodded to both women then retreated behind the sliding door that separated the cabin from the rest of the plane.

Lili lit a cigarette and observed Corey with open curiosity. "This has been a difficult trip for you, hasn't it?"

There was something about a direct question that begged an equally direct response. "Yes," Corey said, careful to keep her tone even. "It has."

"Travel can be an exhausting experience for some." She gestured with the lit Players. "The time changes, different beds, hotel food—not everyone thrives on it the way I do."

Corey nodded, wondering where this was going. "I've noticed that." She was so tired that the dark circles under her eyes had dark circles. Lili, however, seemed fresher and younger than she had when the tour started.

"You're a young woman," Lili went on, her eyes never leaving Corey. "I would think you'd have more stamina—" she lowered her voice to a more seductive, conversational level "—unless, of course, it isn't the travel that bothers you, but your traveling companion."

Corey's breath caught in her throat. This was dangerous territory at thirty thousand feet. She was so tired, both physically and emotionally, that her internal censor might be asleep at the wheel and that could only lead to disaster.

"Are you displeased with my work?" she asked.

"Such insecurity, darling. Your parents should have worked on that and—"

"Don't talk about my parents!" The words tore from her throat with almost brute force.

Lili's eyes widened. "I seem to have hit a nerve."

"If you have a problem with me, then tell me. My parents have absolutely nothing to do with this conversation."

"I understand."

"No," Corey said, her voice trembling, "I doubt if you do."

The girl was too sensitive, Lili thought as the plane touched down in Philadelphia. She was surprised Corey Prescott had made it this far in a business that was most assuredly not for the thin-skinned. While Lili had no complaints about Corey's work, she had hoped for a more congenial traveling companion.

"Would you give me a rundown on the agenda?" she asked as they taxied to a stop.

Corey flipped open her date book and read off the day's commitments. "Your driver is waiting for us in the terminal. He'll take us back to New York this afternoon."

"Excellent," Lili said. She'd promised her pilot that he could take the jet up to Vermont to spend Christmas with his family.

The steward stepped into the cabin. "You can deplane whenever you wish, Mrs. Spaulding."

Lili reached for her coat and bag. "Take heart, Ms. Prescott," she said. "Your ordeal is almost over."

"Merry Christmas, boss." Stephen's assistant Drake stopped at the door to his office. It was a little after two o'clock in the afternoon and the place was emptying for the vacation break. "See you next year."

Stephen got up from his desk and offered his hand. "Have a good one, Drake."

"Any luck finding Frank De Vito?" Stephen had asked Drake to make some phone calls, none of which had turned up any leads.

"Not yet," Stephen said, "but if his wife isn't worried, neither am I."

"Words to live by, boss." Drake offered up a military salute and marched away.

Too bad the words weren't true. Actually Stephen was getting more nervous by the minute about De Vito's whereabouts. He couldn't pinpoint the problem but he had the strong sense that something was coming down and when it did things around Lili! International would never be the same.

Things went well for Lili in Philadelphia, so well that she was back on the highway en route to Manhattan by late afternoon.

Corey Prescott dozed quietly in the back seat next to her. She looked much less formidable asleep than she did awake, Lili thought. She was a beautiful young woman and beauty often isolated. It was a lesson Lili had learned the hard way. There was a gentleness to Corey's mouth when it wasn't pressed into a taut line of disapproval, a gentleness that Lili found touching. It reminded Lili of herself during the early days of her marriage to Carter, when she had been struggling to find a way to fit into his world.

Lili found it hard to believe Corey Prescott had ever had to struggle the way she had. She had beauty, education and ambition. If you needed more than that to succeed, Lili couldn't imagine what it might be. She couldn't help wondering where life might have taken her if she'd been blessed from the start with those same gifts.

She rested her head against a small travel pillow and closed her eyes. Still, she hadn't done that badly for herself. The trashy girl from Euless had come a long way and she was still climbing. The test run of Night-Way would roll out later this afternoon and—

She buzzed the driver from the console phone. "Where are we right now, Ed?"

"A little south of Princeton, Mrs. Spaulding."

"How long would it take us to get to the factory in the Somerset Hills?"

"Maybe forty-five minutes."

"Wonderful," she said. "Let's do it."

The Christmas party at the factory coincided with the first run of Night-Way. Everyone would be there. It would be the perfect opportunity for Lili to thank the staff for the hard work these past few weeks and perhaps show the sleepy Ms. Prescott a thing or two about the way a business should be run.

With a little luck, they'd be home in time for dinner.

* * *

After an early supper, Stephen sent Jessie into the living room to draw thank-you pictures for the Chanukah presents she'd received on Sunday. She fussed a little but before long he managed to get her settled down with construction paper and a big box of crayons.

"Call me when you need the scissors," he said. "I'm going to load the dishwasher."

She nodded but he knew she was so engrossed in her drawing that his words barely registered. Like father, like daughter. He hadn't been able to get Frank De Vito's vanishing act off his mind for days now. He kept telling himself that Frank's disappearance wasn't his problem. For all he knew, Grant Spaulding was right and Frank had a woman on the side.

And maybe he even would've believed it if it weren't for the fact that he knew De Vito was hot on the trail of something a hell of a lot more important than sex.

He switched on the small TV mounted under the cabinet. Time for his daily dose of gloom, tragedy and vice known as the nightly news. He loaded the pots to Hillary's Whitewater troubles, the plates to government shutdowns, and was about to toss in the knives, forks and spoons when the words *Special Report* flashed across the screen. He reached up and raised the sound.

"...a breaking story from our New Jersey bureau. Details are sketchy but it seems there's been an explosion at a cosmetics plant in the Somerset Hills. Emergency vehicles are on the scene. Apparently there have been numerous fatalities. According to our sources, Lili Spaulding was at the site at the time of the explosion and is being rushed to a nearby hospital. Chopper Four is en route to the Lili! International building right now and we'll update the situation as soon as we have more information."

He stared at the screen as the picture shifted from a serious newscaster to a talking pizza.

"Corey," he said aloud to the empty kitchen. *Corey.*

34

Somerset Hills

In the blink of an eye the gentle snowscape exploded into a nightmare. The sky blazed as flames leaped and crackled, dancing across what remained of the factory roof. The fire's roar drowned out everything but the wail of sirens and the screams.

And, oh God, the screams.

Corey tried to close her mind to the screams but they ripped at her skin, tore at her heart. She couldn't think about those screams. She couldn't think about the people trapped in the building, the people that the rescue squad would reach too late. She couldn't think about anything but the fact that the woman she had wanted to destroy was lying unconscious on the ground next to her and it was Corey's choice if she lived or died.

"She's still not breathing!" Ed, Lili's limo driver, yelled over the din. "Do something!"

You don't have to do anything, Corey...let her go...she never did anything to help you...think about Millicent...think about that letter....

"My mother," she whispered, staring down at Lili's still form. "My mother—"

"I can't hear you," Ed yelled. "What are you saying?"

Let her die, Corey...she's nothing to you...she never has been...let her die and you can put the past behind you....

Lilly Ann Barnett had turned her back on her own daughter. How wrong could it be for that same daughter to turn her back on the woman who had given her life?

That's not how your daddy and I raised you, honey. Millicent's sweetly familiar voice surrounded Corey like an embrace. *Lili Spaulding is family. Do this for me, honey...do it for me!*

There was no way Corey could refuse, even if every fiber of her being screamed for her to let the woman die. Corey crouched down next to Lili and searched for a pulse at her wrist, her elbow, the base of her throat. "Come on ... come on ... don't die on me ... don't—" Elation—sudden and surprising—tore through her with the same powerful impact as the blast had only minutes before. "Help me, Ed!" she cried. "I've got a pulse."

"Ah, Jesus," he moaned, wringing his hands together. "Look at her, will you? Look at all that blood! She's gonna die!"

"She's not going to die!" she snapped at Ed. "Don't say that."

"All that blood—"

Corey quickly inspected Lili's still form. "Head wounds bleed like crazy." There were no signs of injury anywhere else.

Ed, however, was beyond hearing. "She's gonna die ... I know she's gonna die—"

"She'll live," Corey whispered fiercely as she cleared Lili's air passages. *You can do it,* Millicent's voice urged her forward. She pinched Lili's nostrils closed and began to breathe air into the woman's lungs. Slowly. Rhythmically. Over and over and over again even though Lili wasn't responding. *One more time, honey. Just once more ...*

"Give it up," Ed said, his voice breaking on a sob. "She's dead—she's dead!"

Ambulances screeched up the driveway. Seconds later EMS technicians scattered in all directions. Too late ... too late ... too late—

"I'll take over." A short, heavyset man tried to push her out of the way.

She elbowed him in the ribs. "Go to hell."

"You've done all you can," he said, his tone curt and professional. "She needs more help."

"No!"

"Joe!" The technician called. "I need help here."

"Give it up, Ms. Prescott," Ed pleaded with her. "You're wasting your time."

A hand clamped down on her shoulder. She swung wide with a fist.

"Shit!" a second technician yelped. "What are you, nuts?"

Corey blocked out Ed's cries and the technicians' curses and the fact that time was running out. She blocked out everything but the fact that all that she was, all that she had ever accomplished, would be worth nothing if Lili Spaulding died.

The sound of sirens pierced Lili's sleep but she refused to give up her dream. Sunshine...blue skies...the warm waters of the Caribbean ... Whit. He'd been standing on the porch of a whitewashed villa on the beach. His hair glittered with silver. His skin was tanned a golden brown. His broad chest was bare and he wore no shoes. A pair of faded jeans rode low on his lean hips.

She called to him but he didn't seem to hear. She cupped her hands around her mouth and called again. He turned slightly in her direction but his gaze seemed focused on some point beyond her as waves gently lapped around his ankles.

Mama, help me.... The child drifted past Whit, her small form carried gently on the waves. The little girl—her perfect little girl—was just beyond Lili's reach. No matter how hard she tried, Lili couldn't grab the child's hand and pull her to safety.

She pleaded for Whit to help but he turned a deaf ear. Carter watched from a distance, his arms folded across his chest. His face was set in stern lines of disapproval and her stomach knotted in response.

My mother...my mother. The voice was so real, so familiar. Suddenly the child wasn't a child any longer, but a young woman. The young woman's face was partly in shadow and the odd tug at the corner of her mouth reminded Lili of Corey Prescott. Lili moved toward the young woman and was only a step away when the siren blared again and she was thrust suddenly, angrily awake.

"Mrs. Spaulding." That voice again, that familiar voice. "Wake up, Mrs. Spaulding."

Wake up? Why was Corey Prescott in her bedroom, telling her to wake up? She struggled to comply but felt as if she were at the bottom of a lake and the surface was a long way up.

She forced her eyes open. Long streaks of black dirt bisected Corey's face and blood smeared the front of her jacket. There was an odd look in the young woman's eyes, a mixture of fear and relief and something Lili couldn't identify. Two men flanked her. Both wore navy pants and matching parkas and sported that taut, professionally worried look she'd come to recognize on medical personnel.

She wasn't in her bedroom—that much was obvious—but what was she doing lying in the snow? It never snowed in New Orleans or Orlando. Or could they be in Chicago? It snowed a lot in Chicago. She struggled up onto one elbow, ignoring the stab of pain beneath her rib. Before she had the chance to open her mouth to speak, the technicians sprang to life, wielding stethoscopes and blood pressure monitors and an arsenal of bandages.

"Wait!" Lili tried to sound imperious but it was difficult from her position on the snow-covered ground. What on earth was that loud crackling sound that seemed to fill the air? She swatted at the men, appalled by the slow, faltering response of her muscles.

"Ma'am, you have to let us do our job," the taller of the technicians said.

"What job?" she asked. "What am I doing here?"

"We can't answer that question," the shorter technician said, "but we can get you to the hospital."

"Hospital!" She ripped the blood pressure gadget from her arm. "I refuse to go anywhere until—"

Corey Prescott blocked her view. "You're going to the hospital, Mrs. Spaulding. There's been an accident and you need to be checked out."

"But I see the car over there—" She pointed toward her beloved Rolls. "It looks fine."

She tried to look beyond Corey Prescott but the young woman crouched down in front of her, blocking her view. There was an odd smell in the air, a sulfurous combination of heat and smoke and an even odder smell, high and sharp and piercing . . . like blood. Bits and pieces of memory spun past— Ben Krementz's laughing face, the cheers as the first bottle of Night-Way rolled off the line, a horrible deafening roar when—

"Oh God!" She looked at Corey Prescott. "Tell me it didn't happen . . . tell me I'm dreaming—"

"I'm sorry." The young woman's eyes welled with tears.

"Ben—?" *Please, not Ben . . .*

"I'm sorry," Corey said again. "He's gone."

"I don't understand." Her words were faint, indistinct. The simple act of breathing took all of her concentration. "Things were so perfect—he was so proud of what we'd done . . ." She couldn't finish her sentence. Her mind refused to accept the horror of what had happened and she tumbled into the darkness.

The ambulance driver tried to block Corey from riding to the hospital with Lili but Corey refused to leave.

"I'm going with Mrs. Spaulding."

"That's against the rules," the driver said.

"I don't give a damn about the rules," she shot back. "She's not going anywhere without me."

He raised his hands in defeat. "I'm not gonna fight you, lady. Have it your own way."

The technicians lifted Lili onto a stretcher. "Be careful," Corey said. "Don't let her slip off."

The two men exchanged glances but Corey didn't care. Let them think she was crazy. She wasn't about to let Lili out of her sight until she knew the woman was going to be all right. She told herself she would do the same for anyone but the rise of emotion in her chest told her otherwise.

She's your blood, honey. Millicent's voice soothed her fears. *Of course you're going to feel this way.*

She's nothing to me, Corey thought as the ambulance sped toward the hospital with Lili's limo in hot pursuit. She would have helped Ben Krementz if she'd had the chance. The fact that it was her mother's life she'd saved was nothing more than coincidence.

* * *

Westchester

Felicia's scream shattered the evening stillness. Grant put down his glass of Scotch and dashed into the great room where he found his wife dissolved in tears and a strange man standing near the mantel, looking horribly uncomfortable.

Felicia threw herself into his arms. "Oh, my God . . . oh, my God . . ." Her words were lost on a tidal wave of tears.

"Felicia!" He shook her. "Stop that crying and tell me what's wrong." He was intensely aware of the stranger's scrutiny. He had to maintain the perfect husband persona.

"It's so terrible—" She gasped for breath. "So awful—"

The baby. Jesus, not the baby. "Is it John Carter?"

"N-no." She met his eyes. "It's Lili, Grant. There's been an accident."

His legs went weak. "The plane—?" The weather was perfect for flying, clear and cold, with little wind. How could anything go wrong?

"Not the plane," Felicia cried. "There was an explosion, Grant! A terrible explosion in New Jersey."

His mind was a yawning void as he struggled to make sense of her words. "Lili was in Philadelphia today, Felicia."

Felicia tried to speak but couldn't. The strange man stepped in.

"Mr. Spaulding?" Grant nodded. "I'm Detective Chase." Chase named some obscure New Jersey police department. "There's been an explosion at your factory in Somerset." The detective had been interviewing someone on Staten Island when he got the call.

The floor shifted beneath Grant's feet. An explosion on the very day Night-Way's test run rolled out. *What the hell have you done, Jarreau?* "Are there any casualties?"

"Four dead, I don't know how many wounded. Your mother—"

"Jesus." He bent over at the waist, his gut twisting with pain. "She wasn't supposed to be there."

"Sir?" The detective's voice was polite but there was no disguising his curiosity. Grant hoped like hell he hadn't understood.

"She was in Philadelphia," Grant said. "Not New Jersey."

"I'm sorry, sir, but she was on the premises at the time of the blast."

The pain gripped him harder. He tried to frame the next question but the bile in his throat made it impossible to speak. *Not this way,* he thought. *Not now.*

The detective cleared his throat. "Mrs. Lili Spaulding is being taken to Saint Peter's Hospital in Morristown."

His blood pounded in his ears. "She's not dead?"

The detective's face turned bright red. "I should have made that clear right up front."

Grant was too relieved to tear a strip off the guy. Lili was still alive. The one person on earth who wanted nothing more than to make him happy. Grant could only thank God that Jarreau's insane scheme hadn't cost him his greatest supporter. Lili was every bit as necessary to his future plans as a full campaign chest or his choir-boy smile. As long as he had her in his corner, the future was still his for the taking.

He turned to Felicia who was sniveling in the corner. "Call the lawyers," he said. "Tell them what happened." The lawsuits would be flying before they knew what hit them. At least their corporate attorneys would get a head start on damage control.

"Where are you going?" she asked, her eyes wide and weepy.

Stupid bitch. Where the hell did she think he was going? "Mother needs me."

The detective jingled his car keys. "You can ride with me, Mr. Spaulding. I'm on my way back to the hospital. It'll give us time to talk."

And if Grant played his cards right, it might even give him time to incriminate Frank De Vito.

The hospital driveway was choked with ambulances, police cars and television news vans complete with traveling satellite dishes. Nothing like a disaster to bring out the best in everybody.

The emergency room teemed with injured factory employees. Cuts, burns, broken bones—the damage ran the gamut. Corey wondered how many other local hospitals were filled to overflowing as a result of the explosion, how many families—like Ben Krementz's—would be shattered by tragedy.

"Room B," a male nurse barked as they rolled Lili through the swinging doors. "We'll give you five. If she's not critical, we move her out." He turned to move on to the next casualty.

"Not critical?" Corey blocked his exit. "She's unconscious."

His sharp eyes took in the blood stains on the front of her jacket. "You hurt?"

She shook her head.

He pushed a piece of paper at her. "Then give blood. We need all we can get."

The curtains were drawn around Lili's cubicle. Corey paced the crowded hallway. *What's wrong with you, Prescott? You know you don't give a damn what happens to her.* She'd been looking to bring Lili's empire down around the woman's perfectly coiffed head and that explosion might very well have done it for her. It didn't much matter if the blast had been caused by one of those animal rights groups or by a faulty steam valve. Production of Night-Way had gone up in flames and with it went Lili's hopes for the future.

In a way, Corey felt sorry for her birth mother. The business was everything to Lili Spaulding. She lived and breathed Lili! International, pouring all of her energies into making sure the company entered the twenty-first century at the peak of its game.

You'll survive, Corey thought as a doctor vanished behind the curtain. Lilly Ann Barnett was nothing if not a survivor. Lili still had the Spaulding name, the Spaulding fortune. She still had the penthouse apartment, the houses, the steely will that was the stuff of legend. She'd faced tougher obstacles before and triumphed.

"Are you the one who saved Lili Spaulding?"

She blinked as a dark-haired woman thrust a tape recorder under her nose. "Excuse me?"

"Dana Anders, Action News." The reporter gestured toward Ed the limo driver who was holding court for a horde of hungry journalists. "Mr. Militello said you saved Lili Spaulding's life."

Corey felt her cheeks redden. "I don't know if I saved her life."

"Mr. Militello said that Mrs. Spaulding wasn't breathing until you performed CPR."

"Well, I—"

"Don't be modest," Dana Anders urged. "Take credit!"

Corey started to back away. "I only did what I had to do. The ambulance crew—"

"Anders!" A male voice called out. "Press conference. Chief of police. Now."

"You stay right here," Dana Anders ordered Corey then hurried toward the nurses' station. "I want all the details on the miraculous rescue."

Corey stared after the woman. Miraculous rescue? She wondered what the reporter would think if she knew that she had almost let Lili Spaulding die.

A young blood technician appeared at her elbow. "Did you fill out the form?"

"Not yet."

She handed Corey a pencil. "ASAP," she said. "The live bodies are piling up. We need all the help we can get."

Corey ducked into the stairwell and sank down onto the top step. She might as well give blood while she waited for the news about Lili.

> First name: Catherine
> Maiden name: Banning
> Last name: Prescott
> Date of birth: 2-14-63
> Name and address of
>   nearest living relative: ~~Millie~~

Reality hit her like a two-by-four between the eyes. Millicent was gone. In the whole wide world there wasn't one single person who gave a damn if she lived or died. For almost twenty-seven years Millicent had been there for Corey as her safe harbor, her anchor, her *mother*. She had been there for Corey through the rebellious years, the scared years, the years when Corey wondered what she'd done to make God so angry with her. Millicent had been there through it all. She'd held Corey's hand, wiped away her tears, celebrated her successes.

And now there was no one left to care. If Corey had died in that explosion, no one would have mourned her passing or shed a tear or raised a glass in her honor.

Haven't you heard a word I've been saying, honey? You're not alone.

You don't understand, Corey thought. *I'm nothing to Lili Spaulding but a paid employee.*

Tell her the truth. She's as lonely as you are, honey. You said so yourself. Tell her the truth and see what happens.

"Oh, Mom," she whispered. "I don't know how."

She could almost feel Millicent's arms around her, warm and loving. *Sure you do, honey. Just walk in there and tell her that you're her daughter. The rest will fall into place....*

Corey hesitated. In every way that mattered, Millicent was her mother. Lilly Ann Barnett might have given birth to her but it was Millicent Banning who had earned the title. No one would ever be able to take that away from her. But Millicent was gone now and the empty space inside Corey's heart was growing bigger every day.

A few months ago she'd wanted nothing more than to see Lili Spaulding destroyed, but the sight of the proud woman unconscious and bleeding had done something to Corey. She no longer wanted revenge. She didn't need to tear down Lili's empire because that empire no longer mattered to Corey.

Take the chance, honey. What do you have to lose?

I'm doing it for you, Corey thought as she moved through the corridor toward Lili's cubicle.

No, honey. If you love me, you'll do it for yourself.

A tall young doctor with a retro Marcus Welby look stepped from behind the heavy blue curtain as Corey approached.

"How is she?" Corey asked.

"Angry," he said, shaking his head. "She won't get off the cell phone long enough to let us do a decent exam."

"She's okay," Corey said, amazed by the sense of relief that flooded her body. "It's when she's not interested in the cell phone that you have to worry."

"Head injuries can be tricky," he said. "I think she should be admitted for observation but she's not having any of it."

"I'll talk to her."

"Good luck," he said. "That's one tough lady."

The doctor strode away to take care of his next patient.

This is it, Corey thought as she drew in a deep breath and squared her shoulders. The moment of truth she'd been heading toward since the day she was born.

She waited until Lili stopped speaking then stepped into the cubicle.

"There you are!" Lili placed the cell phone down on her lap. "I asked the nurse to find you." Her forehead was lightly bandaged and she wore a thin white cotton hospital gown scattered with pale blue asterisks. Corey would have looked like an inmate. Lili managed to look downright regal. "Has there been any news about the explosion?"

"Nothing," Corey said. Her hands were trembling so badly she had to clasp them behind her back. "The police are asking questions but nobody seems to know anything yet."

Lili's dark blue eyes misted with tears. "Poor Ben," she said, fiddling with the hem of her gown. "I had just kissed him goodbye and—" Her words broke off in a muffled sob and she lowered her head.

Corey was overcome with the need to comfort her mother. She stepped forward, heart beating so fast she could scarcely draw a breath, then placed her hand on Lili's head. Her mother's hair was cool and silky beneath her fingers. *My hair is like yours,* she thought in wonder. The same slight wave at the crown. The same tough cowlick, tamed into submission by a high-priced hairstylist.

"Good grief, Ms. Prescott." The tears shifted swiftly into annoyance as Lili removed Corey's hand from her head. "If you're looking to dispense comfort, go outside and dispense it where it can do some good."

Corey told herself the harsh words weren't personal, that it was only Lili's injuries that made her speak to her that way. "I thought you could use the company."

Lili arched a brow. "Really? And since when have we been good company for each other?"

Corey regrouped, struggling to find the way to break the news. "It was a long trip," she said tentatively. "I think we got along amazingly well—all things considered." *All things considered?* What a ridiculous thing to say—even if it was the truth.

"Darling, I may not be at my best at the moment, but I still don't suffer fools gladly." She leaned back against the pillows and met Corey's eyes. "You've done your duty, expressed your concern for your employer's welfare. You're free to go."

"Thank you," Corey said automatically, "but I'd like to stay with you."

"That's not necessary."

Corey drew in a breath. "I think it is."

"Don't worry," Lili said. "The Christmas vacation remains inviolate. Not even you, darling, can put a good spin on what happened today."

"That's not why I want to stay."

"My son is the one who is most badly hurt by this incident. His people will handle the press for Lili! International."

Lili's words hit Corey like a slap in the face. How on earth could Lili possibly think Grant Spaulding was the injured party in this tragedy?

She's frightened, Corey told herself, trying to control her growing anger. *That's why she's not thinking clearly.* Not only had Lili seen part of her empire go up in flames, she'd seen long-time employees lose their lives. That would be enough to cloud anyone's thinking.

"I'd be glad to help," Corey offered.

"That won't be necessary."

"It's my job."

"Not this time, darling. Grant is what's important now. His team will know what to do."

Her words stung but Corey would not be turned away. "I'd like to talk to you about a personal matter."

Lili picked up the cell phone. "It can wait until after the New Year."

"We need to talk now."

"Darling, you have picked a very inopportune moment to flex your corporate muscles."

"This has nothing to do with business."

Again that sardonic arch of the brow. "I didn't realize we had a personal relationship."

"We don't—I mean, we do... or we will have—"

"Darling, I don't have a clue what you're driving at. If you have something to say, then please do us both a favor and say it. Otherwise, let me get on with my business."

"There's something you need to know," Corey began, "something I just found out a few months ago."

"I'm sure whatever it is is fascinating, but I make it a policy to stay out of my employees' personal lives."

"This is different. I—"

Lili raised a hand. "Recitations of thwarted love affairs are terribly tedious, darling. So are domestic squabbles."

"Mrs. Spaulding, please—"

"I've had a difficult day, Ms. Prescott. I don't need—"

"Listen to me, Lili!" Oh God, this was turning into a disaster. She clutched the blood donor form more tightly. "I'm sorry but this is very difficult for me and if I don't just say it, I might never—"

"Mother!" Grant Spaulding burst through the curtain and pushed Corey aside as he made his way to Lili's bedside.

Lili's entire face came to life as if someone had thrown a power switch. "Grant, darling!" She held out her hands to him. "How did you find me? When I couldn't reach you on the telephone, I—"

He clasped Lili's hands then kissed each one in a display of filial devotion that sickened Corey. "Thank the police. They came to tell me about the explosion."

Lili's eyes glittered with tears as she clung to Grant. "It was terrible," she whispered. "All those poor people—"

Grant glanced over at Corey. His expression was oddly bland, considering the high drama of the circumstances. "You can go now."

Her spine stiffened. "Mrs. Spaulding and I were talking."
She looked toward her mother. "This is very important."

Grant's expression didn't change but his anger filled the
room and chilled her blood. "My mother needs her rest."

"She's not—" She bit back the words and turned toward
Lili. "If you would give me ten minutes, you'll understand."
The sound of her own voice sickened her. *What's wrong with
you, Prescott? You're begging for your own mother's attention.*

"Aren't you listening?" Grant's tone hardened. "Not today."

Lili patted his hand. "Thank you, darling. What on earth
would I do without you?"

"We're family," Grant said, closing the circle. "You'll never
have to find out."

Once again Corey was on the outside looking in, only this
time the pain she felt was more intense, more devastating, because she'd been fool enough to allow herself to hope there
might be a happy ending. She bolted from the cubicle, nearly
tearing down the curtain in the process.

"Wait!" The technician grabbed her by the wrist before she'd
gone two feet. "What about the blood donation?"

"Ask him," she snapped, jerking her head in Grant's direction. "I think my mother prefers blue blood to red any day."
She crumpled up the donor form, tossed it to the ground, and
then she walked out the door.

My mother.

The words grabbed Lili by the throat. She sat up and swung
her legs over the side of the bed. *My mother prefers blue blood
to red....*

"Where are you going?"

She stood up, hanging on to the bed rail for support. "Didn't
you hear her? Why did she say that?"

"Mother, what's going on?" Grant placed an arm on her
shoulder.

"You shouldn't have let her leave that way. There was
something she wanted to tell me—"

"Whatever it is, it can wait," Grant said. "She was upsetting you, Mother. I'm glad she's gone."

Lili slid her feet into her suede pumps. *Ask him...my mother prefers blue blood to red any day...* What a strange thing to say. It didn't make any sense at all. *My mother...*

She stopped the first nurse who walked by. "The young woman who was with me," she said, ignoring Grant's dire warnings about her own health. "Where did she go?"

"This place is a madhouse today," the nurse said. Her cheeks reddened noticeably as Grant took his place at Lili's side. "What'd she look like?"

"Slender, dark hair, bright red jacket—" *She looks like me,* Lili thought. *How was it I never noticed?*

"The one who brought you in," the nurse said, nodding. "She hitched a ride with one of the news crews." The nurse's words were meant for Lili but her attention belonged only to Grant.

Lili swayed on her feet.

"Damn it," Grant said as he caught her by the elbow. "You should be back in bed."

"Listen to your son," the nurse said, dimpling up at Grant. "He knows what's best for you."

"You're right," Lili said, leaning on Grant for support. "Of course, you're right." She'd been through a terrible ordeal. Was it any wonder her mind was playing tricks on her? Corey Prescott was an angry, ambitious young woman. How ridiculous to believe anything she had to say. Lili should be home in her apartment, sipping egg nog and looking out on the lights of Tavern on the Green, the way she had every Christmas since she married Carter. "I want to go home," she said to Grant. "Tell Ed to bring the car—" She stopped as a spot of white caught her attention. A crumpled piece of paper was sticking out from beneath a folding chair. Corey Prescott had been clutching a piece of paper, she thought, and she bent down to retrieve it.

"The hospital has a maintenance staff," Grant said. He sounded both curious and a tad concerned. "Why don't you—"

His words were drowned out by a buzzing inside her head, a deep, resonant sound that threatened to overwhelm her senses.

Throw it away, girl. There's nothing you want with that old piece of paper.

Her fingers shook as she smoothed the folds.

You're going to regret this. See if you don't. Don't come crying to Grandma Hattie when your world turns inside out.

A blood donor application form, that's all it was. Some ridiculous piece of bureaucratic red tape designed to give clerks something to do from nine to five. She relaxed. What dangers could be hiding in a blood donor application? There was very little writing on the page, just a few scribbled lines.

> First name: Catherine
> Maiden name: Banning
> Last name: Prescott
> Date of birth: 2-14-63
> Name and address of
>   nearest living relative: ~~Millie~~

"No," Lili said, dropping the paper as if it were on fire. *Banning.* She knew that name . . . Millicent Banning . . . *I know you must think I'm crazy, Mrs. Spaulding, but my daughter Catherine* . . . a perfect blue-eyed Valentine's Day baby girl . . . *she's dead, Carter, my little girl is dead—*

"What is it?" Grant asked. "What's wrong?"

"My daughter," she whispered. "Dear God, I've found my baby!"

35

The truth slammed into Lili with such force that she dropped to her knees. "Oh, God," she moaned, lowering her head so no one would see her tears. "Oh, God . . . oh, God—"

How could she have been so stupid, so *blind?* The same dark hair, the same deep blue eyes . . . the same temper that came and went like a summer storm. She'd known from the start that Corey Prescott was different from the others. It had been there in the way she looked at Lili, speculative and sad and angry, all of it right there in her eyes—

"Mother?" Grant bent down in front of her.

Her heart ached with sorrow and she found it difficult to catch her breath. *You tried to tell me but I wouldn't listen,* she thought, the words harsh and ugly in their bitter truth. She had attributed Corey Prescott's edgy intensity to ambition but she'd been wrong. It wasn't ambition that fueled the young woman but hatred, a bone-deep, irrevocable hatred that Lili could never erase, no matter how hard she tried. The floor seemed to rise up and she rocked back on her heels, struggling to draw in a deep steadying breath.

"Nurse!" Grant's voice rang out above the din of the emergency room. "My mother needs help!"

My mother . . . my mother. Grant said the words with pride and love. She was his mother, certainly in all the ways that mattered. She might not have carried him in her womb the way she'd carried her daughter but she had given him her heart and soul and all the devotion she would have lavished on her own girl if circumstances had been different. For almost twenty years he'd been at the center of her life, the one thing that gave meaning to her days. Nothing meant more to Lili than his happiness. Not even her own.

"I never meant to hurt her," she said, brushing a lock of fair hair back from his forehead. "I only did what I had to do." The *right* thing to do at the time. How could she possibly have known what the future would hold for them both? She'd been seventeen years old, dirt poor and terrified. *And selfish, Lilly Ann?* She couldn't deny it. Maybe she had been, but selfishness wasn't a sin. Sometimes you had to be selfish in order to survive.

"To hell with Prescott," Grant said. "You're the only one I care about right now." How strong his words sounded, how reassuring to know Lili meant as much to him as he did to her. Would he sound as warm and reassuring when she told him the truth?

"You don't understand, Grant. There's something I need to tell you about Corey—"

"Our hot-tempered Ms. Prescott will get over her tantrum, Mother. Some people don't understand when a family needs privacy."

"Oh, Grant," she said, so softly her words were almost lost. "Corey is family too."

Corey exited the news van a block away from her apartment.

"You sure we can't convince you to grab a drink with us?" asked the driver, a good-looking man with piercing green eyes. "Christmas cheer and all that?"

"Sorry," she said, offering up a thin smile. "I've had all the excitement I can handle for one day."

The audio crew was a nice enough bunch, loud and raucous and totally irreverent. She thanked God their interests lay more in sound levels than sound bites. She almost felt sorry for them that they'd let a major coup slip right through their hands.

Lili Spaulding's bastard daughter saves her life in blast ... film at eleven.

Too bad Lili Spaulding's bastard daughter was a damn fool.

You should have let her die, she thought as she unlocked the door to her apartment. She'd been looking for revenge, hadn't she? Lili's death would have been the ultimate triumph. Corey had been a damn fool to think—even for a second—that she and Lili could be anything but strangers to each other.

Lili Spaulding had made it clear that she already had one child and she didn't need or want another. Especially not a scarred and broken child who'd wasted most of her life wishing for things she could never have.

The only thing that surprised Corey was how much the realization hurt.

I gave it my best shot, Mom, but it wasn't enough. She doesn't want me any more now than she did the day I was born.

She waited, but this time not even Millicent could take away the pain.

"Oh, Mrs. Spaulding!" Gretchen, the housekeeper, burst into noisy tears at the sight of Lili. "I was afraid you were—" Her words broke off in hiccuping sobs.

"Mother is fine," Grant said, his arm protectively draped around Lili's shoulders.

Lili nodded. "I'm fine," she said, even though her head was pounding like the very devil.

Gretchen dabbed at her eyes with the hem of her neatly starched apron. "We were all terribly worried about you, ma'am. When the policeman turned up, we—"

"Policeman?" Grant interrupted her. "What policeman?"

Gretchen gestured toward the living room. "He insisted on waiting for you."

Lili and Grant exchanged glances. "Maybe there's been some news," Lili said.

Grant's jaw was noticeably tight but he managed a smile. "I doubt it, Mother. These things take time."

He was being unduly pessimistic, Lili thought as she entered the spacious living room. She knew in her heart there would be a simple explanation for the explosion at the factory, something so straightforward and inarguable that the matter could be put to rest.

"Mrs. Spaulding." The detective rose and flashed his credentials. "I'm Terry Halloran." He named a precinct.

Grant stepped forward. "I'm Grant Spaulding. My mother has been through hell today, Detective Halloran. Is this visit necessary?"

Halloran ignored Grant. "Mrs. Spaulding, when was the last time you saw an employee named Frank De Vito?"

Lili frowned. "I'm afraid I don't know a Frank De Vito."

"He was with your Research and Development department," Halloran said.

"I'm in charge of R and D," Grant broke in. "What about De Vito?"

Something was wrong with Grant's tone of voice. Lili couldn't quite place exactly what but she sensed the detective caught it, too.

Halloran turned toward Grant. "He was found in the rubble."

"So were a lot of people," Grant said. "Is he alive?"

"Barely. He was taken to a hospital in East Orange." Halloran paused. "He had a lot to say in the ambulance."

"I can just imagine," Grant said, frowning. "Probably put the blame squarely on Lili's shoulders."

"No," Halloran answered. "He put it on yours."

Detective Halloran left thirty minutes later, followed quickly by Grant. Lili's head throbbed so badly she was afraid she might vomit.

"Would there be anything I can do for you, ma'am?" Gretchen appeared in the archway to the living room.

"A pot of tea," Lili said, as exhaustion rolled over her. "I'll take it in my room." Every night for the last twenty years she'd enjoyed a pot of tea before bed. Strange that she would cling to that meaningless ritual now in the face of tragedy.

And it was a tragedy. She lived in a world that thrived on hyperbole but no words were strong enough to convey the horrors she had witnessed. That detective must be mad to believe Grant would ever orchestrate something as terrible as the factory bombing. Night-Way was his future, the success story that would carry him through the primary to victory. Why on earth would he, Grant, destroy the company that was his birthright? It simply didn't make sense.

Tragedy had pushed Frank De Vito into madness. That was the only explanation Lili could come up with. Grant had woven a terrible story about a dead child and lost dreams and a need for revenge so strong it couldn't be denied. Halloran had taken notes while Grant talked but Lili found it almost didn't matter to her who lit the fuse. Nothing could change the fact that her factory had been reduced to rubble, that dear friends and employees lay dead or injured. That so many dreams had been destroyed.

Once in her room, she stripped down to her skin then slipped on a turquoise silk kimono. She lit a cigarette then stood by the window and looked out at the city lights below. Grant had been in a particularly uncomfortable mood. She'd never seen him quite that way before and it concerned her. He had promised Lili he would go straight home to Felicia and the baby but she wasn't certain she believed him. So much had happened that afternoon—she felt as if her entire life had been turned end over end. Certainly Grant felt much the same way.

On the surface he had taken her news about Corey amazingly well. He'd listened to her story about Clifford Earle Franklin and Eileen Fontaine without betraying any emotion. When she got to the part about Carter, his jaw had tightened noticeably but he said nothing at all. Not even Millicent Banning's pathetic letter moved him to display anything beyond mild disgust. Still she had sensed something beneath his calm acceptance, a darker pool of emotions that unnerved her. The encounter with Halloran had only added to her unease.

"Ridiculous," she said out loud, her breath fogging a tiny square of windowpane. She was seeing things that weren't there, reading more into Grant's reaction than actually existed. The fact that Corey Prescott was her biological daughter took nothing away from Grant. Lili adored him now as much as she had adored him from the start. There was nothing she wouldn't do for him, no mountain she wouldn't scale to keep him safe and happy.

Would you turn away from your own daughter if it meant losing your son?

A terrible question but it was the answer that almost broke her heart. The daughter she'd carried inside her body was a stranger to her while the son she'd gained through marriage was as dear and familiar to her as her own face in the mirror. *My daughter,* she told herself. *My little girl.* The words held power but no magic. She waited but the rush of maternal affection didn't materialized and she wondered if it ever would.

She had waited too long for Whit and she'd lost him. Maybe it was the same with Corey. There might have been a time, years ago, when a reunion would have been possible between them but not now. Corey had made it painfully obvious these past two weeks that she hated everything Lili stood for, but at least now Lili understood why. Corey Prescott may look like a beautiful young woman but inside she was still the little girl Lili had left behind. Millicent Banning had described scars, terrible scars that held the child back. No scars marred Corey's lovely face any longer but her edgy defensiveness marked her as wounded just the same.

The whole situation had a sense of unreality, as if she were watching someone else's life being played out on a movie screen.

Don't think about it tonight, she told herself. Her head throbbed with pain and it was all she could do to keep her eyes open. She found her way to the bed and lay down across the covers.

"I did my best," she murmured as she drifted off to sleep. Not even Lili Spaulding could do more than that.

There were six messages from Stephen on Corey's answering machine, each one escalating in intensity. At first he tried to mask his concern with a joke but in each succeeding message his fear became more obvious. And there was more than fear in his voice, she realized. There was a deep note of caring—of affection?—that brought her up short.

Bad timing, she thought. Stephen needed a woman who would be around for the long haul. Corey doubted if she'd be around for the weekend. Her days at Lili! International were over. That much was clear. And since Lili! owned the apartment and everything in it, Corey intended to be out of there and on her way home to Boston as fast as possible. There was nothing left for her here. Stephen and Jessie were a lost dream, same as Lili Spaulding.

The telephone rang again.

"Prescott, I know you've gotta come home some time. It's Stephen. Give me a call and—"

"Stephen." Her heart was beating so fast she placed a hand on her chest to steady herself.

"Corey!" His elation warmed her cold heart. "Why the hell didn't you call me?"

"I just got home."

"You're on all the local stations," he said. "They're calling you a hero."

She laughed bitterly. "Fool might be a better word."

"You saved the Steel Magnolia's life."

"She didn't need me to save her, Stephen. She doesn't need anyone but Grant."

"Are you okay?" He sounded concerned.

"I'm fine," she said. "A little dose of reality never hurt anyone."

"I'm coming over," he said. "The housekeeper's still here. I'll leave Jessie with her and—"

"No!" She didn't mean to sound quite so harsh but she was fast reaching the end of her rope. "No," she repeated, more softly. "It's too late. You were right about me that day at Serendipity, Stephen. You and Jess deserve someone who'll be there for you. I'm not right for either one of you."

"What happened, Prescott? Two days ago we were—"

"Two days ago I wasn't Lili Spaulding's daughter. Now I am. It changes everything."

"Lili's daughter? What the hell are you talking about? Lili doesn't have—"

"It's a long story," she said. "You'll probably read all about it any day now."

"I'm not letting you go this easy. We can—"

"No, we can't. I'm not the woman you think I am, Stephen. I'm not even the woman *I* thought I was."

"I'm coming over," he said again. "We'll talk."

"I won't be here."

"Damn it, Prescott. You're not going to walk out of my life. Not—"

"Goodbye, Stephen," she said. "Take good care of Jessie." She hung up before he could change her mind.

The phone rang again a few seconds later. She turned down the answering machine and ignored it. Smart women knew when it was time to cut their losses and Corey was nothing if not smart. She'd been smart long before the doctor made her beautiful and once her beauty faded it would be her brains that would get her through. It had taken her a very long time to learn that lesson and she wasn't about to forget it now.

Her suitcase was still in the trunk of Lili's limo but that didn't matter. She could live without her suitcase and everything in it. She pulled two enormous tote bags down from the top shelf and began tossing lingerie and toiletries into them. Her suits and dresses deserved better than to be shoved into bags but they'd survive. The important thing was getting out of there as fast as possible. Emotion made you vulnerable and right now Corey was more vulnerable than she'd ever been in her entire life.

"She wouldn't let us near Mrs. Spaulding," the burly EMS technician said for the camera. "She was gonna bring her back or know the reason why."

Animal rights groups deny any responsibility but there is speculation that Frank De Vito, a company employee, is—

"Turn that fucking thing off," Grant said, gesturing toward the television suspended over the bar. CNN—it was enough to make him puke. Whatever happened to hockey games and prizefights? The bartender ignored him which irked Grant no end. He could buy the damn place ten times over. He deserved some respect.

"I said, *turn that fucking thing off.*"

The bartender didn't bat an eye as he tossed lemon and orange peels into four old-fashioned glasses. "You don't like it, go somewhere else."

He pushed his glass toward the bartender. "Another Scotch."

"Sorry," the bartender said. "You've had enough."

"I'll be the judge of that."

"If you could be the judge of that, you wouldn't be asking for another Scotch." The bartender met Grant's eyes. "Bar's closed, pal. Go home and wait for Santa."

The one place he wasn't going was home. He'd called Felicia from Lili's apartment and his well-bred wife had screeched at him like a fishmonger's daughter.

"This will ruin us, Grant! Your company...the campaign...what are we going to do?"

He didn't know what they were going to do. If he knew what to do he wouldn't be sitting in some Second Avenue dive, watching CNN, ABC, NBC, and CBS call Corey Prescott a heroine. She'd saved Lili's life, breathed air into her starving lungs, whatever melodramatic phrases the anchor felt like using to hype ratings. Corey Prescott, selfless and brave employee.

Corey Prescott, the boss's daughter.

"Son of a bitch," he swore, draining the rest of his Scotch. Night-Way and the factory explosion were the least of his worries now. Once the shock wore off and he'd realized Lili was safe, he'd seen the beauty of Jarreau's plan. With one masterful blast, Grant's problems had vanished—and if De Vito died as a result, so much the better. CG-47 was history and he'd been ready to celebrate until Lili detonated the second bombshell of the night. He'd maintained a cool facade in front of Lili but inside he was burning with fury. No way was he going to let some bitch walk in off the street and take what belonged to him.

He'd made a few phone calls since leaving the penthouse and he had Prescott nailed to the wall. She'd orchestrated every move, from getting Blake Morrow bounced out on his bony ass to sliding into the man's position before anyone realized what had happened. She might be Lili's biological daughter but she was still a conniving nobody who would be going no place damn fast when Grant got finished with her.

He tossed a fifty dollar bill down on the bar then slipped into his cashmere coat. It pissed him no end that she'd refused his advances. Who the fuck did she think she was anyway? Most women got wet just dreaming about him but that bitch had given him the wounded virgin act. He wasn't buying it anymore. She was a conniving slut who deserved whatever she got.

Corey's phone wouldn't stop ringing. The answering machine was filled with messages from Stephen and various news organizations, all of whom were looking for an interview with the heroine of the hour.

The hell with them. She didn't feel like a heroine—she felt more like a fool. She finished packing her belongings into tote bags then phoned the airlines to see if they had any flights to Boston that night. She'd kept her apartment and she had no doubt she could land a terrific job before too much time passed.

And if she didn't find a job, so what? She needed to put space—both physical and emotional—between herself and Lili. She'd had her chance for revenge and she'd blown it. She hadn't even had the satisfaction of telling Lili Spaulding that she was the child who'd been left behind. Instead of destroying her mother, she'd saved her and now she was paying the price.

The reservations clerk told her there was one more flight to Boston that night and Corey booked a seat. There was another reason for getting out of New York as soon as possible: the longer she stayed here, the harder it would be to turn away from Stephen and Jessie. She knew that life didn't come with guarantees. Great beginnings most of the time ended up in recriminations and goodbyes. Still she had the bittersweet sense that it might have been different for her and Stephen.

"Too late," she said, dragging her bags into the hall. Now she'd never know.

Her intercom buzzed and she frowned. She hadn't called for a cab yet.

"Visitor to see you, Ms. Prescott. Mr. Stephen Gold."

"Tell him—" Her heart lurched and she stopped. "Send him up."

There was nothing he could do to change her mind but she wanted to see him one more time before she left. She wondered if he'd brought Jessie with him, then prayed he'd had the foresight to leave the little girl home. The human heart was amazingly resilient but a child's heart was different. Wounds left scars that followed a little girl all the way into adulthood.

The bell rang. She took a deep breath then reached for the doorknob.

"Stephen, I don't think—"

"Are you going to invite me in for a drink, little sister?" Grant Spaulding loomed in the doorway. His choirboy face was twisted with hatred.

Little sister? Oh God—

"Sorry." How did he know she was Lili's daughter? How *long* had he known? She couldn't let him see her confusion. "You'll have to leave now."

"Five minutes. One drink. It's the least you can do."

She hesitated a second too long. He stepped into the foyer and shut the door behind him. Sweat broke out under her armpits.

He kicked at one of her leather bags with the toe of a hand-sewn shoe. "Going someplace?"

"Yes," she said, reaching for her purse. "So, if you don't mind..."

"I do mind," he said. "I mind a hell of a lot."

"Look, I don't know what your problem is but—"

He closed the distance between them in one long stride. "You're the problem."

"I'm nothing to you."

He chucked her under the chin. "You're my baby sister."

She pushed his hand away. "You're drunk."

"Not yet, but I'm working on it." He backed her against the wall. "You should've told me you were Lili's bastard."

"I don't know what you're talking about," she lied.

"Bullshit." He pulled her crumpled blood donor form from his coat pocket. "Better learn to cover your trail."

Her throat constricted. "Does Lili—?"

"She told me."

She knows, Corey thought. *My mother knows.* So why wasn't it Lili who had come to her door? Why wasn't it her mother?

"How much will it take to get you the fuck out of my life?" He sounded angry and more than a little drunk.

"I'm not in your life," she replied, trying to maneuver toward the archway to the living room. If she could make it to her bedroom, she'd lock the door between them and phone for the police. "I've never wanted to be in your life."

"Bullshit. You're Lili's bastard and you want a piece of the pie."

"You couldn't be more wrong."

"I called Blake Morrow. I know what you did."

Her gut twisted with fear. "You're delusional."

"So are you, little sister, if you think you'll ever mean half as much to Lili as I do. Everything Lili does, she does for me. She rebuilt the company for me."

The truth resonated inside her lonely heart. "Aren't you lucky," she said with a bitter laugh. "Some of us have to work for a living."

"I've worked my ass off." His voice was an ugly rumble near her ear. "I've earned every fucking cent of that trust fund."

"How wonderful for you." She gestured toward the door. "Please leave."

"I don't think so."

"You weren't invited."

"Maybe not," he conceded, "but the doorman announced me."

"He announced you as Stephen Gold."

"Surprise." Grant laughed softly. "You opened your door for him almost as fast as you spread your legs."

Slapping him was a reflex action, one that she regretted almost immediately when he grabbed her wrist.

"Not very friendly, bitch."

In one blinding instant she knew what he was about. Her knees went weak as a buzzing began deep inside her brain. *Terror,* she thought. This was how it felt to be terrified. She could handle it. She could handle anything. "Draw up legal papers," she said, denying the glitter of danger in his eyes. "I'll sign away any claim to my mother's money."

"This is the nineties. Contracts are made to be broken."

"Not this one. Once I leave, you'll never see or hear from me again."

He considered her slowly, his cool green eyes chilling their way down her throat, over her breasts, lingering at the spot between her legs. "There might be something you could do to convince me, little sister." He grabbed her by the hair and started toward the bedroom.

The water was cold and black, swirling dangerous water that could grab you and pull you under before you had a chance to catch your breath.

"Mama!" The child's voice skittered across the surface toward where Lili waited on the shore. "Help me, Mama!"

Even in the darkness Lili could see the child's sorrowful face. Ugly scars ran down her right cheek and tugged at the side of her mouth. My daughter . . . my little girl.

"I need you, Mama . . . I need you—"

Lili's heart narrowed with fear. The girl was in danger. "Stay there!" she called to the child. "I'm coming."

But she couldn't move. No matter how hard she tried, she couldn't move.

The waters rose up around the child's head and—

Lili came instantly and fully awake but the dream didn't fade. She saw her daughter's face, both the child's and the woman's, heard her voice, felt her fear.

"Corey," she whispered. She threw back the covers and grabbed for her clothes.

Corey didn't fight as Grant dragged her toward the bedroom. He was much stronger than she'd realized and she had no doubt he'd hurt her if she gave any resistance. Bile burned the back of her throat but she swallowed it down again.

You can do this, she told herself. *You can do whatever you have to do.* She might not be his match in strength but she was more than his match in intellect. Her gut told her she would have only one chance to escape and it was up to her to figure out when that chance came along. If she could just manage to break free and slam the door closed between them, she would stand a chance.

Stay calm, she told herself. *You can do it.*

He threw her down on the bed, so hard the breath left her lungs in a loud whoosh. Her skirt rode up over her hips, exposing the length of her legs, her panties. His eyes were everywhere and her fear escalated. What if she never got the chance to break and run? What if—

No! That's not going to happen. You'll find a way.

"You can do better than that." He towered over her. "Show me how you are with your do-gooder boyfriend."

"I told you I don't have a boyfriend."

"Panty hose?" His lip curled. "Take them off."

"No."

"Take them off or I'll rip them off."

She didn't want his hands anywhere near her. She hooked her thumbs under the elastic band and began to peel them from her body.

"Ma'am." The security guard beckoned Lili to his desk. "You have to sign in before you can go upstairs."

Lili straightened her spine and met the man's eyes. "I'm Lili Spaulding," she said in her most imperious tone. She wondered what he would think if he knew she had a pistol in the pocket of her frivolous mink jacket. Something was wrong. She could feel it deep in her bones as she gave him the apartment number. "I own that apartment."

"Yes, ma'am." His suspicious smile widened. "Please sign."

She did, noticing that Stephen Gold's signature bore a strong resemblance to Grant's. She wondered absently if they'd gone to the same school.

"Should I ring Ms. Prescott?"

"No," Lili said. "I want to surprise her."

"Better take care," he said with an obnoxious chuckle. "Don't want to interrupt her and her friend."

Lili ignored the leer implicit in the chuckle. "Her friend?" She kept her voice light and teasing.

"Said his name was Stephen Gold."

Lili arched a brow. "Isn't life just filled with surprises."

"Sure will be if you pop in on them at the wrong time."

"Ms. Prescott won't mind," Lili said, aiming a sharp glance at the man. "I'm her mother."

The panty hose weren't enough for Grant.

"The panties," he said, gesturing. "I want to see your pussy."

She came close to vomiting at the thought but refused to give him the satisfaction. "No."

"I don't like the word *no.*"

"I don't like being given orders."

He considered her. "Maybe you're right." He leaned down and ripped her blouse from her body. "Show me your tits."

Her fingers trembled as she struggled to unsnap her bra.

"Not bad," he said. "Not great but not bad."

An ugly embarrassed flush covered her from head to foot. She was fifteen again, scarred and lonely, wondering if she would ever belong. "How about you?" she taunted. "Afraid to show me what you've got?" *Come a little closer, you bastard, and I'll make sure you never father another child.*

She could barely withhold her elation as he unzipped his fly.

Five steps closer... come on... five more steps and I'll—

Her head snapped back as his fist landed a blow to her jaw. "You stupid bitch," he snarled. "You think I'm going to fall for that?"

Her thoughts were jumbled, disoriented. "I don't know what—"

The second blow glanced off her temple. "Shut up!" he roared. "I don't want to hear anything from you."

She tried to sit up but dizziness kept her pinned to the mattress. She noticed a bright red stain spreading across the pillowcase. Blood, she thought. *Her* blood. He wasn't only going to rape her, he was going to kill her.

She threw back her head and tried to scream but her throat was locked tight with fear. If only she hadn't told Stephen to stay away. *Help me! Please, please help me....*

He tore her panties from her body then shoved her thighs apart with his knee.

"You're not wet," he said, fingering the thick curls. "No problem. You will be before I'm finished."

"You bastard!" Her voice was raspy, her words indistinct. "You filthy son of a bitch."

He shoved her panties into her mouth. "You talk too much, Corey Prescott. I don't like that."

Help me... God, please, somebody help me now—

The door to Corey's apartment was closed but not locked. Lili took that as an invitation and stepped inside. A radio played softly from another room, bland elevator music that set her teeth on edge under normal circumstances. Two leather totes sat in the middle of the foyer. One was tipped over on its side. Corey's slate-gray coat was hung carelessly from the closet door. Lili looked inside the closet itself. It was empty, save for a brightly colored down parka. If Stephen Gold was there, where was his coat?

You're thinking like an old woman, Lili. Passion wasn't always neat and convenient. Passion didn't always take time to hang up coats or remove snowy shoes. The puddles on the tile floor told her that.

She had no right to be there. Whatever was going on in another part of the apartment was none of her business. Corey
had managed on her own for over thirty years. She didn't need
Lili's help or advice.

Turning, Lili made to leave, but the sense of urgency, of
danger, wouldn't quite let her go. She drew in a deep breath,
held it, then listened. She couldn't make out the words but the
threatening tone was unmistakable. A man's voice, familiar yet
not so. Not Stephen Gold's, she thought, but Grant's. Her
Grant. Certainly her imagination must be playing tricks on her.
Corey had made her feelings about him perfectly clear on any
number of occasions. The thought of the two of them—

She pushed away the thought. Ridiculous. Too ridiculous to
even contemplate. The doorman had said Corey's guest was
Stephen Gold. She had no reason not to believe him. In her
experience, doormen knew everything there was to know about
an apartment building and its tenants. Nothing escaped the
doorman—

Mama, help me!

She started at the sound.

Please, please . . .

Her imagination was running away with her. Her old dream
come back to haunt her waking hours. Hadn't the doctor
wanted to keep her in the hospital overnight for observation?
Head injuries were tricky things. Next thing you knew she'd see
a line of pink elephants dancing down the narrow hallway.

But she continued moving toward the bedroom. Quietly.
Cautiously. She put one foot in front of the other and kept
moving toward the open door at the end of the hallway.

She needed to see for herself, needed to know everything was
fine. It didn't matter if Corey hated her for invading her privacy this way. There were so many other reasons for Corey to
hate her that adding one more hardly seemed worth the worry.

"You might as well have some fun." Grant's voice, clear and
compelling. Lili's heart sank. *Her son.* Her beloved boy. "Relax and—" His words stopped abruptly as he noticed Lili
standing in the doorway. His angry expression morphed into a
sheepish choirboy smile. "It's not what you think."

Lili's eyes took in Corey's naked body, the blossoming bruises on her cheek and jaw, the way she was pinned beneath Grant's powerful body. Dear God, what was that stuffed in her mouth? "You don't know what I'm thinking."

He shielded himself with the bunched up blankets. "It's a fling, Mother," he said, his confidence returning. "One thing led to another and—" Again the charming smile. "I'm my father's son."

"Leave her alone, Grant." Her stomach was turning itself inside out and she prayed she wouldn't be sick. "Put on your clothes and go home to your wife." She had talked to him that way when he was a teenager. He'd needed a strong hand, someone with vision to keep him in line.

"Private party," he said, an edge of steel in his voice. "You weren't invited."

She met Corey's eyes and the terror she saw in them came close to buckling her knees. *She's frightened but not hurt,* Lili told herself, praying it was true. Praying that it wasn't too late to save them all.

"I want to hear Corey tell me she's okay," Lili said, forcing her voice to remain calm.

"I don't think she's in the mood to talk."

"Take that . . . *thing* out of her mouth and we'll see."

"You're overstepping your bounds, darling Lili. Adult games only make sense to the adults involved."

Corey struggled against him, her dark blue eyes drowning, drowning . . .

"Let her go, Grant," Lili said, more strongly this time. "Let her go *now.*"

He didn't move. The atmosphere in the room grew more charged.

"She's nothing," he said, his eyes locked with hers. "She aced Morrow out of his job. She planned this, Lili. She planned it every step of the way. She's a conniving bitch. Don't waste your time on her. I'm your son. I'm the one who understands you."

"My son wouldn't hurt anyone," she said, her voice breaking. "My son wouldn't do this." Too bad her son had never been anything more than a foolish dream.

He shifted position. Corey bucked her hips wildly. He slipped to one side, cursed, then landed a loud crack alongside Corey's jaw and in that instant all of Lili's fears were realized. Her fingers wrapped themselves around the gun in her pocket and a second later Grant fell to the floor with a bullet lodged in his left shoulder.

"Touch my daughter again," said Lili, "and I'll kill you."

For a moment Corey was sure time had stopped. Terror downshifted swiftly into shock as Grant dropped to the ground, writhing in pain. Blood was everywhere, dark red droplets spotting the pure white sheets. And the most amazing sight of all, her mother standing in the doorway with a gun dangling from her manicured fingertips.

She began to shake uncontrollably and Lili flew to her side. She pulled the undergarment from Corey's mouth then wrapped her in a blanket, all the while murmuring softly in her ear. Words of love? Apology? Regret? Corey didn't know or care. All she knew was that she was safe.

"I have to call the police," Lili said, brushing the hair off Corey's forehead with a gentle hand. "You must press charges against him."

Corey nodded, arms wrapped tightly about her chest. "I know." What was Lili feeling right now? Lili had loved Grant with all her heart and now she'd lost him.

Grant moaned loudly in pain then drifted into unconsciousness. Lili flinched but she didn't acknowledge him. Instead she ran soft, healing fingers over Corey's cheek, her poor damaged cheek.

"You chose me," Corey said, as she searched Lili's face. "When the time came, you chose me." She swallowed hard. "You saved my life."

"You're my daughter," Lili whispered, her voice catching. "I did the only thing I could do."

"I came here to destroy you. I wanted to make you pay for not wanting me."

"Your mother—?"

Corey shook her head. "Last September. She loved me more than anything on earth and I'll miss her every day of my life."

"You're very lucky."

"I know," Corey said. "She was very special."

The words didn't hurt Lili the way she would have thought. Instead they were a healing balm to her soul. Their eyes met and for a moment Lili thought she was back in Atlanta with her baby girl in her arms and a heart filled with hope and dreams. It had been a long strange journey but maybe some of those dreams could still come true.

She held out her hand. Corey's eyes filled with tears. Lili waited, scarcely breathing.

"Corey," she said softly. "I'm so sorry."

And then the most amazing thing happened. Her daughter reached out across the years and took her hand.

"So am I," Corey said. "So am I."

Lili Spaulding bowed her head and cried with joy.

Epilogue

Barbados, Christmas Day

The villa was situated on top of a hill overlooking the bay. Masses of red and pink bougainvillea bloomed around the windows and door and their scent filled Lili's head with hope.

She brought her rented car to a stop beneath a banyan tree and checked her map. This had to be the right place. Dark green shutters, whitewashed walls, no neighbors. It was the perfect beach retreat for a man looking to simplify his life in the lap of luxury.

But, more than that, it was pure Whit.

Her fingers trembled as she reapplied her lipstick and checked her hair. She wasn't a schoolgirl any longer. It was ridiculous that the thought of one man should make her feel so vulnerable, but then hope always made a woman vulnerable.

And, dear God, how she hoped!

Her life seemed new again to her, soft and gentle and filled with possibilities. Possibilities she hadn't dared dream about since those long-ago days in Euless when she'd believed the answer to her prayers could be found in the protective circle of one man's arms. The folly of youth, she thought, and its wisdom, too. Life was sweeter shared and she prayed it wasn't too late for her and Whit.

She tapped on his front door and waited, feeling the way she'd felt all those years ago when she stepped into the foyer of the Franklins' house on the hill. Excited and terrified and more than a little out of place. This was Whit's private world, a world she longed to share with him—if he still wanted her. She tapped again but there was still no response. Curious, she peered into the front window but saw nothing more than a sun-splashed room with flowers and good artwork.

She followed the stone path around the side of the house, breathing in the sweet smells of exotic flowers and hope again . . . sweet sweet hope. She was filled with wonder. After all the years, all the mistakes, she'd found her daughter. Some of the wounds would never heal and she understood that. Two proud women, two battered hearts. It would take time but she trusted the power of love to make them whole once more. Grant would stand trial in the spring and Lili had no doubt that he and Dan Jarreau would face harsh sentences for their act of selfish terrorism. She had loved her stepson without reservation for almost twenty years and he repaid her by sabotaging the empire she'd helped build for him . . . for his children.

There were hard times ahead for all of them but out of the sorrow something wonderful had blossomed between mother and daughter. Lili wasn't naive enough to think it would be easy but she knew it would *be*, same as she knew the sun would rise tomorrow morning.

Corey's heart was a fragile thing—but then so was Lili's. It would take time but somehow the bond they'd forged that terrible night would strengthen and grow. She was glad that Stephen Gold and his daughter Jessie would be there to help Corey heal. Not even Lili would hazard a guess as to the eventual outcome, but miracles happened every day and she prayed that three good people would find a way to become a family.

Time, she thought, as she rounded the back of the house. All they needed was time. Strange to realize that she and Whit had had all the time in the world and they'd somehow never figured out how to use it. Was it asking too much that the fates bless her just one more time?

And then she saw him. He was sitting on an outcropping of rock, staring out at the sea. His silver hair glittered in the Caribbean sunlight. He wore cutoffs and no shirt. His bare back was deeply tanned. He looked younger, more handsome, at peace with himself and his world. He had obviously found what he'd been looking for and suddenly she knew that if she really loved him, the time had come to let him go. He deserved more than the complex, imperfect woman she was.

She turned to leave but there was one more miracle waiting for her after all.

"Took you long enough, Lil," he said, his voice gruff with emotion.

Tears filled her eyes as she walked over to where he sat looking out at the wild and beautiful sea. "I know," she whispered. "Can you ever forgive me?" He was the love of her life, the man who saw beyond her face and into her secret heart, the place where beauty begins and ends.

"I love you, Lil," he said. "Nothing will ever change that."

"Thank God," she whispered back. "I'm only sorry it took me so long to realize how much I love you."

His beautiful smile lit up her world. "I'd say it was worth waiting for."

He opened his arms to her and she rested her cheek against his bare chest.

Home, she thought as she closed her eyes. After all these years, Lilly Ann Barnett had finally come home.

A brutal murder.
A notorious case.
Twelve people must decide
the fate of one man.

Jury Duty

an exciting courtroom drama by

Laura Van Wormer

Struggling novelist Libby Winslow has been chosen to sit on the jury of a notorious murder trial dubbed the "Poor Little Rich Boy" case. The man on trial, handsome, wealthy James Bennett Layton, Jr., has been accused of killing a beautiful young model. As Libby and the other jury members sift through the evidence trying to decide the fate of this man, their own lives become jeopardized because someone on the jury has his own agenda....

Find out what the verdict is this October at your favorite retail outlet.

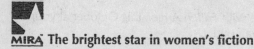

From National Bestselling Author

DEBBIE MACOMBER

Comes a poignant story of an undeniable attraction

Fallen Angel

Amy Johnson was being groomed to take over her
father's company. No one seemed to notice that her
heart wasn't in it, that she was miserable. Until a
handsome stranger gave her some much-needed
advice and a shoulder to lean on. But just when
his tempting kisses made Amy hungry for more,
Josh Powell was sent to the other side of the world.
He left without making any promises or commitments
to her.

When circumstances bring them together again, Josh
must decide whether he'll let this alluring woman into
his life or if he'll let her slip away....

Fall in love with *Fallen Angel*, this October at your
favorite retail outlet.

If you love the romantic style of

BARBARA BRETTON

Then order now to receive more timeless stories
by one of MIRA's bestselling authors:

#66004	TOMORROW & ALWAYS	$4.99 U.S.	☐
		$5.50 CAN.	☐
#66044	NO SAFE PLACE	$4.99 U.S.	☐
		$5.50 CAN.	☐
#66090	DESTINY'S CHILD	$4.99 U.S.	☐
		$5.50 CAN.	☐
#66074	SHOOTING STAR	$4.99 U.S.	☐
		$5.50 CAN.	☐
#66066	STARFIRE	$5.50 U.S.	☐
		$5.99 CAN.	☐

(limited quantities available)

TOTAL AMOUNT	$
POSTAGE & HANDLING	$
($1.00 for one book, 50¢ for each additional)	
APPLICABLE TAXES*	$ _____
TOTAL PAYABLE	$ _____
(check or money order—please do not send cash)	

To order, complete this form and send it, along with a check or money
order for the total above, payable to MIRA Books, to: **In the U.S.:** 3010
Walden Avenue, P.O. Box 9077, Buffalo, NY 14269-9077; **In Canada:**
P.O. Box 636, Fort Erie, Ontario, L2A 5X3.

Name: _____

Address: _____ City: _____

State/Prov.: _____ Zip/Postal Code: _____

*New York residents remit applicable sales taxes.
  Canadian residents remit applicable GST and provincial taxes.   MBBBL6

MIRA

Look us up on-line at: http://www.romance.net